TIMELESS

A STARCROSED NOVEL

JOSEPHINE ANGELINI

LOS ANGELES

ISBN: 979-8-9855810-4-1

Published by Sungrazer Publishing

Cover design by Jenny Zemanek

For my daughter

Content warning:

This book contains depictions of sexual assault, self-harm and bullying.

CHAPTER 1

Helen sat in the guidance counselor's office, trying hard not to gently electrocute her teacher into unconsciousness.

Mr. Summerton was a nice person, and she really didn't want to use her goddess powers on him. She was squeamish in general about using them on full mortals, especially not on the good ones.

Mr. Summerton was a vest-wearing man, and Helen respected any teacher who braved the derision of teenagers to stay true to their own fashion sense. He also had a bald spot on his head that got sweaty when he felt passionately about something. Usually, the gleam on his pate only kicked in when he was giving one of his hell-fire lectures about Jim Crow or the New Deal, or Women's Suffrage. He was a history teacher who absolutely loved being a history teacher. Currently, he also had to be the guidance counselor, not because he knew anything about it, but because Nantucket High was short on staff since a "freak storm" had tragically killed so many people. Mnemosyne, the Goddess of Memory, had altered all eyewitness accounts of the Olympians' descent upon the small island of Nantucket, but she could not erase the lives that had been taken.

But if guidance counseling wasn't Mr. Summerton's initial profession, Helen certainly couldn't tell, because he sure was swinging for the fences. Mr. Summerton was trying so hard to get her to settle on a list of colleges to apply to that his whole head was beaded with sweat. At this point Helen felt like *she* should be the counselor. This guy needed some serious handholding.

"Helen, your grades may not be straight A's, but your teachers rave about you, you've never gotten below a B, and your test scores are really, *really* good. Surprisingly good," he said, glancing down at her file to make sure. When he saw the high scores he'd mentioned, he huffed and started sweating a little more. "There's so much in your file that makes me think you've just been flying under the radar here."

"I had a good day in testing, but I'm not the best student. Homework isn't my strongest suit," she admitted.

"What about your plan for a track scholarship?" he asked.

Helen tried not to groan at his earnest face and sat on her hands. Why the heck did everyone want her to go to college anyway? Her family couldn't afford it. Lucas' family had offered to pay. In fact, his mother Noel had given her this whole long lecture about how much of her own education she'd missed out on because she was bartending and trying to put herself through cooking school, but Helen wasn't comfortable with the Delos family paying for college. It was just way too much money to her, even though it was practically nothing to them.

"I had to work, like, a lot after my dad got sick a few months back and I couldn't make it to track meets," Helen said.

And at that time, when her father was being poisoned by her mother to keep him sedated and she'd missed pretty much every school function, Helen had more on her plate than just tending the News Store or going to track meets. She was saving the world from a catastrophic supernatural war. But she was pretty sure she couldn't put that on an absentee slip.

"I lost my standing," she continued, shrugging. "I'm not eligible for a track scholarship anymore."

Mr. Summerton slumped back in his chair, despondent. "I just don't know how to help you," he said. Helen felt terrible. There's nothing more guilt-inducing than letting down a supportive, caring, all-around good teacher. "You've obviously got so much to offer, Miss Hamilton. I just hate to think that in this country having a sick parent can be so devastating to a potentially bright future like yours."

Oh no, here he goes. He's going to talk about the New Deal, Helen thought.

"You know, when Roosevelt was in office..."

Forty-five minutes later, Helen emerged from Mr. Summerton's office with a glassy look in her eyes. Lucas was waiting for her, leaning against the far wall, one knee drawn up, looking absolutely devastating.

Seeing Helen, Lucas pushed himself off the wall and came to her. "What happened?" he asked, not sure if he should be worried or not, considering her expression.

"He *New Dealed* me," Helen replied, eyes still unable to focus due to the boredom she'd been made to endure.

"On a Friday?" Lucas sucked air through his teeth. "Ouch."

He threw an arm over her shoulders as they started down the hallway.

"Did *you* get *New Dealed* when you had your meeting with him?" Helen asked.

"No." Lucas replied.

"Did you tell him where you were applying to?"

She tried to sound nonchalant. Lucas hadn't told anyone where he wanted to go to college, and she was hoping he would take the opportunity to tell her now.

"No," Lucas replied. "But it's not the same for me. I've only been on Nantucket for a year. These teachers have known you your whole life. They just want what's best for you."

"Maybe what's best for me is to stay on the island and take care of my dad," Helen said.

Nobody knew quite what was wrong with him, but Jerry seemed to be suffering aftereffects from whatever it was that Daphne had given him. Conventional medical doctors said his heart had developed an arrhythmia, and despite the best efforts of Jason and Ariadne—Lucas' cousins, who were powerful Healers—Jerry would occasionally grow weak. Sometimes he would even faint. It freaked Helen out to no end. To the point she didn't like talking about it.

She also didn't like the way Lucas wouldn't take her many hints and just tell her his plans for college.

"Not sure your dad would want you to skip college," Lucas reminded her firmly. "Kate will take care of him while you're gone." He sensed she didn't want to talk about it any further. They walked in silence for a bit. "Did you get your maid of honor dress yet?"

She had never been an "event" kind of girl, and she certainly had never looked forward to wearing any kind of clothing other than a comfy pair of yoga pants, but the fact that her father was going to marry Kate was something she could really get behind.

Their upcoming Christmas wedding to be held at the Delos compound was the one thing that both put a smile on Helen's face and sidetracked her completely whenever Lucas wanted to dodge talking about his plans for college.

"It sold out. The dress that Kate and I picked," Helen said, "the off-the-shoulder one."

"The *sexy* one?" Lucas had mixed feelings about Helen showing extra skin. He enjoyed it, but he was also afraid of it, and for very good reason.

"It looks like we're going to have to go with choice number two."

"The high-necked, long-sleeved one that resembles a Hefty bag?"

"The very one," Helen said, playing along. "And I'll be wearing neon Crocs with it."

His whole face lit up. When Lucas was happy, he glowed. Being a Scion of the god Apollo meant that he was touched with light in a way that others weren't. But Lucas also had another side to him; he was a distant Scion of Hades, and a Shadowmaster. Every now and again lately it was the darkness that Helen saw creeping out of Lucas, rather than the light for which he was named.

But not now. Now he was a breathtaking Son of the Sun, and Helen could have slid right down to the center of world. Every time she looked at him, she fell in love with him a little bit more.

Lucas pulled her tighter against his side. "Don't look at me like that or I'm going to get us in trouble."

Helen laughed low in her throat and tilted her lips close to his neck while she said, "Promises, promises."

Before Lucas could do anything about Helen's brazen

flouting of their No Irresistible Goddess of Love Stuff at School Rule, they arrived at the cafeteria. Just as Helen had planned.

"Luke! Over here!" Jason called.

"I'll get you back later," Lucas whispered to Helen before releasing her shoulders, only to grab onto her hand as they weaved through the tables to join their family.

It really didn't bother her the way every admirer of male beauty stared at Lucas. Helen couldn't blame them, let alone be mad at them. In fact, it made her happy. She loved to look at him so much she felt a kinship with everyone else who did as well, and it made her feel like she was in on it. Sometimes she wanted to gesture at the slack-jawed individuals who ogled Lucas and say, "Right? Isn't he *bananas*?" only because she understood exactly where they were coming from.

Jealousy wasn't her thing, although it was Lucas'—hence their conversation about her maid of honor dress. Secretly, Helen thought it was kind of funny. He feared that her face or her legs or her cleavage would start a stampede or something, which was a valid concern considering her face had once started a war. But ever since Helen had shared in Orion's blood, thus absorbing some of the emotion-reading abilities of the descendants of Aphrodite from the House of Rome, she knew better. There was a perfect partner for everyone, and the faces and bodies that went along with that perfection were as varied as the individuals who dreamed of them. Everyone was someone else's perfect. Helen just happened to be Lucas', for which she was eternally grateful.

"What'd you tell Summer School?" Claire asked, using the nickname she'd given Mr. Summerton. He was a tough teacher and if someone didn't do well enough in his class they ended up in summer school.

Helen sat down next to her best friend. "Nothing. I couldn't get a word in," she replied. "But did you know that the SEC was founded to protect people from stock market fraud?"

"Oh, good Lord," Claire groaned. "How many times are you going to get New Dealed? My ears are bleeding *for* you at this point. Just give him a list. All he wants is to know that you've at least thought about leaving Nantucket."

"I just don't know what to say," Helen replied as she rummaged through her bag for her lunch.

"Tell him you want to go to NYU with Hector and Orion," Jason said.

"Or Columbia," Claire added, gesturing at Jason and Ariadne because that's where they had decided on going. "Or, you know... Parsons. If I get in there. If my portfolio is good enough and my parents don't murder me."

Claire bit her lower lip with worry and Helen reached out to her.

"Claire. You're going to get in," Helen assured her. "And your parents can't murder you. Physically."

Ever since the Final Battle with the gods, when Helen had claimed Lucas, Claire, Orion, Jason, Hector (Jason and Ariadne's brother), Andy (Hector's girlfriend), and Cassandra (Lucas' younger sister) to be her immortal family for the rest of eternity, they'd all changed in remarkable ways, both big and small. While they weren't fully immortal—they could die if they chose to—they could not be killed, nor could they age.

Near-immortality aside, Claire's artistic ability had skyrocketed, and she had completely shifted her focus. Instead of pursuing microbiology as she'd always planned, Claire now wanted to be an artist. But it was all new to her. She'd never even thought about art before, and now it was the most important thing in her world. After years of being preemptively proud of their daughter for the PhD she would undoubtably earn someday, her parents were not likely to understand. And secretly, Helen didn't understand either. She hadn't given Claire these artistic abilities; they'd just shown up on their own and no one knew why yet.

"My portfolio is barely two weeks old, so we'll see," Claire said. She rounded back on Helen. "Just get it over with and tell Summer School you're going to New York."

"I can't," Helen quibbled. "I can't go to school too far from home or it will look suspicious when I'm here all the time."

"Then just *take* an application to U Mass or Boston College —or Wellesley. You could go to school with Andy," Claire said.

"Andy's in the North Pole, doing her oceanography research," Helen said.

"But technically she goes to Wellesley," Claire amended.

Helen looked at Lucas, but he said nothing. Not one word about where he wanted to go or even what city or state he was planning to be in next year.

Helen pulled her sandwich out of her bag and took a bite quickly so she would have an excuse not to talk if Claire kept pestering her. Bad idea. She tipped her sandwich sideways to see whether the visual matched with the train wreck that was going on in her mouth.

"Is that peanut butter and tuna?" Lucas asked, noting Helen's grimace.

"I fink fo," Helen replied, trying to keep the goop in her mouth from touching any more taste buds. She couldn't think of what to do with it, so she just swallowed it. Then she put the offensive sandwich down in front of her and stared at it.

"Are you going to throw up?" Ariadne asked.

Helen shrugged, uncertain. "Maybe?"

Jason stifled a laugh, and Claire smacked him on the arm before turning to Helen.

"How's your dad?" she asked.

"Oh, probably not great," Helen replied, still staring at the sandwich he'd made her.

Helen's father had always been adventurous with the sandwiches he packed for her lunch. It was a running joke between them, but this was not like the pickle and Jell-O monstrosity back in eighth grade. That had obviously been intentional, because he'd also left her a protein bar and an apple to eat instead. Helen didn't know what to think of this one. Was he being funny, or did he forget what he was making halfway through? This was why Helen couldn't leave Massachusetts. Her dad was quietly unraveling.

"Here," Lucas said, sliding his neatly packed Bento box from Noel in front of Helen.

She shook her head and stood. "I'm going to get an iced tea. Anyone want anything from the vending machine?"

When she returned with her drink Jason was talking and Lucas yawned hugely. Jason stopped.

"Am I boring you?" Jason asked.

"Sorry," Lucas replied.

"Did you two fly off somewhere interesting last night?" Jason asked, including Helen in the question.

Helen shook her head, thrown. She hadn't seen Lucas last night or the night before...or the night before that.

"I was in New York," Lucas replied.

"You went to see Hector?" Ariadne asked, disappointed. "I have something for him. I wish you'd told me you were going to see him."

"Next time," Lucas apologized.

"He's so lonely with Andy away," Ariadne said, fretting about her big brother.

"Andy should just marry him and put him out of his misery," Jason said.

"They're way too young," Claire disagreed.

Jason shrugged. "We marry young," he said, leaving out the word *Scion*, though it was understood.

"We are not talking about this again," Claire said.

"I'm just saying, if you're going to Parsons, you should live at our brownstone in Washington Square."

"With *you*," she clarified.

"Yes."

"My parents would die, or kill me. Or kill me and *then* die if I lived with a boy."

Helen leaned forward, shocked. "Wait. You guys are thinking about moving in together next year?"

Claire said *no* the same time Jason said *yes*. Claire crossed her arms and glared at Jason.

"I'm just saying, it's a big brownstone. We wouldn't even have to share a room."

Claire rolled her eyes skyward, whispering, "Help me."

"Leave her alone, Jase," Ariadne chided.

Helen never imagined that Claire and Jason had even discussed such a big step, but it was clear everyone else knew this but her. And one person was staying conspicuously silent on the whole subject.

Helen stared at Lucas' chest, desperately trying to decipher the slow boil of emotions in him. Even though she had the ability to read hearts, emotions never stayed put, they never came one at a time, and depending on the individual, they could mean pretty much anything. Helen could see love, devotion, and commitment in Lucas. She also saw flashes of anger and sadness, guilt, and resentment. She had no idea what any of it meant.

On more than one occasion Helen had told Orion that his emotion-reading talent was useless because now that she had it, she was more confused than ever. Orion usually laughed and told her that it took practice.

Lucas caught Helen squinting at his chest and knew what she was doing. He never tried to avoid her when she was reading him. Instead, he met her eyes, leaned back, and smiled at her in a way that made it clear what he felt for her.

Reading him from that point on would only make her blush, so she rolled her eyes at him and stopped. He'd been a Falsefinder his whole life, so it was practically impossible to outsmart him if he wanted to keep something to himself. Helen just didn't know *why* he wanted to keep his plans to himself, and it hurt her that he did.

Cassandra swept into the cafeteria, and the Scions welcomed her with smiles and waves. Everyone else in the lunchroom did the equivalent of a mental stutter step before going back to their own conversations with an added level of fervor.

Cassandra was the Oracle of Delphi, the mouthpiece of the Three Fates, and because of that she had a way of making everyone around her subconsciously aware of the fact that their lives were a fragile thread that would inevitably be cut.

Most people on the island had grown used to Cassandra and pretended they didn't sense this uncanny aspect of her nature, but even they left her presence with a driving need to live a little more for the rest of the day, like they'd just heard the seconds of their life ticking away on some universal clock.

When Helen had made her friends all essentially immortal, she had frozen them in time. Cassandra still looked like a girl of twelve, though she was almost sixteen. She was naturally small and thin, big-eyed, and pouty lipped, and as such she had always looked younger than she was. Now she was stuck like that, an eternal twelve-year-old who carried the responsibility of Fate within her. Helen had always sympathized with Cassandra, but now she felt guilty about her, too. Though Cassandra insisted that it was the Fates and not Helen's gift of immortality that were keeping her from becoming a woman, Helen hated that she hadn't at least tried to help Cassandra grow up before she'd given up Everyland, the world she'd created. And now she couldn't even try. Without possession of Everyland, Helen was no longer a goddess. She could no longer make her own reality.

Cassandra didn't come to school very often. The Fates could take possession of her whenever they saw fit, so she was forced to split her time between in-person and remote learning. She never knew when she could be overcome unless she was with Orion. He had the ability to shield her from the Fates so they could neither see the actions of the human world through her or take over her body and speak through her in prophecy. If Orion was close, she was safe from the horrid possessions that left her battered and sickly, but he couldn't be in Nantucket all the time.

Orion was a leader of two Houses—the House of Athens and the House of Rome—and he had to be in New York to integrate their affairs. And, even though Orion already had more than his share of responsibility, he wasn't twenty yet. He also had to get an education. He and Hector went to NYU together, and most of the time Orion stayed with him at the Delos brownstone on Washington Square Park unless he swam back to Nantucket to be near Cassandra.

When Orion wasn't around, Cassandra was frayed and scattered, and she usually stayed home. Coming to school while he was in New York was dangerous for her.

"Don't forget we're meeting at the house after school," she announced, shifting from foot to foot.

"Do we have some work to do?" Ariadne asked excitedly, her eyes darting around to make sure they were not overheard.

Ariadne was the only one among them who was not immortal. When Helen brought the Scions to Everyland and granted them near immortality, Ariadne had not been with them. She was still one of them, though since Matt's death she had often seemed apart.

"Possibly," was all Cassandra would say in answer.

The Scions didn't want to waste their talents while they were going to high school, pretending to be normal. They recognized that they had been given gifts that they should use to benefit others. But it appeared that the Fates did not want the Scions to make the world a better place. Every time a Scion tried to intervene in a situation and do something good for the world it blew up in their face. The Fates made sure that if a Scion did so much as try to stop a traffic accident that was occurring in front of them, they'd have to kill an innocent bystander to do it. The older Scions—the cousins' fathers, Castor and Pallas—had told them that that's the way it had always been for Scions. Try as they might, Scions only made mortal's lives worse when they intervened.

So, the Scions were still working on a system that allowed them to do as much good as they could without causing more harm in the process, but they hadn't entirely figured it out yet. As the Oracle, Cassandra was at the center of it, and she had many reasons for wanting to find a way to work around the Fates. Freedom from them, for starters.

"Good," Jason said, smiling at Ariadne, his twin. As Healers, they felt the need to help others more keenly than the rest of them. It was literally what they were born to do.

"Okay, but later," Claire said. "Helen and I have try-outs for Holiday chorus."

"Seriously, Gig?" Helen complained. She'd thought Claire had given up on that bad idea. "You're really going to make me do this?"

"Yes. We're trying out," Claire insisted, and then turned back to Cassandra. "We can come after dinner."

Cassandra tossed her thick black braid behind her shoulder and looked around anxiously. "Fine," she agreed, and then left them.

"You're going to *sing*?" Lucas asked Helen tentatively.

Helen was quite possibly the worst singer in the world. Not only was she tone deaf, but she also had terrible timing. She was always the person singing the chorus during the refrain or belting out a few off-key notes a measure or two before she was supposed to.

"Luckily, everyone has to audition, so I know I won't make it," Helen said as the bell signaling the end of lunch rang.

"Thank the gods," Lucas whispered under his breath.

Helen wrinkled her nose at him as he tucked her under his arm for the short walk to the hallway, where they separated—Lucas, Claire, Jason, and Ariadne to their advanced placement classes, and Helen in the other direction to her totally regular classes.

She glanced back once to see if Lucas was looking at her. And, of course, he was.

Chapter 2

"Well, that was utterly humiliating," Helen said, still mildly shell-shocked.

"Come on, it was great!" Claire enthused.

"For you! You sounded amazing. I never knew your voice was so pretty." Helen frowned over this. She knew Claire's voice better than her own, and just a few weeks ago Claire's singing had been decent at best. It was strange, but she couldn't think of anything malignant about this ability, so she let it go.

"You sang, good too," Claire replied.

Helen couldn't figure out if Claire was being supportive or sarcastic, but she did know that was a bald-faced lie. She entered the combination on her locker, opened it, and did a complicated juggling act to catch about five different things that fell out at her. Bobble heads, glittery framed pictures of her and Claire from middle school, a silly pen with a giant, goofy-looking alien topper that had been Matt's, and several other bits of memorabilia from Helen's long residence at this one particular locker—including a squeaky rubber chicken that had just appeared in there as if it had spontaneously coalesced from the ether—all tried to run for freedom every time Helen opened the door. Her locker was a mess, but she loved it because it was full of stuff that her friends had either made for her or given to her over the years. Sure, it was getting somewhat unruly, but she wasn't about to throw any of it away.

"Gig. People literally covered their ears," Helen continued as she shifted some books around.

"Who cares? You still made it into the Holiday Chorus!"

"As the *jingle beller*! All I do is stand there and shake these." Helen took the noise makers out of her bag and waved them around. "You don't even need to have rhythm to be the jingle beller! You just have to keep moving your arm!"

"But you're still going to be part of the caroling," Claire said, trying not to laugh at her musically challenged friend.

"And why do I want that, again?" Helen asked, tortured.

"Because it's our senior year," Claire lectured sternly. "We're leaving soon, and if we don't say yes to everything this year has to offer, we're going to regret it."

Even though she had just made a total ass of herself, Helen knew her best friend was right. The more average high school stuff Helen did, the more connected to the world she felt, and Helen needed to stay connected. Some of the things she could do were scary, and sometimes she did them without thinking. The more normal she acted, the more normal she would be.

"What's high school without a little humiliation, right?" Helen complained as they went outside to the parking lot.

Helen shivered and suppressed the feeling that someone was watching her. A glance around told Helen that they were alone. It was just the cold that made the back of her neck prickle.

"We're making life-long memories!" Claire shouted to the dark sky. This deep into the winter the sun went down before five o'clock.

Helen stuffed the jingle bells back into her bag. "Yeah." She laughed darkly, still struck with the feeling that they weren't alone. "We've got to hurry up and live before you become a teen bride."

She cringed as soon as the words were out of her mouth. She saw Claire deflate and reached out a hand to stop her from walking away.

"Sorry. I don't know why I said it like that. It sounded less mean in my head. That was terrible."

Claire nodded, accepting Helen's apology. "But you are right in a way—even though it was terrible," she conceded. "It's like, I know I want to be with him forever, but do we have to start forever right now? Can't we have a minute?"

Helen shrugged and got into the passenger side of Claire's car. She understood where Claire was coming from, of course, but at least Claire knew what Jason intended for their relationship. Helen didn't even know what Lucas wanted to do next year, let alone for the rest of their practically eternal lives.

"It's so frustrating," Claire said, starting her car. "What do you say to Lucas when he brings up, you know, the future?"

"He hasn't brought it up," Helen replied quietly as they drove off school grounds.

Claire glanced over at her, confused. "I thought—I mean, you know how Jason is always saying Scions marry young, and I just assumed, *you* and *Lucas*..."

"It's fine." Helen ended the conversation before the tightness in her throat got any worse.

. . .

They drove in uncomfortable silence to the Delos compound which was situated on a pristine part of prime Nantucket beach in Siasconset. It was a new construction on a large strip of beach, and though the property had many modern touches like the walls of glass that opened beach side, it was based on the whaler design like most properties on Nantucket. The scale of their property, however, was colossal. Letting themselves in like they lived there, they followed the sound of voices to the library.

"Sparky!"

Helen almost melted with relief when she saw Hector striding toward her, his smile as bright as his blond curls and nearly as broad as his shoulders. He gathered her up in a big bear hug, lifting her off the ground and making a gravelly sound in the back of his throat as he held her.

"I missed you," she said against his neck. It had only been a few weeks since he had moved out to the Delos brownstone on Washington Square Park to attend NYU, but there was something about Hector's presence that made Helen feel better. And seeing him made her realize that she really needed to feel better right now.

Hector tilted his head back to look at her. "What is it?" he asked quietly.

Helen shook her head. "Later."

When Hector put her down it was Orion's turn. He approached her with narrowed eyes, reading her heart. He hugged her in a softer, less demonstrative, but no less caring way than Hector had.

"Someone needs a cry," Orion whispered knowingly. Helen chuckled.

"Maybe that's it. I just need a good cry," she said, downplaying it. She pulled out of his embrace to look him over. "And you need another haircut."

"Nah," Orion said, shaking out his glossy mane. "I'm thinking of growing it out."

Hector rubbed his eyes in a long-suffering way. "So help me, if I see you wearing a man bun..."

"Who says I'd put it up in a bun?" Orion asked him defensively.

"Orion. You are *such* a man-bun kind of guy," Helen said before abruptly switching sides. "But I think it'll look good on you."

"Ha!" Orion said, pointing at Hector like he'd just won a bet.

The guys greeted Claire with hugs before she moved to Jason. Helen looked around the room. Castor and Pallas were talking quietly in the corner. Ariadne was standing a little apart, just staring out the window, waiting for the meeting to begin. She'd been doing that more and more since Matt had died.

Jason and Claire went to her and the three of them took places near each other. Cassandra sat in a large chair that swamped her tiny body, her eyes drawn to Orion's tall, lithe frame.

"Where's Lucas?" Helen asked no one in particular.

"He had to leave," Cassandra answered from across the room.

"To go *where*?" There was an uncomfortable pause, and Helen realized her voice was louder than it needed to be.

"He didn't say," Orion replied softly.

He brushed the inside of her wrist with the tips of his fingers. Helen instantly felt calmer, and she knew that Orion was subtly altering her emotions.

"Lucas doesn't need to be here. He already knows what I'm about to tell you because he was the one who came up with the plan," Cassandra said, her gaze drifting down to Orion's fingers on Helen's pulse point. "We should get started."

Helen followed Orion over to the sofa. "Thank you," she whispered as she sat down in between him and Hector.

Orion tilted his head close, his green eyes peering at her. "Any time."

He turned his attention back to Cassandra. Helen reminded herself that Orion was unintentionally sexy, but she glanced down at his chest anyway, just to make sure he wasn't flirting with her. The slow throb of his heart was thick and rich with attraction, but he was always like that. Orion was wired for love, but he was comfortable with being single for now, and that was probably the sexiest thing about him. Cassandra had a devastating crush on him, though he scarcely glanced her way. Cassandra's mind was mature beyond her years, but her body was still too young, and apart from one befuddled kiss he'd given her when it looked like the world was about to end, Orion didn't consider her as a partner. She was never going to grow up, so what was the point? He cared about her, and he was careful to take her feelings into account because he didn't want to hurt her, but that's where it ended for him. Helen knew that deep down they were perfect for each other. Or they would be if Cassandra ever reached adulthood.

Helen forced herself to concentrate on the meeting rather than the spicy smell of Orion's skin. He was attractive, but that didn't mean that she was attracted to him. They'd been down that road and Helen knew it was a dead end. Lucas was the only one she really wanted. She moved away from Orion ever so slightly and tuned in to what Cassandra was saying.

She'd already missed a ton.

"Since Orion seems to be the only one who is hidden from the

Fates, you're all going to have to work with him if you want to use your powers to help people," Cassandra said. "But in order to do more than just whatever bad things happen directly in front of you when you're with him, you're going to need to use my prophecy."

"So, Lucas has a plan. And we think it'll work," Orion said, taking a turn at explaining. "Cassandra will foresee things that are supposed to happen, and on my own—without telling her or anyone else—I'll pick which event I think I can stop, or fix, or even just make a little better."

"What about the rest of us?" Ariadne asked.

"At the last possible moment, I'll come and get whoever has the talents I think can help me best. Your job is to be ready for anything."

"It's like a shell game, but for the Fates," Cassandra said, looking pleased.

Castor and Pallas exchanged doubtful looks.

"*What*, Dad?" Jason asked, annoyed.

Him and his father's relationship had become strained ever since Pallas sided with Tantalus and the gods during the last battle—and against Helen. Though Pallas had refused to directly fight, Jason had never really forgiven his father, though he had forgiven Claire and Ariadne for making the same choice. They had done so out of loyalty and love for Matt, who had challenged Helen because she was the Tyrant.

In a way, Matt had been right. Helen was too powerful. She understood why everyone had chosen what they had in the moment. Also, she couldn't carry a grudge in a bucket. It just wasn't her style.

"Usually when we get involved with mortals it doesn't end well for them, even when we have the best intentions," Pallas reminded them. He looked at Jason and Ariadne. "And I'm not just talking about your mother."

Ariadne looked away. It had only been a few months since Matt had died. Helen still had trouble accepting that her life-long friend was gone, but for Ariadne it was worse. She had loved Matt.

"But that was before, when the Houses were too busy fighting each other," Hector argued, eager to move past the fact that his sister was still mourning a guy who had, in fact, killed him. Hector had died, and Lucas had descended into the Underworld and made a deal with Hades for Hector's revival. Hector had forgiven his father, but he hadn't forgiven Matt for that stunt. Helen suspected it was less about what side Matt had been on and more because Hector had lost, which still bugged the crap out of him.

"Things are different, and we can finally focus on something other than the survival of our Houses," Castor said. "But the House Wars weren't what kept us from doing more for humanity in the past. When I was a kid, I wanted to be like Superman."

"Pretty sure it was Green Lantern," Pallas corrected.

"That was *Ajax*," Castor said. "Remember that stupid t-shirt?"

"Oh yeah." Pallas said, realizing. Then he chuckled at a memory.

"The point is, the Fates won't allow Scions to be heroes, no matter how much we want that." Castor looked at his daughter. "Do you really think you can use the Fates in a way that *they* haven't already designed?"

Cassandra looked down, nodding. "You meet your fate on the road you take to escape it. I know. *Oedipus*. And maybe it won't work, but we've never had a Shield from the Fates on our side before, and now with Orion... I think it's worth a try. What good is being what we are if we can't use it to help people?"

"Agreed," Jason and Ariadne said together.

Castor and Pallas looked at each other. A decision passed between them in silent conversation. "You sure?" Pallas asked his brother.

Castor nodded, "It's time."

He stood, facing Orion as he shook out his arms, like he was about to do something athletic with them. "Since you're set on going forward with this, you should probably know *all* of our talents, so you can decide how best to use *us*."

"What do you mean, *all* of your talents?" Hector said carefully, because Castor looked like he was bracing himself for a fight.

Castor got a wicked glint in his eye. And then he turned into a wolf.

"Holy shit!" Hector yelled.

Everyone exchanged shocked glances.

Jason looked at his father. "He said *us*. Does that mean you *both*...?"

"Yes," Pallas answered for them, since his brother was currently shaking off his clothing and couldn't exactly turn back into a naked man in the present company to speak.

"I don't know why only Jason inherited the ability," Pallas continued, "but Apollo was even called The Lycian—the wolf-god—which is why some of our cousins have that last name. The wolf is one of Apollo's many avatars, along with the mouse, crow, and dolphin."

As he spoke, Castor changed into a mouse, then a crow, and then back into a wolf.

"Obviously, the dolphin isn't too practical on dry land. And the crow is hard to maintain. I myself can't do that one at all.

We've rarely taken these forms in twenty years because we're vulnerable as animals. When we used to use them, we did it to deceive and kill other Scions." Pallas turned to Orion, whose mouth was still hanging open. "Your father, especially, might not take it well if he finds out about this."

"Why's that?" Orion wanted to know.

"Castor has history with your mother, Leda."

Wolf-Castor snapped at Pallas.

"*Before* your parents were together," Pallas added quickly. He seemed to understand his brother's signals even in Castor's changed form. "Let's just say, Daedelus might remember a wolf being around Leda. So be careful how you present this information to him if you ever choose to."

"Wow," was all Orion could say.

"Uncle Caz," Hector drawled appreciatively.

"We're not proud of how we used this ability, or most of the things that we did back when we followed Tantalus," Pallas continued. "Which is why we've kept it a secret."

There was a long pause. Too long. They all needed a minute.

"Does Lucas know?" Helen finally broke the silence.

"Actually, yes," Pallas answered. "He figured it out a while ago. He is a Falsefinder..."

Helen breathed a laugh. She knew all about that. Helen was a Falsefinder too, but somehow Lucas seemed to be much better at it than she was.

As the meeting broke up, Orion went to talk to Cassandra while Jason, Ariadne, and Claire splintered off into a group of their own. Jason was not taking the news of his father hiding his shapeshifting talent very well, and Ariadne and Claire seemed to be talking him through it. Helen touched Hector's arm and gestured for him to follow her out of the room.

"Are *you* okay?" she asked when they got out into the hallway.

Hector shrugged. "I don't know."

"It doesn't bother you, that they kept the fact that they're shapeshifters a secret?" she asked him, leaning her back up against the wall.

Hector put his shoulder against the wall, facing her, and thought about it for a moment. "Not really," he said, deciding. "They're our parents, but they're still people. Everyone has secrets."

"Does Lucas?" she asked with a smile.

Hector chuckled softly. "Seriously?"

"Was he with you last night in New York?"

A blank look flashed across Hector's eyes, and that answered her question.

"He lied to me," she whispered. "Well, he didn't lie to me—he can't. But he let me believe a lie, so same thing."

"Helen—" Hector began, straightening up.

"You don't have to cover for him."

Hector took her shoulders in his hands and looked at her sternly. "Lucas is *not* cheating on you."

"I never said he was," Helen replied, dropping her gaze. "But he still lied to me."

Hector pulled her against his chest for a hug. "You want me to talk to him?"

"No," she replied, taking the hug. "I will. Or maybe I won't. I'm not going to force him to be open with me," she said, standing up straight. "When he's ready, he'll tell me. Or he won't. And that's his choice too."

Hector gave her an uncertain look. "Why do I have a bad feeling about this?"

"If he wants a relationship with secrets in it, that's what he's going to get."

"Yeah, this is bad."

"What's bad?" Orion said, butting in as he came into the hallway.

"Lucas screwed up," Hector told him.

"Yeah, he did," Orion replied, reading Helen's emotions. "That's cold anger. He must have *really* screwed up."

Helen took a deep breath and smiled. "Anyway, I guess I'll fly home now." She said as she headed for one of the beachside exits.

"Must be nice," Orion said wistfully as he followed her outside. "I've got to swim home. Up the Hudson. It's not so clean."

"You're not staying?" Hector asked Orion, coming outside with them.

Orion shook his head. "I have to leave so Cassandra can make prophecies."

"Right," Hector replied musingly. Then, he suddenly burst into motion. "Race ya!" He ran straight for the ocean, getting the jump on Orion.

"Sometimes it's like living with a fifth grader," Orion said, shaking his head while he watched Hector plunge beneath the waves.

"I wish I enjoyed it as much as you both do. Even though I can do pretty much everything you can do underwater now, the ocean still *freaks* me out," Helen admitted.

"Why?" he asked.

"Sharks are creepy."

"Nonsense."

"Says the Son of Poseidon."

He brushed the side of her cheek with his fingers. "Call me if you need me."

"You too," she said, frowning that she was only now considering his feelings. "That was quite a bomb Pallas and Castor dropped on you."

Orion laughed. "Yeah, no one wants to think of their mom like that, but..." He looked back at her. "She could control hearts *and* calm the Furies. Why wouldn't she date other Scions? Makes more sense than only being with one person your entire life. That way you find out what you really want."

"I guess," Helen agreed, somewhat unsure.

Orion locked eyes with hers. "Good night, Helen."

She waited for Orion to dive beneath the water, and then once again felt that prickling feeling on the back of her neck, like she was being watched. She looked around, but there was no one else on the beach. She soared up into the air, not wanting to take any chances.

The next morning Helen turned away from the counter at the News Store to blow her nose. Though it had been a short flight from the Delos property on the beach to her dad's house in the town center, Helen had felt the cold seep into her, which was unusual. She had gotten such a chill that she had to wear socks to bed and pull on an extra blanket. Even still, she couldn't seem to get warm for some strange reason.

The Saturday afternoon rush was just thinning out after two solid hours of non-stop work for Helen and Kate. There were still a few customers in the News Store checking out the salt-water taffy or grabbing bottles of the kombucha that Helen had made her dad order, and none of them were at the register yet, but still. It was gross to blow your nose at work. Helen threw out her tissue and pumped a dose of hand sanitizer into her palm.

"So, I'm thinking I'm going to have to shell out for that bartender, the one that makes all the specialty drinks like the rum punches and the gin fizzes." Kate said, swinging behind the counter to stand next to Helen.

"Handlebar Mustache?" Helen asked dubiously. "The one with the pocket watch in his waistcoat?"

Kate nodded painfully. "He's really good. And he knows all of these old-timey seasonal drinks. Also, he kinda looks like a young, hip Santa. You know, before the pot belly and the red and green color scheme took over."

"He kinda does," Helen agreed, then turned to smile at an approaching customer. "Five-twenty-five," she said, ringing up the kombucha.

The customer swiped his card and left. Helen turned back to Kate.

"I still can't believe people are willing to pay so much for fizzy, flavored bacteria in a glass jar," Kate said.

"Says the woman who is about to pay double for the bartender at her wedding because he makes rum punch and looks like Santa," Helen rejoined.

"Touché." Kate cocked her head and crossed her arms, watching Helen. "Have you been crying?"

Helen shrugged and took her credit card slips off the spike, idly riffling through them. "Possibly," she admitted. "Or maybe it's allergies?"

Kate was momentarily thrown. "Can you get allergies? I mean, with your..." she gestured to Helen's whole body in a swishy way that Helen understood to mean "goddess-ness."

Helen shrugged. "I've been off lately. I'm..." she paused and thought about it. She did feel weak and shaky physically for some reason she hadn't figured out yet, but her emotional state was even worse. "Disappointed," she finally decided.

Kate stepped closer to Helen and touched her arm. "With what?" she asked.

Another customer came to the register and Helen turned to her with a bright smile. "Is that everything?" she asked, ringing up the assortment of candies and soda pops.

The customer asked a few questions about the foliage, but unfortunately it was too late in the season for that. Also, Nantucket didn't have many trees. It wasn't really a foliage kind of place, like Vermont was. And it was winter, not fall. This person had obviously booked the wrong vacation at the wrong time, but still Helen was cheerful and helpful, and the customer left seeming like she would come back tomorrow if she needed anything, which always made Helen feel good.

"Seriously. Disappointed with what?" Kate asked when the News Store was empty again.

Helen sighed. She wasn't getting out of telling Kate. "Lucas," she admitted. "He's hiding something from me."

"Huh," Kate replied, raising an eyebrow. "The good kind of hiding because he has a surprise, like, jewelry? Or the bad kind of hiding, like a secret wife?"

Helen couldn't help but laugh at that. "Pretty sure it's not the second one, but it almost doesn't matter. I feel like he's pulling away from me."

Kate weighed her words before continuing. "You know, your father and I don't know every last little detail about each other, and that's okay. It doesn't mean we don't love each other, or that we aren't a team."

"Am I overreacting?"

Kate shrugged. "Maybe?"

The bell on the door rang and Lucas came into the News Store, still holding his car keys. He wasn't in a rush as he crossed to Helen, a smile starting in his eyes and slowly moving down to his mouth.

"Hi," Helen said. Her voice cracked and she wanted to kick herself. How did he do that to her? She considered it abnormal to still get butterflies looking at her boyfriend.

"Hi," he said back.

She stood there staring at him, grinning like an idiot before she remembered it was her turn to talk.

"Did we make plans for this afternoon?" she asked.

"No." He looked at Kate. "Do you need her?"

"Nope," Kate answered quickly. "Have fun!"

Kate shoved Helen's bag, phone, and jacket at her and leaned close. "You have nothing to worry about," she whispered into Helen's ear.

Helen knew that Kate was trying to be quiet, but Lucas was a Scion. She may as well have shouted it.

Lucas helped Helen into her jacket and then opened the door and waved goodbye to Kate. He took Helen's hand, walked all the way to his car, and *then* asked.

"What did Kate mean by that? Worried about what?"

Helen shook her head, refusing to say anything as she got into the passenger seat.

Lucas started driving them toward 'Sconset. "I'm not going to stop asking until you answer."

"Yet, I'm the one with the questions that aren't getting answered," Helen remarked.

"What questions?"

Helen glared at his profile. He glanced back and forth between her and the road.

"Okay. We have to stop," he decided, pulling off the road. He put the car in park and turned to face her. "What is it?"

"I don't want to ask!" she nearly shouted. "I want you to *want* to tell me where you've been going and what you've been doing."

Lucas made a frustrated sound and dropped his head for a moment. When he looked back up, his bright blue eyes pinned her.

"I'm working."

That definitely wasn't a lie. It just didn't make any sense. "What? Like at a job?"

"Sort of." He ran a hand through his hair. "I'm preparing... for the future."

"Am I included in this future?" she asked.

He narrowed his eyes at her, a little bit scared now. "What's going on?"

She threw up her hands. "I don't know. You won't even tell me where you want to go to school next year."

Lucas thought about it for a moment. "Do you trust me?"

"That's not fair."

Lucas took her hand. He fiddled with her fingers, rubbing the pad of his thumb over her skin. "You're right. It's not."

He suddenly looked so sad. Helen reached out and put her hands on either side of his face, leaning close to him.

"Just tell me."

"Gods, I want to," he whispered, leaning his cheek into the palm of her hand. "But I can't. Not yet."

He wasn't lying. His heart was a tangle of fear and resentment and anger and frustration, like too many clothes shoved into a washing machine. He was in pain, and he was scared, and Helen simply couldn't bear it.

"Okay," she said suddenly, as she moved into his arms and held him. "I trust you."

He relaxed into her, relieved, and Helen realized that what he feared most were her feelings. Her frustration. Relief folded into something else, and Helen felt Lucas' body go from unspooling into hers to tightening against it. His mouth found the curve of her neck and his hand the curve of her hip. He pulled her around in her seat until she was facing him and kissed her. Easing her back and moving over her, his hand slipped under her shirt and up the side of her.

A horn honked as a car passed them. They both jumped, looked out the front windshield, then laughed. It was still broad daylight, and they were very visible on the side of the road.

"Was that Jason?" she asked.

"Jackass," Lucas said.

"What are we doing, by the way?" Helen asked.

Lucas looked over at her. "Movie at my house."

They normally did "movie night" at night, but she didn't really care what time it was. She just wanted to turn off the lights and lay under a blanket with Lucas until she could hardly stand it, and then she would pretend to fly home, only to come right back in his window. Or he would fly in hers if Jerry was complaining about how much time she was spending at Lucas' house.

When Helen and Lucas arrived in the family room Jason, Claire, Ariadne, and Cassandra were already there, arranging pillows and blankets and finding spots for bowls of snacks and drinks. Castor, Noel, and Pallas joined them, which was not unheard of, but not usual either. Helen noticed Noel watching Ariadne closely, asking her questions, basically trying to draw her out.

Lucas watched Helen watching them. "Ari isn't doing well."

Helen nodded. She had seen the widening pit in Ariadne's heart. Time wasn't healing her wounds from Matt's death, and there was less of her because of it.

"Is that why we're doing 'movie day'?" Helen whispered back. He nodded in reply. "Has anyone suggested therapy?" she asked.

"There's so much she wouldn't be able to tell a therapist. Would it even help if she couldn't be completely open?"

Helen frowned. "All those Healers in the Hundred Cousins, and not *one* of them studied mental health? There must be a Scion Ari can talk to. A professional—if not in your House, then maybe Orion knows someone in the House of Rome."

"Humm," he hummed in his throat, his eyes growing hazy. "Did I mention that I love you?"

"Not today."

He pulled their blanket up over them so he could touch her beneath it.

Helen had no idea what movie they watched. When it was over, she couldn't have even recalled the title if it were the only question on her college entrance exams. They opened the blinds and stretched as a group. The sun was going down.

"Are we going to watch another?" Claire asked dreamily. She and Jason had been sharing a blanket of their own.

"I could make sliders," Noel offered, heading toward the kitchen. "We could keep snacking through dinner."

Lucas wrapped his arms around Helen after his stretch. He held her for a few minutes, swaying back and forth.

"I have to go. Stay here with everyone if you want," he said. "I'll see you Monday."

He let her go and headed for the door. Helen was so thrown she just stood there for a moment. Then she caught up to him in the hallway outside the family room.

"What do you mean, you'll see me *Monday*?" she demanded.

He went to one of the seaside doorways and opened it. Night was falling. "Trust me." He gave her a sad smile and flew away.

Stunned, Helen wandered into the kitchen to find Noel.

"Hey," Noel said warmly while she pulled food out of the refrigerator.

Helen cut right to the chase. "Do you know where Lucas goes at night?" she asked.

Noel stopped, her hands full of cheese. "No," she replied, looking worried. "It used to be just once a week or so. At first, we thought he was with you..." she trailed off and put the cheese down. "He won't talk to me or Castor about it."

"He asked me to trust him. I told him I would." Helen felt cold creeping into her. A shiver shook her from head to toe, and she wrapped her arms around her middle to stop it. She had no idea why she felt cold all the time now. "Should I be worried?"

Noel smiled knowingly. "Delos men don't cheat."

"That's not—why does everyone think that first?" Helen wondered aloud. "What I mean is, should I be worried about Lucas being in trouble somehow?"

Noel shrugged. "I don't know. He said I shouldn't worry, but you know how he is."

"Yeah," Helen replied.

She mumbled some goodbyes to the rest of the family and then flew home. On the way, it started to snow.

Chapter 3

She dreamed about Everyland.

The cities were bombed-out wastelands. The forests were clear-cut mud washes. The fields were toxic dumps. Zeus, beautiful and vengeful, floated above it all, screaming Helen's name.

She shook herself awake.

"Woah!" shouted Orion. She saw him ducking down to avoid her punch, which she stopped in mid-air.

"What the hell!?" Helen said, jumping out of bed.

Orion was crouched down, holding up two travel cups to shield his head. "I bear an offering of coffee! Don't kill me!" he pleaded jokingly.

"What are you *doing* here?" Helen asked, helping Orion back up to standing.

He handed her a travel mug. Coffee, heavy cream, no sugar, just like she liked it. She took it and had to sit back down on the edge of her bed to relieve her shaky legs.

"I'm here to do a thing with you," he said, sitting down next to her. His heart was still pounding. He gave an uneven laugh. "You know, the thing we discussed? I told all of you to be ready for anything?"

Helen slumped with relief, until she realized that she was in a tank top and a tiny pair of underpants, and it was still dark out. "What are you doing in my bedroom?"

"Your dad let me up," he said like it was obvious.

Helen guffawed. "No, really."

"No, *really*," Orion said honestly. "He sent me right up."

"Huh," Helen mused. She took a sip of her coffee. "He's never let Lucas come into my bedroom. Knowingly, that is."

Orion looked at Helen out of the corner of his eyes. "He doesn't trust Lucas."

"And he trusts *you*?" Helen said, gesturing at Orion and his disconcerting hotness.

He nodded. "It's not your body your dad is trying to protect."

Helen looked at him disbelievingly.

Orion paused, debating whether to continue.

"Just say it," Helen dared him.

"I make you laugh. Lucas makes you cry. Who would you pick for your daughter?" Orion asked simply.

Helen stared at Orion, stunned. "That's *not* true," she said. "I mean, yeah, I've cried over him, but that was because we couldn't —" she broke off, frustrated. "It's not the whole story!"

"I know." Orion smiled and stood up. "Get dressed."

Still cold and muttering to herself about what Orion had said, Helen put on several layers and brushed her teeth before meeting him downstairs. He was chatting with her dad and Kate in the kitchen. The sun was barely up. Her dad looked tired as he tightened his robe around his thinning shoulders.

"What time is it?" Helen asked.

"Almost too late," Orion replied. "You still can't use your portals, can you?"

Her ability to teleport anywhere had been lost when she'd given Everyland to Zeus because of how portals work. Even if she was trying to teleport across her bedroom, she needed to open a portal into Everyland, go into it, and then open another into wherever she wanted to end up. She didn't know that was how the portal system worked before she created her world, because it always seemed to her that she was traveling through cold, blank space—blank space being all Everyland was before she'd built it. Now she understood that if she tried to teleport, she would have to open the borders of Everyland, and Zeus could use that opening to escape if he timed it right. It was too risky to even try.

"No," Helen replied, deflating.

"Didn't think so," Orion said, sounding annoyed. "Come on. You have to fly us there."

Helen chugged her coffee and put the mug down. "Where are we going?"

Orion led her outside. "I'll tell you in a bit," he said, then he turned to Kate and Jerry and said a polite goodbye to them. Carefully watching them interact, Helen noticed that her dad really did like Orion better than Lucas.

"Be careful," Jerry called out to Helen.

"Sure, Dad," she said, though it was kind of ridiculous considering she couldn't die. Her father *could*, however, Helen thought as she noticed how pale he was.

"Where to?" Helen said, irrationally annoyed with Orion because her dad liked him better.

Orion put his arms around her, which felt nice. But only because they were standing in a foot of snow and he was warm, she told herself, and not because his body felt freaking amazing. He was smiling mischievously down at her. Of course, he knew what she was feeling whether she was willing to admit it or not.

"West," he directed, easing her closer against him.

He was being intentionally saucy, Helen realized. "That's enough of that," she grumbled, releasing gravity abruptly. As they rocketed into the air, Orion swore and clutched at her in fear.

They flew far. Orion didn't tell her where they were headed, he just told her to keep going. Finally, somewhere above the Great Plains, they spotted a stormfront on the horizon.

"This should be it," he said.

They landed in a huge field of dry grass. There was no one around for miles. "Well, this is beautiful, but why are we here?" Helen asked. She didn't see anyone there to rescue.

Orion laughed nervously. "You *can* stop lightning, can't you?"

Helen could both generate and absorb lightning, and she explained it to Orion as best as she could. He sat down on the parched ground and Helen pulled up a tuft of hay next to him. It wasn't dawn yet this far west, but it would be soon.

"I'm guessing Cassandra made a prophecy about a wildfire?" Helen asked.

"Hundreds of miles are supposed to burn. People die," he answered.

Helen frowned and looked down. "Must be hard for her to see those things. To know they're going to happen and also know she can't do anything about it."

"It is." Orion pulled up a bit of hay and started breaking it to bits in his fingers. "She needs this to work. She needs to know that something she does matters."

Helen glanced down at his heart. It was swirling with emotions. "How are things between you two?" she asked.

Orion let out a long breath and flicked the last bits of hay in his fingers away. "They *aren't.*" He shook his head as he spoke. "I know she's sixteen, and emotionally she's, like, sixty, but she looks so young. I just... don't feel that way about her."

Helen breathed a curse and looked away.

"It's not your fault," Orion said.

"Yeah, it is," Helen started to argue, but he took her hand and stopped her.

"Cassandra told me that the Fates never let the Oracles mature. She said it had something to do with the first Cassandra, at Troy. They allowed her to become a woman and she betrayed them for a man."

Helen remembered. Or at least the part of her that was Helen of Troy remembered following Aeneas—who had been a dead ringer for Orion—to Cassandra's temple. She'd seduced him and because of that he had to leave Troy before it was sacked. She'd saved his life by destroying his honor.

Helen sighed heavily. "Do you have feelings for her at all?"

He considered this. "There are a lot of ways to love a person. It doesn't always have to be physical."

"Yeah, but I've seen how she looks at you," Helen countered. "It's physical for her."

Orion shook his head again. "It's not going to happen. And I know that hurts her, but this is not something I can change about myself."

She gave him a sad smile. "I'd be worried if you could."

"Some of us just don't get to be with the one we want."

Helen didn't think he was still talking about Cassandra. Before she could formulate a question for him, or decide if she even wanted to, the sky above them darkened ominously. A thundercloud moved overhead, and then it kept on going without shedding any bolts. It passed them. Orion and Helen gave each other a panicked look as they realized they were in the wrong place.

"Stay here!" Helen yelled over the rushing wind. "I'll catch the lightning in the clouds."

Orion grabbed her before she took off, stopping her. "If you can't get to all of it, and a fire starts, I'll make the earth turn over and put it out!" he yelled over the wind.

Helen nodded in understanding and jumped into the air.

She could feel the static building like a scream in the back of her throat. Every hair on her head and her skin stood on end and began to sparkle with white-blue light. There was an enormous amount of energy already there, and her presence became the seed the cloud needed to release it. Electricity sought the earth, but Helen tethered it to her body until a dome of lightning surrounded her.

As the electricity reached the fourth state and became plasma, the heat, hotter than on the surface of the sun, was almost intolerable, even for her. Her clothes disintegrated in a puff of smoke as plasma forked over her body like veins of pink light. She had never tried to take in so much energy before.

Before it blinded her, she thought she saw a face among the clouds. He had amber eyes, like hers.

Helen felt herself getting tossed about. She tumbled through the thunderhead and got blasted by the ice crystals inside. They scoured her skin, making a thousand little cuts. She threw her arms up to protect her head.

Feeling herself expelled from the storm cloud, Helen dared to open her eyes. She was still aglow with plasma, and she was falling from the sky like a comet.

"Helen!" Orion screamed from the ground.

She couldn't stop her fall. Orion threw his arms out wide, and as he did, the topsoil rippled and folded over like waves hitting a beach. He turned over acres of dry scrub, summoning up soft earth to cushion Helen's fall.

She hit and sank down deep. The earth smothered the fire in her skin, and everything went dark as she was buried.

She felt arms reaching around her. Hands smoothing over her face, brushing away grit.

"It's okay," Orion murmured. His voice sounded high and tight with fear. "It'll be okay. I'll get you to Jason and Ariadne."

Orion wrapped her in his jacket, lifted her into his arms, and started to run.

"It's too far—" Helen murmured, but Orion either didn't hear her or he wasn't listening. There was no way he could run halfway across the country while carrying her, even at Scion speed. She tried to get him to stop, but he kept on going.

She must have passed out because when she opened her eyes it was dark. Orion was panting and Helen could feel his body shaking with fatigue as he strode out into the Atlantic. They were nearly home. Cold saltwater washed over her. It flooded her nose and her throat, closing off her airways. She struggled in a panic, kicking to the surface. Orion surfaced with her, his arms keeping her afloat.

"I can't breathe!" Helen gasped, coughing violently as her head got repeatedly dunked under the water by dragging waves. "I can't breathe underwater anymore!"

Orion held her head above water. She noticed the scared look on his face before he could quash it.

"I'll breathe for you," he said, sounding calm. He covered her mouth with his and they sank below the waves. As he swam for them both, she gave herself up to the kiss and fell back into the darkness.

When she woke again, she was inside the Delos house. Ariadne and Jason were holding their glowing hands over her, their eyes screwed shut in concentration as they healed her. Helen became aware of shouting.

"You let her go up into a storm cloud alone!?" Lucas was yelling.

Helen turned her head to see Hector and Castor holding Lucas back as he lunged at Orion, who was backed up against a wall, hardly able to stand. Orion was bare to the waist, shoeless, and still soaking wet. Normally he could banish water immediately, but he was so spent he couldn't even summon the power to do that.

"Hey!" Hector shouted in Lucas' face. "This was *your* plan. Orion didn't do anything wrong."

That caught Lucas' attention. He went slack, defeated. Helen tried to pry her dry mouth apart to speak.

"What we need to do is figure out why Helen was so affected by the lightning," Castor said.

"Lucas..." Helen croaked.

"She's awake," Jason called.

Lucas' face was before hers in a moment, his hand smoothing back her hair. "What happened?" he asked. He saw her trying to swallow and he turned away. "Water!" he called.

Lucas helped her sit up and drink until she'd had her fill. Using electricity always drained her of fluids. She looked across the room at Orion, who had slid down the wall. He could barely lift his head he was so exhausted. Cassandra and Hector were crouched next to him, trying to hold him up.

"Help him," Helen said, pointing toward Orion weakly. The twins went to him immediately.

"Orion said you fell from the sky," Lucas whispered, his face a mask of worry. "What happened?"

"He blindsided me," she murmured, her eyes closing.

Helen felt herself being lifted and cradled against Lucas' chest. She turned into him, breathing deeply of his scent, while the muffled sound of him saying something to his father reverberated through her. Then, she floated until she felt herself being stretched out on cool, familiar sheets. She was in Lucas' bed. She gave herself up to sleep with Lucas curled against her back.

Helen felt a thigh between hers, and smooth skin under her cheek. She spent one moment in between, unsure who was holding her, and then she knew. Her cheek was in the same place where she'd once made a Helen-shaped dent in him.

She ran her hand down Lucas' chest to his stomach, where he stopped her from going any further.

"Who blindsided you?" he asked.

"I didn't really see him," Helen mumbled.

Lucas turned them over and moved away to prop himself up on an elbow. "Who?" he persisted.

Helen sat up suddenly, worried. "How's Orion?"

Lucas frowned. "He's fine."

"And the fire? Did we stop it?"

"You did."

"Good," she said, relieved. "That means it worked. We might not be able to beat fate, but at least we can dodge it."

"But we didn't, not really, when you think about it. You got hurt, Helen," Lucas said, frowning. "We've all decided to back off my idea for now. Until we can figure out what went wrong."

Helen deflated. She knew Ariadne and Cassandra needed this, and now her failure was holding them back.

He sat up opposite her in bed. "Why won't you tell me whose face you saw?"

She rolled her eyes at him. He never let anything go.

"I thought I saw Zeus in the thunder cloud," Helen admitted, feeling silly to even say it. "But he wasn't there." She reached out for her world. She controlled the borders of Everyland and in that way she was still connected to it. She could feel the unmistakable presence of her prisoner inside. "He's definitely still in Everyland. I must have been hallucinating."

Lucas' lips tilted in a doubtful smile. "So, next question. How did you get injured badly enough to hallucinate?"

Helen shrugged, thinking of how cold she'd felt lately and how every now and again she felt weak. She thought of the lightning in her mind, and fearfully pushed away the possibility that these things were tied to Zeus.

"Maybe even I have limits?"

He didn't look convinced. Neither was Helen, but she wasn't going to say that and freak him out. She leaned forward to kiss him, and her stomach growled.

"You're hungry," Lucas said.

"Very," she replied, still going for the kiss.

He chuckled, stopping her. "You need to eat."

He stood, pulled on a pair of sweatpants, then went to his dresser to get Helen some clothes. He kept a drawer for her with some of her clothes in it. He brought her a pair of soft leggings and an oversized sweatshirt.

He leaned down and gave her a kiss. “I’ll be right outside,” he said, before leaving her to change in privacy.

They went down to the kitchen to find Orion demolishing a plate of baked ziti. Cassandra sat next to him silently watching him eat with wide, owl eyes. On the other side of the table Hector sat with Jason and Ariadne, who were eating as well. They had spent a lot of energy healing Orion and Helen the night before, but they looked like they had nearly recovered.

“There you are!” Noel called out, relieved when she saw Helen and Lucas. She stopped chopping vegetables to give Helen a hug and clung to her a bit longer than usual before letting her go. “I already called Kate and told her you were better. Sit. I have more food coming.”

Orion leaned back from his plate, smiling at Helen as she slid onto the banquet next to him.

“Thanks,” Helen said as she butted her shoulder against his.

“I would say *any time*, but I really hope that never happens again,” he replied, his smile fading. There were dark shadows under his eyes.

“Here,” Lucas said, sliding in on the other side of Helen with a plate for her. She dug in immediately.

“So, Sparky,” Hector began, stretching his big arms up over his head. “Any idea why you fell from the sky like a flaming rock?”

She shrugged and swallowed at the same time. “There was a lot of lightning in that thunder head. All that electricity must have scrambled my brain.”

Not exactly a lie, but not the whole truth. She didn’t want to make anyone panic, though. She’d deal with Zeus on her own. She was immortal. How bad could it get?

"Can you still fly?" Cassandra asked.

Helen disengaged gravity and floated up for a moment, proving she could.

"You couldn't breathe underwater, though," Orion reminded her.

Helen shrugged, not sure what it meant. But she knew how it felt, though she would never say it aloud. It felt like she was losing her powers.

Chapter 4

Helen shook her jingle bells. And shook them. And shook them some more.

After three hours of standing there like a doofus while everyone else sang, she was ready to kill Claire for making her join chorus. Her boredom had reached critical mass. Her head was buzzing, she felt hot, and every now and again she thought she saw a flash of lightning in her mind's eye.

"Miss Hamilton?" Mr. Abebe said, one of his dark eyebrows arched.

Helen realized that everyone had stopped singing. Probably a while ago. She put her hand over her jingle bells, silencing them.

"Sorry," she replied, shrinking. Then she laughed, slap-happy with non-stop jingling. "Once you get going it's tough to stop!"

Mr. Abebe gave her a strange look. "Don't lock your knees," he told her, apparently assuming she was feeling lightheaded. Which...she was. These bouts of weakness were beginning to alarm her, but she told herself to pull it together. She was a freaking goddess, for crying out loud. She smiled at Mr. Abebe brightly and he turned to address the rest of the chorus.

"Good job, everyone. I've been told it's snowing pretty hard outside so be careful getting home. Practice tomorrow, two to five, IF we have school! It might be a snow day!" he shouted over the sound of chatter, cheers and moving bodies as the Holiday Chorus broke up.

Helen made her way across the tiered risers to get to Claire. As a soloist, Claire had a special spot in the first row on the left side of Mr. Abebe, the choral conductor. Helen stood all the way to the right, practically in the aisle, just under the exit sign. She was more of a mascot than a member.

"Your solo was amazing!" Helen called as she made her way through the departing crowd to Claire.

Claire grimaced, waiting where she was for her best friend. "You just like *Oh Holy Night* because there are no jingle bells in it!"

Just as Helen reached Claire, she overheard Gretchen speaking to someone a few risers above them.

"Lucas has a voice that's to *die* for. But he's a mess right now because she's been *cheating* on him with his *cousin*, Hector. Do you remember him? Oh my god, light my *panties* on fire, he's almost as hot as Lucas..."

"Don't, Len," Claire was pleading in her ear.

Helen realized that she had started to climb the risers to get to Gretchen, and Claire was hanging on to her like a barnacle to stop her.

Gretchen looked down at Helen, still two levels away, with an expression that was equal parts disgust and horror.

"What did you say about me?" Helen asked, her voice dangerously low. Thunder rumbled outside.

Gretchen had hated Helen since they were kids and Helen had once frightened her by accidentally tearing off the door to the bathroom. While Gretchen had been using it. Helen had tried to apologize, but Gretchen wasn't the kind of person to forgive and forget. Especially not someone she envied as much as Helen.

"It's not worth it." Claire knew all about Gretchen's grudge. Helen looked at Claire's upturned face and nodded, knowing her best friend was right.

"Okay. Let's go," Helen said, spooling back the lightning mounting inside her. She had to get ahold of herself. She might dislike Gretchen, but she didn't want to actually hurt her. Helen and Claire turned as one and started down the risers.

"What a freak," Gretchen hissed.

This time it was Claire who snapped. She whirled on Gretchen, and it was Helen's turn to hold Claire back.

"You're talking out of your ass, Gretchen! You're just jealous because you couldn't catch a Delos boy with a net!"

"Whoa! What's going on here?" Mr. Abebe asked, vaulting up the tiers to stand between Gretchen and Claire.

"She was starting a rumor about Helen," Claire said, gesturing to Gretchen.

Gretchen couldn't have looked more shocked if an alien had plopped down in front of her and called her mama.

"What!?" she said, turning frantically to the person she'd been gossiping with, but whoever it was had abandoned her. "I was talking to a friend about her parents' divorce!"

Claire narrowed her eyes at Gretchen. "Playing the victim when the adults showed up worked when we were kids. We're not kids anymore."

Gretchen turned to Mr. Abebe with tears in her eyes. "I have no idea where this is coming from. Helen attacked *me*."

Claire faced Mr. Abebe. "Really?" she asked him. She gestured to Helen who was shifting from foot to foot anxiously, which made her look like a baby giraffe. "You think *Helen Hamilton* would attack anyone?"

Gretchen huffed, but Mr. Abebe held up a hand.

"That's enough," he decided. "It's late, it's snowing, and if we don't get home soon, we'll be stuck here, and I do not want to be stuck here. You feel me?"

Gretchen said nothing. She crossed her arms and glared at Helen.

"Let's go," Helen said in Claire's ear.

She had to physically pick Claire up and turn her around. Helen gathered their things and hustled them out of the auditorium.

"What the hell?" Claire exclaimed as they walked together to the student parking lot.

"Gretchen hasn't gone after me like that since Zach died."

"Right?" Claire said, still fired up.

"And what was she even talking about? Lucas isn't a mess."

Claire went quiet.

"What?" Helen asked defensively.

"He hasn't been himself. He never speaks in class anymore. I mean, he always cheers up when you're around, but...," Claire added quickly. "Whatever's going on, he won't talk to Jason about it. Lucas keeps telling him to focus on Ari and Cass."

Helen thought about Ariadne and Cassandra...and her dad. "Why are we all falling apart? Except for you, thank God. You're like, blossoming, with your singing and drawing. You've got all these hidden talents that are bursting out of you. It's wonderful."

Claire smiled and put her arm around Helen. As they looked across the white-blanketed parking lot for Claire's car, they noticed a man in a long, dark overcoat on the edge of school property.

"Who's that creeper?" Claire asked, pointing at him. But he disappeared almost instantly.

Helen thought about going after him, but that would have left Claire alone in the storm. "Let's get out of here," she said instead.

They got to Claire's car, or where Claire's car should have been, and it was just a white mound of snow.

"Crap," Claire said.

Helen looked around. "I could dig it out, but it probably wouldn't be safe to drive. Do you want to go back inside, or would you rather walk?"

"Walk," Claire answered, preferring a blizzard to a night snowed in with Gretchen. "My house is closest."

Helen hesitated, looking around for the creeper in the overcoat, but it's not like she couldn't handle him, so she didn't object. She didn't want to spend the night at school either. She took out her phone to call her dad but saw only a red X where the signal bars should be.

"The tower must be down," she said.

"You can use the land line at my house." Claire suggested, and the two of them started walking.

It was cold. Helen tried to burrow deeper into her coat.

"Are you okay? You're shivering like crazy," Claire noticed.

Helen hopped up and down while she walked. "I've been cold a lot lately," she admitted. She tried not to sound as worried as she felt about that.

"Do you want to run it?" Claire asked her.

"Maybe." Helen sniffed, looking around to get her bearings. It was dark, and the snow was falling hard. She didn't recognize their location. She held out her arm and stopped them. "Where are we?"

"We're still on Surfside. Wait, no. Is this Prospect?" Claire asked, spinning around.

"Neither," Helen answered. "Did we go right onto Sparks?"

Claire shook her head, confused. They were at a crossroads where three streets met—Surfside, Sparks, and Prospect—but on the island that Helen and Claire knew, those streets didn't meet exactly. What they were standing in now was the perfect intersection of three streets that seemed to stretch out forever. It was like no place that existed on Nantucket.

"This isn't real," Helen whispered to herself as she rotated around.

"Who's that?" Claire asked, her voice shaking.

Helen spun and put Claire behind her. She cupped a ball of lightning in her hand, ready to hurl it. Across the intersection from them stood a tall woman in a long, dark gown that spread out across the snow at her feet. Helen recognized her.

"Hello again, Helen Hamilton," the non-human said in a deep voice.

"Hecate," Helen breathed regretfully. The Witch Titan, goddess of the crossroads, keeper of boundaries, locks, and doorways, had helped Helen in her battle against the gods. And for that, Helen owed her three tasks. Since Helen hadn't summoned her, she could only assume that the Titan was there to collect.

The two goddesses tipped their heads in mutual respect.

"You know that whole thing about selling your soul to the devil at the crossroads?" Claire whispered in her ear.

"Yeah?" Helen replied.

Claire gestured widely to where they were standing.

"I don't want your soul, Helen," Hecate said, looking amused by Claire.

"But you do want something," Helen clarified.

Hecate nodded. "And I'm here to help you." Then she narrowed her eyes at Helen. "How are you feeling?"

Helen shifted on her feet. How could anyone, even the Witch Titan, know that she'd been struggling?

"That's an odd question," Helen remarked.

"You are in an odd situation," Hecate said in a no-nonsense way. "Zeus is killing you. He is tearing down your world from the inside and it is draining you. Eventually he will weaken you so much that you will no longer be immortal. You, and all the friends that you blessed with immortality, will die."

Helen heard no lie in Hecate's voice and instead felt the sinking truth of it.

"Lennie," Claire said, reaching out and taking Helen's arm.

Helen looked back at Hecate. "Why are you telling me this?" she asked.

"You can't fulfill your promise to me if you are dead," Hecate replied, like it was obvious.

"Right." Helen nodded.

Zeus. Killing her. That explained a lot. If Helen thought about it, she could hear him screaming her name down the bombed-out streets of her former heaven. For a moment, she saw him as if they were meeting in Everyland. He stood amongst the rubble, beautiful and vengeful. He strode forward, and she thought she heard him say, "*You can't hide or run or fight. I'm in your head.*"

Helen felt a shiver go down her spine and snapped back to reality. Claire was shaking her arm. "Len? *Helen*?" Claire said sharply.

"What?"

Claire sighed, relieved. "You've just been standing there *forever*. I thought I was going to have to unplug you and plug you back in."

"I'm okay," she lied. Her head was throbbing. Helen turned to Hecate. "Do you know how I can stop him? Zeus?"

Hecate shook her head sadly. "That's why I must insist you begin on the three tasks you promised to perform for me."

"Now? Like, *right* now?" Helen replied, incredulous. "Isn't it customary to give me a few days or something?"

Hecate thought about it. "Since you do not appear to be at death's door, and since, for whom we are going to see, time is of no consequence, I can be lenient." Hecate tilted her head down, in acquiescence. "I'll give you two days."

The wind blew and the snow swirled. When it settled Hecate was gone and they were across the street from Claire's house.

Claire looked at Helen. "Are you really going to die?" she asked, her voice tremulous.

Helen shook her head in confusion. "I don't feel like I am," she said.

"You'd tell me if it started getting bad, right?"

Helen nodded. "Promise."

Claire laughed to let out some tension. "I guess this is our life now, right? Freaky witches and gods trying to kill you?" Helen could tell she was making a joke because she was scared.

"Looks like it. But at least we're not sleeping in the gym. On the nasty wrestling mats that are definitely covered in staph. With *Gretchen*," Helen joked back. She was scared too. The lives of everyone she loved hinged on her.

. . .

They went inside and started peeling off snowy layers while Claire's mom fussed.

"Did you girls walk?" she exclaimed. "Why didn't you stay at school?"

Helen went to go use their landline while Claire got a lecture about the Donner party. She reached her dad and told him that they were at Claire's.

"Jason and Lucas were here looking for you two," he replied. "They specifically said they *weren't* worried. So, of course they were."

Helen chuckled at that. "We're fine, dad." She twisted the phone cord around her finger. "How are *you*?" she asked.

"Pissed I didn't get the snow blower fixed," he remarked. "Other than that, I'm okay."

"Would you tell me if you weren't?"

Her dad was quiet for a moment. "I'm home. I've got my feet up. I've been worse."

Not the answer Helen was looking for, but she knew it was the best she was going to get out of him. Helen promised to shovel around the house when she got back home and said goodbye. She tried Lucas' phone, and then Jason's, but all she got was a series of beeps in reply.

As she was considering whether she could fly to the Delos home in this snowstorm, she heard someone at Claire's front door.

She went to the front of the house, already hearing the low rumble of Lucas' voice. When he saw Helen, she thought he looked far more relieved than he should have. Jason was already arguing with Claire for walking home.

"We had to," Claire was replying defensively.

"Why didn't you just stay at school?" Jason scolded as they all went into the family room.

"Because! We'd just gotten into a huge fight with Gretchen and if I didn't get out of there, I was going kick her in the—"

Claire's grandmother *tisked* from her chair on the other side of the room, and Claire stopped immediately.

Claire turned to her grandmother and bowed. "*Gomen nasai obachan*," she said in Japanese. Helen knew that phrase. It meant *sorry, grandma*. They'd had to say it a lot in their lives.

"Why are you fighting with Gretchen again?" Claire's mom asked, confused. "I thought you girls were staying away from each other."

"*We* were," Claire said indignantly, gesturing to herself and Helen. "Anyway, I'm really hungry and tired and cold and I don't want to talk about Gretchen."

"You didn't see anyone else?" Lucas asked, like he already knew they had.

Helen looked at him, bemused. How did he always know stuff?

"No," Claire said, huffing. Lucas cringed slightly at the lie, but Claire kept going. "Not a lot of people out. Can we make hot cocoa?"

While Claire and Jason went into the kitchen, Helen and Lucas sat down with Grandma in family room. They said things loudly for her to hear, and they were also able to quietly say a few things to each other in between. Helen's family knew what she was, but Claire's family hadn't been told yet. Claire was certain it would make them disapprove of her relationship with Jason even more than they already did, so they were waiting to spring the whole "we're kind of immortal" thing on them.

"You drive here?" Grandma asked disapprovingly.

"Yes, we have a big truck with chains on the tires," Lucas said in a raised voice for grandma. Then he lowered his voice so only Helen could hear. "Cass *saw* you at the crossroads."

"Hecate came to collect," Helen whispered back to Lucas.

"Very dangerous." Grandma did not like Lucas and Jason driving.

"Yes. It is very dangerous out tonight," he agreed with Grandma while looking pointedly at Helen. "That's why Jason and I went to find Claire and Helen."

Grandma *harumphed* with approval. Apparently, she wasn't okay with Jason and Lucas risking their lives unless it was to retrieve her granddaughter. Oh, and her granddaughter's friend, if she happened to be along.

"You stay tonight. No more driving," Grandma decided.

"Thank you," Lucas replied politely. Then under his breath he ground out, "Cass said the Fates were screaming. I thought you were hurt."

He took her hand and held it, even though Grandma looked daggers at them for the overly intimate contact. Helen could see the strangling fear in Lucas and moved closer to him until the side of her body was against his, figuring what the heck? Grandma had never approved of her anyway, and Lucas needed her. While Grandma pretended that they weren't there, Helen quickly told Lucas everything that had happened at the crossroads.

"I have two days and then I have to start completing Hecate's tasks—whatever they are," she finished.

"Before Zeus kills you." Lucas' heart was beating too fast.

"Before he kills all of us," Helen stressed, pressing closer to him. "Everyone's immortality relies on mine, and Everyland is my power source. It's where I made you immortal," she whispered. "Zeus just wants out. I can open the borders of Everyland before he kills me—and I will. But then how do we stop him from destroying *this* world?"

During Helen's last encounter with Zeus, he had made it clear that the modern world didn't please him, and that once he was done with her, he was going to send the rest of the world back to the Bronze Age where he liked it. That included culling the population back down to the ten million individuals that then existed planet-wide; the "extra" seven and a half billion currently alive would be eradicated.

Lucas nodded, sinking into thought. The flashing lights of panic in his chest quieted, and the lights in the room dimmed almost to black.

"Power out," Grandma said.

"I've got to speak to my dad," Lucas said quietly to Helen before he stood. "I'll fix it," he told Grandma, and then he glanced at Helen, including her problem in that statement. As soon as he left the room the lights brightened as if they'd been let off a leash.

Helen spent a few uncomfortable moments trying to make conversation with Grandma, until everyone else came back to the family room with hot cocoa and a board game. Claire's dad lit a fire in the fireplace and Jason and Lucas pretended to be impressed with how quickly he did it, though either one of them could have done it in a fraction of the time. During all this, Helen kept catching Lucas staring at her with a worried frown.

"It'll be okay," she whispered to him.

Eventually, Claire's parents and grandmother said they were ready for bed and insisted that everyone go up at the same time. Claire's mom set Jason and Lucas up in the guest room while Helen and Claire shut the door to Claire's bedroom.

"They know we're just going to sneak into each other's beds

later, right?" Claire whispered to Helen while they were brushing their teeth.

"I think trying makes them feel better," Helen said around her mouthful of foam.

"So ridiculous," Claire said, rolling her eyes. "I mean, Jerry knows you and Lucas are having sex, right?"

Helen stopped brushing and spit. "We're not."

Claire's eyes popped. "You're not?" She stopped brushing and spit.

"Well, not *yet*," Helen said defensively. "You and Jason have been together for nearly a year but up until a few weeks ago, Lucas and I still thought we were cousins."

"Wait until you're ready,"

"Oh, I'm ready." Helen let out a breath. "I don't think he is. I feel like he's holding back. Am I crazy?"

Instead of disagreeing with her, Claire said, "He's not nesting the way Hector and Jason are."

"Right?" Helen was almost relieved to know that her doubts were not totally unfounded, even if that meant they were real.

"But Lucas has always been different." Claire shrugged. "And maybe that's not such a bad thing. Maybe it's okay to want to live your life for a while first."

"It is," Helen said, mostly because she knew this was how Claire was feeling and she wanted to support her. "But if that's what he wants, he should tell me instead of stringing me along."

"He's not stringing you—" Claire started angrily, and then stopped herself, remembering that they were talking about Lucas, not her. "He loves you. Talk to him."

They got into bed and turned out the lights, but no one was sleeping. Helen made up her mind to get some answers out of Lucas that night. She knew he loved her. Just like she knew Claire loved Jason. But that didn't mean either of them were ready for anything permanent, and why should they be? They were all still way too young for this kind of talk. If Lucas wanted space, she'd give it to him. If he didn't want space, then she was ready for the next step in their relationship. And she was going to tell him that tonight, she decided.

It wasn't long before Helen saw Jason creeping into Claire's room.

"That's my spot," he whispered, grinning. "Lucas is waiting for you."

Anxious and excited, Helen disengaged gravity and floated into the air as Jason slid into Claire's bed beneath her. She flew silently into the guest room, using the shadows in the peaked ceilings of Claire's house to hide in, and stopped above Lucas. She floated there, watching him watch her.

"Hi," he breathed, reaching up to her.

"We need to talk," she said.

He caught her hands in his and pulled her down to him. "Sure," he said, gathering her against his body and pulling the covers over them. "How do you feel?"

This was not what she wanted to talk about. "Lucas—"

"You should rest," he said, turning her over and spooning against her back. "Your feet are cold."

"I'm fine." She squirmed out of his grip so she could turn and look at him. "This is not what I—Lucas." She made him stop snuggling into her neck and look her in the eye across the pillow. "Do you need space?" she asked.

He laughed. "No." He tried to pull her closer, but she stopped him.

"Then why won't you tell me where you want to go to school next year?"

"This is what's bothering you? With all the things you have to deal with, you're worried about where I'm going to school?" he asked teasingly.

While she knew he had a point, she was determined not to get sidetracked this time. "Yes," she answered firmly.

He looked up at the ceiling and sighed in frustration. Then he looked over at her. "I'm not going to college next year."

Helen sat up. "What?"

"I want *you* to go wherever you want," he said firmly. "But I'm not going."

Helen gawked at him. "Your parents are going to freak out."

He nodded. "They will. But I'm eighteen now, and I've made my choice."

"Does this have anything to do with where you go at night?"

"Yes," he admitted, sitting up opposite her. He looked down at the sheets between them. "You're worried I'm plotting my escape. That I'm trying to get away from you, but you couldn't be more wrong." He reached out to her, and she went to him the way left follows right. He caught her close and guided her back down onto the bed, laying himself on top of her. "I never want to be farther away from you than this."

He kissed her, and Helen couldn't think of anything more she could possibly want.

"Beauty, you haven't been sleeping well, which means I hardly ever see you," complained a gentle voice.

Helen turned over, sliding easily through the dark silk sheets, and found Morpheus propped up on his elbow, looking down at her. His long hair flowed to the pillows, ruffled gently by the breeze that stirred through the four-poster bed, and his moon-white skin nearly glowed in the almost-darkness of his land.

Helen sighed with relief to see him. "I'm having man troubles," she admitted.

Morpheus smiled and rolled on top of her. "So I sense," he purred, turning into Hector.

Helen stopped him from kissing her. "Wait—I didn't mean *that*. I was talking about Lucas!"

Morpheus-as-Hector smirked at her. "You thought of this body today. You can't hide it from me." He dropped his lips to her neck and slid his knee between her thighs.

Helen shifted under Morpheus-as-Hector. "First of all, get off me because you're huge and you weigh a ton," she said. "And second, I only thought about him in passing because Gretchen brought him up."

Hector shifted back into Morpheus, and he sat back, laughing good-naturedly. "Unfortunately, I can't make love to you in any form. Lucas would be angry."

She sat up and faced the God of Dreams. "He's hiding things from me again."

Morpheus' smooth brow wrinkled slightly in a frown. "While Lucas *is* quite the handful, your real problem is Zeus. You're avoiding it, Beauty."

"I know," Helen said, looking past Morpheus to the dim follow-me-lights that drifted on the breeze like tiny golden spheres. "And I have no idea what Hecate will make me do."

The corner of Morpheus' lips tilted up in a half-smile, recognizing that she had avoided speaking of Zeus again.

"Hecate won't make you do anything odious," he assured her.

Helen cocked her head at him. "How do you know that?"

"Because I know her. We're neighbors, in a way." Morpheus

nodded his head across the fields of poppies and in the direction of the nightmare tree, which grew on the border of his land and Hades. "She resides in the Underworld." He reconsidered. "Some of the time. For the most part, Hecate goes where she's needed."

"Can I trust her?" Helen asked. Strangely, she had never questioned whether she could trust Morpheus. She simply knew she could.

He narrowed his hypnotic eyes in thought. "I would never presume to speak for a Titan," he said. "But I can tell you she needs you as much as you need her. Keep that in mind while you go about these tasks. Don't let her get more from the exchange than you." He smiled at her, brushing his fingers across her cheek. "Though I like that you've stayed your sweet self, you must remember that you are immensely powerful now, and the other gods are plotting ways to use you."

Helen raised an eyebrow. "But not you?"

"I have exactly what I want from you when I have you in my arms," he replied, shrugging.

Helen heard no lie in him. He lowered his head to kiss her, and this time he did not stop. When his lips touched hers, she awoke.

"Sweet dreams?" Lucas drawled knowingly.

Helen opened her eyes to the sun just coming up in Claire's guest room to find Lucas was awake and lying under her. She pushed herself up over him.

"How'd you know I was with Morpheus?"

He pulled a face. "How is it possible that you still don't know you talk in your sleep? Especially when you're with Morpheus."

Helen blushed furiously. "So, what'd you hear?"

Lucas ground his teeth. "I heard you say *not Hector.*"

"That sounds really bad," she agreed, chuckling. "Yesterday, I overheard Gretchen starting a rumor about me cheating on you with Hector. I had one image *reluctantly* flash through my head, and Morpheus ran with it."

"This was the fight after chorus?" he posited.

"Yep," Helen said. Then she giggled. "Even in dreams, fooling around with Hector is like getting mauled by a bear."

Lucas rolled them over and looked down at her, his eyes pinched with anger. "And just how far did Morpheus run with it?" he asked.

"Totally PG-13," Helen assured him.

Lucas relaxed, hearing the truth.

"Sorry, you guys," Jason whispered from the doorway. "Claire's parents are waking up."

"Time to go," Lucas said, reluctantly getting off Helen.

She released gravity and floated up. She had to fly over Grandma to get back into Claire's room and dove into bed just as Grandma pushed through the half-open door, clearly intent on catching Jason there.

"*Baa-baa*!" Claire scolded.

Grandma harrumphed when she saw that Claire's bedfellow was Helen, but she did not apologize.

Lucas used the landline first thing to reach his dad, and then came back to Helen looking concerned. "He's called a meeting of the Houses," he whispered to her, Claire, and Jason at the kitchen table.

"Why?" Helen asked. "Doesn't he remember how horribly the last one went?"

The last time the Houses had convened, Phaon, from the House of Rome, had tried to knife Orion in the back. Helen had created a magnetic field to snatch the knife out of Phaon's hands. It was the first time she'd ever used her lightning like a magnet, and she'd overshot it, ending up encased in ball lightning with the residual energy. At the same moment, Lucas had wrapped his arms around her to restrain her from killing Phaon with the blade she'd taken from him. She'd nearly killed Lucas. He was horrendously burned, and his heart had stopped. She'd had to build Everyland to save him because nothing in this world could have.

"I'm sure he remembers," Lucas said, giving Helen a wry smile. "But Zeus' possible return endangers all the Houses."

It took a little convincing to get Claire's parents to allow them to leave. The storm had passed, the sun was bright in the sky, but the roads hadn't been plowed yet. It was still unsafe, according to Claire's parents, who had no idea that they were having breakfast with demigods.

After much arguing, and a few stacks of pancakes, Claire's parents suddenly relented. They let the teens go but only if they promised not to drive.

"How did we get out of there?" Lucas asked as they tromped through two and half feet of snow in Claire's front yard to get to the road— just a slightly lower ribbon of two and a quarter feet of snow.

"Um...I may have used a little bit of Orion's talent," Helen admitted.

Normally, she avoided at all costs using the emotion-swaying powers she had received when she became blood brothers with Orion. She thought there was something wrong about being able to manipulate people's hearts.

"You didn't," Claire scolded, glaring at her.

"I couldn't do morning with Grandma," Helen replied defensively. "Sorry, but the woman hates me."

"She does," Claire admitted. "But my parents..."

"...will be fine," Helen finished for her. "I put them in a fantastic mood. They'll probably come running out here in a few minutes to play in the snow." Helen gestured broadly at the sparkling wonderland around them.

Lucas shook his head at Claire, smiling. "Why don't you just tell them what you are?" he asked.

"Yeah. Why don't we tell them, Claire?" Jason asked. Except he wasn't smiling.

Helen looked between Jason and Claire. She'd thought they'd both wanted to keep their immortality a secret, but apparently not. They were obviously at odds about this.

"Claire. They're going to find out," Helen said seriously.

"I know!" Claire shouted back. "Just let me tell them my own way, okay?" She stormed ahead of them. Helen went to follow her, but Lucas stopped her. He met her eyes meaningfully and shook his head.

"I didn't know it was a touchy subject," he said in apology to Jason.

"Everything's a touchy subject with her lately," Jason grumbled back, and then he sped up to catch Claire.

Lucas gave Helen a look. "What's going on with her?" he asked.

Helen threw up her hands. "I mean, *should* I tell you? You're just going to tell Jason."

"Helen," Lucas said, stopping her. "We both know you're going to tell me."

"Fine. She's not ready for forever. She's not ready to get

married, or to talk about being practically immortal, because she's thinking things over," Helen said.

"Thinking *what* over? Being with Jason?"

Helen rolled her eyes, knowing she'd said too much. "See? This is why I didn't want to tell you." She tried to stomp away from him, but Lucas caught her.

"Oh, no-no-no-no. You can't leave it like that," he said. "Jason would literally never get over it if she broke up with him."

Helen crossed her arms. "And don't you think that's a lot to pile on a girl when she's trying to figure out how to tell her very traditional parents that she doesn't want to be a microbiologist after all? That instead, she wants to go to *art* school?"

Lucas looked dumbfounded. He ran both his hands through his hair and started pacing in a circle. "They have to be okay. I can't—" he broke off and ran his hands down his face. Helen knew that gesture. Lucas did it when he wanted to stop himself from saying more.

"You can't *what*?" she asked, taking a step toward him, and hoping he'd finally say everything he had been holding back.

Lucas chose his words carefully. "I can't let Jason ruin his relationship with Claire. I'll tell him to back off."

Helen narrowed her eyes at him. What he'd said wasn't a lie. But it wasn't the whole truth, either. She kept walking, leaving him behind.

"Helen," he called.

She spun around. "What?" she asked, daring him to talk.

His lips twitched. "If you want to go to art school, go to art school," he said, barely making it through without cracking up.

Helen almost laughed at Lucas' reminder that Jason and Claire's relationship was not theirs. But she wasn't going to let him win this time and stormed off.

Something smacked into the back of her head. It was cold. So very cold.

Stunned, Helen turned back slowly as the snowball started sliding down her hair and under the collar of her coat. Lucas stood at the ready. One hand loaded with another snowball.

"You did *not* just throw a snowball at me," Helen said, incredulous.

He threw the other snowball.

"You're dead!" Helen shrieked.

She didn't fly or use Scion speed or strength. Instead, she ran straight at him like a normal mortal would, gathering up a snowball of her own as she went. Lucas dodged it and then circled around, heading to Jason and Claire.

Lucas yanked Jason out of whatever serious conversation he was having with Claire and used him as a shield. Helen's next two snowballs hit Jason. She did a stutter step to get around him and tried to grab Lucas, but he'd already moved on to Claire, who he pushed into Helen, knocking the two girls into a deep, fluffy snowbank.

Then, it was anarchy. Completely NFL-illegal leg tackles. Snow shoved up shirts and down pants. Writhing and screaming. There were no teams—it was every snowballer for themselves. Claire won, in that she was the least wet and cold when they arrived at the Delos compound.

"Where have you been?" Castor asked as he opened the door for them, obviously not happy. "The other Houses are already gathering in the Great Room. Go get changed and get down there. Now."

They dashed upstairs without arguing. Helen and Claire both had to borrow something nice from Ariadne, as neither of them kept semi-formal wear in their boyfriends' dressers. They met at the top of the stairs, groomed and ready. Helen was supposed to enter the room second to last—Cassandra, as the Oracle, was the most highly honored, and she always joined the meeting last. Or whenever she felt like it.

"See you in there," Jason said, and he and Claire went down first.

Helen and Lucas stood at the top of the stairs for a while, just looking at each other.

"You look nice," Helen told him.

"So do you. You know, we never went to prom?" Lucas said like it had just occurred to him. He held out his arm for Helen.

"Oh, I know," Helen told him as she took it. They started down the steps together. "I think one of us was dead that weekend."

Lucas' shoulders shook with laugher. "Don't you regret that we haven't done normal couple stuff like that?"

"What, like junior prom and homecoming dances?" she asked. He nodded and she shook her head. "You?"

He shrugged. "A little."

"I think there's a senior cotillion." She watched him carefully while he smiled expectantly at the floor. "Lucas, would you go to senior cotillion with me?"

"I thought you'd *never* ask," he burst out, so overly relieved she knew he was joking.

They came to the paneled double doors of the Great Room and stopped.

"Just don't burn me to a crisp this time," he teased, right before he pushed the door open for her.

They entered the room, arm in arm and smiling, and everyone present turned to look at her and Lucas.

The formality of these events still felt foreign to Helen, probably because it was the only time in her life when she was treated differently. On a usual night for her, she'd be bussing tables at Kate's Cakes and trying, and usually failing, to get her homework done during her breaks. Here, she was treated like a goddess. It made her laugh, actually, because she was the only goddess she knew who had to mop floors and take the garbage out before she went to bed.

Cassandra was already in the room, standing close to Orion rather than occupying the only chair. Usually everyone but the Oracle had to stand. Cassandra was supposed to sit, but Helen knew she wanted to be as close to Orion as she could be and sitting would put him too far away from her. The chair was offered to Helen, but she shook her head uncomfortably.

The Heads of the Four Houses stood in a circle. Helen was Head of the House of Atreus and there was no one behind her because she was her whole House. To her right was Lucas, Heir to the House of Thebes. To his right was his father, Castor, who was Head of the House of Thebes, and behind him was Pallas, Hector, Jason, Claire, Ariadne, and a few big blond members of the House who used to be part of the Hundred Cousins. Helen didn't know them very well.

To Castor's right stood Cassandra, the Oracle of Delphi, always a little apart and alone. To her right was Orion, Head of the House of Rome on his mother's side, and Heir to the House of Athens on his father's. Behind him stood a woman Helen didn't know. To Orion's right was his father, Daedelus, the Head of the House of Athens, and behind Daedelus were a few of the black haired, blue-eyed members of his house.

Castor took one step forward into the center of the circle. "Thank you all for getting here so quickly. I briefly informed every Head of House about the new danger we're facing, and you all expressed an interest in hearing it from Helen herself. Helen?" Castor turned to her.

Helen stepped forward with a reluctant grimace. She'd never liked public speaking, probably because her mother had cursed her to feel overwhelming cramps when she used her Scion powers in front of mortals. As a result, she'd developed an ingrained aversion to the spotlight. She touched her hand to her belly just to reassure herself that the cramps were not there before she began.

"The battle on the beach with the gods ended in a stalemate. Zeus knew I wanted to stop the fight before it spread, and he wanted to possess the world that I created when I became a goddess. So, to end the war before it started, I gave it to him. But I also tricked him. With Hecate's help, I kept the borders of my world for myself. Zeus can do whatever he wants inside Everyland, but he can't get out while I'm alive. And Zeus wants out," she said simply. "He's doing everything he can to destroy my world, and even though I'm immortal, wrecking my world weakens me because it's the source of my immortality. I've spoken with both Hecate and Morpheus about it; and this is just a theory because it's not like this has ever happened before, but we think that if he manages to destroy enough of my world before I can rebuild it, he might be able to kill me. If he does, my world will fall, Zeus will be free, and he will come for all of you."

Helen looked around at everyone's faces. She considered telling them that she could rebuild Everyland with the briefest of thoughts just to put them at ease, but stopped herself. She didn't know how hard it would get to rebuild if this continued. Even now she felt a little dizzy and could see lightning flashing in her head.

"It will be a second Titanomachy," said the gorgeous woman standing behind Orion. She was tall, in her thirties, had skin that was so black it had a blue hue to it, and cheekbones so high and sharp they looked like folded crow wings. She was powerful, too. Helen couldn't read her heart, though she could tell from her voice that she was scared.

"I'm sorry, I don't know who you are," Helen told her honestly.

"This is Niobe. Heir to the House of Rome," Orion said.

"Just let Zeus out," Hector insisted loudly while Helen did some mental gymnastics about Niobe—who, apparently, was Orion's heir. "Pick a spot, we'll all be standing there ready, open the boundary, and we'll jump him together."

"Would that work?" someone from the House of Athens asked Daedelus uncertainly.

"Hector...that's...no," Helen said, shaking her head to clear it. "As soon as Zeus is free, he can portal away. He'll just go back to Olympus and then attack us whenever he feels like it. I have to defeat him—not just trick him and settle for a stalemate. It has to be a fair fight and I have to put him in Tartarus. That's the only way to get rid of him."

Everyone was silent for a moment.

"We've all read Hesiod. A fight with the gods would destroy the world," Niobe said.

Helen nodded, though she had *not* read Hesiod. There was just too much homework being a teenager and a goddess.

"That's why I avoided a real fight with him," she replied. "Look, I feel fine right now." She saw Lucas frown and his eyes flash as he heard her lie, but Helen plunged forward anyway. "And I'll hold Zeus inside Everyland for as long as I can, but—" she looked around and shrugged.

It was clear that no one had a solution to this problem. Her eyes landed on Lucas last. The natural shadows in the room were starting to lean toward him. She stepped back and stood next to him, taking his hand; and the shadows went back to their proper angles.

Daedelus stepped forward. "Helen," he said, tipping his head to her respectfully. "As bad as this news about Zeus is, it's not the whole story. My brother, Ladon, has come to explain. Castor, will you help me?"

Castor nodded and went to one of the many sets of tall French doors that opened out onto the terrace to the beach. He and Daedelus pushed open the doors, plowing through the new snowdrifts that blocked them.

Something moved outside in the snow. A massive, hulking shape lumbered toward the doors from the ocean.

Lucas drew Helen behind him. Hector, Orion, and Ariadne angled themselves in front of her as well. Helen weaved behind all the shoulders that had suddenly sprung up in front of her, frustrated. She could barely see what was happening.

"Please don't be alarmed," Daedelus said when he heard everyone murmuring. Then he smiled suddenly. Helen was sure she'd never seen him smile before. It made him look even more like Lucas than he already did. "My brother is more frightened of all of you than you are of him."

Helen could see a light that was warm and golden inside Daedelus' chest. He genuinely loved his brother, so when Ladon entered Helen knew she had nothing to fear, despite what he looked like.

Ladon was twelve feet tall, with a hunched back that had a row of spikes running down its spine. The spikes poked through the long, oversized coat he wore. His stride was strange, but Helen couldn't make out the shape of his legs under his clothes. The skin on his face was a patchwork of iridescent scales and olive-toned skin.

"Helen Hamilton, do you know me?" he asked in a gentle voice.

Helen shook her head at him dumbly and he frowned pensively, as if filing away that bit of information for some other purpose.

"I am Ladon. First Son of Bellerophon, former Head of the House of Athens, Son of Poseidon. My nephew has told me many great things about you."

Helen shut her mouth, which was hanging open, and looked at Orion accusingly. "He hasn't told me even one thing about you," she replied. She was starting to feel like he'd been hiding things from her.

Orion shrugged at her sheepishly as if to say, *not my secret to tell*. Helen looked back at Ladon, who smiled at her. He had a nice smile, just like his brother.

"Very few know I was ever even born," he said, shrugging.

"Wait—he said *First* Son. I thought Daedelus was the Head of the House of Athens, and you were the Heir," Niobe said to Orion.

Orion nodded at her. "I am, Niobe," he replied, sounding sad. He turned to his uncle. "Go ahead," he urged.

Ladon turned to face Niobe and she couldn't help but take a slight step back. Helen startled, too, when she saw Ladon's tail slither under him as he turned. It looked like a python flowing across the floor.

"The House of Poseidon has carried two burdens in its bloodline," Ladon explained quietly. "Earthshakers and monsters. When I was born half dragon, my father, Bellerophon, followed the old ways. He cast me out and left me exposed, but I did not die. I was formally disowned. So I was never his Heir. When Daedelus was born he was named Heir, and he is rightly the Head of the House of Athens."

Helen looked at Daedelus. He was supposed to have left the infant Orion exposed on a mountainside to die when it was discovered he was an Earthshaker, but he didn't do it. Daedelus didn't disown his son in the old way. Helen had never liked Daedelus, but the more she learned about him, the more she respected him.

"How long have you known?" Helen asked him.

"Most of my life," Daedelus replied. He shook his head quickly. "But this isn't why I've brought Ladon here to speak to all of you." He turned to his brother. "Tell them."

Ladon turned to Helen. Again, his snake tail slithered over the floor like it had a mind of its own.

"I've come to tell you that Poseidon has taken Hera and Apollo into his domain, deep in the ocean." He turned to Helen. "The three of them are plotting against you. If you take to the sky, you are vulnerable because that is Apollo's. If you go into water, you are vulnerable, because that is Poseidon's. And Hera—I don't know what she has planned for you. But she is the worst of all of them."

Several people started talking at once, and the barrage of sound hit Helen harder than it should have. Lightning flashed in her mind, and her field of vision went blank. She felt a cold sweat start to prickle her upper lip and between her brows and dabbed at her face as unobtrusively as possible.

"We have to level the playing field," Castor said.

"Where are they?" Orion asked his uncle.

"Yeah, let's take the fight to them," Hector added eagerly. "I get Apollo."

"Are the Olympians going to attack us?" asked Niobe.

"No," Helen said, to answer Niobe. "When I tricked Zeus and locked him in Everyland, I made him swear on the River Styx that he and the other Olympians would not attack any of you or this world if I gave him Everyland. That was the whole point of the trade to begin with."

"But what about *you*?" Lucas asked Helen, his eyes wide because he already suspected he knew the answer. "Aren't you included in that oath?"

"I was supposed to be allowing him to send me to Tartarus," she tried to explain. "I was pretending to give myself up...how could I ask that?"

Lucas closed his eyes and took a deep breath, like he was searching for patience. Then everyone started talking at once again.

Helen turned away from the noise to think. What Ladon told her made sense. She'd fallen from the sky when she tried to fly during a storm, as if it had rejected her. She'd nearly drowned in the ocean when Orion tried to bring her through it. Apollo and Poseidon couldn't remove her powers over these elements, but they could work against her to nullify them if she were already weakened from within by Zeus' attacks. The Olympians were ganging up on her, and their attacks had to be coordinated.

Hera was the wildcard. She had no domain or specific talents, but Helen knew from the small fraction of reading that she had done on Greek mythology that Hera had tortured every mortal she'd considered a threat, and each time she'd done it in a strange and horrifying way. Helen was afraid of Hera. She was vindictive and her attacks were always personal.

Helen's ears were ringing. More lightning flashed inside her head. A beautiful man burned her fields to cinders and ripped her heaven apart as fast as he could. He was laughing at her. The buzzing in her head flatlined, telescoping in until she was back inside the here and now again, with a raging headache in tow.

"...Because if Zeus is weakening her from the inside, and the Olympians can attack her, she needs to be protected!" Hector was yelling at Lucas.

"What do you think I'm doing!?" Lucas shouted back at him. The noise was too much. Helen had to put a hand to her throbbing head.

"Um...leaving half the time!? And where the hell do you go anyway!?" Hector challenged.

Lucas stepped up to Hector. Orion and Jason immediately jumped in between the two of them.

"Stop!" Helen demanded. Maybe a little too loudly.

Everyone was on the ground. They'd been blown back away from her in a perfect circle. Only Ladon had kept his feet under him against the gale force wind that had spiraled out of Helen. He faced her over the wash of bodies and tumbled furniture and smiled at her like he understood.

"It was just wind. They aren't injured," she insisted, paralyzed with guilt, while everyone started to pick themselves up.

"I know," Landon replied sympathetically. "We're monsters, Helen. That means that we're both too strong *and* too vulnerable. Take the help they offer you. You can't do it alone."

Ladon slithered out through the French doors, heading right for the ocean. Helen followed him outside into the night. She felt Lucas grab her arm to stop her.

"Don't, Helen," he pleaded in her ear. "I can't protect you in the water."

"He said we were monsters," Helen murmured. She turned to look at Lucas and saw that they were almost to the water's edge.

Ladon had vanished into the sea. Startled, she stepped back before the foamy line of surf could touch her borrowed dress shoes. "I'm starting to get a little flakey," she admitted with a shaky laugh.

"Tell me."

"It's like a dial tone in my head. It happens when Zeus throws a fit. My head hurts and I lose control, and I..." she trailed off.

He nodded and put his arms around her. "It's going to be okay." He held her for a while, watching the sun go down over the snowy dunes. "And you're not a monster."

"I'm scared I'm going to hurt someone."

Lucas stopped trying to convince her otherwise. Instead, he led her back up the slippery sand and inside. She shivered from head to toe when the warmth of Noel's kitchen hit her. Her arms felt heavy and her legs rubbery with weakness. Claire was there, looking disheveled.

"I'll be back to help you with your tasks for Hecate," Lucas promised, sitting her down next to Claire. He gave her a quick kiss. "I'm already late."

"Wh—" Helen began, but Lucas went back out through the door they'd just come in and was airborne. She sat there, staring after him long after he had disappeared, fuming.

"Wow, that sucks," Claire said, stunned. "He really does just *go*. And he won't say where?"

"Nope. He asked me to trust him, and I'm trying to." Helen turned to her, feeling horrible for losing control during the meeting. "Are you okay? Did I hurt you?"

"I'm fine," Claire said, shrugging. She found a basket of nachos on the table and took one. "You didn't light anyone on fire this time, so that's progress."

They shared a wan smile, but Helen knew it wasn't funny. Claire had been in the room because now that she was immortal, she was like a new kind of Scion that they hadn't figured out yet. She wasn't strong or fast, but not being able to die had given her the right to attend. Now Helen was reconsidering that. Claire had a bunch of new abilities that baffled Helen, but she didn't have the ability to avoid pain.

"What if I'd hurt you? What if Noel had been in there?" Helen asked.

Thinking of what could have happened to Noel made them both silent for a moment.

"It's not like there's a guidebook for becoming a goddess," Claire sympathized. "You'll figure it out."

Helen could hear raised voices in the next room. "I should go back out there," she said reluctantly.

"Don't," Claire urged. She pushed the basket of nachos at Helen. "Just sit here and wait for Hector."

It wasn't long before Hector and Orion came into the kitchen with Niobe.

"Where's Luke?" Hector asked.

Helen was silent.

Orion and Hector shared an angry look. "One of us has to get him in line," Hector practically growled.

"I'll talk to him again," Orion soothed. "We can't start fighting amongst ourselves right now, okay?"

Hector nodded, tightlipped. The trio looked down at Helen like she was a problem they had to solve.

"Nacho?" Helen asked, pushing the basket toward them.

Hector took one and pointed at her with it. "You're coming with us back to New York."

"We can't leave you alone," Orion explained. "We'll drive. No flying, no swimming. We'll just take a car, like normal people do."

Niobe huffed disbelievingly. "Did you all just see what Helen did out there?" she asked.

"That was *nothing*, Fancy Face," Hector commented to Niobe. "You should see her light show."

Niobe rolled her eyes at him though she was charmed, as most people were, by Hector. "I think it more likely that we need protection from her."

Her English was excellent, but Helen noticed that she did have a slight accent.

"Hi," Helen said, holding out her hand to Niobe. "I'm Helen."

"I know," Niobe replied, giving her side-eye. She still took Helen's hand, though, and shook it. "I knew your mother," she said, peering at Helen closely. "It's uncanny how much you look like her."

Helen didn't know what to say.

"Niobe is my cousin," Orion interjected when Helen faltered.

"*Distant* cousin," Niobe amended.

"And the Heir to the House of Rome," Orion said, confirming Helen's theory.

"Until Orion has a child," Niobe finished for him. He smiled at her doubtfully.

"You never mentioned you had a cousin before," Helen said, trying to sound neutral and failing.

"I asked him not to," Niobe said, clearly capable of speaking for herself. "Hiding was how my family survived the Scion war, and you were too close with the Delos family." She glanced into the next room where Castor and Pallas were talking. "The Delos brothers were considered like the Boogie Men when I was young, but they're nothing compared to how scary you are."

Helen's eyes widened. "You are direct, aren't you?"

"We don't know what Helen's capabilities are anymore," Orion interjected before their exchange had a chance to turn sour.

"And that's more dangerous than her not having any," Hector added. "Helen could try to summon a bolt and find out she's not fireproofed anymore, or something." He looked at her. "You need protection."

"But I have school," Helen complained weakly.

"You're coming with us for a few days while Orion and I sort out our school situation," Hector grumbled as he left the room. "Grab some of your things from Lucas' room, Princess. We're going."

Helen pursed her lips and looked at Claire. "I hate it when he calls me that."

"That's why he does it," Claire replied, nodding.

Helen sat there while Orion brought Niobe to confer with Pallas and Castor, trying to imagine what it would be like if just once she convinced Hector that she didn't need protecting. But her head still hurt, and she couldn't imagine him ever saying, "you're right," so she gave up and went upstairs to call her dad and pack a bag.

Chapter 5

They caught the last ferry off Nantucket. Then Hector, Orion, and Helen drove and slept in shifts.

The ocean turned into neon strips of highway with nothing but trees on either side. They shared I-90 with giant snowplows and pressed vending machines buttons at interstate rest stops, dialing up fizzy caffeine drinks and fried triangles of salt. Every time they stopped, Helen couldn't shake the feeling that someone was watching her.

When they finally crossed the bridge onto Manhattan, they left the Delos Range Rover at the secure parking lot that the family owned, walked four avenue blocks carrying their stuff, and arrived at the brownstone on Washington Square Park, exhausted and cranky right before dawn. Though Helen had been to New York with Lucas a few times before, for one reason or another she had never been inside the house that she'd heard so much about.

The Delos brownstone was the largest on the Square. Hector punched in the security code and opened the double doors into a front room that was filled with antiques. There was an ancient Kouros on a plinth, and a gold-leafed couch with red silk cushions that looked extremely uncomfortable, which had pride of place for some unfathomable reason. Priceless works of art hung on the walls, protected by special glass cases. The pristine marble floor stretched back to the kitchen. It was very elegant and spacious, but it was a museum, not a home. Helen trudged in and looked around blearily. She was far more tired than she should have been.

"Nobody really hangs out down here," Hector said as he passed Helen on the way to the stairs. He stopped and pointed at a place on the marble floor. He looked back at Helen apologetically. "Your great uncle, Polydeuces Atreus, died right there. My uncle Ajax killed him."

Helen didn't even know she'd had a great uncle Polydeuces. Her mother had never mentioned him.

A thought occurred to Hector. "We should probably give you back the Aegis."

"Of Zeus?" Helen asked, eyebrows raised. "Like, the shield that strikes terror into anyone who sees it?"

"Spoils of war." Hector shrugged. "You want it back?"

Helen considered the dull headache building up behind her eyes. She didn't want anything that belonged to Zeus. "Nah. You can have it."

"We usually skip right over this floor unless we're going to the kitchen. I've never even sat on that couch," Orion said as they passed the lumpy thing. "I think a god was conceived on it, or something like that," he added.

"Ew," was all Helen could say. She saw Orion's shoulders shake with laughter as he climbed the steps in front of her.

The second floor looked like a real home. This was obviously where the family spent time together. There was a music room, a

TV room, and a slightly more formal but still welcoming library with a pool table and a wet bar that was perfect for entertaining. There was also a room full of comfortable couches, all facing each other so the people sitting on them could talk. Or nap, considering the number of throw pillows and blankets scattered about.

"Bedrooms upstairs," Hector called when Helen slowed to look over the nap room. It looked cozy.

As soon as she got to the third floor, her eyes were drawn to a door at the end of the hallway. While the rest of the Delos house was painted in tasteful shades that brought out the wainscoting and the molding, and complimented the deep-pile runners that protected the glossy hardwood floors, this door was a riot of graffiti.

It was chaotic, grungy, and beautiful.

"What's that?" Helen asked, already drifting down the hallway toward it.

"That was Ajax's room," Hector called.

Helen stopped at the door. She stared at it for a long time. There were so many images and colors and letters that had been attenuated and pulled out of shape it was hard to find a place to let her eyes rest, but it did have a rhythm to it—a kind of angry logic she could nearly understand.

She felt Hector's warm, heavy hand on her shoulder. "No one's allowed in there, not even to dust."

Helen blinked her eyes to clear them of the images that were burning into them.

They turned away, and just as Helen took her eyes off it, she saw it.

"Daphne!" she shouted, turning. "He wrote *Daphne* on his door!"

The three of them stood in a line and backed up until they

were all the way up against the opposite wall. They squinted. The shapes blurred and the images became letters.

"What the..." Hector cursed, and gave a strange laugh.

"Oh, wow. Now that I see it I can't unsee it," Orion said, tilting his head left and right. "How did he do that?"

"It's like one of those visual tricks. It's a cup, no—it's a couple kissing, no—it's a cup," Hector said, bobbing his head forward and back again.

"But way more complicated than that," Helen added. She pinched her tired eyes closed. "It hurts to look at."

Orion hummed in his chest, considering it. "He was hurting when he painted it."

Helen gazed at Hector and Orion. Daphne had taken care of Hector after he'd become an Outcast. She'd been the only family he'd had for months. She'd done the same for Orion when the Furies had driven his family apart and he was left to fend for himself as a small boy. Daphne had only been there for Helen, however, when she was very young; she barely remembered her mother from that time. Both Orion and Hector had had more adult conversation with Daphne than she'd had, and both had loved her. She could read it in their hearts. Helen didn't know what she felt for her mother.

"I have to go in there," Helen said, struggling to both understand and convey why this was suddenly so important to her. "My mom lied to me and told me Ajax was my father. I thought he *was* my dad for months."

Hector looked at Orion with a raised brow, asking what to do.

"I'm a guest here, and I've always respected this rule. But now I think I need to see this, too," Orion told him.

"Yeah. So do I," Hector admitted. He looked at the door. "It's like she's still in here," he whispered, seeing and unseeing the hidden name written there.

Helen tried the knob, and she pushed the door open.

Inside, the walls of Ajax's bedroom were covered in graffiti. Colors and sharp shapes pushed up onto the ceiling. In the center of the room was a mattress on the floor that was sheathed in black sheets, surrounded by books that were piled haphazardly at the corners. Closer to the window was an easel and a stool. And that was it. Art, books, and a mattress.

Helen walked to the easel first. There was an unfinished oil painting on it, long dried now. It was a self-portrait. Ajax looked so much like Hector they could have been twins, but the expression on Ajax's face was not like anything she'd ever seen on Hector. Ajax looked so vulnerable, and his hands were different. Slimmer, and infinitely more graceful. Even as paint, she could see how deeply his hands felt everything they touched. Helen wondered how Ajax could use his hands to paint hands that looked like they could still reach out and touch her. They broke her heart.

Orion squatted by the books beside the bed. He lifted one that was named *Art and Physics*. "Daphne had me read this," he said quietly. He pointed to another book on the stack. "And that one."

Hector went to the large closet that took up one wall and opened it. There weren't many clothes in there: everything was either a school uniform or splattered with paint. Three quarters of the closet was used for storage for art supplies and finished works. Helen joined Hector at the closet. A green t-shirt hung there, dusted with blowback from a spray can. She touched it, turning it towards her.

"Green Lantern," she whispered, recognizing the symbol on the front.

"Look at these," Hector said, holding out a sketchbook.

Orion came up behind Helen and the three of them flipped through the drawings. Some of them were completed charcoals and pastels, and some of them were just studies of body parts. All of them were of young women, usually nudes.

"So beautiful," Orion said.

Hector agreed. "It's like I can see what they're thinking and feeling."

"They're all in love," Orion decided.

Something caught Helen's eye. "Wait," she said before Hector could turn the next page. She felt a chill wash through her.

The drawing was set in Ajax's bed, in the same black sheets. The subject, a nude girl, was turned away. The sheets threaded around her long, slack limbs. Her hair was shorn, and the back of her exposed neck looked fragile—almost like it was in danger. She was sleeping deeply, her whole body given up to the boy who was drawing her.

"That's *me*," Helen said, scared that someone could draw, not just the shape of her, but the way she felt when she slept in Lucas' bed.

"It's Daphne," Orion corrected.

"They're all Daphne," Hector realized. "Look." He passed the sketchbook to Helen and took down another. He randomly opened the pages to a sketch of a laughing girl. Her face radiated such joy that it was impossible not to smile back at her. Hector pointed to the necklace she was wearing. The same one was around Helen's neck.

"She used the Cestus to pose for him as other girls," Helen mumbled, understanding. She looked down at her teen-aged mother sleeping in Ajax's bed. "Except for this one. This is her, but he didn't draw her face. She probably didn't let him."

"He drew her trust," Orion said, looking at Helen. "Much more precious."

"It looks like all of them were done in this room," Hector said. "She must have been changing her face and coming here for weeks—maybe months. I don't know, how long does it take to do these many drawings?"

Orion shrugged in answer. "Daphne did tell me that she practically lived here after she and Ajax got rid of the Furies. Before they had to run away."

"Do your dad and uncle know about that? That my mom had come here looking like other girls?" Helen asked Hector.

He shook his head absently. "I don't think so."

They gently closed the sketchbooks and put them back where they'd found them. Every image was so intimate, so filled with life and feeling that they couldn't look at too many of them in one sitting. It was too emotionally exhausting. Helen's eyes were beginning to unfocus and the headache that had been threatening earlier had completely moved in.

"If no one knew, then why did Ajax and my mom have to run away?" Helen asked as they left the room.

"Your grandmother, Elara, had arranged a marriage for Daphne. She was promised to another man," Orion replied, closing the door respectfully behind them.

Helen gaped at him. She hadn't known. "What are you talking about? She was a teenager in the *nineties*, not Elizabethan England."

"Your mom said all Atreus women were married at seventeen, just like Helen of Troy," Hector said. "Someone else had to decide who 'got' her, or men would start killing each other over her."

"The guy Daphne was supposed to marry was Mildred's brother. You remember Mildred, right? Tantalus' wife, Creon's mother?" Hector said darkly.

Creon Delos, son of Tantalus Delos, had been Heir to the House of Thebes and Hector's cousin. Creon had hunted Helen down back when she barely knew what a Scion was. He'd killed Hector's aunt Pandora—no one really knew why because the only three people present when it happened—Pandora, Creon, and Daphne—were now all dead. When Creon killed Pandora, he became an Outcast for killing his own kin, and the Furies had incited Hector to kill Creon, making Hector an Outcast. That's when Daphne stepped in and took Hector away before the rest of the Delos family were driven mad by the Furies. Lucas would have killed Hector if Daphne and Helen hadn't gotten between them.

Hector stopped in front of another closed door down the hallway. This one had a big, pink "P" on it. He put his paw of a hand on the P, touching it lovingly. "This was Pandora's room. Are you okay sleeping in there?"

Helen took an automatic step back. Hector had been especially close to his aunt Pandora. The Delos family didn't talk about her very often anymore because she had violated the sacred laws of hospitality when she'd kidnapped Daphne and given her to Creon to kill. She had dishonored their family, though Pandora had done it because she believed that Daphne had killed Ajax all those years ago when, really, he and Daphne faked their deaths to run away together. Ajax had died later. Pandora had never gotten over losing her brother. None of them had.

Ajax had always been the piece of the puzzle that was forever lost, leaving the picture incomplete. He'd been special, and after just twenty minutes in his room, Helen could feel why. He'd had a gift that could have stretched beyond their closed world of demigods, blood feuds, and Fate. Everyone loved him. His brothers Castor and Pallas still didn't let anyone into his room, not even housekeepers to clean. Pandora had broken the sacred oath of hospitality to avenge him. Daphne had lied to Helen about Ajax being her father in a convoluted bid to bring him back from the dead. Helen remembered Castor telling her that even Tantalus had loved Ajax the most. And Tantalus had murdered Ajax over Daphne, because of her face. The Face that Launched a Thousand Ships. The same face that Helen now wore. Helen did not want to sleep in Pandora's room.

"Do I have to?" she asked, so body and soul tired she could barely form sentences anymore.

"There are two beds in my room," Hector offered after a moment. "But I snore."

Helen turned to Orion. "Where do you sleep?" she asked him, hoping to trade with him.

Orion gave a weird laugh. "Er, Tantalus' old bedroom."

Helen sighed out the last of her strength. "Now I know why Lucas never took me here," she whispered. She pushed open the door to Pandora's room and went inside.

Helen thought she'd be tired enough to sleep through anything, but she was wrong.

The bed she slept in was made for a 'tween. It was a romantic jumble of white fluffy pillows and princess-like drapery. The inside wall sported a poster of the boy band N*SYNC. The young male singers tugged at their clothing and pouted sensually. This was the bedroom of a person Helen had cared about and who had died because of other people's loves and lies.

The thing that kept Helen awake, besides her throbbing head

and the bright flashes of lighting she saw every time she closed her eyes, was knowing that one of those "other people" was her.

Just days after the Delos family arrived on Nantucket, Daphne had tried to kidnap Helen in the back room of her father's shop. Helen had ripped through her shoes in order to shake her attacker off her back. But now Helen wondered what would have happened if she had allowed herself to be taken by her mother back then. Would Pandora, Creon, Matt, Zack, Mr. Hergesheimer, and all the other people who had died still be alive? Would her dad be healthy?

What if she had just *gone* with her mother when Daphne had tried to get her off Nantucket all those months ago?

If she had just gone, she never would have fallen in love with Lucas. Though it made her feel like she was somehow being unfaithful to him, given the choice between loving Lucas and saving all the lives that had later been lost or ruined, Helen knew she probably should have left with her mother that night. But the Fates hadn't given her a choice. Daphne had electrocuted Kate and tried to kidnap Helen rather than sitting her down to talk like a rational human being. That was the moment Helen's life had changed. She'd been backed into a corner and despite all the god-like things Helen could do, it was the definition of powerlessness. Having no choice.

The sun came up shortly after Helen laid down. Light now streamed through the leaded panes of glass in the five-by-five-foot window that dominated an entire wall of Pandora's childhood bedroom. Helen threw off the stifling heat of the fluffy comforter and put her feet down on the floor, nearly burning the side of her leg on the old-fashioned steam radiator next to the bed. She quickly snatched her bare skin away from the angry thing. It hissed and rattled beneath the cold window. Above the radiator the corners of the windowpanes were frosted with spiky lattices of ice. Helen regarded the pair of them, window and radiator forever working against each other, and got out of bed shaking her head.

She went into the bathroom and drank sweet New York City tap water right from the faucet until her front teeth went numb and her belly felt swollen. She angled her hot, sleep-deprived eyes under the stream for a few minutes to soothe them. There were no towels in the bathroom, which shouldn't have surprised her. Towels were for living girls, not dead ones.

Helen drip-dried, dressed, and went downstairs, sniffling as she followed the smell of coffee. She found Orion in the kitchen standing at the counter eating a bowl of cereal.

"I don't know about you, but I'm wiped out," he moaned when he saw Helen.

"Yeah? Try falling asleep with a poster of a hormonal boy band staring down at you."

"How do you know I didn't? You have no idea what Tantalus was into."

She chuckled and started opening cabinets. "Mugs?"

Orion pointed, and Helen took down a mug that said, *And on the Eighth Day She Created Wellesley.*

"How long are we going to stay here?" she asked, thinking of Andy as she filled her mug.

"One of us will drive you back tomorrow, then we planned on staying with you in shifts," Orion answered.

Helen sipped her coffee. "You know, it's not like I'm alone on Nantucket."

"Castor, Pallas, and Ariadne are not immortal, Jason is much more important to us as a Healer than a fighter, and Lucas disappears every night," Orion said. "One of us has to be with you all the time. Hector and I just came back to New York to get our schoolwork sorted out. We're going to be living with you for however long it takes to get this resolved."

Helen chuckled over the rim of her mug. "My dad's going to love that."

Hector came into the kitchen stretching his big body, yawning loudly. He saw Helen using Andy's mug and his mood immediately darkened. She noticed.

"When was the last time you spoke to her?" Helen asked Hector.

He sat down heavily at the table. "The satellite phone on the smaller research boat she's on is for emergencies only. She calls when she can."

"Must be hard."

"What day is it?"

"Thursday," Helen said.

"She usually calls on Sundays. We'll see," he answered.

Helen could see ropes of frustration tying knots around Hector's heart. They kept tightening until he stood up to distract himself. He opened and then shut the refrigerator door. He pushed some furniture around. Hector was probably the most physical person Helen had ever met. If he felt something deeply, his whole body responded, and he missed Andy so much he didn't even know what to do with himself. She and Orion shared a look. Orion put his bowl down in the sink and sighed.

"You two up for some sparring?" he asked like he was already regretting it.

Hector raised an eyebrow in reply.

"Right." Helen mumbled, putting her coffee down. "Let's go punch each other in the face. Because that's what regular people do to help someone deal with frustration."

"Don't worry. I'll go easy on you," said Hector with a grin.

There was a door in the kitchen that led to the basement levels. Hector entered a security code into the panel next to it and led them down. The first lower level was an office, library, and master suite, all of which were so lavishly furnished it was easy to forget that they were underground.

"My grandfather Paris' rooms. I guess they're Uncle Castor's now. Anyway, they're reserved for the Head of the House," he said.

They went down one more flight of steps to a second basement level. "The armory," Hector said, as they passed a room full of suits of armor, swords, shields, and spears. "The really expensive art and sculpture," he said as they passed a vault, "and the gym," he finished.

He burst through the doors at the end of the hall and started stripping on his way to the men's locker room.

"What's this about Andy not calling?" Helen asked Orion when Hector was out of earshot.

"She must be really caught up in her research, I guess," Orion replied. "Hector knows it's what she loves, but it's hard for him to understand."

"Anyway, since both of us are super frustrated with our relationships right now, rather than dealing with them, we've been sparring. A lot," Orion said, squinting thoughtfully, like he was second-guessing some of his life choices.

She'd had no idea he was dating someone. She tried not to get jealous. Failing that, she tried not to show just how jealous it made her.

"What relationship?" Helen asked quietly.

"Exactly."

Helen grinned at his sardonic expression, far more relieved than she should have been that he was still single. She broke away from him on her way to the women's locker room. She found some clothes on a shelf and changed into a pair of bike shorts and a sports bra, then met the guys in the fight cage.

"Now, what are the rules?" Helen said, tying her hair back in a ponytail.

Hector shot in to take her legs out and she hit the mat with a *thunk*.

"*Melee*!" Orion howled, tackling Hector.

It was a three-way fight for a while, but the natural dynamics of their relationships led to Hector coaching Helen as she and Orion worked on grappling. Helen started in control with Orion on his hands and knees under her, but he quickly had her on her back.

"Watch it, Helen!" Hector warned, but it was too late. "Use your legs!" he shouted at her.

Helen wrapped her legs around Orion's waist. He didn't start raining down hammer fists, which Helen knew was the best move in this position. Instead, he pressed his shoulder into her chest and throat, trying to cut off her air. Helen worked to get him in an armlock.

"Careful. He's more flexible than Lucas," Hector warned. Orion wriggled out of it.

Helen finally managed to overpower him from the bottom. She basically crushed his ribs with her thighs until he tapped out. Orion lay on top of her for a minute after.

"Ouch," he groaned in her ear. Helen started laughing. Orion pushed himself up over her. "That's going to leave a mark."

"What I lack in skill I make up for in brute strength," Helen admitted, though it had taken more out of her than it should have. Her strength was definitely waning in an alarming manner, but she wasn't about to tell Orion that.

"I'll get the honey," Hector said as he left the cage.

Orion eased himself off her, taking his time and cringing a lot.

"Why didn't you hit me?" Helen asked, propping herself up on her elbows.

Orion shook his head and put a hand over his ribs. "I'm not going to hit you, Helen," he said, like his mind was made up about that.

"Hector hits me all the time when we spar."

"I'm not Hector."

"But you could have won," Helen pressed.

"I don't need to," he said, resting back a bit on his heels, but still between her legs. Helen could have inched away from him and sat all the way up if she'd wanted to. But she didn't. Even when Orion was sweaty, he smelled amazing. Maybe even more so.

"What do you need to win at?" she asked. "And don't tell me nothing. Everyone has their thing. With Hector it's boxing, with Lucas it's Jiu-jitsu. What's your thing?"

Orion looked at her, a half-smile parting his full lips. "Stiletto," he said.

"A knife fight?"

"It's a House of Rome thing."

"Teach me."

"I will," he promised quietly.

Helen could see he was aware of where he was, that she hadn't moved away from him; and she could tell that he was reading her heart. She had no idea what it was telling him. His heart was shifting through emotions too quickly for Helen to keep up, but she saw lust there, sharp and searing, before he stifled it.

Helen sat up. "Where's that honey?" she asked, looking at anything but Orion.

"I think Hector forgot us," Orion said, getting up painfully.

They went upstairs. As Helen reached the security door a heated conversation was abruptly ended. She opened the door to find Hector and Lucas in the kitchen.

"Lucas," Helen said, frozen with surprise.

Lucas stood arms crossed over his chest, leaning back against the counter. His icy blue eyes were narrowed but his lips curved in a smile underneath, warming them.

Helen went to him, and he opened his arms wide for her, unblocking her view of his heart. It was full of love, and something else that was akin to love but darker. She pressed her heart against his in a hug and realized with surprise that the other emotion was longing. Lucas really missed her.

"He just appeared... kind of out of nowhere," Hector commented strangely.

Lucas glanced at Orion before he gave Helen a little kiss hello. "Today is the day, right?" He asked her.

"What day?" It dawned on her. With everything else that had been going on and the distracting, insect-like whine of a headache now couched permanently behind her left eye, it had slipped Helen's mind that her two days were up in just a few hours. "Hecate! Right. I have to start my tasks." She looked around the room at a loss. "So, how do you clock in for a shift with a Titan?"

Lucas shook with silent laughter in her arms. "We have to get to a crossroads," he answered.

"And how do you know that?" Hector asked confrontationally.

"Ah—common sense?" Lucas replied. "We could summon Hecate here, but I think it would be more respectful to," he glanced at Helen and smiled, "clock in on her own turf."

Helen tisked jokingly at Hector. "You don't make the boss

come to you, *obviously*," she said, though she secretly agreed with Hector. How Lucas had figured that out was beyond her.

"Looks like Luke has all the answers," Hector said, still challenging his cousin. He had a bone to pick with Lucas.

"Bro. Where the hell's the honey?" Orion demanded, interrupting the stare-down. He pointed to his ribs. "Cracked. Remember?"

"Such a baby," Hector teased as he took a jar that was behind him on the counter and threw it at Orion. "You gotta hit Helen or she'll wreck you."

Orion shook his head as he opened the jar. "Such a jackass," he grumbled, taking a swig of honey.

"Let me go change," Helen told Lucas, trying to pull out of his arms, but he didn't let her go.

"Okay," he said, holding onto her hand. They went upstairs together, stopping at the linen closet to get towels. Lucas balked at Pandora's door.

"I know," Helen said. "But it was either here or I was sleeping with Hector."

Lucas opened the door and went in saying, "Definitely here then." They had barely closed the door when Lucas folded her into another hug. "I've missed you," he whispered.

He curved over her, holding her up and against him as if he couldn't seem to get close enough. It was like he was starved for her, but they had just seen each other the day before. She pulled back, confused, and really looked him over. He didn't look tired. There were no bags under his eyes and his skin didn't look pale or anything, but something was off. He seemed worn down.

"I need a shower. I smell like a dude."

"*Two* dudes," he joked, still clutching her tightly.

Finally, he released her.

Helen sped through a shower, barely dried her hair, and rushed out with just a towel covering her. Lucas was sitting on the edge of Pandora's bed, fully dressed. He looked tense.

Helen paused. "Is something wrong?" she asked.

"Come here," he said, holding out his hands.

She stood in front of him, and he wrapped his arms around her waist. He turned his face to the side and tilted it down so she couldn't see his expression. She ran her fingers through his hair, worried about him.

"Lucas—" she began.

He pulled her down onto the bed before she could finish, and he quickly went from kissing her to something more serious. Helen could feel how much he needed her, but he held himself back.

"It's okay, I want to," she told him, in case he was waiting for verbal consent.

"Me too," he said. "But not now." He rolled off her and let his breathing settle.

Helen's heart sank in disappointment. She pushed herself up on his chest and pointed at the poster. "It's Justin Timberlake, isn't it?"

His eyes sparkled. "Lance Bass, actually. He looks like he's about to cry."

They laughed and laid down together, doing quiet things like looking at each other's hands and tracing constellations in each other's freckles, until she felt Lucas really relax and let go of whatever it was that had been wearing him down.

. . .

When it was time, they went downstairs and found Hector and Orion on the second floor sitting on opposing couches in the nap room. They were already wearing their coats.

"Where're we going?" Hector asked.

"It's just me and Helen on this one," Lucas replied.

"You think that's smart?" Orion asked.

"You're the cavalry," Lucas said, shaking his head like they were misunderstanding him. "If we all go together, we could get cornered together."

He took a thick square of paper out of his coat pocket and handed it to Hector. "This is where we're going to meet Hecate."

Hector opened it. Orion joined him on the couch so they could both look at it. It looked old. The paper was yellowed, the folds were worn, and the writing on it was in minuscule, ornate cursive.

"What is this? An old blueprint?" Hector asked. Lucas nodded.

Orion studied it intently. "This is *under* the subway lines. Where did you get this?" he asked, looking just as taken aback as Helen felt. She had no idea how Lucas had come up with any of this.

"That's not important," Lucas replied. "If we're not back by tomorrow morning, that will be a good place to come looking for us." Hector and Orion just stared at Lucas, their mouths agape. "Okay?" Lucas asked.

Hector's eyes narrowed mistrustfully, and he sat back, crossing his arms. "Sure, Luke. Anything you say."

Lucas sighed and dropped his head. Helen heard him whisper a curse under his breath before looking up again at Hector.

"Please?" he asked.

Hector relaxed his combative posture and nodded because he

would never say no if someone in his family asked him for something, no matter how strange or difficult.

"Dawn," Hector said, like he was giving Lucas an ultimatum.

Lucas silently agreed and drew Helen toward the steps.

"Helen," Orion called. She looked back at him. "Be careful," he warned.

Helen frowned. Lucas was still holding her hand as she followed him down the steps.

"That was weird," she said as they stepped outside.

"They're just trying to protect you," he said, tucking their intertwined hands into his coat pocket to keep Helen warm. They jaywalked across the street to cut through the park. It was so cold out that the snow squeaked under the soles of their boots.

"But not you?" she asked.

"I think I'm one of the things they've decided you need protection from," he replied with a tilted smile.

"Because you won't tell them why you keep disappearing, or where you're going," Helen inferred.

He drew them to a stop by the Washington Square Arch and turned so Helen could face him. "I can't tell anyone yet. Especially not Hector."

Helen nodded and didn't say anything.

"Do you still trust me?" Lucas asked, almost scared of her answer.

Helen smiled at him, like he should know better. "I haven't asked again, have I?"

He reeled Helen inside his open coat, wrapping her up against his warm body. "Gods, I love you," he breathed. "I promise I'll find a way to make you happy. No matter what."

He kissed her under the arch before she could tell him that she already was.

. . .

They had to run to the West 4th Street Station. Helen reckoned that she'd made her deal with Hecate at sundown, and in New York in mid-December, the sun set before five o'clock. That meant they had about an hour to find Hecate.

The subway station was getting crowded as rush hour approached, and already people filled the platform. Lucas took her all the way to its end. A train arrived, but Lucas held her back.

"We have to go down onto the tracks," Lucas told her.

"Won't people see us and freak out?" she asked.

Lucas shook his head, looking around. As the train pulled out, it seemed like the world dimmed and a gray veil had been pulled around them.

"Let's go," Lucas said, holding Helen's hand. She had no choice but to jump down onto the tracks with him.

Helen looked back at the commuters on the platform waiting for the next train, but no one saw them. When Lucas used his Shadowmaster talent to make them invisible, it was as if they were separated from the world. She glanced at him and noticed that he was perfectly comfortable with this, and she wondered how often he used this talent.

They stopped at a padlocked service door that was recessed inside a niche. Lucas pulled Helen into the niche with him and waited.

"What are we waiting for?" she asked after a moment.

"Train," Lucas said, glancing down at her with a little smile on his face. "I can make us invisible, but doing a whole door is bit trickier. We'll wait for the next train to block us."

"Have you done this before?" she asked, both amused and

confused. He shrugged, pursing his lips together. "Can't tell me, huh?" she said, disappointed.

Lucas shook his head, frowning. "I can't tell you how I know the way to Hecate without telling you everything."

"Okay," she agreed, determined to keep her promise to trust him.

They waited for another train to come into the station. When they were blocked from view, Lucas twisted the deadbolt off the door, and they went into the service shaft. He pulled out his phone and used it as a flashlight.

"It might be better for us to fly down," he said, shining the light on the rusty metal staircase that was rickety with disuse.

"Do you think it's safe for me to fly?" she asked.

"Technically it's not the sky, which is Apollo's domain," he said thoughtfully. "Apollo can't touch you here."

They soared down the stairwell until they landed on a metal gangplank that went horizontally into the bedrock. They followed the rough-hewn tunnel until it became so dark they could barely see more than ten feet in front of them.

There were gouges in the walls and on the floor. Helen raised a hand to touch one of the long trenches scored into the bedrock.

"Are these claw marks?" she asked, afraid they were. The gouges were ten feet long, a foot wide, and at least a foot deep each. They looked unmistakably like scratches.

Lucas shined his flashlight around the rock tunnel. "Yep," he replied, revealing them even on the ceiling.

Something above them scuttled away out of the light. Helen jumped back. Strangely, the thought of the giant thing that had made the claw marks didn't bother her as much at the little thing that was scurrying.

"It's probably just a rat," Lucas said, smiling. His smile faded as he saw more shadowy shapes lingering just on the edge of his flashlight beam. They had too many legs to be rats. "Or maybe not."

Lucas tried to put Helen behind him, but she shook him off. "You get behind *me*. I'm the one with the lightning."

"Don't hurt them," Lucas replied with genuine sympathy as the creatures picked their way forward into the circle of light.

Helen couldn't help but cringe away from them. They looked like rotting hands and heads. The hands used their fingers to crab-walk across the walls, floor, and ceiling, but the heads were far more gruesome. They moved atop what looked like starfish feet. Tiny tentacles shot out from underneath the decayed flesh and pulled them along. There were hundreds of the creatures.

"What are they?" Helen asked, detaching gravity, and floating above them. One of the heads had nearly crawled across her boot.

"The Hecatoncheires. The Hundred Handed Ones—or what Zeus left of them," Lucas said. His voice held considerable compassion. He floated up next to Helen, took her hand and led them deeper down the rock tunnel. "In the war between the Titans and the Olympians, the Hecatoncheires fought for Zeus. But when Olympus won, Zeus pulled them apart and left them like this to punish them."

"He punished them for helping him?"

"Them and any being related to the Titans—even the ones who fought for him, like Prometheus."

"That doesn't make any sense," Helen whispered.

"No." Lucas looked at her meaningfully. "If Zeus wins, everyone but him loses."

The tunnel ended and opened into an enormous room that appeared to be the junction for many tunnels. Large arches supported the cathedral ceiling, and buttresses held up what looked to be three different subway lines that passed overhead. It was a subterranean crossroads.

Lucas took Helen's hands in his before he let her descend. "Please let me take the lead in this one?"

Helen frowned at that. "You don't think I can handle this?" she asked, offended.

"I've had more practice dealing with beings like her. Just let me do this, okay?"

"Practice? When did you get practice?" she pressed.

"Please?" was all he would say.

Helen gave him an odd look but nodded tightly. They alit in the center of the room. The Hecatoncheires swarmed around them but did not try to crawl too close.

"Hello again, Helen Hamilton," Hecate's voice floated out. She emerged from a tunnel opposite Helen and Lucas, dressed in a blue-black gown.

"I've come to fulfill my end of our deal," Helen said, stepping forward.

"But not alone," Hecate noticed.

"We're sort of a two for one," Lucas said.

Hecate stayed on him. Her face flashed around her head, prism-like, as if she were looking in every possible direction.

"Our bargain does not include him." Hecate started walking in a deliberate circle around them.

"It doesn't *not* include me." Lucas replied calmly.

"Lucas," Helen hissed in his ear. "What are you doing?" Though it was obvious. He was challenging an enormously powerful being. He didn't even look nervous about it, either. That worried her the most.

Lucas gazed at Helen, his eyes like two blue stones. "Don't be afraid," he said before looking back at Hecate.

"You are not the *right* one," she told Lucas.

"What does that mean?" Helen asked.

"Look, you can try to make me leave, but I don't think you'll like what happens next," he said to Hecate.

"If you want to accompany the young goddess you must strike a bargain with me," she said to Lucas.

"No bargain," he replied with finality. "We do this my way or not at all."

Hecate kept circling them. "Your goddess owes me."

"And she will pay what is owed and nothing more."

Hecate stopped and regarded Lucas with a knowing half-smile. "Three tasks."

"And no more."

"As you say," Hecate agreed, tipping her head.

She then looked at Helen. "You will go to the Titan Cronus, and he will give you your first task."

Lucas held up a hand to intercede. "That's *two* tasks," Lucas objected. "Go to Cronus—one. Do as he orders—two. Possibly more, depending on what he says. And to be clear, what Cronus tells Helen to do will count as *your* tasks. Correct?"

Helen could practically hear Hecate grinding her teeth. "Correct," Hecate said in a clipped voice.

Lucas tapped his ear. "Correct—what? Say it."

Hecate regarded Lucas for a long time. "We want the same thing," she began, trying to reason with him, but Lucas cut her off impatiently.

"*Say* it," he demanded.

Hecate sighed. "Every individual task Cronus gives the goddess Helen will count toward the fulfillment of her debt to me."

Orange fire ran around the ring that Hecate had drawn to encircle them.

Lucas bowed formally to Hecate. "Thank you for your clarity, great goddess. Or whatever you are."

"And yours, young Scion. Or whatever *you* are," Hecate replied, her eyes sparkling with something that was torn between amusement and bitterness.

"We're ready to fulfill your first task," he informed her. "You may send us to Cronus now."

Hecate smirked at him knowingly. "You know the way—or doesn't your goddess know that about you?" She smiled cat-like at Lucas while he glowered back at her. Then Hecate disappeared. Abandoned by their mistress, the forlorn Hecatoncheires swarmed off in streams down every tunnel, leaving Helen and Lucas alone.

Helen turned slowly and looked at Lucas. "What the hell?" she asked quietly.

"I know, I'm sorry," he pleaded, reaching out for her. Helen moved away from him. "I had a feeling she was going to try to get more out of you than you owe her, even though she is usually one of fairest of the immortals. You're too big of an opportunity for her." He was still trying to get nearer to Helen, but she was fighting him off.

"What the *hell*, Lucas?" Helen shouted.

"Please," he said, still tugging at her. He looked so anxious and lost, Helen finally relented and let him draw her close.

"I can speak for myself," she bit out.

"I know," Lucas said, relaxing now that she was allowing him to hold her. "I know you're clever. You tricked Zeus, which was epic. But you aren't devious, and they're all looking for a way to hurt you, or use you." He leaned back and looked her in the eyes.

"I just want you to stay the way you are. Let me be the devious one, okay?"

Helen studied him for a moment. "Morpheus said something very similar. About how all the gods are trying to use me," she admitted.

A muscle in Lucas' jaw jumped as he clenched it. "Morpheus adores you and he'd do anything for you." He smiled ruefully. "It should make me happy, but it just pisses me off."

"Why?"

"Because he's a sneaky bastard," he said, angry. "He visited you as *Hector* when you were sleeping with me. Such a dick move."

Helen laughed, despite herself. Then she took a deep breath and reminded herself that she wasn't going to ask him a bunch of questions about how he knew so much about the gods and what they wanted. She was going to trust him. Because he'd asked her to.

"Ready?" he asked.

Helen wrinkled her brow, confused. "For what?"

"For Cronus," Lucas replied. He sighed heavily. "I didn't want to do this in front of you but... just hold onto me." He looked at her pleadingly. "And don't think about this too much."

And with that Helen entered the frigid cold, the absolute silence, and the utter darkness of a portal.

Only Worldbuilders could make portals, and Lucas was not a Worldbuilder. She had no idea how he had gotten this talent. She hadn't given it to him—she didn't think she could if she'd tried. Of all the strange things that were occurring in Lucas' life, this newly revealed ability unsettled her the most.

. . .

They appeared in a sylvan landscape, next to a river. The sun was pleasantly warm. The breeze was gentle. Helen knew exactly where they were because she'd been there before.

"The Elysian Fields," she whispered. Flash-frozen blades of grass crunched under her feet as she stepped out of the portal circle. She looked up at Lucas. She wasn't going to ask. She wanted him to be ready to tell her, but he wasn't yet and so she held back her questions and nodded at him in silent agreement.

"This way," Lucas said, dropping his eyes. He took her hand, and she considered pulling it away from him, but she'd promised to wait, and waiting did not mean holding him hostage with her anger. She gave him her hand.

He led her across a bridge over the River of Joy and toward an enormous olive tree. Its leaves were silvery spearheads, and its trunk looked like ropes of drooling clay that had been woven together haphazardly. It was an ancient tree with roots that clawed the ground like fingers, but the canopy was covered in tender shoots and new growth. It was both old and young at once.

Beneath the tree sat an enormous man. He was sitting cross-legged like a limber yogi, and his hands were resting in his chiton-covered lap. Even seated, he still loomed over Helen and Lucas who stood, and Lucas was over six feet tall.

His bare torso was amply muscled but wilting with age. The skin around his joints was baggy, but his forehead and cheekbones were taunt and smooth. His hair and long beard were snowy white, but his eyebrows were black as coal. When he opened his eyes and looked at Helen, his eyes were solid black with swirling galaxies in them. He could have been fifty years old, or a hundred and fifty, or a hundred and fifty million for all Helen could tell.

"It's always nice to see you, grandchildren," he said.

Helen shifted uncertainly from foot to foot and couldn't find a good place for her free hand. "Have we met?" she asked.

"We will had been meeting many times," he replied.

Helen paused, trying to untangle his tenses. Lucas gave his head a little shake, as if to tell her it was useless.

"Great Cronus," Lucas said formally. "We come in fulfillment of the first of the goddess Helen's three tasks for Hecate. We have been instructed that her next two tasks will be given to us by you."

The Titan turned his galaxy eyes on Lucas. "Ah, yes," he said, as if finding the right page in a book. "This is when I tell you the second half of what you have already done."

"Um—what?" she asked.

Helen and Lucas shared a look. Helen was relieved to see that Lucas was just as lost as she was.

"What came second must have been done before the first or it could never have happened at all. And of course, it will, and it did," Cronus said.

Lucas looked askance at Helen. "What is the second half that must have been done before the first?" he tried. She could hear him absolutely hating himself for his tortured grammar. Lucas was a very good student.

Cronus smiled at Lucas. "Grandson, you must have steal the Omphalos from your family and brought it to me."

Helen gasped. "I actually know this one! The Omphalos. It's a rock, right? The rock you ate... instead of... your son. Zeus."

Helen's enthusiasm wore thin when she heard the words she was saying. Cronus *ate* his children because he knew of a prophecy that said they would replace him. They didn't die, obviously, but it was still a disturbing thought—for her at least. Cronus did not seem phased by it at all.

Cronus turned his whirling eyes on Helen. "Yes, granddaughter. I did have eaten it." He touched his belly proudly. "This making it the strongest thing in the universe. For the first part, you need to have get the Omphalos."

Lucas frowned in thought. "It was at Delphi, and it belonged to the House of Thebes, but no one knows where it went." He turned to Helen. "The Omphalos disappeared from my family's collection. I don't know when."

"You must tell me when. I will have send you," Cronus said.

Lucas nodded. "We'll find out when and where the Omphalos disappeared. That will count as Helen's second task. Then we will come back to you and retrieve it, which will be Helen's third task."

"No," Cronus said. He held up three fingers. "Come to me." He held up two fingers. "Retrieve Omphalos." He held up one finger. "Last thing—most important." He dropped his fist back into his lap. "Then the past will have been complete, as are Helen's tasks. The Hand is not faster than Time," he said, smiling at Lucas fondly.

Lucas smiled back, like he got caught doing something naughty.

"What's the third task?" Helen asked.

Cronus turned his whirling eyes on her. "If I had told you, Fate would make it not so."

She felt uncertain about this. She was still thinking about how he swallowed his children, and how Morpheus had warned her that the other gods would want to use her.

"But why are we doing this for you? What do you want so badly that you would cash in two favors from a goddess?" she asked, hoping to divine if his intentions were good or bad.

"Family. Love. Always these things," Cronus answered.

He was not lying. To be extra sure, Helen read his heart and saw that it was open to her, though nearly inscrutable anyway. Cronus' heart was like a hall of mirrors and reflected in those mirrors was everything he felt, which seemed to be everything at once. He wasn't hiding anything from her. In fact, just the opposite. Helen saw that he was in overwhelming pain.

"You're very hurt," she said, cringing away from the gaping hole in him.

"Someone I love had been suffering. More suffering than anyone ever," Cronus replied. "This you must end."

Both she and Lucas could hear the truth in what he said. She looked at Lucas and nodded. "I think this is something I would want to do even if I didn't have to," she told him, greatly moved by the depth of Cronus' feeling. Lucas leaned a little closer to her in comfort, then faced Cronus.

"We will return when we know where the Omphalos is, and we will tell you when to send us," Lucas agreed. Then his eyes narrowed. "But I think you already know when and where it is. Why not just tell us if this is so important to you?"

Helen saw Cronus' heart suddenly choke with frustration.

"I already have known all *always*," Cronus replied in a booming voice. His expression suddenly softened, almost like he was pleading with them. "Is, was, will be Fate set, then?" he asked them, like they still had a choice.

Lucas' eyes danced around as his thoughts flew together. "Wait, it's not?" he asked. "Fate is not set?"

Cronus shrugged. "Will you had find that out if I have had giving you all the answers?" he asked, raising a tantalizing eyebrow.

Then he shut his galaxy eyes, and their interview with the Titan Cronus, God of Time, was ended.

. . .

Lucas took Helen's hand and opened a portal directly into Pandora's bedroom in the Delos brownstone on Washington Square.

"I have to go," Lucas said quickly. He took her face in his hands and kissed her. "I'll find it," he promised before pulling away.

"Wait... just stop," she pleaded. The portals, the way Hecate had spoken to him like they were on equal footing, the way Cronus had hinted at something else in Lucas, all of it was too much for Helen, but he was already shaking his head.

"It's late," he said, looking out the window at the rising moon. "I have to go."

Helen shut her mouth and balled her fists rather than ask him why. Because she'd promised.

He grabbed her and clung to her tightly, his need so blatant it stunned her. "I'll be back before *you* know it," he said.

He released her suddenly, stepped back, and looked at her with such longing it was as if he were boarding a ship that was about to sail away for years. Then, he disappeared.

Chapter 6

Helen stood in the ice-crusted room. In the dark. For a while. Then she turned around and went downstairs. She found Orion and Hector on the second floor, doing schoolwork.

"What the hell?" Orion said, jumping up from his laptop.

"The alarm's on—how'd you get in?" Hector demanded, striding toward her.

Orion glanced down at her heart. "Are you okay?" he asked.

"Ah... nope?" Helen replied.

Hector and Orion shared a look.

"Helen, how did you get into the house? Can you make portals again?" Orion asked.

"No. But Lucas can now." She gave a borderline hysterical laugh. "Can we get pizza? I'm starving."

"Sure," Hector said, looking her over. He waved her to him. "Come here."

Helen sighed as she dropped her forehead against Hector's

meaty chest and rubbed her face in his soft t-shirt. Her head hurt and her ears were ringing.

"Did you find out what's going on with Lucas?" Orion guessed.

"Not even a little bit," Helen replied, her voice muffled in Hector's chest. She pulled back and looked at Orion. "Pizza *and* a cannoli. Then I'll talk."

While they waited for their food, Helen recounted everything that had happened and the three of them kept talking about it while they ate.

"I'll call my dad and ask him about the Omphalos. Maybe he knows where it went," Hector said, pulling out his phone.

While Hector spoke to his father, Orion stared at Helen. "So. Lucas," he began leadingly.

Helen rubbed her face with her hands before leaning into the table toward Orion. "Remember when we became blood brothers?" she asked him.

"Vividly," he replied with a half-smile that was part amused, and part saddened.

Though it had brought them closer together, it wasn't a happy memory. Ares had been using Helen as bait for Orion and Lucas. He'd tortured her at the edge of a standing portal into the Underworld, in the icy nowhere between one place and another where there are no godly powers, to draw the three Heirs to the Four Scions Houses together, mix their blood, and release the Olympians.

It had worked, too. Helen had managed to put Ares in Tartarus, but too late. Orion, Lucas, and Helen had become blood brothers and the gods had been freed. In the process, Helen had absorbed some talents from Orion and Lucas. Through

Lucas' blood she had gained the Falsefinding talent. Through Orion's blood she had become an Earthshaker, and she could read and influence hearts.

"Did you ever get any of my abilities?" she asked Orion. He shook his head. "Did Lucas ever mention to you if he had?"

"No," Orion answered. "And he didn't have the ability to portal during the battle with the gods, or he would have used it," he added, guessing why Helen was thinking in that direction.

"So, it's new. And I didn't give it to him, which means another god must have."

Orion stared at her blankly, shaking his head slightly. He had no answers.

Hector joined them back at the kitchen table with a disappointed sigh. "My dad said that they couldn't be sure exactly when the Omphalos disappeared. It was part of their inventory one month and the next month when they did inventory again it was gone. Security cameras showed nothing."

"When?" Helen asked.

"About the time Ajax died—or when they thought he did back in '93. It fell through the cracks because they had other things to worry about."

Helen rolled her eyes. "That narrows it down a bit, but it still means I've got to wander blindly around the early nineties for a whole *month* looking for the right day."

Orion narrowed his eyes. "Whatever day you go will be the right day because it already happened. You can't change the past. All you can do is show up and let it unfold."

Hector leaned close to Helen. "He's sensitive *and* deep."

"The only thing missing is the man bun," Helen added, nodding sagely and taking the last bite of cannoli.

Orion threw a crumpled napkin at them as he stood up. "I'm going to finish writing my paper. A very deep and sensitive piece on man buns." He paused to kiss Helen on the top of the head before he left.

They both watched him go before Hector turned to Helen.

"He's really worried about you," Hector told her.

Helen shrugged. "I feel fine," she lied. Actually, despite the pizza, she felt weak and jittery, and if she let herself think about it, she could see Zeus setting fire to her sky.

"I don't want you doing these tasks with Lucas," he said. "If you want someone with you, it should be me or Orion."

Helen turned her hands up. "I don't think I could stop Lucas from coming even if I wanted to."

"What if one of your tasks goes down at night and he ditches you?" he asked, purposely characterizing Lucas' behavior in a harsh way to make his point.

Helen stood, getting angry. "He's not going to 'ditch' me."

Hector caught her arm before she could walk away. "Lucas knew you wouldn't need a cavalry," he said, looking up at her. "He didn't want Orion and me along to see what he can really do, because he knew we wouldn't let him get away with it like you do."

"I'm not letting him get away with anything. I'm trusting him because he's earned my trust." She sniffled, suddenly feeling stuffed up. "Weren't you the one who told me people were allowed to have secrets?"

Hector smiled ruefully. "Yeah, but this secret is making him unreliable, and that endangers all of us." Then he let his hand slide down her arm as his expression changed. "Why are you so sweaty?"

"I don't know," she said blearily, as flashing lights blanked out her vision. "Aw dammit," she mumbled, and then she fell into Hector's arms.

He caught her and lifted her up, calling for Orion.

"No—I'm good. I just got dizzy," Helen protested as Hector carried her up to the nap room.

"What happened?" Orion asked.

"She fainted."

"I did not *faint*," Helen complained as Hector put her down on the couch.

"Oh right. Then you threw yourself at me," Hector said sarcastically. "Is it Zeus?"

"Yeah. He's angry," she answered. She held her aching head while Orion and Hector exchanged worried looks.

"Should we call the twins? Have them get here as quickly as they can?" Orion asked.

"No," Helen insisted with closed eyes. "I'm going to go to bed, and we'll drive home tomorrow. If I still feel like garbage after that, then we tell everyone. Okay?"

"Fine. But you're sleeping with me tonight so I can keep an eye on you," Hector said. "I don't mean with me—like we're *sleeping* together. I mean in my room. In the other bed."

Orion clapped Hector on the shoulder bracingly. "That wasn't awkward at all. In case you were wondering," he told him. "I'll pack our stuff. You watch her."

Hector helped Helen upstairs and sat on the edge of the tub while she washed her face and brushed her teeth. When she was done, he took her place in the bathroom. She closed the door behind her and stripped down to a t-shirt and underwear on her way to bed, leaving a trail of clothes behind her. She slid between the cool sheets, but she couldn't fall asleep right away. She was acutely aware of the disconcerting fact that she was in her boyfriend's father's bed.

When Hector came out of the bathroom a few minutes later, Helen asked him, "Don't you think it's weird that this house is frozen in time?"

"Huh," Hector said musingly. He switched off the lights and started taking off his clothes. "My dad and uncle left the Hundred Cousins when my mom got pregnant with me, and they took Pandora with them." He folded his clothes neatly and left them on the dresser. "After that, Tantalus just closed this place up and my dad, aunt, and my uncle never saw him again. Until the last meeting of the Houses—well, before the one we just had."

"When I fried Lucas." She grimaced, remembering.

"My dad had a hard time accepting that Tantalus had killed Ajax," Hector said, like he was trying to explain. "That's why he took Tantalus' side in the battle with the gods."

"I know. You don't have to apologize for him. I get it," Helen said.

"Jason doesn't," Hector replied, trying to sound mocking but sounding sad.

Out of the corner of her eye, Helen saw the shape of Hector's mostly bare body lit up by the moon as he got into the other bed. When he was under the covers, she rolled onto her side to face him. "And now this house belongs to Castor, but you live here. Did he ask you to keep everything the same?"

Hector pillowed his head on his thick arm. "No," he whispered. "I haven't changed anything because... it's not done yet. Whatever happened here is still happening." He smiled and tilted his face into his arm, embarrassed to be speaking in such a vague and non-Hector way. The gesture made him seem vulnerable. Like Ajax in his self-portrait. He looked back up at her.

"I know exactly what you mean," she said, feeling the weight of history pressing down on her. "Being in this house makes me feel like everything I'm doing has been set up for generations. Like we've all been forced into our roles. Into our relationships."

"No one's forcing me," Hector said across the five feet of dark and winter moonlight. "It's not your face, you know."

"What?" Helen asked, confused.

"You *are* beautiful," he whispered. "But it's not why they love you." His big shoulders rose as he filled his lungs and sank as he let his breath go. "It's not why I love you."

He rolled over before she could see his heart.

Eventually, Helen fell asleep. She dreamed of big, blond men with swords who burned whole cities to find her. Some of them were coming to save her. Some of them were coming to kill her. One was her soul mate, and she gave herself to him on black sheets with the smell of spray paint all around them.

"Helen!" Lucas was shouting down the hallway.

Hector was at the door before Helen could reach it. He opened it as Lucas came running from Pandora's room. Fear for her safety was quickly replaced by confusion as Lucas saw Helen and Hector in the same bedroom, both barely dressed, and Helen's clothes scattered on the floor. Then, his confusion crumbled into betrayal.

"It's not what you think," Hector said, looking desperately guilty.

Orion appeared behind Lucas. Past experience had taught him to put himself between the cousins, ready to break up a fight before it could start. Hector and Lucas usually beat the hell out of each other first, and then talked about it later.

Helen stepped in before it came to that. She put her hand on the bottomless hole she saw opening in Lucas' heart.

"Two beds," she said, pointing with her other hand behind her so he could see. "I almost fainted last night, and Hector didn't want me sleeping in a room alone in case I got worse. That's all this is."

Relief washed through Lucas as he heard the truth, and he pulled Helen into a hug.

Hector and Orion both let out held breaths, looking at each other like they'd just dodged a bullet.

Lucas pulled back and looked Helen over. "You almost fainted?"

She shrugged. "It comes and goes," she admitted. "Zeus is like a big baby. He throws tantrums." Her face fell. She knew she couldn't keep this hidden any more. "And they're getting worse. I've never felt physically weak before if I wasn't injured. This is new."

Lucas' face hardened and the light dimmed around him. "How much worse?" he asked.

"I feel fine right now," she said. "Like I said. It comes and goes."

He glanced back at Hector and Orion. "I'm taking her home," he told them.

He opened a portal and took Helen through it.

They appeared in his bedroom in Nantucket.

"You just *left* them there?" Helen asked disbelievingly.

"I'm not in the mood to get grilled by Hector," he mumbled,

pulling her close. He wrapped his arms around her waist and buried his face in her neck.

Helen sighed and held him. "You're just delaying the inevitable. And pissing them off in the process."

"I don't care," he said. His hands fanned out over her body, pressing her tighter against him as he edged them off the disk of ice on the floor and toward his bed.

"Wait, Lucas," she said, pushing him away. "I also know *when* we need go. To get the big rock I need. I know when it disappeared."

He looked confused for a moment, then light dawned. "The Omphalos," he said. "New York, 1993."

He kissed her and backed her up against his bed. Helen stopped him as he pulled her down with him. "Hold on," she said, wriggling out of his grip and sitting up. "Why are you acting like this?"

"Like what?" he asked, kissing her ear.

"Like we haven't been together in months," she replied.

He flopped back onto his bed in frustration. "Can we pretend I already answered you, and we had a long conversation about it, and now we're at the part where I get to hold you?"

Helen turned away from him. "This isn't right. I feel like... I don't even know what's going on with you anymore."

He sat up next to her. "Here," he said, taking off his shirt and facing her so she could read his heart. "You tell me what's going on with me."

There was still some lingering black smoke of fear and the bruise-purple of hurt from finding her with Hector. But mostly there was love and *need*, pulling on his heart. It was overwhelming. She looked back up at his face.

"It doesn't make sense how much you need me," she said.

He smiled wanly. "It never has."

And then he was kissing her again and shifting her underneath him. There was nothing but Lucas above her, straining closer like he could never get near enough until her need matched his own and he had to cover her mouth to keep her from screaming his name.

"My parents are home," he whisper-laughed in her ear.

"Then you shouldn't have done that thing."

"What thing?" he teased, rolling off her.

"*That* thing—you know the thing," Helen said, looking for her shirt. She could hear Noel coming up the stairs, talking on the phone.

"Here," Lucas said, passing Helen a pair of jeans and a sweater out of her drawer.

They pulled on their clothes and were still buttoning this and zipping that when they heard knocking on Lucas' door.

"Lucas? Are you home?" his mom asked uncertainly.

"Yeah!" Lucas called, kissing Helen one last time on his way to open the door.

Noel looked between Helen and Lucas, surprised. Helen saw Lucas' flushed cheeks, shining eyes, and disheveled hair and knew they were busted. Her hand shot up to her hair to smooth it.

Noel smiled knowingly at Helen's lame attempt to fix herself up before turning back to Lucas.

"Hector called and told me you were home—when did you get in? I didn't hear you," Noel asked, confused. She turned to Helen. "I thought you weren't supposed to fly. Weren't you in New York with Hector and Orion?"

"I brought Helen back to see Jason or Ari. She fainted last night," Lucas said, sidestepping his mother's questions.

"She looks fine now," his mom said, sardonically lifting an eyebrow. Helen wanted to find a nice rock and crawl under it.

"What's really going on, Lucas?" Noel asked.

"Helen fainted last night. I want someone to check her."

His mom's face fell with disappointment that he still wouldn't explain. "Okay," she said, though it obviously wasn't. "They're getting ready for school. You guys better get it together or you'll be late," she said before leaving them.

She stopped at Cassandra's bedroom and knocked. "Cass? Are you feeling up to going to school today?" she asked gently.

"No," came Cassandra's immediate reply.

Noel hovered outside the door for a moment, weighing whether she should go in. She touched the tips of her fingers to Cassandra's door before walking away.

Helen shot Lucas an angry look. "You shouldn't have lied to your mom. She's going through enough right now."

"I know. That's why I lied," he said.

Helen had no idea what he meant. "They're all going to find out you can make a portal in a few hours when Orion and Hector get here."

He reached out and smoothed her tousled hair. "I'll take every hour I can get."

Helen started down the hall to Ariadne's room, but Lucas caught her arm. "No, don't be angry," he said, drawing her near, backing her against the wall, and brushing his lips over her temple. "Just one more day, okay?" he pleaded.

Helen saw the spark of need in him again, too bright, and too soon after she'd put out the last one. She realized his need—as blinding as it was—was masking something much deeper and darker. It was covering his sadness. Lucas was so sad it was sinking him, and the only thing left were these signal flares of need. Helen would have done anything to take his sorrow away, so she put her arms around his neck, softening against him.

"Let me help you," she whispered.

"You are helping me," he said as his lips ran across her neck. "*This* helps me."

Ariadne's door opened forcefully, and they broke apart as she rushed forward, and then stopped. She looked between them and gestured with her phone.

"Helen—Hector just texted me and told me you might be here and that you fainted last night," she blurted, studying them. She shook her head, puzzled. "Are you okay?"

"I don't know," Helen admitted. "It's hard to explain."

Jason met them in the hallway, and they all went downstairs together. They ate a quick breakfast standing in front of the refrigerator while discussing what Helen had been experiencing.

"So, Zeus is using his lightning bolts," Jason said, thinking it through.

"And his strength," Helen clarified. "Sometimes he gets so angry when I rebuild a forest or a mountain that he just," she paused, searching for words, "pushes it over with his bare hands."

Lucas and Jason shared a scared look.

"I know," Helen said, understanding their fear. "And if you thought that maybe you could take him in a fight, I want to let you know that you can't. Zeus is stronger than all of you put together."

"But is he stronger than you?" Lucas asked.

Helen shook her head uncertainly. "I don't know. But I do know that if I fight him and lose, none of you can stop him." She swallowed, her yogurt sticking in her throat. "He'll tear you apart. Even Hector. I know he thinks he stands a chance. He doesn't."

She saw them sink into themselves. But they needed to know.

"I can't let Zeus out," she said, stabbing at the berries on the bottom of her yogurt cup. "I just have to... put up with it."

Ariadne rolled her eyes. "Why do New Englanders always think that stoicism is the right answer? Is it the snow?" she complained. "Seriously, I asked Matt this once, and he usually had answers for everything, but he could never explain to me why you're all so pig-headed."

"We've got good schools here. We *should* be smarter," Helen joked, just happy Ariadne was talking about Matt and smiling at the same time.

Jason and Lucas had noticed, too. They shared a hopeful look before Jason turned serious again.

"Helen, you're not in pain, right?" he asked.

"I get headaches. My nose gets stuffed up. I get weak, and I feel faint, and time goes by without me being really present," she said honestly. "But I'm not in real pain."

The twins nodded in unison.

"Is it getting worse?" Ariadne asked.

Helen had to admit that it was. "Yes, but slowly."

The twins looked at each other.

"If it's getting worse, we can only assume there will be a limit to how much you can take," Jason said.

Lucas went to the sink and rinsed off his spoon. "We'll find a solution before that," he said.

"We've got time," Ariadne offered confidently, but Helen noticed that behind Lucas' back the glance she shot Jason was very concerned.

"You have to tell us if it changes," Jason told Helen carefully. "If this escalates, we need to know."

Helen nodded, knowing they couldn't help her even if she did. A thought occurred to her. Their immortality came from her world, which was now under attack. "Have any of *you* felt weak?" she asked.

Lucas, Jason, and Ariadne thought about it for a moment. "I know I'm not one of the immortals, but I have felt more tired than usual," Ariadne admitted.

Jason looked away pensively. "I thought it was just because Claire and I—" he broke off, unwilling to talk about the problems he was having with Claire in front of her best friend. "Yeah," he said. "I've been dragging." He looked at Lucas. "You?"

Helen knew that Lucas had been sad, and that sadness often translated into a lack of energy, but he didn't give them a straight answer.

"We should ask everyone—Claire, Hector, Orion—and find out how they're feeling," Lucas replied evasively. He started gathering up his stuff. "We gotta go."

Helen grabbed an extra coat on the way out the door, and they all headed to school together.

Claire met Helen at her locker with a dozen questions. It took Helen all of homeroom, and they were both nearly late for their first classes, but she managed to tell Claire everything about Hecate, Cronus, fainting, and Lucas' new ability to create portals.

"Don't tell Jason about the portal stuff yet. Lucas asked me to give him one more day before I blabbed," Helen told her before they separated.

"Shouldn't be hard," Claire said, laughing in an unhinged way that crept up on crying. "Jason's not speaking to me."

"What?" Helen exclaimed, stopping dead.

"Later," Claire called over her shoulder.

Helen took a step to chase after Claire and force her to talk, but the bell rang, and she had to use a little Scion speed to make it to class on time. But it was a disaster because Helen hadn't done any of the reading.

After class, Lucas was waiting for her in the hallway.

"I thought you told Jason to back off, not break up with Claire," she said angrily as she rearranged the stack of assignments she hadn't completed on time.

Lucas looked stunned, and then he groaned. "He's an idiot. I'll talk to him, okay?" he promised. He put his arm over her shoulder, noticing what she held. "Did you do *any* of your homework?"

"Of course not," Helen snapped, stressed out. Lucas just laughed. Then she laughed under her breath with him. "Why does that make you happy?"

"I don't know," he mumbled, smiling at the floor. "*You* make me happy."

They got to Lucas' next class and saw Jason chatting up Gretchen and Amy outside the door. Gretchen and Amy were in hair-flipping, eyelash-batting heaven and Jason was encouraging it. Helen and Lucas shared a look. She didn't see Claire anywhere, and this was her next class, too.

Bathroom, Helen thought, shooting Jason a dirty look. She shrugged off Lucas' arm and ran down the hallway.

Claire was crying in the girls' room next to the biology lab. No one used that bathroom at this time of year because it was usually when the AP bio class started dissecting fetal pigs, which made the whole corridor stink like formaldehyde.

The bell rang for the start of class as Helen went to Claire, who was standing by the paper towel dispenser, blowing her nose. She gave her friend a huge hug and asked, "What happened?"

"After you left for New York, Jason came to me and said that if I wanted space, it was fine with him, but that I should remember it goes both ways. And for the past two days he won't talk to me, won't return my texts, and he's been flirting with every girl in the school. So, I guess that means we broke up." Claire replied, sniffling.

"He's hurt—I can see it in his heart," Helen said. "He wants to hurt you back because he thinks you don't love him as much as he loves you."

"Why? Because I want to figure out what's going on with me, rather than pick out engagement rings?" Claire asked flippantly. "All of a sudden, I can draw and paint and sing and play instruments and I love being able to do these new things, but that doesn't mean I don't love him. *God*, it smells bad in here."

"Yes, it does," Helen agreed plainly.

Claire threw her paper towel into the waste basket. "And why is he flirting with *Gretchen* of all people?"

"That's just tacky," Helen said. She put her arm around Claire. "Wanna play hookie?"

Claire smiled. "I do."

Helen grinned, as they started for the door. "Two hall passes, coming up."

Helen went directly to the office and told a convoluted story about fumes in the bio lab bathroom while influencing all of the office administrators' hearts. Not only did she get hall passes for them both for the rest of the day, she also obtained an extension on a few of her class assignments. She felt a little guilty about that, but not really. She figured all her Scion extra-curricular activities had earned her a couple of days to write a paper or two.

Instead of going to lunch, the best friends went on a vending machine rampage and brought their chips and sodas to the auditorium.

"Are they ever going to put on this play?" Claire asked.

Helen looked around at the set of *A Midsummer Night's Dream*. "They keep having to delay it," she said, recalling one of the morning announcements.

"Because of all of your shenanigans," Claire said, giving Helen a half smile.

"Not *my* shenanigans. I have no shenanigans," Helen said.

"Why do you keep saying shenanigans?" Ariadne asked as she joined them from the backstage entrance.

Claire's eyes darted behind her hopefully, looking for Jason.

Ariadne shook her head. "He's not coming," she said apologetically. "Lucas is talking to him, though."

"Is anyone bleeding?" Helen asked.

"Surprisingly? No," Ariadne said, sitting down between them.

Claire rubbed some set glitter off her arm rather than look Ariadne in the eyes. "How'd you find us?" she asked, repositioning herself on Queen Titania's hillock to give Ariadne some room.

"Oh please. Like I don't know where you'd be if you're not in the cafeteria for lunch," Ariadne replied, smirking. "So. What are we doing?" She helped herself to some chips.

"We're taking an emotional day off," Helen replied. She read Ariadne's heart and saw that it was still heavy, but it wasn't quite so empty. "How are *you* doing?"

Ariadne smiled and shrugged. "One of Orion's distant cousins from the House of Rome is a grief counselor. We talk."

"Good," Helen said. "I'm proud of you for getting help."

Ariadne tilted her head to the side and rested it on Helen's shoulder. "Thanks. I'm glad I'm doing it. Lucas had to practically drag me the first time. He's trying to get Cassandra to do it, too," she admitted. She picked her head up as a thought occurred to her. "It's like Lucas is trying to fix everyone."

Claire guffawed. "He's got some more work to do on Jason, then."

Ariadne shook her head, smiling. "Jason's not broken, he's just... a good Scion boy. Scions fall hard when they fall in love." She paused and smiled sardonically at her own situation. "And my brothers were raised to think that was exactly what they should do. Fall madly in love with a nice mortal girl, get married, and bring her into our world so they can have Scion babies. And the sooner the better. So, you're shit out of luck, Claire."

"Maybe not. He might ask *Gretchen* to marry him," Claire replied dourly.

"Oh, god, please no," Helen groaned.

Ariadne laughed and leaned back, but quickly sat up again. "Ew! What the hell is *that*?" she said. She turned and looked behind herself while wiping the heel of her hand with a disgusted look on her face.

Helen spun around the fastest and was on her knees reaching for what looked like a shiny round white ball.

"Don't touch it!" Ariadne warned. "It's all squishy and it *moved*. I think it's alive."

Confident that it couldn't kill her, no matter what it was, Helen picked it up and turned it over. "Oh gross!" she squealed, dropping it again. She rubbed her hand repeatedly on her jeans. "It's an *eyeball*!"

"No way!" Claire said, inching toward it.

"Yeah, way," Helen said. "Hand me that chip baggie."

She used the empty bag to pick up the eyeball. The girls

pulled into a tight huddle and examined it. The iris was a beautiful cobalt blue.

"What are you doing?" asked a voice from the shadowy backstage.

Startled, the three girls shrieked, and Helen dropped the eyeball again. "Lucas, you scared the crap out of me!" she said when she saw him coming toward them with a bemused look on his face.

"We found an eyeball," Ariadne said, pointing at the thing on the ground.

Lucas crouched down to inspect it. He picked it up, using the bag. Lucas suddenly jumped and practically threw it across the room. "Holy shit, it moved!"

"Ha!" Ariadne said, pointing at Lucas. "I told you!"

"Okay," Lucas agreed, laughing abashedly. He picked it up and held it out for Ariadne. "You have to take it home. Show our dads."

"Why can't *you* take it?" she argued. The bell rang, signaling the end of lunch and Ariadne moved toward the door.

"Because Helen and I have something else we have to do right now, and I'm not keeping that thing in my pocket the whole time," Lucas replied.

Claire groaned in frustration. "I'll take it," she said, stomping over to it and picking it up. "Like we haven't seen worse," she grumbled, putting it in her bag on her way out of the auditorium.

"Claire?" Lucas called. She paused at the door. "Jason is going to be waiting for you after chorus. Please talk to him."

Claire nodded, suddenly serious, and then went through the doors with Ariadne.

"Do you *have* to go to class?" Lucas asked, facing Helen and taking her hands in his.

"Not especially," Helen admitted, moving closer to him.

He laugh-groaned like he was in pain. "Helen—we can't."

"What?" she teased, draping her arms across the back of his neck and pressing herself against him. "Can't what?"

He muttered a curse and kissed her, but before it got too interesting, he broke away. "Orion and Hector are going to be back soon, and we still have to get ourselves ready."

He took her hand and they walked to the door. Helen saw the gray veil drop around them, making them invisible.

"What do you mean, get ready?" Helen asked as they slipped, unseen, through the hallways.

"We can't go back to 1993 dressed like this," Lucas said. "And we have to figure out what to do about money. All the bills are different now and it's not like we can use an app."

Helen chuckled. "Savages. How did they survive?" She had an idea. "You know, I think my dad and Kate still have clothes from the nineties. My dad never throws anything away."

They ran to her house still hidden. Lucas dropped the veil of invisibility when they were inside.

"Let's check the attic," Helen said, heading for the stairs.

"Helen? Is that you?" Kate called from the kitchen.

Lucas and Helen shared a surprised look. "Yeah!" she called. She lowered her voice for Lucas. "She's usually at the store now," she said defensively as he shook his head at her.

"What's wrong?" Kate asked.

"Nothing. Why are you here?" Helen asked in return.

"Wedding stuff. Why aren't you in school?" Kate fired back, joining them at the foot of the stairs.

"We gotta do this thing," Helen admitted. "We can't tell you what it is or why we're doing it, or anything like that. But we need clothes from the nineties."

Kate stared at them for moment, and then sighed resignedly. "Styles come back around so, Helen, you're dressed mostly right, except for your jacket," she said, leading them upstairs. "Lucas, you're all wrong."

Kate went into the back of Jerry's closet and pulled out a button-down flannel and white, long-sleeved thermal. She held them out to Lucas. "Extra points if you tie the flannel around your waist," she told him. "The jeans are an issue. Not going to lie. Men wore really baggy jeans—like, hanging off their butts baggy."

Kate went up into the attic and passed down some jeans, a boxy brown jacket for Helen, and a black peacoat for Lucas. He changed while Helen tried on the jacket.

"I mean, I think it's okay? It's kind of drab," Helen said, turning around as she looked in the mirror.

"It's grunge, sweetie. And your hair is too smooth," Kate told Helen as she tied a black leather-corded choker around her neck. "You'll have to wear it back in a ponytail."

Lucas finished dressing and joined them in Helen's room, holding out his arms. "What do you think?" he asked.

"It's looks like you're going to a Pearl Jam concert," Kate said. "So, perfect."

"Thanks, Kate." Helen gave her a hug.

"How long are you going to be gone?" Kate asked, concerned. "Your dad doesn't complain to you. He complains to me, though. He never sees you anymore."

Helen glanced at Lucas, feeling horrible.

"Helen will be back before Jerry gets home," Lucas answered.

"Good," Kate replied. Then she brightened. "When you're back you can try on your maid of honor dress."

"It's *here!*?" Helen squealed, grabbing Kate's hands and jumping up and down. "Where is it?"

"Helen," Lucas interrupted, smiling at her. "Later."

Kate told the two of them to be careful and returned to the kitchen. Lucas stacked his and Helen's phones together and left them on her dresser. "Ready?" he asked, taking her hand.

"Let's do it," Helen replied.

Lucas opened a portal to the Underworld and brought them directly to Cronus, sitting cross-legged under his olive tree with his eyes closed.

"Right on time," the Titan said, smiling.

"Ha," Helen whispered to Lucas. "Dad joke."

"*Granddad* joke," Lucas countered.

Cronus opened his galaxy eyes. "Are you prepared?"

"We are," Lucas replied.

"You will spoken to your uncle Ajax. He will have been informed he must helped you," Cronus said. "Other events you will had seen, and you will have been tempted many times to interfere, but you have not yet interfered. This is as it always must be."

"I understand," Lucas replied.

Helen smirked at him. "Good thing one of us does." She stopped Lucas before he could explain. "But I get the gist of it. Grandfather paradox—given to me by my grandfather, ironically. Don't do anything but take the Omphalos."

Lucas turned back to Cronus. "How will we signal to you that we're ready to come back to this time?" he asked.

Cronus gave him an odd look. “Come here.”

“But back in 1993, will you be expecting us—oh, I get it,” Lucas said, nodding sheepishly. “You were had always been expecting us.”

“Geeze, Lucas. Catch up,” Helen teased.

Lucas narrowed his eyes at her, like he was thinking of all the fun ways he was going to make her pay for that. Then he took her hand and faced Cronus.

“We’re ready.”

CHAPTER 7

The Titan Cronus, Lord of Time, opened his black eyes wide. Helen could see the whirling galaxy in the center of them grow closer as if they were drawing her near, and then there was darkness and bitter cold.

Helen and Lucas appeared across the street from the Delos brownstone on Washington Square Park in Manhattan.

As they looked around, Lucas took a deep breath. "This is so weird," he said, letting his breath out in a gust. "It's the same, but different."

It was nighttime. There were still a few people about, but they were going somewhere else and not there to linger. Helen and Lucas looked at the Delos' front door.

"Is it just me, or is 1993 a little dirtier than now?" Helen asked.

The streets weren't as well-tended. There were cracks in the sidewalks and the black railing around the park was old and bent in places. Even the buildings looked slightly less scrubbed and polished compared to how they were in Helen's time. It was still a lovely neighborhood, but it wasn't perfect. It wasn't pristine. It looked a bit more lived-in, a bit more approachable, and Helen found herself rather liking it.

Lucas laughed under his breath. "Grunge," he said.

There were lights on inside the Delos brownstone. Every floor blazed with activity. Using their Scion hearing, Helen and Lucas could hear the low rumble of many male voices, and every now and again the high, piercing laughter of a young girl.

"Pandora," Lucas whispered, hearing his aunt's voice from when she was a little girl.

Helen turned her head to watch Lucas. He'd spoken of his aunt Pandora only maybe once or twice since she'd died, but Helen knew he missed her deeply. The color of his heart was a dull, bruised red.

"Do we wait for Ajax to come out?" she asked, mostly to give him something else to think about. Lucas operated best when he had a problem to solve.

He shook his head. "We'll probably be here until morning if we do," he replied.

"Ring the doorbell, then?"

Lucas' brow furrowed in thought. He looked up at the building's façade. He pointed at a window on the third floor. "That's Ajax's bedroom," he said. "We could fly up, hidden, and..."

"Freak him out when we suddenly appear in his bedroom, and either have to knock him unconscious so he won't shout for help, or get into a giant fight with him that brings everyone running?" Helen asked sardonically.

"Good point," Lucas admitted.

Helen chuckled. They both perked up when they noticed the door opening. Lucas quickly veiled them in invisibility.

"Oh my god," Helen gasped. She saw what looked like herself and Hector, though of course it wasn't either of them.

"Tomorrow?" Ajax asked.

"Tomorrow," Daphne agreed. She went down the steps, but Ajax didn't close the door. He watched her, heading for the park.

"He's going to go after her," Lucas whispered, his eyes glued to Ajax.

He was right. Just as Daphne was alongside Helen and Lucas, Ajax jerked forward and followed her, like an invisible string between them had pulled taut.

"That wasn't enough," Ajax said, as he turned Daphne around and kissed her.

Helen and Lucas stayed very still, though Ajax and Daphne could have been hit by a car without noticing. Helen couldn't take her eyes off them. It really looked like her and Hector, and she could feel Lucas getting irrationally angry as he watched them kiss.

"You're not wearing a coat," Daphne said, pulling away from Ajax and trying to chafe some heat into him. "Or shoes," she added, gesturing down to his bare feet. Daphne laughed and untangled herself from his big arms. "You're going to get a fungus!"

Lucas and Helen both breathed out matching surprised laughs. Helen had never seen her mother smile this much.

Ajax and Daphne kissed their last goodbye, and Ajax started back for his door. But as Daphne illegally cut through the park after dark, striding with New Yorker purpose, he stayed and watched her until she was all the way across before he turned and slowly made his way back to the front door.

Lucas looked at Helen. "Disguise yourself," he whispered. She nodded and he unveiled them.

"Ajax," Lucas called.

Ajax was at the base of his steps. He spun around quickly, immediately taking a fighter's stance. Lucas held up his hands in a placating gesture.

"Daedelus," Ajax growled, then he looked closer, confused. "Wait. Who are you?"

Helen could see Ajax's heart racing and his hot blood fanning out to his muscles, ready for a fight. Lucas was reacting too, even though he didn't mean to; it was just too engrained in him to stand his ground when facing aggression. Helen stepped forward before things got out of hand.

"I'm Helen, this is Lucas. Hecate should have told you by now that you're supposed to help us steal something," she told Ajax.

It was disorienting to be talking to someone who looked so much like Hector but was not him. Certain details were different, like his hands, his movements, and the sound of his voice. Speaking to Ajax was akin to being on this street in another decade. Ajax was close, but not exactly what Helen knew. Daphne, on the other hand, had been an identical copy of Helen physically, except for her cropped hair. Helen didn't know what to think about that yet.

Ajax dropped his stance and cursed under his breath, taking a few calming breaths. "Your name is *Helen*?" he asked, unable to help grimacing. He glanced anxiously up at his door. "My brothers are going to notice I left the door open soon, so talk fast. What do you need?"

"The Omphalos. It's a rock," Lucas replied, glancing up at the door with dread.

Helen knew he was picturing seeing his dad come through it and squaring off with him as Ajax had done. Lucas looked like he was from the House of Athens. Even without the Furies, his father or uncles would attack him on sight.

Ajax shook his head, confused. He had no idea what they were talking about.

"It's about this big. It's mostly round. It just looks like a regular stone," Lucas said, describing it quickly with his hands. "Check around the house. It could be there."

"And if it isn't?" Ajax asked, his eyes darting to the door. Someone was coming. "Meet me in the park after school tomorrow," he said hurriedly, and then he flew up to his bedroom window so quickly a human couldn't see him do it in the dark.

Lucas veiled them just as *his parents* came to the door.

Helen took Lucas' hand. They watched an early twenty-something Noel and Castor come outside, in the middle of what seemed to be an argument.

Helen and Lucas weren't stunned simply because Noel and Castor looked so young. It was how raw they both seemed emotionally, that came as the greatest shock. Neither Helen nor Lucas was used to seeing either of these people so tangled up in their feelings.

Noel was carrying a large duffel bag. A look of determination was fixed on her face. Castor chased after her. Noel paused when she noticed that the front door was already open. This gave Castor a chance to touch her arm and turn her around.

"You don't have to go," Castor said. "Just quit."

"I'm not quitting my other job!" she told him angrily, throwing off his hand. She tried to go down the steps, but Castor reached for her again, like he couldn't stop himself.

"We'll pay you whatever you're making at *Lush,* and then some," he promised.

She dropped her head back for a moment, like she was asking

the stars for help. Then she looked directly at Castor and said, "So this can be my only job, and then I'm screwed if the Delos family decides to fire me? No, thank you."

"Where does that mistrust even come from, Noel?"

"Practice!" she shouted back at him. "I've been taking care of myself and my dad my whole life, and the one thing I know for sure is that you can never rely on anyone." She poked him right in the middle of his chest. "*Especially* not the people who promise you that you can."

She tried to leave again, and Castor followed her, stopping her at the bottom of the stairs right next to Helen and Lucas. Helen could feel Lucas' heart thrumming. She could also see the wildfire of longing and fear in Castor. And she could see the hurt, the want, and the rage boiling away in Noel. Lucas' mother had been an angry young woman. Helen never would have guessed that.

"Adonis and Leda Tiber are dangerous, Noel," Castor said, gripping her by the shoulders and nearly growling at her. "The only reason they hired you was because of me."

Noel laughed in that way people do when they want to scream instead. "That's just... unbelievable," she said coldly. "I've been slinging drinks since I was sixteen, and you think I got my job at the hottest nightclub in town because of *you*?"

Castor let her go. "I have history with the Tibers, okay?" he admitted.

She smirked at him suggestively. "Which one? Leda or Don?"

"Our *families* have history," he clarified, obviously in no mood to banter.

Noel made a dismissive gesture. "Look, I've never talked to them about you, and they've never asked questions about you, so you don't have to worry about me telling them private things about your family, if that's what this is about."

"It's not," Castor replied. "I'm not worried about you saying anything. I'm just worried about *you*."

"I can take care of myself. And I barely know you," Noel shot back. "What do you care where I go to work when I leave here?"

He threw his arms wide, like he was giving up. "I've never cared about anyone outside my family, but I care about you—and *they* know that."

Knowing the situation had deepened, Noel didn't attempt a sassy comeback. She stood there, staring at him, like she could nearly figure him out, but not quite.

"*Flaca*!" called a young woman. She came striding up to them, wearing lace-up platform combat boots, torn fishnets, a tiny miniskirt that puckered around her bodacious backside, and a cropped leather motorcycle jacket. She snapped her gum behind her deep wine-colored matte lipstick, lined in black.

"Hey, Castor," she said, her full lips sliding apart in a knowing smile.

"Aileen," Castor said, tipping his chin up at her in greeting.

Helen had to cover her mouth to keep herself from gasping aloud. Aileen was Pallas' wife—and Hector, Jason, and Ariadne's mother. She'd died years ago. The firecracker in front of her was not what Helen had imagined.

"*Mami*," Aileen scolded, taking Noel's hand. "You better have something else to wear in that bag," she said, her voice sliding up and down and all around with her New Yorican accent. "We're working the same well. No tits, no tips." She pulled Noel away. "'Bye," she singsonged over her shoulder to Castor. "Oh, and tell your brother he can kiss my ass."

Aileen's laughter floated through the air, as Castor went inside, his eyes hungrily following Noel's every step, like his worry for both of them was dragging him down.

Helen and Lucas waited until the door closed. Then Lucas let out a held breath.

"That was so bizarre," Helen said, turning Lucas around and having him sit down on the Delos' stoop. "Are you okay?" she asked, sitting next to him.

Lucas shrugged. Then shook his head. And then laughed. "I don't know what I am. It's so strange to see all of them like this."

Helen curved her hand over his bicep and leaned her head against his shoulder. But they didn't get much of a chance to process what they had just seen. Not three minutes after Castor had closed the front door, it opened again.

"It's like Grand Central," Lucas complained.

Still veiled, he and Helen turned to see a girl—black-haired, blue-eyed, painfully skinny—tiptoe out of the brownstone and close the door silently behind her.

The girl, who resembled Cassandra and had the same haunted look, rested her hand flat against the door.

"Goodbye," she whispered, and then she tiptoed down the front steps. Helen noticed she was wearing slippers, and underneath the black wool overcoat that was several sizes too large for her, Helen saw the hem of a white nightgown.

Helen felt Lucas' hand tense around hers so tightly it was painful.

"Pandora?" Helen whispered, though she knew it couldn't be her. She just couldn't think of any other young girl in the Delos family at this time.

Lucas shook his head, his eyes wild. "Antigone. The Oracle before Cass," Lucas whispered back. "We have to follow her."

Helen nodded. Something seemed terribly wrong. There was no way they weren't going to see where Antigone led them.

. . .

Helen and Lucas stayed veiled as they followed Antigone to the 8th Street N/R subway station. They stood near her on the train while she sat, curled tight inside the enormous man's overcoat she wore. Her eyes were hollow, and her face was gaunt, like she was used to staring down demons, but her legs were too short to reach the ground. Her little white bedroom slippers with pink bows dangled childishly beneath her. The whole ride downtown Lucas never took his eyes off her.

Antigone got off at South Ferry, the very bottom of Manhattan Island, and the territory of the House of Athens. In 1993, Helen remembered, Athens and Thebes were bitter enemies. If Antigone were to encounter anyone from the House of Athens, the Furies would possess them, and the girl, who was no warrior, would surely be killed.

Helen could hear Lucas' breathing rasping in and out with anxiety as they followed Antigone to the water. She stayed small as she passed through the station so no one would see her. She crept closer to the long wooden pilons that stretched out into the water and demarcated where the ferries made berth at South Ferry Station. She paused, feigning nonchalance until no one was looking. She squeezed through a fence and hid, waiting.

Then she started to walk out onto the pilons, jumping wildly from one to the next. The wind snatched at her frail body. Her huge black overcoat flapped around her girlish white nightgown.

Lucas strained to chase her down and grab her, but Helen stopped him.

"She's planned this," Helen whispered to Lucas.

He nodded and squeezed his eyes shut for a moment. When he opened them again, he looked at Helen.

"So, we have to stand here and let her kill herself?" he asked, his throat working like the words were too bitter to say.

"I don't know," she replied.

Helen knew why this was hurting him so much. Instead of Antigone, this could easily be his sister. Helen searched her mind, looking for anything that would comfort him. "When did Antigone die?" she asked.

Lucas brightened. "After Ajax," he said.

"That means she doesn't die tonight," Helen said optimistically.

Lucas' eyes scanned around. No one was anywhere near them. "Who saved her, then? Did *we* do it?" he asked desperately.

Helen shrugged and shook her head at the same time. She didn't know. But she did know that Cronus had told them to get the Omphalos. And *nothing* else.

"I don't think so," she replied.

Antigone had reached the end of the pilons. She held out her arms like she was going to hug that famous, sparkling skyline. And then she toppled forward, into the cold, black water.

Lucas charged down the pilons and Helen followed. She caught him before he could dive and held him back.

"Wait!" Helen hissed in his ear. She clamped her arms around him, stopping him from saving Antigone, and hoping he wouldn't hate her for this. "Please, Lucas. Just trust that this is exactly what's supposed to happen."

Lucas went slack in her arms as they watched Antigone's white nightgown get sucked beneath the surface, her pale face sinking like the moon into the sea.

Suddenly, they saw the flash of iridescent scales, and an enormous creature with triangular spikes sticking out of his back breached the surface and dove after her. The creature took Antigone in his arms and darted down beneath the waves with her.

Helen and Lucas shared one shocked look, and then—without thinking—they both jumped into the water.

Helen found that she could swim and even breathe underwater again and sensed why. In 1993 Poseidon was locked up on Olympus and not actively working against her. She assumed the same would hold true if she tried to fly.

She saw an iridescent flash of scales in front of them and took off after it, with Lucas right behind her.

They almost couldn't keep up, but as they chased the sea monster and the girl he had stolen from death, Helen recognized him. It was Ladon, First Born to the House of Athens, Disowned Son of Bellerophon, and most importantly to her, Orion's uncle.

It wasn't long before they were swimming through old brick tunnels and sunken supports—the flooded bones buried under New York. Some of the submerged chambers were long tubes with train tracks at the bottom. The ornately tiled walls were crumbling from the water, but the style put them somewhere in the mid to late 1800's. In some places barrel vaults were all that remained where the ribbing of arches held; the walls had collapsed. They breached in one of those forgotten chambers.

Helen and Lucas stayed just beneath the surface as they swam to the edge of Ladon's subterranean cove, and then Lucas veiled them as they came silently up from the water and onto the stones that sloped up into an Art Nouveau style subway station, complete with stained glass panels in the ceiling. They heard Antigone scream and turned to see her skittering away from Ladon on the heels of her hands and kicking at him with her tiny feet.

Ladon cringed away from her, trying to tuck the most monstrous bits of him out of sight so as not to scare her.

"Please—I won't hurt you," he begged. "But you must stay still, or you could injure yourself on me."

Down Ladon's back and tail were scales that were so sharp they gleamed. Ladon tried his best to keep these parts of himself away from her.

Antigone rolled over and, bracing herself on her thin, shaking arms, wretched several times to clear her lungs. Ladon slithered closer, his human torso and head hovering above her anxiously, but not touching her.

"I will bring you a blanket," he said, his long, draconian lower body undulating across the brick floor toward what appeared to be a very refined living room, right in the middle of a sunken early 1900's subway station.

Helen and Lucas moved closer, dodging crumbled bricks and loose subway tiles as they made their silent way around the edge of the subterranean cove that was Ladon's lair.

While Helen and Lucas inched closer to the comfortable and tasteful living space that he had amassed for himself, Ladon gathered blankets and lit frosted kerosene lamps for Antigone. He paused briefly to put on clothing. Helen observed him. From the waist up Ladon was very much a man in his late twenties. He looked like Lucas. They had the same black hair and blue eyes of the House of Athens, and most of him was covered in the same smooth skin. But there were patches of iridescent scales on his handsome face and torso, and from the waist down and across his back, Ladon was a dragon. He had crooked legs, talons, and a tail. His spine had a row of wicked-looking spikes sticking out of his fiery-blue hide, and his tail seemed to snake about on its own.

He was monstrous. And beautiful. And he had a problem dressing himself. His dragon scales seemed to slice his clothes to shreds. He tried to cover his bare chest and his lower half, but it was a losing battle. Finally, he gave up and went back to Antigone, cringing in on himself so he didn't frighten her with his huge body.

Antigone had pulled her knees up to her chest. She was shivering and crying quietly.

"Why didn't you just let me die?" she sobbed.

Ladon laid a blanket near her and backed away quickly. "Why would someone as young as you want to die?" he asked.

Antigone heaved a sob that was almost a laugh. Tears slipped in curtains down her cheeks, and she brushed them away heedlessly with the back of her hand.

Ladon nudged the blanket closer to her, his hind talons prancing with worry because she hadn't put it around her yet.

"You're cold," he offered. "The blanket will help."

She pulled the blanket up over her bare legs. "Are you House of Athens?" she asked, sniffling.

Ladon nodded. Then shook his head. "I am Disowned."

Antigone hiccupped as she stared at him. "Why don't we feel the Furies?" she asked.

Ladon backed away from her and curled his lower body in a coil. He rested his human torso on top of his dragon half.

"I think the Furies are gone," he replied, sounding quizzical. "But they have never bothered me much to begin with."

She took a deep, shuddering breath and snuggled down into her blanket. "I'm so tired I could die," she said. "The Fates haven't let me sleep in weeks."

"The Fates?" he repeated, then he froze. "You're the Oracle." His voice was low and unsteady.

"I am," she said. "I wish I wasn't."

"Why won't they let you sleep?" Ladon asked, approaching her cautiously.

She laid her head down. "They've been punishing me for disobeying them. They want me to say something, but I won't."

"It must be very hard to fight them," Ladon said, sympathizing.

"It's torture." Antigone rubbed her eyes. Then she looked around. "The Fates aren't here with you, either." She let out a long sigh. "They're silent. Finally." She yawned so hard her whole body shook.

"You can sleep. I'll watch over you," he told her.

She stared at him with owl eyes.

"I have tea," he said. "I'll make you tea."

Ladon rushed off again to his living area and lit a small camp stove. He put a kettle on and fumbled with a mug while Antigone fought to keep her eyes open.

She laid her head on the crook of her arm. "I've never seen you before in any of my visions. I thought I saw everything," she said. "What's your name?"

"Ladon," he replied over his shoulder.

"Ladon," she sighed, her eyes closing. In a few more breaths, Antigone fell asleep. Ladon gave up on the tea and went back to Antigone. He watched her until he was satisfied that she was sleeping deeply, then he came right for Helen and Lucas.

He moved surprisingly fast, darting forward to corral them against the wall of the cavern. His sharp scales flared out from his skin, creating a gleaming ruff.

"Though I cannot see you, I can smell you and I can feel the heat of your body. Reveal yourselves," Ladon called quietly, looming above them. "I don't need to see you to kill you."

Helen and Lucas didn't have a choice. Helen used the Cestus to change her face and Lucas unveiled them.

Ladon gasped and startled back, before snaking closer to

Lucas. "What is this, a trick?" he asked. "Invisibility is not a talent of any of the Houses. Are you Athenian?"

"We aren't here to harm you," Helen said. "We saw Antigone jump and followed you when you took her."

"Antigone," Ladon whispered to himself as if locking the name in his mind. His eyes landed on Lucas. "You look like my brother, but you're too old to be his son."

"I'm not," Lucas assured him.

Ladon glanced over his shoulder at Antigone. "Did you follow us to make sure that she lived—or that she died?" he asked.

Lucas' eyes flared. "We don't want her dead," he replied.

Ladon nodded, believing him. "Then you must use your powers of concealment to bring her back to her family as soon as possible. If she goes missing, many will die."

"We can't interfere," Helen said, stopping Lucas before he could agree.

"But *we're* not interfering," Lucas argued. "*He* saved her. She's got to go home, one way or another. What difference does it make if we take her?"

"I could bring her back to her territory, but she would not like the path we must take underground," Ladon said, and then he grimaced. "There are things scarier than I down here, and I think she's been frightened enough for tonight."

Lucas turned to Helen, who was torn. "The war doesn't start tonight. It's too early," he reminded her. "She has to go back."

Helen tipped her head to the side, considering. It was true that if the Oracle went missing the House of Thebes would tear the city apart looking for her. It would be cause enough to start the war, and the war between the Houses wasn't supposed to start for another year or so.

She turned to Ladon. "You can't tell your family about us, or about her. If you promise not to speak of this, we'll take Antigone home."

"I promise," Ladon agreed.

They all looked over at Antigone, who was sleeping deeply. "We'll have to wake her," Lucas said.

"Let her rest a while longer," Ladon said.

Helen shook her head. "The sooner we get her home the better."

Lucas and Helen went to Antigone and shook her awake. She sat up, startled, but her expressions changed quickly when she regarded Lucas more carefully.

"Do you have any idea how long I've been wondering when this was going to happen?" she asked, seeming much older than she looked. Then she chuckled at their surprised expressions. "I know who you are, Lucas."

Helen and Lucas shared a sidelong glance while Antigone pushed herself up to standing.

"We have to take you home," Lucas said.

"I *know*," Antigone replied tiredly, like she was sick of having to remind people that she knew way more than they did. She turned to Ladon, who hung back in the shadows, outside the circle of lamplight. "I'll see you soon, Dragon," she told him.

Ladon shook his head, cantering toward her anxiously. "No. We should never see each other again," he said, but he didn't sound convinced.

"I think I'm past *should* and *shouldn't*," she said. She turned to Lucas. "Let's go," she said with a level voice.

Lucas took Antigone and Helen by the hand and concealed them. Ladon undulated forward nearer the spot where Antigone stood, a searching look on his face as he tried to see her through

Lucas' veil. Ladon had saved Antigone's life. He was freed of the Furies toward the House of Thebes, though she still owed her debt to Athens. It was not the same bond that had had been forged between Helen and Lucas when they had saved each other's lives, but it was no less strong. Helen couldn't see romantic love in Ladon towards Antigone when she looked into his heart, but what she did see was deep devotion—an overwhelming instinct to protect her. It was something Helen had never seen in a human before, and she supposed that kind of devotion could be part of his dragon nature. Whatever the source, Antigone and Ladon were locked together now, like she and Lucas had been after they saved each other's lives and freed themselves of the Furies.

Lucas opened a portal and brought them back to the Delos brownstone on Washington Square Park. Antigone made a startled sound to find herself instantly transported to another part of the city.

"Amazing the things your generation can do," she whispered, looking around. Her gaze finally rested on Lucas. "But this is the wrong place. Take me to my house on Perry Street."

"Oh, that's right," Lucas said, remembering. He looked at Helen and explained. "Antigone isn't a Delos, but a Lycian—our cousins. They live nearby."

"Aren't they expecting you to be sleeping here?" Helen asked Antigone, considering that this was the last place she was seen. In her nightgown, no less.

"Trust me," Antigone replied, smiling knowingly.

Lucas took their hands again and opened a portal to the stoop of the townhouse the Lycians owned in the West Village. It was a bit smaller than the brownstone on Washington Square, but it was no less stately. The townhouse was thin and tall and made of red brick. Antigone went up the stairs, then stopped at the door and turned to face Helen and Lucas.

"You're coming in," she told them, like she already knew they would.

Helen looked at Lucas and shrugged. "I guess if anyone would know what we're supposed to do..."

"...it would be the Oracle," Lucas finished. They shared a smile and followed Antigone inside.

"No one's here," she said, flicking on lights. She went back to the kitchen and made a phone call.

"Hello, Uncle Paris," she said into the receiver. "No, I'm fine, I just wanted to sleep in my own bed tonight." She paused and listened. "No, don't. I'd rather be alone, actually. Yes, I walked—I needed air—no, I'm fine. I'm *fine*," she stressed. "Tell my mother not to come, and don't send anyone else, either. I'd like some time alone, okay? Thank you."

She hung up and faced them, her eyes taking on a thousand-yard stare as the events of the night caught up with her. She wrapped her arms around herself and shivered.

"I need a hot shower," she said.

They followed her upstairs, where she let them into the largest of the guest rooms. It was stocked with everything they could need to wash the night off and sleep comfortably. Before she left them Helen stopped her, worried.

"I'll come with you. I'll just sit outside the bathroom door while you bathe to keep you company," Helen told her.

Antigone smiled at Helen, her teeth chattering. "I'm not going to try to kill myself again," she said. "It would hurt my dragon."

Helen studied Antigone carefully. There was a golden glow in her chest. The color was pale, brand new like a bud and not vivid like an open blossom yet, but it was definitely present when Antigone thought of Ladon. She loved him in the same innocent way that Cassandra loved Orion. And with the same lack of reciprocation. Helen felt sad for Antigone, but there was nothing she could do about it.

"I'm going to stay with you anyway," Helen insisted.

Antigone narrowed her eyes at Helen distrustfully. "Who are you?" she asked. She gestured at Lucas. "I know he's Castor's future son. But your face—I've never seen it, and I'm not like the other Oracles. I see things They don't want me to see sometimes. Though I didn't see Ladon. Maybe because I died? Did Atropos cut my string, or did she refuse to?" She frowned suddenly. "Anyway." She threw a hand as if she were pushing that complicated tangent to the side. "I'm not going anywhere with you unless I know who you are."

Helen looked pleadingly at Lucas.

"I think this is a special case," he offered. "How can we mess up the future if Antigone already knows it?"

"Good point," Helen admitted. She revealed her true face.

"Wait—are you Daphne, or Helen?" Antigone asked, intrigued.

"Helen," she replied, intentionally only answering the latter question.

Antigone sighed, like that was a relief. She took Helen's hand. "Sure. You can come with me. It's just I've been trying *not* to tell Daphne something for days now and I can't be around her or They are going to get their way. But I'm fighting it. And losing. Obviously," she said, laughing darkly.

Helen glanced back at Lucas while Antigone led her down the hallway.

"Go with her. I'll find us some clean clothes," he said.

"Your dad and uncle's stuff is in the dresser for when they stay over to watch me when my mom goes out. Second drawer," Antigone told him from her doorway. Helen smiled at the thought of Castor and Pallas babysitting, although who else could? It's not like Antigone's mom could leave the Oracle of Delphi alone or with some random teenager. Helen got the feeling that Antigone didn't get a lot of alone time, and that when she did, she had to insist on it. Like tonight on the phone with Paris.

Helen went into Antigone's bedroom with her and was startled at what she found inside. Half of Antigone's bedroom was like a ninety's teen wonderland. There were fuzzy pink throw rugs, suede bean bag chairs, a brand-new stereo system with a fully stacked CD tower, and elegantly carved white wood furniture.

The other half of her bedroom looked like a ward. She had a hospital bed with thick canvas straps on it. There was a heart monitor, an IV scaffold, and a cold fridge that was filled with saline bags, plasma, and chilled doses of medicine. The juxtaposition of the two worlds was jarring. No young person should be so sick that she needed to sleep in a hospital bed with restraining straps on it.

"I know. I'm a total freak," she said self-consciously when she saw Helen's expression.

"You're not a freak," Helen replied angrily. "And you shouldn't be embarrassed. The Fates have no right to do this to you. Or to anyone."

Antigone laughed mirthlessly. "They think they have the right. Even now, they're trying to tell me what to say."

"Don't listen to them," Helen said. "You can speak for yourself."

"It's hard to do when They're always whispering in the back of my mind." Her face fell. "The only moments I haven't heard Them since They first came to me was tonight, when I was with Ladon." She got a dreamy look on her face and went into the bathroom.

They took turns showering. Helen borrowed a much-too-tight nightgown, and Antigone pulled down a Murphy bed for Helen to sleep on.

"I've never had a sleepover," Antigone said, fluffing a pillow from the top shelf of her closet and handing it to Helen. "Ceyx—our House's head Healer—sleeps in that bed all the time when I'm ill, but I don't think that's the same thing."

Helen wrinkled her nose. "Probably not," she said. They shut off the lights and the girls got into their separate beds.

Curiosity was eating Helen up inside. "What is the thing you're trying *not* to tell Daphne?" she asked, though she knew she probably shouldn't.

"I don't really know," Antigone said, turning sad. "It's a prophecy about you, I think. I never hear my own prophecies beforehand, but I do know you only happen if Ajax is dead. I don't want to deliver it because I don't want my cousin to die."

"Me neither," Helen whispered, thinking about Ajax and the hole he'd left in so many lives.

Antigone laughed, in that slightly drunken way that very tired people do. "That's ironic. Capital I."

"I know," Helen said.

"And all of this is useless anyway, because here you are," she said, sounding defeated. "The Fates win again."

"There's nothing useless about fighting against them," Helen said.

Moments later, Antigone rolled over to face Helen. "You and Lucas are in love, aren't you?" she asked.

"Definitely," Helen replied.

"What's it like?"

Helen thought about it. "It's the best," she said simply. "And the worst. It's everything. And sometimes everything can be a bit overwhelming, you know?"

Antigone yawned. "Doesn't sound like you enjoy it very much," she observed blearily.

"I do," Helen objected. "I wouldn't trade it for anything."

Antigone made a humming noise, her eyelids closing. "Other girls want unicorns. I've always wanted a dragon," she mumbled, already falling asleep.

A few minutes later Helen saw their door open and Lucas creep in silently. Helen pulled the covers back for him and he slid into bed behind her. He tucked her tightly against his chest, sighed deeply, and fell asleep almost instantly.

Helen, however, laid awake half the night. When she finally fell asleep, Morpheus sent her a nightmare about a girl in a white nightgown, tied to a stake and left as a sacrifice for a dragon. The girl screamed and pulled at her bonds until her wrists bled. The bleeding kept getting worse the more she struggled until rivers of blood ran in thick ropes from her slit wrists, drenching her virginal white nightgown in gore.

The dragon never appeared. It was being bound that had killed her.

And the girl wasn't Antigone. It was Cassandra.

Chapter 8

Helen woke. She was lying on Lucas' chest.

Sometimes, on the edge of sleep, she had to remind herself that she hadn't done this as many times as she thought she had.

Every now and again the other Faces' memories she had experienced when she had touched the waters of the river Lethe resurfaced in her mind, and Helen felt as if she had awoken with the Lover's chest beneath her cheek thousands and thousands of times before. But it was also always the first time, when she'd found herself pressed into him after they had fallen from the sky. They had awoken in a crater after they'd both died hating each other; and they'd been reborn in love.

Helen looked up at Lucas. He was staring at the ceiling, thinking.

"She's still sleeping," he whispered.

Helen piled her hands on his chest and rested her chin on the backs of them. "You okay?" she asked him quietly.

"Thinking about Ladon," he replied. Then he glanced at Antigone. "And her."

Helen's eyes rounded in sympathy for them. "They'll be like Orion and Cassandra. In love, but never really together."

He swallowed his anger and looked back up at the ceiling. Helen's stomach growled embarrassingly loud.

Lucas smiled at her. "Let's get up," he said.

They went downstairs to the kitchen and helped themselves to bowls of cereal. Lucas sat at the table while Helen hovered at the counter, as if her presence could make the coffee brew faster.

Lucas regarded her with a bemused smile. "What are you wearing?" he asked.

Helen laughed and stretched out one of her long arms. Her sleeve ruched up nearly to her elbow. "You like it?" she teased, modeling the high-necked flannel nightgown for him.

"Come here, Granny," he joked back.

She strutted toward him, sliding her socked feet across the floor and he chuckled, reaching for her. He pulled her onto his lap and kissed her sweetly, but quickly pulled back, his expression changing.

"I wish we could do this all day," he said.

Helen nodded. "But we have to meet Ajax in a few hours," she finished for him.

"And we have to get out of here before anyone comes home," he added.

Antigone entered the kitchen and went straight for the cereal. "We'll leave soon," she told them. "You will take me back to Ladon."

Helen and Lucas shared a surprised look.

"We can't," Lucas said.

Antigone whirled around, angry. She gestured to Helen, still sitting in Lucas' lap. "You two are from different Houses, and you figured it out."

"We're not talking about that," Helen said, standing.

"You're talking about my age? I'm going to be *seventeen* next month."

"The same as my sister, Cassandra," Lucas said quietly. "She's the Oracle in our generation, and she's in love with a great guy. But he won't allow himself to go there because the Fates won't let her become a woman."

Antigone crossed her arms and turned her head to look out the window. Her lower lip trembled, and she clamped it into a thin line. "This is the deal. You show me how to get to Ladon, or I tell my mother about you."

"You wouldn't," Helen breathed, shocked.

"She would," Lucas replied, resigned. He stood up, glaring down at Antigone. She glared right back up at him, even though she had to tilt her head back to do it. "Get dressed," he told her.

She scurried past him, and Helen followed her upstairs.

Antigone started talking while she looked through her dresser, probably to fill up the guilty silence. "There are clothes in my mom's room that will fit you. She won't notice if stuff goes missing, and she dresses really nice, too—"

But Helen wasn't about to let her chat herself off the hook after playing hardball with them.

"You know, after Lucas and I freed ourselves from the Furies my mother lied to me and told me that I was Ajax's daughter," Helen said. Antigone paused in what she was doing, her lips parted in surprise while Helen continued. "For months Lucas and I thought we couldn't be together because we were cousins. Remember when I told you last night that being in love was the worst? This is what I meant. It was the *worst* to be near him and know I couldn't be with him—for Lucas too. Are you sure you want to do this to yourself?"

Antigone shifted from foot to foot. "I know Ladon won't want me. Not like *that*," she said. "But as soon as he touched me, the Fates went away. Finally, I was by myself, and yet for the first time I felt like I wasn't alone. Isn't that strange?" Her big blue eyes searched Helen's.

Helen had no idea what Antigone had been through, and she didn't know what it was like to be forced to share her mind and body with three all-powerful beings who treated her like a walkie-talkie and not a person.

How could she say no to anything that obstructed that kind of violation?

"Dammit," she huffed, relenting. "You're lucky Lucas and I have a few hours before we have to be somewhere."

"It's not luck, though, and it's not fate—the Fates hate Ladon," Antigone said, suddenly looking frightened. "I don't know what this is. Do you think the Fates can't reach me when he's near because he's a dragon?"

"Actually, it might be a family thing, and that's why we thought our generation was the first time it had happened. But if the Oracle is always House of Thebes and the Shield is always House of Athens..."

"The Furies would keep them apart," Antigone said as she figured it out. She was as bright as Cassandra. "But every generation has someone who could block the Fates."

"In my time, it's Ladon's nephew. Orion. Maybe that's part of the reason Cassandra loves him, too."

Antigone frowned. "Ladon's nephew is the one the next Oracle loves? Is he a dragon, too?"

"No," Helen replied, laughing. "He's just... gorgeous."

"Like Lucas?" Antigone giggled. "He looks like House of Athens."

Helen shook her head. "No one is like Lucas. But Orion is... yeah. I'm going to shut up now. Where's your mom's room?"

Helen raided Antigone's mother's wardrobe. She did have some very nice clothes, though Helen limited herself to a functional outfit of jeans, and a sweater. As she dressed, she thought about Antigone and Ladon, Cassandra and Orion, and how those pairings, as doomed as they were romantically, had the potential to thwart Fate. That an Oracle and a Shield became intertwined with each other two generations in a row couldn't be coincidence. There had to be an element missing, something working against the Fates that Helen didn't know about yet.

She met Lucas in the hallway, both dressed in borrowed clothes. Lucas felt something in the front pocket of his dad's jeans. He pulled out a handful of folded twenties with raised eyebrows.

"I don't think he'd mind if we borrowed this," Lucas said.

"He probably would have lost it in the dryer anyway," Helen said, rubbing his arm and starting downstairs.

"You know what's weird?" he asked her. "These clothes smell like my dad, so that means he still smells like he did when he was in his twenties."

"That is weird," Helen agreed. "I have a feeling neither of us are going to be able to look at your parents the same way."

"I wonder how your dad is doing," Lucas mused as they entered the kitchen.

"Me too?" Helen said, but she didn't want to think about her dad. She had enough things to worry about.

They made sure they cleaned up the kitchen, gathered their dirty clothes, and erased any evidence that they had slept there.

Antigone left her mom a note on the kitchen table and Helen changed her face before they set out. It would have been much easier to portal there, of course, but Antigone insisted on being shown the way.

"Are you sure you know how to get there?" Helen whispered to Lucas as they walked east, thinking of how they had traveled underwater. "In a way that doesn't include half-drowning Antigone?"

Lucas nodded but didn't elaborate.

"Does this have anything to do with how you also knew where to find Hecate?"

He sighed, frustrated. "Yeah."

Helen let it drop. He'd asked her to trust him, and she did. No matter how hard he was making it.

They arrived at the subway station before eight in the morning, well before rush hour. The platform was nearly deserted, but there were still enough people around that Lucas had to veil them in invisibility for them to get down onto the tracks and into the service tunnels without being seen.

"This isn't going to be easy for you to do on your own if you ever try to see him again," Lucas told Antigone as they made their way down the rusty metal stairs and into the subterranean world.

"I'll figure it out," she replied, looking determined even though she was also obviously frightened.

They walked for a long time, longer than it took them to get to Hecate's underground crossroads, and it wasn't a straight path. Antigone had come prepared, though. She had a notepad, pen, and a box of multi-colored chalk in the pocket of her jacket. She wrote directions in her notepad and marked the walls according to a color-coded system on a three-dimensional level—red for left, blue for right, green for up, and white for down.

"Don't be surprised if someone or something wipes those off before you come back. Ladon isn't the only one down here," Lucas said when they paused so she could scribble in her notepad. "Take good notes and memorize them before you try to come back. This place is much more dangerous than the Labyrinth."

Antigone looked up at him, momentarily frozen with dread. "I will," she replied, taking his advice seriously.

As they continued, Helen began to question whether they were still beneath Manhattan. They crouched through low tunnels, climbed up and down metal ladders and stone stairs, jumped over crevasses, and edged their way past seemingly endless holes in the ground for so long that Helen was beginning to worry that they were running out of time to meet with Ajax.

"What time is it?" Helen asked Lucas.

They had left their phones at Helen's house because no one had touchscreen anything back in '93, and portable phones were only for ER doctors. Luckily, Lucas and his cousins always wore fancy, waterproof wrist watches. Helen had teased them in the past for their redundant bling, accusing them of all wanting to be like Orion with the Bough of Aeneas around his wrist, but right now she was very grateful that Lucas had on the heirloom Blancpain Fifty Fathoms that his father had given him. He glanced at his wrist.

"We have time," he said.

"We've been walking for hours," Helen said. "This can't all be abandoned subway tunnels."

They passed a series of tumbled-down columns that had graffiti on them. Some of the graffiti was very old and carved into the white barrel stones. Helen squinted at some of it. One said *Glaucus + Lucinda.* She recognized it.

Helen stopped and looked around. "Wait. I've been here before. But... that's impossible."

"Why?" Antigone asked.

Helen thought back to all those sleepless nights when she'd trudged through the Dry Lands. "Because it was in the Underworld. And I never felt us go through a portal," she said, confused. She looked at Lucas, demanding an answer with her stare.

"There wasn't one. We're not in Hades—there's only three ways to get *there*. Death, a portal, or Aeneas' bough," he said, continuing on. "But beneath all the old cities, if a Scion goes down enough layers, they can find the edge of the Underworld, which is made up of many lands. Morpheus' land, Hecate's, Cronus'. The Furies and their Dry Land. They're all in the Underworld, and the Underworld brushes up against ours in places where a lot of people have lived and dreamed and died."

"That makes absolutely no sense, but I think I understand it," Antigone said musingly as she followed him.

Helen held her tongue, determined not to ask Lucas the obvious question. Like how the hell he knew all of that.

A few minutes later, Lucas slowed and motioned for them to be quiet. There were faint voices ahead. The glow of kerosene lamplight flickered across the rough-hewn granite walls, and there were the sound and smell of water lapping gently against a small shore.

Antigone tried to rush ahead, but Lucas grabbed her before she could enter Ladon's subterranean cove and pulled her back against his chest.

"Someone is with him—probably someone from his family,"

Lucas whispered in her ear, his hand clamped over her mouth. "Ladon is free of the Furies with anyone from the House of Thebes because he saved your life, but you didn't save his. He might have to *fight* someone he cares about to protect you. Do you want that?"

Antigone shook her head, her eyes wide.

Lucas released her and moved away, looking at Helen. "Did you get the ability to control the Furies from Orion?" he asked her, gesturing to Antigone. They didn't feel the Furies toward anyone anymore, but Antigone would if they got close enough.

"I think so," Helen replied tentatively, reaching out with her least-used talent to control hearts to stop the effects of the Furies. "But Ladon will be able to smell us and feel our heat soon. Should we stay here or move closer, veiled?"

Lucas nodded, thinking about what she'd said. "Veiled. He won't give her up," he replied, tilting his chin at Antigone. Then, he reached out for both of their hands and veiled them.

Ladon's brother Daedelus was there with him. Both Lucas and Helen slowed and stared when they saw him. As a young man, he looked so much like Lucas that it was difficult for Helen to see him and not like him. And for the first time in her memory, Daedelus wasn't curt and confrontational, as he always seemed to be around her. Here, he was vulnerable and thoughtful, probably because he was with the person he trusted most in the world. It was like looking at a different Daedelus altogether.

"...and Nilus won't stop talking about her. Like our father needs another reason to get angry," he was saying, pushing a hand through his wet black hair as he paced back and forth in front of Ladon. Like Orion did.

"The other Houses will not claim her?" Ladon asked. "She sounds like a great warrior. You would think they would be proud of her. Especially if she were Theban. Paris loves to display his weapons."

"He does. But Castor was the one at the meeting. He's not vain like his father, though he's just as big of an asshole."

Helen felt Lucas stiffen in indignation and repressed her grin as she squeezed his hand.

"You only dislike Castor because it seems Leda has feelings for him," Ladon teased. "Anyway, the girl—the blonde Nilus won't stop talking about even though she nearly killed him," he reminded, getting his brother back on track.

"She could still be House of Thebes, even if Castor denies it."

"But you don't think so," Ladon offered gently.

"I think she's something else. Something that could ruin us," Daedelus said quietly. "Father told me about another girl, about twenty years ago. She had blonde hair, brown eyes, and everyone who saw her became obsessed with her. Paris, especially, if you can believe it. Do you remember any of this?"

"I was still quite young, and living at sea," Ladon replied, shaking his head. "Father had ordered me to stay away. This would have been just before the last period of unrest between the Houses, right?"

Daedelus nodded.

"They can't be the same girl," Ladon pointed out.

"Whoever she is, whatever House she's from, I'm going to find out," Daedelus said. "And I think Adonis might know something."

Ladon picked up his head, and looked right at Helen, Lucas, and Antigone as if catching their scent. "You should go," he said.

"What? Why?" Daedelus asked, perplexed, as he watched Ladon uncoil himself.

"I have to hunt," Ladon said. Both Helen and Lucas cringed at the lie.

Daedelus stood reluctantly. "Do you want me to come with you?" he said, seeming as though he just wanted to hang out a little longer.

"I'd rather hunt alone."

"Alright," Daedelus said as he strode out into the water. Ladon glanced back anxiously at where Helen, Lucas, and Antigone were hiding.

"I'll see you in a few days, brother," Daedelus said over his shoulder, and then he dove beneath the surface.

Ladon watched Daedelus' wake to make sure he was completely gone before appearing frightfully fast before the hidden trio.

"What are you doing here!?" he hissed, cornering them with his long body, looming above them. Lucas unveiled them, holding up his hands to shield Antigone.

"I made them show me the way," Antigone said, stepping forward before either Helen or Lucas could speak.

Ladon seemed to shrink, trying to pull his large body in on itself so as not to frighten her. "You shouldn't come here. It's too dangerous," he told Antigone. He looked at Lucas pleadingly. "Why did you bring her?"

"I'm sorry," Lucas said. "But she didn't give us much of a choice. You can bring her up to the surface after dark. We have somewhere else we need to be right now."

"It's not safe for her to stay here that long," Ladon said.

"Fine. We'll return for her when we finish our business," Lucas agreed. He stood back and held his hand out for Helen's.

He opened a portal and brought them to Broadway and 8th street. They turned the corner just as they appeared, joining the flow of foot traffic as if they had always been a part of it, making it so that no one noticed that they just had materialized out of thin air.

They walked the four blocks to Washington Square Park and crossed to its far end. Helen saw Daphne and Ajax, sitting on the top level of a sunken stone amphitheater. Her feet slowed as she watched the way they seemed to always be falling toward each other. Their hands were always touching some part of the other, or pulling the other closer. Helen knew she was looking at herself in more ways than one.

"Ajax is completely different from Hector," Lucas began, agitated.

"Night and day," Helen agreed, already knowing where he was going with this.

"And you and your mom..."

"...nothing alike," Helen finished, shrugging.

"It kills me how perfect they are together when it's so easy to see you and Hector there."

"I think it's easier to see you and me," Helen said, kissing his shoulder.

Lucas watched Daphne as she got annoyed with Ajax and tried to scoot away from him across the stone bench, and how Ajax ate it up, wanting her more now that she was running from him. Lucas glanced down at his hand, linked with Helen's, and rolled his eyes.

"We're that annoying, aren't we?" he asked.

"Worse," Helen replied, edging closer to him. She was getting nervous.

Helen knew that Daphne wouldn't be able to tell who she was. She had picked a face and a hair color that didn't fit into any of the Scion archetypes, and the Cestus—both halves of it—were completely hidden under Helen's turtleneck. Her concern was that she would say something to give them away. She had so many things she wanted to ask her mother that she was scared to open her mouth at all.

"It's okay," Lucas said, sensing Helen's trepidation. "I'm anxious too."

They joined the couple who stood to meet them, looking them over mistrustfully. Helen tried not to stare at her mother too much while Ajax and Lucas spoke. Then they heard someone calling to Daphne and Ajax, and when they were joined by a teen called Harlow, Daphne's friend, Helen couldn't have been more relieved. She needed someone else there to diffuse the tension.

When Harlow asked to come along with them, Helen invited her immediately before anyone could say no. At this point, Helen was more worried about accidentally revealing herself to her mother than Harlow figuring out that they were casing a gallery for a potential robbery. Also, she'd had no idea her mother had a best friend in high school—or any friend at all. It made Daphne more human, and Helen was fascinated. Her mother had been a *person* once.

The afternoon went surprisingly fast. Helen enjoyed Daphne's company, and that was definitely a first. Ajax's, too. She knew he was a great artist, but he was also kind of a troublemaker, which was surprising. The way Castor and Pallas spoke of him Helen would have thought Ajax was this perfect angel, yet he couldn't wait to spray-paint his father's office at the slightest suggestion that it would provide cover for Lucas as he looked for the Omphalos in the back storeroom.

. . .

Running to the subway station afterwards was the most fun Helen had had in longer than she could remember. She watched Lucas as he shouted excitedly with Ajax; it was so starkly different from how he had been for so long that it saddened her. When was the last time Lucas had been allowed to be a regular teenager? He was helping to vandalize some expensive property, and he was just about to commit robbery, but still. This was how they *should* be at this time in their lives. Pulling pranks, jumping turnstiles, and screaming in the streets.

They made it onto the subway car and Helen, Lucas, and Harlow grabbed yellow and orange seats right next to each other while Ajax—still rushing with adrenaline—embraced Daphne against the closed doors.

"I want to come here after high school," Helen said, watching Ajax and Daphne kiss. She turned her head to look at Lucas. "I want to go to NYU."

He smiled at Helen in a wistful way. "You should," he said, taking her hand.

"If you kiss her too, I'm going to have to throw myself off the train," Harlow groaned.

Helen laughed and pointed at Ajax and Daphne, who were still at it.

"We'll spare you. We've got to get off at the next stop anyway," Lucas said. He nodded at Helen, and they stood.

"Take care of them for us," Helen said.

Harlow waved as they stepped off the train. "I'll see you guys soon?" she called after them.

They didn't reply as they blended in with the crowd.

"I moved one of the cameras while I was in there, just a little bit," Lucas told her. "I don't think they'll be able to see the Omphalos disappear when we come back for it."

"Tonight?" Helen asked.

"Right after we bring Antigone home," Lucas replied.

Helen saw his veil drop over them, felt the cold of a portal, and then they were in the rough-hewn passageway that led to Ladon's cove.

"I've decided that's weird when someone else does it," Helen whispered as they approached Ladon's cove. "Portaling, I mean."

Lucas chuckled, shaking his head. "You scared the hell out of me the first few times you did it," he admitted quietly.

"I've been trying to be *whatever* about it, but it really is sort of freaky," she said, cracking up, as she tried to stay quiet inside the veil. As their laughter died down, his expression fell.

There were times when it seemed to Helen that Lucas got caught on something in his head, like he had walked into a web of emotions that was so sticky he couldn't move. Lucas grabbed her face and kissed her desperately. But just as quickly as he had seized her, he eased away.

"Gods, I love you," he said so quietly she almost couldn't hear him, even though his lips were still brushing against hers. "I wish—"

Helen waited for him to finish his sentence, but he didn't. Tensing, he turned away from her as they heard more voices in Ladon's cove than they expected. They were still veiled and didn't have to hide, but they did have to move silently as they crept closer.

There was a group of dark-haired, blue-eyed people inside the well-appointed living area of Ladon's cove, and it seemed as if they were interrogating Ladon. Five Athenians skulked menacingly in a circle around Ladon who was curled tightly around himself. Helen searched for Antigone but couldn't see her anywhere.

"The next time Daedelus comes here, you back us," a big

woman was saying as she limped around Ladon. "No more of this shit from the House of Thebes. Bellerophon has spoken."

"Yes, I understand," Ladon said.

She didn't seem satisfied with his answer. She conferred quietly with one of the other members from her House—a tall, sullen young man who was maybe a year or two older than Lucas—and then turned back to Ladon.

"Lelix thinks you can find this girl," the big woman said.

Ladon looked between them like they were crazy. "And how would I do that, Doris?" he asked.

"Smell this and sniff her out," Lelix said, throwing a long, black jacket at the base of Ladon's coils. "It's the jacket Nilus was wearing when he fought her. Father says you can smell better than a bloodhound."

Ladon lifted the long coat to his nose, then tossed it aside. "It smells like the East River," he said dismissively.

Doris turned to Lelix and crossed her arms.

Lelix frowned, stymied. "Father said he can follow smell through water. That's how he hunts."

Doris held up a hand to silence Lelix. "If I can get you a piece of clothing that *didn't* go in the river after the fight, will that work?" she asked Ladon. When Ladon didn't comment right away she continued. "Look, if we find this girl and bring her to Bellerophon, that might satisfy him. If we don't, we'll have to find another way to make Thebes pay." She shrugged like her hands were tied. "You tell me what you want to do here."

Ladon dropped his head. "How am I supposed to *sniff her out*," he said, offended to even say the words. "My father has forbidden me to come above wave or ground."

"I'll deal with that," Doris promised. Ladon still looked torn.

She circled a finger in the air. "Everyone out," she said. Then she grabbed Lelix. "Not you," she said, like that should have been obvious.

The other Athenians headed toward the water's edge, leaving her and Lelix with Ladon. She approached the half-dragon with a trace of a limp, looking much more tired than she had just a moment before. Helen thought she looked like she was still healing from a bad injury, and now that most of her warriors were gone, she let her guard drop a little.

"If you do this for your father, we might not have to go to war. This week, anyway." She chuckled sardonically. "So, how 'bout it?"

Ladon gestured at the jacket. "I can't work with that," he told Doris. "But bring me something that hasn't changed hands and been in and out of the river multiple times, and I will help you find the girl who injured you."

Doris smiled. "It's good to have you in the fight. I've always thought you were wasted down here." She hit Lelix on the arm. "Take the jacket, dum-dum," she told him. He scooped it up, scowling.

Doris continued to berate Lelix on their way to the water's edge. "It didn't occur to you to put in a baggie or something before you swam all the way here?"

"What do you mean?" he asked.

"Haven't you ever watched *Law and Order*?"

Their conversation ended when the two of them dove beneath the surface. Ladon watched the water for a few heartbeats before calling out to Helen and Lucas.

"You may reveal yourselves," he told them.

They did so, and started running toward him, about to ask what had happened to Antigone, when he uncoiled himself.

From inside his wrapped, iridescent body, two people flopped forward onto the ground, gasping for air.

One of them was Antigone. Ladon lifted her up, anxiously looking her over, before Lucas could dart in and grab her. The other person looked so much like Orion Helen nearly called his name as she rushed to help him to his feet.

"That was one crevice I've never been in before," he said drolly, and Helen knew it wasn't Orion. He was a few years older, and his voice was different. He still made her laugh, though. He held out a hand to steady himself and Helen braced him. "I need to sit. I'm seeing stars, and not just the ones in your eyes, Lovely," he said to her.

Helen felt a flood of warmth push through her. He was definitely House of Rome, and unlike Orion, he had no moral qualms about using his heart-swaying talents on others.

Helen shook her head, working hard to block Orion's twin. She looked at Lucas, her eyes watering. "He's quite powerful."

Lucas looked between them, catching on, and she saw his heart flare with anger at the newcomer.

Orion's naughty twin held up his hands and Helen felt the soothing feelings flooding her; Lucas obviously did too, because he immediately relaxed.

"No offense, Lovely," he said invitingly—this time to Lucas.

Helen didn't like seeing Lucas' emotions influenced. "Just stop it," she demanded, catching his power in her own and throwing it back at him. "Who are you?"

"How did you do that? You're not House of Rome," he said, suddenly frightened. He peered at Helen as if he could see through the disguise of the Cestus. "Are you *her*?" he asked.

Helen looked at Ladon. "Who is he?" she asked.

"Adonis. He's my friend," Ladon replied.

Adonis—brother of Leda Tiber, Orion's mother. Helen had been told that Orion's uncle looked surprisingly like him. Like Ajax and Hector, it shocked her once again that someone could look so much like someone she knew and loved, and yet be so different in spirit that it was impossible to compare them. Secretly, that comforted her. Daphne looked just like her, and yet they were nothing alike either. It was good to know that who she was inside was entirely up to her.

"I had invited him here to... to meet Antigone, and then my family came by unexpectedly. Thank the gods he was here. Antigone and I don't feel the Furies around each other, but it appears that the rest of my House does around her. Adonis controlled the Furies while I hid them in my coils."

"You must be quite good at it," Helen remarked. She had heard that Adonis was one of the strongest Romans ever, and this proved it.

"I am. It's lucky I was here to end her love for Ladon," Adonis said dramatically, like he was poking fun at Ladon.

Antigone looked horrified. She punched Ladon's chest, which was like flicking a pebble at a mountain for all the physical pain it caused him, but he still seemed wounded by her action.

"Is *that* why he was here?" she asked, her eyes widening with hurt.

"You have to stay away from me," Ladon said in a rush, trying to explain. "You're too young to understand—"

"I'm seventeen!" she shouted back at him.

"There's nothing I could have done about it," Adonis interjected, looking at Helen as if to gauge her assessment.

She nodded in agreement. The pure golden love in Antigone was not something either of them could take away, nor was the shining silver of devotion she saw in Ladon. He would do anything to protect her, and that urge to make sure she was safe would drive him back to check on her again and again. They were bound together, though in an unbalanced mix of platonic and romantic love that would suit neither of them.

Embarrassed and desperate to get away from Ladon, Antigone flailed, surprising all of them. Ladon tried to snatch his tail out of harm's way as she jumped down, but too late. Antigone stumbled over his tail and let out a high gasp of pain. She went still, and then blood started spraying everywhere. She dropped to the ground as one of her legs gave out.

Ladon lunged to pick her up again, but Adonis pushed him back. "Don't." Adonis said.

Ladon had to force himself to stand back. Helen could see that the protective urge in him was nearly overwhelming. She, Lucas, and Adonis quickly knelt around Antigone and tried to staunch the bleeding. From what Helen could see as she pressed down on the wounds, Antigone had three slashes across the inside of her thigh. It was as if a surgeon had cut her three times with a scalpel almost down to the bone. It looked like a giant artery had been severed because blood was fountaining out of Antigone.

"She's not going to make it if we don't get her to a Healer fast," Adonis said grimly as he pulled his shirt over his head and tied it around Antigone's leg.

"Antigone. Where's Ceyx?" Helen asked in a level voice.

"You can't take me home like this," Antigone pleaded.

Of course not. If the House of Thebes knew that Antigone had been injured by an Athenian, even accidentally, they'd lose their minds. And it's not like they could just bring a Scion to a mortal doctor. Adonis shared a look with Helen and Lucas.

"Rome has its own hospital, but it's all the way uptown," he said.

"Where?" Lucas asked urgently as Antigone fainted.

"92nd and Central Park West," he answered.

Lucas veiled Adonis, Helen, Antigone, and himself.

Adonis looked around at the strange gray film that seemed to separate them from the world. "Oh shit, you're a Shadow—?" he began.

Before he could finish, Lucas opened a portal and brought them to the corner of 92nd and Central Park West.

Chapter 9

"... Master," Adonis finished weakly a solid three seconds after they had arrived. He looked around, his face immobile with shock.

"Where to?" Lucas asked. He looked down at the blood still flowing out of Antigone. "I can't hide the mess we're leaving on the street," he pressed.

Adonis pulled himself together. "This is the building. We have to buzz in."

Lucas picked up Antigone, Helen kept applying pressure, and Adonis went to the call box on a downstairs entrance. A fuzzy voice asked, "*Who's there*?"

"It's me. Don," Adonis said.

"*Why can't I see you on the camera*?" the voice asked. Lucas unveiled them. The voice yelled, "*Bring her in!*"

The buzzer went off and Adonis led them down to the subbasement where a door at the end of the hallway opened. A man in his late forties, bearded, a little soft around the middle, although otherwise tall and fit, held the door ajar while he waved them forward. He was wearing a long white jacket over his button-down shirt and khaki trousers.

"Bring her straight on through—all the way to the back. What have gotten yourself into, Don?" he scolded, reminding Helen very much of her father.

"I didn't do this," Adonis protested with genuine offense.

The doctor shook his head disapprovingly but didn't say anything more. Helen and Lucas brought Antigone through a small hospital ward that had six beds. Each had its own IV and heart monitor equipment standing by, and a curtain that could be pulled around it for privacy. In the back were two swinging double doors that opened into what looked like an operating room. They went through the doors.

Lucas laid Antigone on the operating table while the doctor pulled on some gloves.

"No, don't let up the pressure. I'm going to need you to twist that bit of cloth and cut off the blood or she's going to bleed out."

Helen did as he instructed.

"Push that cart over to me," the doctor told Lucas, indicating a stainless-steel rolling cart with all kinds of medical instruments on it.

Helen turned her face away while the doctor seemed to dig under Antigone's skin with his tools. Mercifully, Antigone stayed unconscious. It didn't take him long to find what he was looking for. After a few moments he told Helen she could step back. A clamp held the severed artery, and after a beat, most of the bleeding stopped. He put a few more clamps in and then started sewing her up. Only then did he seem to let out a breath and relax.

"She's good for now," the doctor said. He looked up at

Adonis sharply. "Take your guests to get cleaned up, but don't go anywhere."

They shuffled out of the operating room, shell-shocked and covered in blood. They stood outside the operating room for a few moments, just staring at each other. Belatedly, Helen's heart started pounding with adrenaline.

"She'll be fine," Adonis said. "He's one of the best doctors in town. Human—but my sister owns him. He won't talk no matter what he sees." He thought for a moment, considering. "Though, he *does* seem a bit upset about how young she seems."

"No, that's a good thing," Lucas said, still staring blankly at the wall. "That means he has limits."

"Right," Adonis agreed thoughtfully. "Well, come on. I'll show you where the showers are."

They left the subterranean hospital and Helen glanced up at the words written in black and white mosaic above the double doors. It said *Valetudenaria.*

Back toward the entrance, she saw several rooms that they had run past on their way to the ward. One of those doors had the word *Thermae* written above it.

"What is this place?" Helen asked.

"It's like a scaled down version of a forum. Basically, the things we can't do with mortals around, we do here in this building," Adonis said. He led them to the *Thermae,* and pushed through a set of padded, red double doors into a spa.

There was a lounge area complete with cushy club chairs, side tables, a full bar, and an impressive espresso machine. Adonis walked right through the lounge to the back wall which bifurcated into two tiled hallways. One had a large W written in gold cursive, and the other had a large M.

"The gendered locker rooms are more of a suggestion than a

rule by the way," Adonis said, rubbing at a bit of blood that was drying on his forehead and becoming itchy. "Go down whatever path feels like yours," he said in an offhand way as he took the M hallway.

Lucas followed Helen down the W hallway. She glanced over her shoulder at him, surprised.

"I think I'm in more danger showering with him than you are with me," Lucas explained innocently. "I promise I won't peek."

They looked like the last two surviving characters in a horror movie, and romance was the last thing on her mind.

The showers had separate stalls, which were each larger than Helen's entire bathroom at home, and stocked with everything they could need: shampoo, conditioner, soft and hard soaps, loofas, nail brushes, and salt scrubs.

"You know, this place looks like a fancy spa when you come in, but it's little *too* set up for getting gore out from underneath your fingernails, don't you think?" she called out.

She heard Lucas laugh from the stall next to hers. "I saw a sauna, a steam room, a whirlpool, *and* an ice soak room. It's a spa for gladiators."

"How very Roman," Helen commented drolly, though she was still shaking with adrenaline.

It took a long time under the luxurious spray of the shower for her to calm down. Finally, she turned off her water and stepped out of the marble water section of her stall and into the teak drying section. Hot, dry air that was scented with herbs radiated up from the floorboards, evaporating the water off her lower body. Feeling much calmer, she wrapped herself in a white terry-cloth towel before stepping out of her stall.

Lucas sat on the bench in the middle of the changing room, wrapped waist-down in a towel of his own.

"I peeked," he admitted, looking adorable.

Helen smiled and came towards him, needing comfort. He pulled her down onto his lap and dropped his forehead against her neck, just holding her.

"For a moment there I thought she might die," Helen said.

"Me too," Lucas said, burying his face more deeply into the crook of her neck.

"Hey, no time for that!" Adonis yelled from outside the changing room. "Get dressed and get out here. There are clean clothes in the lockers."

Lucas lifted his head. "How did he know?"

"House of Rome?" Helen replied, shrugging.

Helen opened a few lockers to find something that was suitable for her, but nothing fit Lucas, so he had to go to the men's side. After she got dressed, she noticed a small metal door in the wall, labeled *Incinerator*. She opened the chute and fed it her bloodstained clothes. It unsettled her to think that burning clothes was something that apparently happened a lot here.

A woman was in the lounge with Lucas and Adonis. She was in her mid-twenties, with long, thick auburn hair and a slender yet curvy body. She was one of those all-black wearing New Yorkers, yet there was nothing somber about the long leather duster and thigh-high boots she wore.

Helen had spent her whole life knowing the frustration of being reduced to the single dimension of her beauty, but seeing this woman gave her an inkling of the power that could come with beauty, too. There was nothing one-dimensional about her, and the way her eyes narrowed intelligently at Helen warned of a woman who would be reduced at everyone else's peril. Helen saw that she wore a gold signet ring on her pinkie finger. It bore the letters *SPQR*.

Physical traits didn't always pass down from parent to child, but this woman looked so much like Orion Helen guessed that she was Leda, his mother. In the future, Helen knew, Leda would kill Adonis to protect Orion, and she would be driven insane by the Furies because of it. Helen approached her, shielding her emotions, which were careening all over the place. She knew she couldn't interfere, yet it was horrible to know Leda's fate.

"What House are you?" Leda asked, peering at Helen in the same way Adonis had, as if she could almost see through the illusion of the Cestus.

"As I told Adonis, we can't answer any questions," Lucas replied patiently.

Leda chuffed at him. "Then why should we help you?"

"You're not helping us. You're helping yourself," Helen countered.

Leda's green eyes met Helen's. They were so like Orion's, she thought with a pang, except Leda's were calculating and full of mistrust.

"And how's that?" Leda asked, trying repeatedly to break into Helen's heart and either read it or sway it. She wasn't as strong as her brother and Helen easily swept her attempts aside.

"Delaying the war is the only chance your House has of surviving. You know that. And you know *who* we brought here and what will happen if we don't bring her back to her family as soon as possible." Helen met Leda's gaze. "Your brother did the smart thing for your House by helping her. Now let us bring her home."

Helen saw doubt flash in Leda's eyes before she returned to calculating calm. "If we return the Oracle to the House of Thebes, we're giving back their greatest weapon."

"Their 'greatest weapon' will be very grateful to you for what you did today," Lucas reminded them. He looked at Adonis. "And what you might do for her and your friend in the future."

Adonis nodded, understanding that Lucas was referring to Antigone and Ladon, and how they would need his help.

"Friend? What friend?" Leda asked.

"Let them go," Adonis said quietly.

"And what if Thebes blames us for her injury?" she exclaimed.

"They'll never know about it. That girl is going to do everything she can to hide the fact that this ever happened," Adonis replied.

Leda rolled her eyes at Adonis just like countless other big sisters had at their little brothers when they were being annoying. "And how do you know that?" she asked him.

"Will you just trust me?" he said through a laugh.

She crossed her arms. "What aren't you telling me?"

"A lot. Like for instance, *that* girl right there," he said, pointing at Helen, "is letting you think you're in control here, but you're not. She is. These two don't have to ask us for permission to take anything. They're being polite, I think, which is interesting."

"What are you talking about?" Leda asked, confused.

"You'll see," Adonis promised, already leading them to the *Valetudinaria*.

They found Antigone struggling with the doctor. He was trying to give her a shot, and she was fighting him.

"You need to let me go home right *now*," Antigone pleaded through lips that were paper white.

"Stay still," the doctor was saying. "A little help!" he called to the group. "She needs a sedative before she tears her sutures!"

"My mother will be home soon! You have to take us right into my bedroom!" Antigone begged Lucas.

"If she's torn a suture, and she starts to bleed internally, she will die within the hour," the doctor said gravely.

Antigone looked at Lucas, her eyes filling with tears. "If I'm not home at six when my mother walks through the door, you *know* what my family will do."

Lucas looked at his watch, then up at everyone else. "Can we take her for a few minutes?" he asked the doctor.

"You certainly cannot," he insisted. "She's going to need intensive care for the rest of the night—at least."

Antigone looked up at Lucas. "Please," she whispered.

"We'll bring her right back," he promised the doctor, scooping Antigone up in his arms. The doctor stood to stop him.

Helen touched the doctor's arm. "Unless you want this hospital full of bodies by morning, you'll let us do this." The doctor's eyes widened, and he backed off. Helen placed a hand on Lucas' shoulder, and he swiftly opened a portal.

They appeared inside Antigone's dark bedroom, keeping the lights off as Lucas carried Antigone to her bed.

"Hurry," she urged.

"Handy that you're the Oracle and can see when your mom is coming home," Helen said, helping get her situated beneath the covers.

Antigone laughed weakly. "I just know her schedule," she replied.

As if on cue they heard the front door open. Helen and Lucas darted into Antigone's bathroom as her mother called for her from downstairs.

"I'm trying to sleep!" Antigone yelled back.

Antigone's mother came upstairs, cracked the door, and looked in.

"What's the matter?" she asked her daughter.

"Aunt Jordana," Lucas whispered in Helen's ear.

"I'm just tired," Antigone replied, sounding like a cranky teenager. "Don't turn the light on."

"Is it—"

"It's not a prophecy, Mom," Antigone snapped.

"Did you eat dinner?" Jordana persisted, sounding worried.

Antigone pulled the covers over her head. "Good night, mom."

"Alright," Jordana said defensively, backing out of the room. "Call for me if you need anything."

As soon as Jordana was gone, Lucas brought Antigone and Helen back to the *Valetudinaria*. The doctor was now standing, speaking with Leda and Adonis, but otherwise they hadn't moved. They looked on with wide eyes as Lucas laid Antigone back in the hospital bed.

Helen drew Lucas aside while the doctor bent over Antigone. Their plan to get the Omphalos that night would have to be shelved, but she knew Lucas would already assume that.

"I'll stay here and watch her. You'll have to go back and sleep in her bed in case her mom checks on her again," she said quietly.

"No, I'll bring you to Antigone's. I don't want you spending the night here without me," Lucas insisted.

"That won't work," Helen argued. "How will I get word to you if we need to portal Antigone back into her bed? What if her mom tries to talk to her? We need you there because you can bring Antigone back in case something comes up."

Lucas knew she was right, but he wasn't happy about it. He let out a tense breath and ran a hand through his hair.

"I'll be fine," she said, tipping her face under his to get him to look at her. "It's *me*."

"You haven't been yourself lately," he reminded her.

Now that he mentioned it, Helen realized that ever since they had time traveled, she hadn't had one of those episodes where she saw lightning in her mind and felt weakened from within. Her nose wasn't even stuffed up anymore.

"I feel like myself here, actually," Helen replied, purposely being unspecific because she was sure Leda and Adonis were trying to listen in on them. "I think what was ... bothering me back home can't reach me right now. Because ... they're all on top of a mountain at this particular moment."

Lucas considered this. "Do you think you could make a portal?"

Helen reached for that place inside her that was Everyland. She felt nothing. She shook her head, frowning. "I have all my other powers, but Everyland hasn't been made yet, and I need it to portal."

Lucas nodded in understanding. He relented. "Okay," he said, pulling her against him. "I'm not going to get any sleep tonight, am I?"

Helen smiled. "I'll see you in the morning," she replied.

He kissed her briefly before stepping back and portaling away. Helen turned to face Leda and Adonis who were watching her very closely.

"What's with the ice on the ground?" Adonis asked, pointing at the circle of frost beside Helen's feet.

"I can't explain it," she replied apologetically.

"Of course you can't," Leda retorted. She spun on her heel and strode angrily out of the *Valetudinaria*.

"She's stable now," the doctor interjected as he stood. "But she needs to rest."

"Thank you," Helen replied with genuine gratitude. He nodded briskly and left her with Adonis. Helen turned to him.

"What does your sister have on him?" she asked, meaning the doctor.

He rolled his eyes. "My sister is very good at doing the right people really big favors and then demanding even more in return. Also, she pays well." He eyed her. "Who do *you* go to when you get injured?"

"Who says I ever get injured?" she parried. Adonis chuckled at her evasiveness. She looked down at Antigone, who was already drifting off to sleep and changed the subject. "Is it okay if I stay here tonight?"

"You're asking like I can say no. That's cute." He stared at her with a little smile that was probably thrilled to find itself on his gorgeous mouth. "You hungry? We could grab dinner."

Helen was starving. But he was dangerous. "I have to stay here," she decided, declining.

"We won't leave the building." His smile grew wider as he held her gaze. When Helen felt herself smiling back at him, he turned, knowing she would follow him. Which she did.

"What's your name?" he asked, leading her back to the *Thermae.*

"You're not going to like it," she replied.

"Come on," he goaded, opening the door for her. "I won't tell."

"Yes, you will." She stopped and thought about it for a moment. "It's Helen," she said as she passed him to go inside.

Behind her, she heard his breath rushing out of him in a reverse gasp. She went to the espresso bar and peeked over its counter. She could see refrigerators with food and drinks in them. Adonis swung behind the bar, like it was second nature for him, and faced her across it.

"So. *Helen*. You gotta let me see your real face," he said seriously as he started taking cheeses, olives, and fruit out of one of the refrigerators. "I can almost see it and it's bugging the hell out of me. Do you like salami?"

"Yes, to the salami," she said, watching him put together a meat and cheese board. "But no, to showing you my face."

He stopped and looked up at her. "That's a shame," he said, peering at her. "From the little I can see it's definitely worth looking at."

Helen laughed and shook her head. "Knock it off and feed me."

He laughed and put the cheese board up on the bar. "Look, I know you're in love with him—whatever his name is. It's really beautiful to see. Normally, you know, love like that doesn't end well for our kind." He took up a bottle of wine and glasses and put them down between them. "Drink?"

"Water," Helen replied.

He grinned like he'd been caught trying to do something naughty and fetched her a water. He poured himself the wine. "To love," he said, lifting his glass.

"To love." Helen touched her glass to his and drank.

They ate and chatted about New York and the nightclubs he and his sister owned. He was easy to talk to, and surprisingly soulful. Even if he hadn't looked like Orion, she still would have felt like she could talk to him all night. Helen excused herself when she realized that she was starting to enjoy his company more than she probably should and went back to the *Valetudinaria*. She laid down on the bed next to Antigone's and tried not to think about the fact that love like hers and Lucas' never ended well for their kind.

. . .

She awoke to the feeling of a hand wrapped around her arm. Her eyes flicked open to find Lucas hovering over her. Dark shadow tendrils were wrapping around him like fingers of smoke. Helen knew the shadows in him only seeped out when he couldn't control his emotions. She uncurled from her sleeping ball and sat up abruptly, kicking something that groaned.

"Ouch," Adonis complained.

Helen looked down. Adonis was unraveling from a ball of his own at the foot of her narrow, short hospital bed.

"What are you doing down there!?" she demanded.

"Oh, you didn't know he was there?" Lucas asked accusingly.

Helen looked up at him, shocked.

"Of course she didn't know, you idiot," Adonis said, in a foul mood. "We're both on top of the covers, completely clothed, and she just kicked me in the neck. Pretty obvious I snuck in here while she was sleeping."

"And why'd you do that, again?" Helen asked.

"Because the Head of my House ordered me to watch you and make sure you didn't..." he gestured at Lucas, searching for the right words, "...*poof* out of here. I either had to stay awake all night, which wasn't happening, or..."

"Okay," Helen interrupted, rolling her eyes. She almost said TMI but stopped herself because she didn't think that acronym was around in 1993.

Lucas turned away from them and toward Antigone who was waking up in groggy, drug-addled stages. "It'll be light out soon. We need to get you back home," he told her.

"Okay," she agreed, and Lucas scooped her up. Helen stood and they all faced Adonis, who was still sitting on the bed.

"I want to thank—" Antigone began.

"Don't thank me," Adonis said, cutting her off.

She looked taken aback for a moment. "Well, I just wanted to say that if you—"

"No." Adonis raised a finger to silence her. "Don't thank me. Don't promise me anything. Don't say you'll repay me. Because if you do, I'll have to tell my sister and then you'll be at her beck and call. That is *not* something you want. Got it?"

"Got it," Antigone replied. She frowned in thought. "See you around?" she tried.

"Better." Adonis smiled up at them, leaning back on his elbows, completely at his leisure. "I hope to see all of you around," he said, staring at Helen. "But I doubt I will."

Lucas laughed at a thought in his head.

"What?" Adonis asked.

For a moment it looked like Lucas wouldn't answer him, but then he changed his mind. "You never lie, do you?" he asked.

"*Almost* never," Adonis admitted.

"That's worse," Lucas said. "Will you do me a favor?"

Adonis smirked. "Another one?"

"Stay away from Noel."

While Adonis regarded Lucas with surprised amusement, Lucas opened a portal and brought them to Antigone's bedroom.

He put Antigone in bed carefully and then stepped back. They could hear the water running in another room. Aunt Jordana was awake and getting ready for the day.

"You should go," Antigone told them.

Helen reached down and squeezed her hand. "You can't walk yet, and you can't ask your mom for help, but you need to eat to heal. We're staying for a bit," she said. She pushed two beanbags together and sat down with Lucas.

When Jordana came down the hall and knocked on Antigone's door, Lucas veiled himself and Helen and they waited silently while Antigone told her mom she was still tired and that she'd eat breakfast later.

"I'll see you after work," Antigone said, closing her eyes. "I'm sure you're up to your ears in research. I'll be fine."

Jordana brightened at the mention of her research. "I can't wait for you to see. There are so many magical pieces from the Argo site coming into the lab right now. Your cousin Tantalus, he's just..." she stopped when she realized that Antigone wasn't listening. "Anyway. I'll let you rest."

Jordana closed the door with a disappointed look, as though she would have liked to have told someone what she was doing with her day. She seemed lonely. Helen felt sorry for her.

They waited for Jordana to leave the house before Helen and Lucas went downstairs to make breakfast. Lucas started opening cabinet doors, looking for something.

"I'll bring her some honey now, then go to the store to get more food," Lucas said. He found the honey and turned to leave, but Helen stopped him with her hand on his chest. She could see anger, loss, frustration, and jealousy in Lucas' heart.

"Is this about Adonis?" she asked.

"Do you realize how many times this week I've woken you up and found some other guy, or god, sleeping with you?"

"Three?" Helen guessed cheekily. She reached out for him, trying to get him to laugh with her. "Come on, Lucas, you know I would never—"

"I know," he said, stopping her. "But it's not a coincidence, either. Nothing in our lives is."

"What do you mean?" she asked carefully.

Lucas shook his head and sighed, taking her in his arms and holding her. "I'll always love you. No matter who you wake up with."

"I love *you*. I don't want to wake—" she began, but he stopped her with a kiss. When they broke apart, he slipped out of her arms and went upstairs with the honey.

They spent the day caring for Antigone, which meant they kept feeding her, ordering more take-out, and getting rid of the garbage in creative ways so that when Jordana came home, she wouldn't know that her daughter had eaten her weight's worth in food.

"We have to get the Omphalos tonight," Lucas said to Helen as he handed her a bowl he'd just washed.

"Don't we have all the time in the world?" she asked, drying the dish. "We get back to Cronus' world as soon as we left. No matter how much time it takes us here *it will has already been done.* Or however Cronus said it when he mangled all those tenses."

Lucas washed another dish, thinking. "I can't stay any longer," he finally said after a long pause.

Helen waited, but he did not offer any more explanation. She didn't want to feel angry at him for keeping his secret, but the more they stumbled over the edges of it, the harder it was for her to keep her promise and wait patiently for him to be ready to reveal it.

"Okay. We'll do it after the gallery closes," Helen agreed tersely. Lucas handed her another plate. She took it but she didn't look at him. They finished the dishes in silence.

By sundown, Antigone's wound was mostly healed.

"I don't see any limp," Lucas said, watching her walk across the room. He looked at Helen.

Helen nodded and turned regretfully to Antigone. "We've got

to go," she said, shrugging. "I wish I could say we'll see you again..."

"You will," Antigone told her with certainty.

Helen smiled and hugged her. "I'm glad to hear it."

Lucas took a turn hugging her. "I plan on seeing Ladon before we go. I'll tell him that you've recovered."

"Thank you," Antigone said uncertainly. "Are you telling me this so I don't have an excuse to see him?"

"We both know you will anyway." He said with a smile.

Lucas then took Helen's hand and portaled them to the street outside the Delos gallery.

Helen stared at him while they stepped to the edge of the sidewalk and allowed the heavy early-evening foot traffic to flow by. "Do you know how she dies?" she asked.

"It's unclear if the cause was drowning or some kind of poison she apparently took," Lucas said. "But she will be found in the Hudson, not far from the Village."

"That doesn't mean Ladon does it," Helen countered quietly. "Or that she does it to herself because of him."

"I know," Lucas said. "Maybe they never see each other again. That's what I'm hoping, anyway, because that would be a terrible thing for him to have to carry with him for the rest of his life."

Helen doubted that yesterday would be the last time Ladon and Antigone ever saw each other, which meant that Ladon was probably involved somehow with her death.

They stayed veiled, holding hands and watching the Delos gallery. They'd timed it well; it wasn't long before they heard the beeping of an alarm being set inside the building. Pallas came through the front doors and locked them carefully behind him. He looked up at the front camera, checked that the red recording light was on, and then walked right past them.

Lucas looked at Helen. "Ready?"

"Yeah," she said, and he portaled them into the warehouse at the back of the Delos gallery.

Right at their feet was a round rock about waist height. It was a dull yellowish color, and its surface was worn smooth by the touch of many hands. Helen and Lucas picked it up, and then he portaled them into the tunnel at the back of Ladon's cove. The actual theft had taken them a fraction of a second, which they both found anticlimactic.

"Kind of boring, isn't it?" Helen asked as she regarded the stone.

"It's rather ugly, actually," Lucas replied.

"One man's trash..." Helen said.

Lucas unveiled them, and they went down the tunnel to greet Ladon in his cove. He rushed forward as soon as he detected them, his face blanched with worry.

"She's fine," Lucas said immediately.

Ladon let out a held breath, but he did not relax fully. "Is she safe, though? What of the House of Rome? Adonis would not hurt her, but Leda can be ruthless," he fretted. His back talons scraped the rock beneath him, sending up sparks.

"Adonis seems to be protecting Antigone from his sister. For now, anyway," Helen said, trying to ease his anxiety.

"And Antigone's family? Do they know about me?"

Lucas shook his head. "As long as you stay away from her you should be fine."

"Right. Yes," Ladon said, distracted. His tail thrashed about. "I will certainly stay away from her."

Lucas didn't contradict him. "Do you mind if we leave something here for just a few minutes?" he asked.

"What is it?" Ladon asked, looking at the Omphalos.

"Just a rock." Lucas replied as he set it down, like it was obvious, even though it was far from an ordinary rock.

Helen shot Lucas a look. "Aren't we going back now?"

"I want to say goodbye to someone first," Lucas admitted.

"Lucas—" Helen began.

He turned to Ladon. "Do you mind?"

"Not at all," Ladon said.

He was still distracted. Helen saw a chaotic swirl of worry in Ladon's chest. He was even more over-protective than Lucas, which she hardly thought possible. Ladon's feelings for Antigone might be platonic, but his possessiveness would never allow him to stay away from her. She looked around at all the curios carefully placed inside niches carved into the granite walls. He was a dragon, predisposed to hoarding things, and it appeared he now included Antigone among his treasures.

They left the Omphalos with Ladon and went to the Delos brownstone on Washington Square Park.

"I'll just be a minute," Lucas told Helen as they stood outside, looking up at the light in Ajax's bedroom. She realized that she was being disinvited.

"Sure," she said, letting go of his hand.

"I'm not going to tell him anything," Lucas said, facing her and trying to take her in his arms.

"I know," she replied, wriggling out of his hold. "Just go."

"Helen," he pleaded. "I need to ask him something. It's—" he broke off and swallowed. "It's going to be over soon. No more secrets," he promised.

Shadows started winding out of him like black lace. It used to be rare to see him lose his grasp on his Shadowmaster talent, but it was happening more often lately.

He was starting to come apart in front of her, she realized, and he wouldn't even let her help him.

"I'll wait here," she said gently, letting it go.

She stepped back outside of the veil and allowed Lucas to fly up to Ajax window. She saw him unveil himself, tap on the glass, and be quickly let inside by Ajax.

A few moments later a young woman strode up the Delos' front door and knocked. Helen knew instantly that it was Daphne wearing a different face. She could see the projection of that other person on top and, like a palimpsest, see right through it to what was written beneath. She touched her own cheek reflexively, reminding herself that she was still wearing the other face she had adopted since she had come to 1993, and that the only person who could see through it was Lucas. Because he loved her.

Helen realized that meant she loved Daphne. She loved her mother, and she was dead. She was used to feeling ambivalent about that. Sometimes she even felt angry, like her mom had died as selfishly as she'd lived by taking on Tantalus as she had, but now all Helen felt was sadness.

She stayed in the shadows Lucas had left behind while Noel answered the door, and she watched a younger version of her mother and a younger version of Lucas' mother talk to each other. They seemed to get along, even like each other, though Noel had no idea who Daphne really was.

Daphne turned away from the door, disappointed, and started wandering aimlessly away from the steps. Helen knew this would be the last chance she'd ever have to talk to her mother. She went up to her without even thinking about it.

She had no idea what to say, or what to ask, so she just blurted out the first few questions that came to her mind. She asked Daphne about music and books and hobbies, questions that someone would ask a new schoolmate that they'd been randomly paired up with for a dreaded school project.

Her mother liked sad and angry music, which made sense to Helen. She'd have been surprised if her mom had listened to pop. Her mother did not have hobbies. She didn't read, or watch TV, or go the movies. Daphne had one friend, and she had Ajax. The rest of the world either envied her or coveted her.

Daphne was the loneliest person Helen had ever met and when Lucas appeared next to them and said it was time for them to go, Helen was relieved. The more time she spent talking to her mother, the more she wanted to help her, or at least warn her about what was to come. She got to say goodbye, at least, though it didn't really feel like a proper one. Then Noel appeared at the Delos' front door and waved Daphne over to her.

As Daphne walked away, Lucas veiled himself and Helen. "Are you okay?" he asked, watching Helen see her mother go inside.

"Not really," Helen admitted, wiping away a few stray tears. She looked at Lucas as his mother locked the Delos' front door behind her and descended the steps carrying her huge duffel bag over her shoulder. "Are *you* okay?"

He shook his head absently as Noel passed them. "It's just so strange. They're all hiding something."

"Yeah," Helen agreed, thinking that their parents' generation wasn't much different from theirs.

Lucas opened a portal to Ladon's cove. They looked around and called out for him, but he wasn't there. Lucas laughed ruefully, shaking his head.

"You don't think he went to go see Antigone, do you?" Helen asked.

"I know he did," Lucas replied. "If I'd seen you bleeding like she was, there's no way I could take someone else's word for it that you were okay. I'd have to see you."

He bent down and reached around the Omphalos.

"Goodbye, 1993," Helen said, crouching down to help Lucas.

"Why do I get the feeling we're never really going to say goodbye to '93?" Lucas commented as they stood, hefting the Omphalos.

"You sound like a lyric in a Cure song," Helen said. Lucas looked at her quizzically "I just found out my mom liked *The Cure*," she explained.

"That makes sense," he said. "My uncle was listening to *The Beastie Boys*."

"A goth girl and a hip-hop boy? And we think Ladon and Antigone have problems," Helen joked.

Lucas smiled with her. But there was a hint of sadness hidden behind his smile. Helen wanted to ask what was wrong, but before she got a chance to do so he portaled them to Cronus' grove.

Cronus sat on the ground beneath his ancient olive tree. His swirling galaxy eyes were open. He'd been expecting them.

"You will have been changed, but all is as it always was," Cronus said beatifically.

"Does that mean we didn't mess anything up?" Helen asked. She and Lucas lowered the Omphalos onto the ground in front of the Titan.

"All is as it always was," Cronus repeated, then turned his eyes on Lucas. "But there is... a mess."

Lucas nodded and looked down at his hands as he brushed them together. "Do I have time to say goodbye to her?" he asked.

Helen turned to him. "What do you mean, say goodbye?"

"Time is. Take it or leave it. That is always up to you," Cronus replied.

"Helen and I will return to complete the final task after I fulfill my obligations to Hades."

"Wait, what obligations?" Helen demanded.

Cronus sighed. "You are not the right boy. You will have not completed the final task with her."

"I'm going with her wherever she goes," Lucas insisted.

"You do not. Now you will have parted," Cronus informed him. He smiled sadly and closed his galaxy eyes. "Your master awaits."

Lucas faced Helen and took both of her hands in his.

Chapter 10

They were standing in a field at night. The dark grass was speckled with little white flowers. Helen knew where they were—the Fields of Asphodel in Hades. For the first time she realized that she had recreated this very field in her Everyland, except in daylight; and that the star-like flowers that speckled her sun-drenched land were asphodels.

She looked around, dread suddenly dragging down on her. There were only three ways into Hades, and Lucas had used none of them. He didn't have to, Helen realized, because Hades was his.

Faced with the unavoidable, Helen had no choice but to start putting the pieces of the Lucas Puzzle together.

"Only a Worldbuilder can make portals," she said, looking right into his eyes.

"Or someone who had sworn on the River Styx to *replace* one of the Worldbuilders," Lucas replied in a dull voice. "I wouldn't make a very useful Hand of Darkness if I wasn't given all of Hades' powers."

Helen nodded. This explained how he navigated the Underworld so well. How he knew where Cronus and Hecate were, and even Ladon. Anything that brushed against the Underworld was a part of Lucas' world now.

"Your vow to replace Hades, when you traded yourself for Hector," she whispered. Her breath seemed to shrink in her lungs. "When did this start?"

"My eighteenth birthday. When I reached the age of manhood—for Scions, anyway—the dead judged me again and decided that my compassion for others had grown. And I was found worthy." Lucas breathed a laugh. "Hades tried to help. He argued on my behalf, so that I could get to ease into it slowly, and so the dead are letting me live the daylight hours with you. For now."

Helen's eyes were hot and the image of him blurred with fast-rising tears. "For *now*? How long do we have?"

"Until you go off to college," he said, keeping her gaze as Helen's tears spilled over and she sobbed aloud. He didn't look away.

"And then?"

"And then that's it." He swallowed hard. "I won't be able to leave again."

"Why?" Helen bargained. "Time doesn't matter here. We could go back and forth."

Lucas shook his head. "Hades isn't like Olympus or Everyland. The place is him. That's why they have the same name. When I replace him, I become *this*." He gestured to the Fields of Asphodel. "There's no leaving myself. Have you ever seen Hades anywhere but Hades?"

Helen shook her head. "There has to be a way out if it."

"I swore on the River Styx to replace Hades," Lucas said, his voice shaking. But he still didn't look away. "There is nothing anyone can do to get me out of it. It's done, Helen."

She dropped her head. "I thought we'd have years—centuries—to figure it out," she sobbed.

"I did too," he said, his eyes remote, though they never left Helen. "I didn't want to tell you because I kept hoping I would find another way. But there's nothing..."

He trailed off, still holding Helen's hands in his as he watched her weep. Helen realized he was punishing himself this way. He was making himself watch her suffer and not allowing himself to help her because that was his worst nightmare. And soon it would be what forever would feel like for them both. She stepped into his arms and took the comfort he wouldn't offer either of them.

Helen felt a long breath drain out of him, his arms wrapping tighter and tighter around her until he had nearly dug himself inside her.

"I thought I was so clever. What did I care if I had to trade my eternity for Hector's life? I thought if I couldn't have you, I'd be miserable no matter where I was," he confessed. "But then we found out we weren't cousins. And now I can't have you because I thought I knew better," he whispered, his voice breaking. "I'm so sorry, Helen."

Helen pulled back and looked up at him. "It's not you, it's the Fates. I dodged fighting Zeus, and that made them angry. I didn't complete their plan, and now you're being punished because of me."

Lucas laughed through his sadness. "How is this your fault?" he asked, baffled. "I did this to us. I thought I had it all figured out."

"You saved Hector—" Helen began.

"Hector." Lucas sighed. "He's one of the main reasons I've kept this a secret. If he knew, he'd do something brave and stupid, like kill himself and try to fight his way out of the Underworld."

Helen chuckled because she could totally see Hector trying that, though it would be useless. She turned serious again.

"You can't keep this a secret anymore. We have to tell everyone," Helen said.

"Do you have any idea how many times they've called me selfish in the past few weeks? Do you know how many times Hector and I have gotten into physical fights over my leaving every night?" Lucas said, barely keeping it together. "If they find out now why I've been disappearing, they'll hate themselves. I can't do that to them. Especially Hector."

"But they're going to find out eventually!" She caught his face in her hands and made him look at her. "Lucas. No more secrets."

He dropped his head into her hands and nodded. His eyes filled up and his chin quivered for a moment before he regained control.

"I'm sorry I didn't tell you. I just wanted more time for us to go to school, and watch movies on the couch, and be ... a regular couple for once."

"I get it," Helen whispered. "I'm not angry."

"And I know it's selfish of me to have kept this secret, but I need everyone to be okay before I go," he continued. "I've been staying down longer and longer, but time down there is so much harder to do if I'm worried about someone. It drives me crazy to know someone I love is unhappy."

Helen peered at him, recalling how Lucas seemed starved for her lately.

"How long are the nights for you when you go down?" she asked after a moment.

He looked up at her. "The last night... was eight months."

"Eight *months*?" Helen repeated. Her vision wavered through a fresh upwelling of tears at the thought of how lonely he must have been.

"Please don't cry," he said. He threaded his fingers through her hair and lifted it off her hot neck, kissing her wet cheeks. "I can't stand to see you like this."

His mouth found hers. His hands moved out of her hair, down her back, across her throat, and up the side of her. He cupped every curve, as if he could gather the pieces he'd broken her into and put them back together.

"I'm so sorry," he whispered again and again, his hands slipping under her clothes and his mouth moving over her bared skin.

Helen leaned back, trying to pull him down onto the ground with her, but he stopped her.

"Lie down with me," she begged.

"I can't," he whispered, like it was killing him to say no.

Helen narrowed her eyes at him. "Is this why you've kept me at a distance?"

"I didn't want us to have our first time when there was still a secret between us. It didn't feel right."

"There are no secrets now." She said, pulling on his hands.

He shook his head and sighed. "I'm being called down early. Punishment for not going down while I was with you in '93."

Helen was confused. "But... we're returning the moment we left. No time passed."

"My time did." Lucas looked down at her hands in his. "That's all the dead care about. My time."

"I'll come with you," she said.

"No. You won't."

"Like you said. I'll be miserable no matter where I am without you."

"This is different," he insisted. "You have to complete your tasks and then you have to deal with Zeus. You can't do that from Hades. You have no power here." He took a deep breath and shook his head. "You are the ruler of Everyland. That's where you belong. Not Hades."

He was right. She didn't mean to cry because she knew it hurt him, but the tears kept flowing no matter how hard she tried to stop them.

"How long will you be gone this time?" she sobbed.

"You'll see me in the morning," he said, his eyes filling too.

"No—I mean for *you*."

Lucas shook his head and let her go. "Don't worry about me," he said, stepping away from her. "I'll be back tomorrow morning to help you with your final task." He took three paces away from her. "I love you, Helen."

He lifted a hand. She felt cold air envelope her. Then she was back in her bedroom, standing on a disk of frost.

Helen sat slumped at her kitchen table. She'd hit empty.

The room was stuffed with family. Cassandra, Castor, and Noel sat beside Jerry and Kate at the table with Helen. Orion and Hector stood side by side, leaning against the kitchen counter across from her. Jason, Claire, and Ariadne were behind her, and Pallas had a shoulder propped against the doorframe into the living room.

After she'd arrived back in her bedroom—a moment after she and Lucas had left it on Friday afternoon—she'd immediately picked up her phone and started calling everyone, telling them to come to her house. She knew she'd only have the strength to explain it once. Now that it was done, she had nothing left.

Everyone was silent and still for a while, and then Noel started shaking her head.

"But Lucas will be back tomorrow morning to help you with the last task for Hecate, right?" she asked. "That means he's only in Hades for one night."

"To us it will be one night. To him it could be months," Helen repeated.

"Every night there can go on indefinitely," Orion added from his spot next to Hector. Helen's eyes fell to the Bough of Aeneas, wrapped around his wrist in the guise of a thick golden bracelet. Orion had spent quite a bit of time in the Underworld with her, and he knew what it could be like.

Helen had seen Noel upset before, but this was different. She stood up from her chair reflexively, like she was snatching her fingers away from a flame and stumbled blindly for the door. Orion caught her before she got there. His hands wrapped around her wrists and Helen saw him take away some of the intolerable pain she was feeling. But he could only ease her suffering temporarily. He couldn't get rid of the cause.

"Castor," Orion said, passing Noel off to him. "You should take her home." But Castor had turned in on himself, and it was like he could barely see.

"Pallas?" Helen asked. Pallas didn't need to be told what to do. He stepped forward, ushering his brother and sister-in-law out to the car.

Helen turned around and looked at Ariadne and Jason. "Go with them," she said. "Take Cassandra." The twins nodded in unison, too devastated to do anything else.

"I've got them," Claire said, taking the twins and Cassandra on her way out. "Do you need me?" she asked at the door. "I can come back."

"Don't leave them," Helen replied, looking pointedly at still-fragile Ariadne.

Claire nodded in understanding. "Love you," she said as she herded them out the door.

Helen and her dad stared at each other. He didn't even know where to begin to help her.

Kate put her hand over Helen's. "What do you need?" she asked.

As usual, Kate asked the toughest question. "I need to think," Helen replied honestly.

Hector pushed himself off the counter. "Stay with Helen," he said to Orion as he headed toward the door. Orion stopped him.

"Where are you going?" he asked.

"To fix this," Hector growled.

Helen was on her feet and pushing against Hector's big chest in an instant. "Do you know why Lucas didn't want me to tell anyone? Because he knew *you'd* try to do something stupid," she said, getting in his face.

"It's my fault!" Hector yelled back at her. Orion got between them, but Helen wasn't afraid of Hector attacking her.

"It's no one's fault!" she yelled back at him. "It's *fate*. My mother told me that the Fates wanted the Scions to replace the Olympians, like the Olympians replaced the Titans. Lucas was set up, and so were you, and if you were thinking of killing yourself and fighting Hades to get Lucas back, *it won't work*. You'll just be dead."

Hector slouched in Orion's arms, defeated, and Orion released him.

"Please tell me that wasn't your plan?" Orion asked.

"I have to do something," Hector said. He took an uneven breath and looked at Helen. "I can't let this happen."

"We might have to."

Her head ached. She rubbed her eyes and saw lightning flashing in her mind.

"Are you okay?" Orion asked, touching her arm.

"My head," she replied.

"Your head hurts?" her dad repeated disbelievingly. "You haven't had a headache since..." he trailed off, trying to remember.

"Yeah. About that," Helen began.

She went on to explain in the least inflammatory language as possible that the Olympians were ganging up on her and that as soon as she finished all of Hecate's tasks, she was probably going to have to fight Zeus to the immortal's equivalent of death—which was an eternity in Tartarus. In the meantime, Orion and Hector had to watch over her because she was too weakened by Zeus' assaults on Everyland to defend herself. That meant that Jerry and Kate had two very large houseguests staying with them indefinitely.

"Why don't you go lie down?" Jerry suggested gently when she'd finished talking. He looked so tired and sad. Helen hated that she was putting him through yet another ordeal, but there was no help for it. She was just as trapped as he was.

She trudged upstairs and laid down on her bed, but sleep wouldn't come. It was still light out and when she closed her eyes it was too bright on the inside of her eyelids. She rested and stared at the ceiling, weathering the storm Zeus was creating in Everyland until it had passed and she could stand up again.

She went up to the widow's walk and sat down on the snowy floorboards, threaded her legs through the railings, and looked out at the ocean. The sun was setting. It wasn't long before she felt someone standing behind her. She knew it was Orion.

She patted the snow next to her. "Saved you a seat."

Orion put his legs through the railing and sat down next to her, his warm shoulder barely touching hers. She looked at his profile as he watched the sun go down, waiting for him to say whatever it was that he'd come to say to her.

"I can go to the Underworld and try to get him out," he offered at last. He twisted the Bough of Aeneas around his wrist with his other hand. "I can go tonight."

Helen shook her head. "He's not a prisoner. He's there because he made a vow. I don't think anyone can get him out of it."

Orion hesitated. She could see a war going on inside his heart. "I could trade myself for him," he said.

Dumbfounded, Helen started shaking her head with her mouth agape, but Orion continued. "You told me that the dead have to accept whoever becomes the Hand of Darkness, and that Lucas initially didn't pass their test because he wasn't compassionate enough." He leaned back and held his hands out as if to display his big heart to her.

"No, that's not... that's an oversimplification," Helen said, backpedaling.

"I have the Bough of Aeneas and I've traveled through more of the Underworld than anyone but you. I can read hearts and judge the dead. I even look like Hades. I think it was always meant to be me," he said, turning away from her to look out at the sunset. "Your mom thought so. And I think she was right. I was supposed to become the Hand of Darkness."

"No. Daphne was *not* right. No one has to take over for anyone. Fate, and my mother, can kiss my ass." Helen made a frustrated sound and pushed away the mental image of her mother laughing up at Ajax on the subway. So young and happy and full of love. "And what makes you think it would be okay for you to trade yourself for Lucas anyway?"

Orion grimaced. "You saw down there... what losing Lucas has done to everyone. They were destroyed."

"And you think you matter less than he does?"

He looked at her. "I can't have what I want, so the next best thing is to make someone I love happy."

Did he really love her that much? She shook her head. It was just Orion being selfless again.

"And what if we find out after you trade yourself for him that you can be with Cassandra?" she asked. Though he started to protest, she kept going. "Lucas traded himself to get Hector back, thinking he had nothing to lose. *Half an hour later* we found out we weren't cousins. If you trade yourself for Lucas, I guarantee you that somehow Cassandra will wake up the next morning a fully grown woman and you'll fall madly in love with her. The Fates love irony more than anything. Don't play their game."

"Shit," he mumbled to himself. "Half an hour? Really?"

Helen grimaced, nodding. "No joke."

"That's just... offensive."

They shared a little laugh, looking at each other for a bit too long after their smiles waned. Helen felt her breathing deepen and her cheeks flush. She saw the iridescent sparks of desire flaring under his skin. At the same moment, they turned their heads abruptly back to the sunset.

And noticed there was a huge man in a long, dark overcoat that bunched over his shoulders like a cowl and hung all the way to the ground. He was standing on the edge of Helen's yard, watching them. It was the same guy she and Claire had seen at school.

"Who the hell is that?" Orion asked.

The guy made a run for it, and Orion jumped off the roof in pursuit. "Hector!" he shouted back toward the house as he ran after the man.

Helen dove off the roof and landed in the yard in a crouch, but as she stood, Hector was already there to stop her from running after them.

"You don't leave my sight," he ordered, keeping her clasped tightly to his chest. "Orion will handle it, whatever it was."

She knew he was right, but it was still frustrating. She was used to being the strongest, the least vulnerable of them all, but that wasn't the case anymore. After weathering Zeus' most recent lightning storm, she was still so drained she couldn't even budge inside Hector's arms.

"Let's get inside," he said, keeping her close as he scanned the fast-growing darkness around them.

Helen slipped on something and fell back against Hector. He steadied her and they both looked down to see what it was.

"Is that...?" Hector said, disbelievingly.

"Another eyeball," Helen finished for him.

"*Another* eyeball?" he repeated.

Helen had to remind herself that it was, in fact, just earlier that day when she, Claire, and Ariadne found the first one in the auditorium. She felt a weird kind of vertigo as her time and real time readjusted themselves around her. She thought of Lucas having to go through this every day.

Hector grabbed it, not bothered at all. "It's frozen," he said musingly as he gave it a quick look. "Come on." He took Helen's arm. "Inside."

Orion joined them moments later, soaking wet and smelling like the ocean.

"What happened?" Hector asked.

"Someone was casing the house. Bastard got away," Orion fumed. "I couldn't feel him running on land, or swimming in the ocean. I think he must have flown, but I didn't *feel* it—and I can feel when Helen or Lucas leaves the ground."

"How so?" Hector asked, intrigued.

"They sever themselves from the earth—it's actually quite shocking," he replied, glancing at Helen.

"We release gravity to fly," she explained. "To an Earthshaker I imagine that would feel very strange."

He nodded in assent. "And it didn't happen with this guy." He ran a hand through his wet hair, instantly drying himself all over. "There's something different about this—whatever he is."

"Could you read his intentions?" Helen asked.

Orion scowled and nodded. "He would have killed all of us if he'd had the chance. But you're his main target, and he's definitely going to come back. His emotions were focused on you like a laser."

That was enough information for Hector.

"Okay, I'll take first watch. We'll switch off at two a.m. One of us has eyes on Helen, and the other is watching the perimeter at all times," he said decisively.

Orion nodded, like there wasn't even a question about the justness of Hector's orders.

"Am I allowed to pee by myself?" she asked sarcastically as they entered the house.

"No," Hector replied, completely serious. While Helen blustered, he put the eyeball down on the kitchen counter. "Now. Someone tell me what the hell that is."

They heard someone approaching the house from outside and Helen was instantly sandwiched between Orion and Hector. Orion stayed with her as Hector ran to the door. He pulled it open, but then angled it shut. It was Pallas, naked.

"Dad!" he exclaimed. "Why are you naked?"

"I've been out scouting, in my animal form," Pallas answered from the darkness. "Get me some pants, son."

While Hector dithered, still shocked to see his nude father on Helen's doorstep, she went into the living room and pulled a throw blanket off the back of the couch.

"Here," she said, looking away while she passed the blanket out into the darkness where Pallas stood.

"Thank you," Pallas said in a nonchalant way as he covered himself and entered.

He looked completely at ease with only a blanket wrapped around his waist, and Helen was not at all surprised that Pallas was comfortable with being partially naked. After encountering him as a young man in the early nineties, she knew that he was not bashful.

"I was tracking *that* scent," he said, gesturing to the eyeball on the table. "Claire gave me the other eyeball you found in the auditorium today. We should probably put this one away so it can't watch us." He picked it up with a dish towel and put it in the freezer.

"Why'd you put it in there?" Hector asked his dad.

"In case it can hear us, too. I would assume it can't, but best err on the side of caution."

The four of them went into the living room and kept their voices down so as not to disturb the whole house. Jerry needed his rest.

"I had to wait until after sundown to change, but as soon as I did, I smelled that scent everywhere," Pallas explained. "Whatever this being is, he had hundreds of eyes planted around the island. They're gone now. He must have gathered them up as soon as you found that first one in the auditorium, but their scent is still in the places where you frequent, Helen. Like your house, our house, the News Store, and your school."

Hector regarded his father strangely.

"What?" Pallas asked.

"How does changing *work*?" Hector blurted out.

"Physically, I become a wolf, which is why it's only useful for certain things. Otherwise, I'm faster and stronger as a Scion."

"So, do you think like a wolf?" Hector pressed, still fascinated. "Do you... eat like a wolf?"

"I'm completely myself," Pallas said. "Just on four legs. I don't want to eat raw bunny rabbits, if that's what you were picturing."

"So cool," Hector mumbled.

"Anyone have any ideas as to what this eyeball being could be?" Pallas looked pointedly at Orion.

"*No* idea," Orion replied, startled to be put on the spot.

"It's just that there are a lot of sea creatures with multiple eyes, and your House is known to have many different types of—" Pallas began delicately.

"Monsters," Orion finished for him, not taking offense. "I'll ask my uncle Ladon, but I don't think it's a House of Athens thing. Whatever that guy was, he flew away when I chased him."

"I've never heard of any fliers in the House of Athens," Pallas agreed.

"There are none. Never have been. We're earth and sea only," Orion confirmed.

"Maybe Hecate knows. She hangs out with a lot of monsters," Helen said thoughtfully. "I'll ask her, and Cronus. They both need me to finish my tasks, so they have a vested interest in making sure I stay alive."

"Good idea," Hector said.

They stood awkwardly for a moment, trying to ignore the fact that Hector's dad was naked except for a blanket wrapped around his waist.

"Well, I should be getting back," Pallas said. "Castor and Noel are—" he paused and looked at Helen, troubled. "How are you doing, Helen?"

Helen felt everyone's pity, and it made her angry. "I'm not giving up," she said defiantly. "I don't care if this is supposed to be Lucas' destiny, or some such nonsense. I'm not going to roll over and let the Fates take him."

Pallas gave her a small smile. "Good," he said quietly. He looked down at his mostly bare self. "I should go."

"Can I watch you turn back into a wolf?" Hector asked eagerly as they followed Pallas to the door. "Does it hurt, or tingle or something?"

Pallas smiled, amused. "Just a little itchy, maybe."

"Why did both you and Uncle Castor get the cool shape-shifting talent and none of us got it?"

"Every generation is different," Pallas replied. "Your generation is stronger, ours was weirder."

"Yeah," Helen said, eyes wide as she thought back to what she'd seen in 1993. "You were all definitely weirder."

Pallas opened the door but turned to narrow his eyes thoughtfully at Helen. "Did we meet?" he asked.

Helen shook her head, blushing for some reason. She supposed it was because seeing him as he was when he was younger allowed her to know him in a way she couldn't before. It was an intimate thing to get a glimpse of someone in their youth.

"Lucas and I stayed hidden," she said. "But we saw you and Castor and Noel."

He smiled back at her candidly, as if he understood her discomfort. "Weird, right?" he said.

"Definitely," Helen agreed, and then in a flash Pallas turned into a wolf and ran off into the darkness.

"Helen, when you get Everyland back, you have got to give me the ability to do *that*," Hector said, and then he climbed up to the widow's walk to take first watch.

Helen and Orion went upstairs to brush their teeth and get ready for bed. The light in the hallway woke Jerry. He came to the bathroom, blinking, and saw them together standing over the sink. He took a breath to say something, and they both stopped brushing to listen.

"Never mind," Jerry said, thinking better of it. "Sleep well."

"You too, Dad," Helen replied.

Orion spit and looked up at her. "I think having two guys crashing in your bedroom is harder for your dad to accept than your being immortal."

Helen laughed through a mouthful of toothpaste and rinsed.

She blew up the inflatable mattress for Orion, gave him some blankets and one of her pillows. She waited to start crying until she thought he was asleep.

A few minutes later she saw the shape of him in the darkness, lifting the corner of her blankets, and felt him slide into bed with her.

"Come here," he whispered, pulling her into a hug. Helen laid her head on his chest, and he ran his hand over her hair while she cried for a while. "My offer still stands," he said after a long silence. "I could take Lucas' place."

Helen pushed herself up on her arms and looked down on

him. "Whatever I do, it won't be at the expense of someone else. Especially not you. I can't lose you."

She could feel want building in him like a held scream, and an echo of it in herself answering him. He felt it too, but instead of acting on it, Orion went back to smoothing her hair under his hand until she fell asleep.

Chapter 11

When Helen awoke the next morning, she was alone in her bed.

"Don't step on me," Hector warned from the floor.

Helen sat up and looked down at him. He was lying on his back, his hands threaded behind his head, wide awake. "You must be exhausted," she said.

"I was kinda hoping Luke would show up at dawn so I could get some sleep," he answered.

Helen looked out the window at the rising sun. "Why isn't he here?" she wondered aloud. "Maybe he went home first?"

He looked doubtful. "I'd go to you first if I were him." His eyes tracked down her body, and he quickly pulled them away, but not before she saw desire pulse through him, deep red and honey-thick.

Helen's skin tingled as she flushed all over. She was only wearing a thin tank top and she could see iridescent sparks scintillating under her skin. She made a lame attempt to cover herself with the sheet, wondering why in the world she was reacting this way to him. It was Hector—he was totally off limits.

Hector flicked his blankets aside and growled something profane about the Arctic under his breath. He got up from the air mattress and stalked out of the room.

Orion entered moments later. "What's wrong with him?" he asked.

"Andy's been away too long," Helen said.

"Yeah. I'm sure that's all there is to it." Orion looked pointedly at Helen.

She threw her pillow at him. "Knock it off," she said, but her blush only deepened and the iridescent sparks under her skin shone brighter. She knew he knew what they meant. "A little privacy?" she asked, annoyed.

"Sure," he said quietly, closing the door behind him.

Confused, she picked up her phone and called Ariadne, who was not happy to be awoken just after dawn on a Saturday. Helen asked her to get out of bed and check Lucas room and then the kitchen, but he wasn't in the Delos house.

Helen showered, dressed, and ate breakfast expecting Lucas to walk through a portal at any second. But he didn't. Kate returned from her early-early shift at the bakery preparing the first batch of pastries for the morning rush at Kate's Cakes.

"Do you need me to work today?" Helen asked hopefully. Anything to get her mind off waiting.

"Actually, I was wondering if you'd like to get your maid of honor dress fitted when the tailor opens?" Kate asked with a sheepish grin. "If it's too much—"

"No! Wedding prep is perfect," Helen replied gratefully. "I need something to cheer me up."

Her dad left for the News Store at the same time Ariadne,

Jason, Claire, and Cassandra pulled up in the Delos Range Rover. They assumed, like Hector had, that Lucas would go to Helen first. After about an hour of waiting anxiously to no avail, they started discussing options.

"He's got to still be in Hades," Orion said, twisting the thick golden band around his wrist. "I'm going down to find him."

Helen's brow furrowed. "But that's it, right? You're just going to go look for him."

"What else would he do?" Cassandra asked, glancing between the two of them with mounting suspicion in her eyes.

Though Helen and Orion hadn't discussed it aloud, they both understood that it would be better not to tell anyone about Orion's idea to trade himself for Lucas. It would put everyone in the position of having to choose between the two of them, even if only in their minds, and Cassandra especially shouldn't have to make that kind of choice.

"I'm just going to try to find out why he hasn't come back yet," Orion said calmly.

"Which portal are you going to use?" Helen asked, moving the conversation along so Cassandra wouldn't have a chance to question them further.

Orion couldn't create portals the way she and Lucas could, but the Bough of Aeneas allowed him to pass through natural portals that stood in thin spots between the earth and Hades, like the ones in the old subway tunnels under Manhattan.

"I'll have to use one on the mainland since the one on Nantucket was destroyed," Orion said, giving Helen a small smile. They'd destroyed it with Lucas when the three of them sent Ares to Tartarus. "I can be there and back in a couple of hours."

He looked at Hector, tacitly waiting for permission to leave Helen. Hector frowned but nodded.

"Do it," he said. "Jason. You'll guard Helen with me while Orion is gone. Claire and Ari, can you take Cassandra back home?"

"Wait—why?" Cassandra started to protest.

"I don't want your mom and dad waiting around for Lucas all by themselves," he told her. Cassandra didn't look happy about being sent home, but she couldn't argue with Hector's reason.

"I can stay with them until this afternoon, but Helen and I have chorus practice later," Claire said.

Helen froze. "Wait—on a Saturday? And didn't I get kicked out of chorus for not showing up when I was in New York?" she asked, grasping at straws.

"*Yeah*, on a Saturday because the concert is Friday night and we had all those snow days, and *no*, you didn't get kicked out. You're still the jingle beller," Claire replied, grinning, like she was enjoying Helen's agony.

Helen didn't complain. Chorus practice was something to do rather than go stir crazy at home.

Kate, Helen, Hector, and Jason walked to the tailor's shop. It was a unit on the top floor of what was usually a summer rental, only a few blocks away from where Helen lived. Outdoor steps led up the side of the whaler-style cottage to the spare but cozy shop above. A pen and ink sign in the window read *by appointment only* in elegant calligraphy.

Inside, the shop was divided into two rooms. The main room contained a fitting platform and three-way full-length mirrors, as well as a large settee with a coffee table in front of it; and the other room was a changing room with a curtain hanging in the doorway for privacy. In between the two rooms was a small galley for refreshments.

A man came out from behind the curtain and kissed Kate on both cheeks. "There's the blushing bride!" he said enthusiastically.

He was about Jerry's age, with black hair that was silvering in an attractive way; and though not especially handsome, he was tall, broad, and impeccably dressed. His suit was expertly tailored, and he wore it with the casual grace of someone so accustomed to flamboyance, that the royal blue velvet vest he wore buttoned over the slight curve of his taut potbelly seemed muted on him. He extended a polite hand and Helen shook it.

"And you must be Helen," he said with just a hint of a Southern accent.

"This is Gus," Kate said, introducing him.

"Winter weddings always make the best parties," he replied, eyes sparkling as he took her maid of honor dress down from the rack and led Helen over to the privacy room. "You get into that and then come and stand on the box," he said, and then he closed the curtain for her.

While Helen changed as quickly as she could, she overheard Gus say, "Well, it seems like she'll have her pick of handsome beaus to dance with."

"Actually, there's another one that's usually with these two. He's Helen's beau," Kate corrected with a laugh.

Gus gasped. "Another one, and just as easy on the eyes I'll bet? My, my. She better pack a pair of tennis shoes, or she'll never make it through the reception. Well, come in," he called out to Hector and Jason. "Don't let that cold in... how *do* you stand it?" he muttered to no one in particular. "Kate, you'd better open that champagne in the 'fridge. I need something to put a little heat in my cheeks."

Kate gleefully popped a cork and filled two flutes, and Helen emerged wearing her gown. Kate wanted a white winter wedding, which meant everyone in the wedding party was to wear white, not just the bride. Helen's dress looked very much like a bridal gown, and though she was there to get it tailored, it already hugged her perfectly.

Gus walked all the way around Helen, held her arms out from her sides and then stood back with a look of rapture on his face. "Aren't you just the prettiest thing I've ever seen?" He turned to Hector. "Isn't she the prettiest thing you've ever seen?"

"Yup," Hector replied a little too quickly. He glanced sidelong at Jason who was staring at him, surprised, and shrugged. "Well, she is," he said like it was a well-known fact. Jason let it go without comment, but he looked unsettled.

Helen stepped up on the platform while Gus evaluated her. Kate handed him his champagne. He clinked glasses with her, and she took a seat on the settee.

"You can't perfect perfection, but I'll do my best," he muttered, pinching at a small fold of fabric at her waist and marking it with tailor's chalk. "Sit down, boys," he called in an offhand way over his shoulder. "This house has stood for hundreds of years. The walls don't need you to hold them up."

Hector and Jason took places on either side of Kate. In the mirror Helen could see Hector looking at her, and his heart peeling back for her, layer by layer, like an opening rose. When their eyes met in the glass, he looked away quickly and stood.

"Is there any water?" he asked, already headed to the kitchen.

"Right in there. Help yourself," Gus replied. He pursed his lips and looked up at Helen with a twinkle in his eye. "I'm sure I don't know your boyfriend, but I wouldn't kick *that* one out of bed for eating crackers," he whispered in a scandalous tone.

Helen smiled at his charming turn of phrase but didn't comment. She didn't blame him for stirring the pot. Everyone loved drama—if it was happening to someone else, of course.

She saw Hector check his phone, then hurry outside to take a call in private. Andy. Had to be. No one else made Hector's inside light up like a Christmas tree. Except, Helen had to admit, maybe her.

She told herself that she didn't want Hector, and that the thrill she felt was not attraction but rather anxiety over knowing he was attracted to her. She *couldn't* want Hector because she loved Lucas.

Of course, she loved Hector in a way too. And Orion. She loved all three of them for different reasons, but Lucas was whom she was meant to be with.

Except for the fact that everything in their relationship up to that point had indicated that they couldn't be together. In fact, their relationship had been nothing but one obstacle after another. Helen gritted her teeth and banished that thought. She made her own choices, and she chose to be with Lucas, no matter how many obstacles the Fates put between them.

By the time the fitting was over, she was exhausted from fighting the thoughts in her head, and her nose was getting stuffed up. She squeezed her eyelids together and saw lightning flashing in her mind.

"You okay?" Hector asked as they walked back to Helen's house.

Helen shook her head but incongruently replied, "Yeah. Was that Andy that called?"

Hector let Kate and Jason get a few steps ahead of them

before answering.

"She spared me five whole minutes," he said through tight lips. "Just long enough to tell me her professor asked her to stay on and that she was going to be gone another month."

"Another *month*?" Helen exclaimed. "That's... wow."

"I don't want to talk about it," he said. Helen peeked at his chest. His heart was a dead, gray color but underneath it was a simmering bile green. She waited and he eventually exploded, like she knew he had to. "I get that her work is important! I get that her research can help the environment and it could save a bunch of animals—and I care about that stuff too! I even get that she loves it. In fact, I love that she loves it, but there's no balance anymore. I asked her if she was still coming back for Christmas and your dad's wedding, and you know what she said?"

Helen shook her head.

"She said 'I have to *go*. Bye.'" He looked so sad. "Is she ghosting me?"

"No way. Andy loves you," Helen insisted when Hector didn't look like he believed her.

"I just don't know anymore. I don't need her with me every second of the day, but I do need her sometimes. Does that make me an unreasonable jerk?"

Helen shook her head. "It makes you human."

He laughed bitterly as they arrived at Helen's house. Jason and Kate went inside, but Helen lingered with Hector on the front steps. "That's another thing. She's *not* entirely human, and sometimes I have no idea what she's doing with me."

Helen stared at him. She'd never heard him comment about the fact that Andy was half siren in a negative way before. "What do you mean?" she asked.

He sighed heavily. "I mean—all this," he said, gesturing to the garment bag draped over Helen's arm. "Sirens aren't big on commitment, or ceremony, or settling down, and I want..." he broke off and stared longingly at Helen. "I want all of it."

Claire pulled open the front door, yelling, "Lennie! Oh, there you are." She looked between Hector and Helen. "It's time for chorus," she said, trying not to seem suspicious, but failing.

And rightly so. There was something going on between them. Nothing had happened, but Helen couldn't lie to herself about it anymore.

She ran up to her room to hang her dress in her closet, then sat down on her bed, taking a moment by herself to recalibrate. She watched the light change as it slid in slits across the walls and furniture that had surrounded her all her life. She missed Lucas.

Claire called her name again and Helen met her outside, getting in the car with her, Hector, and Jason.

Hector started up the car and the radio came on, playing an old song by Crosby, Stills, and Nash. Helen recognized it because her dad liked to listen to classic rock sometimes. Strident singing blasted out of the speakers:

...And if you can't be with the one you love, honey, love the one you're with!

Hector's hand shot out a little too fast as he turned off the radio. There was a titter of nervous laughter in the backseat from Claire. Helen didn't crack a smile. Nothing was funny.

When she walked into the auditorium next to Hector, Helen heard Gretchen hiss and squeal under her breath to whomever was standing close enough to her to be in range of her newest gossip bomb. Helen suddenly found herself the recipient of many hateful stares.

"Don't worry about it," Claire said. "This is just like in the fourth grade when you wore that t-shirt with the unfortunate piece of fruit on it."

"What are you talking about?" Jason asked.

Helen rolled her eyes and spoke quickly to get it over with. "I wore a t-shirt with a watermelon on it and Gretchen got everyone in the school to start calling me Helen-Helen-Watermelon."

Hector snorted a laugh. Claire smacked his arm. "Sorry," Hector apologized.

"And now no one calls you that," Claire said.

"Yeah. Because you beat them up."

"My point is, who cares what Gretchen says? Everyone will forget it by tomorrow." Claire left to go take her soloist place on the risers.

Doubtful, Helen went in the other direction to her place in Siberia and took out her jingle bells. She could hear Hector and Jason laughing at the revelation that she was, basically, the chorus mascot. She flipped them both the bird and resolutely shook her hated handful of holiday cheer.

They'd made it past Claire's solo when Orion sauntered into the auditorium and sucked all the air out of the room. He was being as unobtrusive as possible, but even still that meant every eye flew to him.

As he slid into a seat next to Cassandra, Helen gave Orion an expectant look, silently asking if he'd found Lucas. Orion nodded and mouthed the word *later*. Helen took that to mean Lucas' absence wasn't because of something urgent, which was good news. Sort of. Because she couldn't think of anything non-urgent that should keep Lucas away from her, especially since they had so little time left together. Unless she figured out a way to get him out of his oath, which she *would,* she promised herself.

The music teacher, Mr. Abebe, approached Orion with his brow furrowed. "Excuse me, but you need to go to the office and get a nametag to be on school grounds," he said.

"It's okay, I'm supposed to be here," Orion said, smiling. Helen could feel waves of calm hitting her, and everyone in the room suddenly believed that Orion belonged there.

"Great," Mr. Abebe said, smiling back at Orion warmly. He turned to the chorus with a gooey smile on his face. "All right, let's get back to work!" he boomed happily.

Helen met Orion's gaze across the room and tipped her chin up at him in recognition of his impressive handiwork. He nodded back at her as he settled into his seat. He was obviously feeling himself. Orion was rarely cocky, though, she had to admit, it suited him. It reminded her of Adonis, but better because it wasn't watered down with overuse. Orion was dead hot on an off day. On a good day he was frigging lava.

Helen shook her head and her jingle bells a few times to clear one and check that the other wasn't dented. Which was which she had not yet determined.

She jingled her way through three more carols, mentally berating herself. What was wrong with her? Lucas was missing, but she was thinking about every guy except him, which had never happened to her before. Sure, there was a minute there—when she and Lucas had believed they were cousins—that she'd entertained the notion of being with Orion. But even then, when she'd thought that being with Lucas was impossible, she couldn't imagine really being with Orion physically. She was imagining it now. In technicolor. With him *and* Hector. Helen was so distressed she dropped her jingle bells. Twice.

Unfortunately, her inability to even hold on to her jingle bells, which is literally the only thing required to be a jingle beller, did not get her kicked out of chorus. Mr. Abebe finished off rehearsal by complimenting Claire on her brilliant solo and suggesting that Helen put some sticky tape on her palms before the recital on Friday. Helen grumbled to herself and went right to Orion.

"Woah!" he said, looking down at her heart and then quickly away as he suppressed an embarrassed smile.

"Did you do this?" she demanded, pointing to her chest.

He looked back at her, stunned. "No. I'd never—"

"Do what?" Cassandra asked, appearing at his elbow.

Orion mentally fumbled and decided to simply ignore Cassandra's question. "It's not me," he told Helen. "I mean, maybe it's me," he added, that cute-cocky thing coming back. "But I'm not trying to influence you."

"What do you mean, influence her?" Cassandra asked, her eyes bouncing between them.

"What's up?" Hector asked, making his way down the row. Helen immediately looked away from him.

"You stay over there," she demanded, stopping Hector.

"Why?" he asked.

Orion covered his grin. "This is really interesting," he said, glancing down at Helen's body. "*Both* of us?" he asked, pretending to be scandalized.

Helen grabbed the sleeve of his jacket and dragged him a few paces away from the group. "I am not in control of this!"

"Apparently." Orion couldn't stop smiling.

Helen crossed her arms tightly over her chest. She felt like screaming. Orion could see that he'd taken his joke too far.

"I'm sorry," he said, barely touching the tips of her elbows with his fingertips in apology.

"Where's Lucas? Why hasn't he come home?" she asked.

His face fell. "The dead have insisted that he make up the

three nights he spent with you by spending three days with them."

Helen frowned, thinking. "How long will that be for him?"

"He wouldn't tell me," Orion replied.

"You spoke to him?" she asked excitedly.

"Yeah." He looked troubled. "Helen—we have to talk. In private."

"Okay," she whispered. She caught herself watching his mouth and realized that they were standing too close together and she was leaning toward him. She jerked away. She'd almost kissed him.

Helen turned abruptly and went back to the group. She saw Jason and Ariadne exchange suspicious glances. Cassandra's cheeks were so red it looked like she'd just been slapped. Helen felt horrible.

"Lennie!" Claire huffed, joining them. "What the hell was up with the jingle bells? You dropped them during *Silent Night*!"

Helen stared at her for a moment. "I can't even," she said, and went back to her unglamorous spot under the exit sign to get her bag.

As she bent down to pick it up off the ground, she overheard Gretchen gossiping. "...Ryan, I think? Looks like she's doing him, too..."

It took every ounce of self-control Helen possessed not to vault up the risers and punch the freckles off Gretchen's face. As she stood upright and spun around to get away from Gretchen, she ran into Hector. He'd followed her. He caught her shoulders in his hands and she looked up at him.

"Are you okay?" he asked quietly. She saw longing tug at him and felt something inside her tug back.

"Damn it," Helen breathed. Tears welled up in her eyes. She

let her forehead thunk into Hector's chest and he put his arms around her, swallowing her up. She felt like she was drowning in her own overheated body.

She heard him say defensively, "I didn't do anything to her, Jace—she's just upset!" and she pulled out of his arms and headed for the door. She heard snatches of the conversation behind her as she walked.

"...She's worried about Lucas," Jason was saying sharply to Claire. "Who cares about the Christmas recital?"

Helen knew that wasn't fair of him. She stopped and turned around, taking a deep breath. "Sorry, Claire," she said. "I'll staple the bells to my hand if I have to, but I won't ruin this for you. I promise."

Claire looked embarrassed. "No, I shouldn't have—" she began, but Helen didn't need an apology in return.

"We're all worried about Lucas," she interrupted. "But that doesn't mean you're not allowed to care about anything else."

"Yeah," Hector said, taking Helen's side. He looked at Orion. "Didn't Luke tell you that he wanted all of us to keep living our lives?"

Orion's eyes darted to Helen. "Well, kind of," he replied cautiously, like he was considering her talent for Falsefinding.

Helen saw that he was snatching his emotions away before she could read them. She took a step closer to him. "What did he say, exactly?"

Orion rolled his eyes. "Please don't make me repeat it right now," he begged.

"Is it about me? He wants me to keep living my life?" she pushed.

"Shit, Helen," Orion said, running a frustrated hand through his hair. "Later."

"Why can't you say it in front of all of us?" Cassandra asked.

"Because it's private, Cass!" he snapped back at her.

"Private for my brother, or for you?"

Orion looked trapped. "For both of us," he replied.

It occurred to Helen that, like Adonis, Orion never lied. He was too honorable to lie, and she loved that about him. She kind of loved everything about him, which was a huge problem.

She needed some space. She went down the back hallway and pushed her way out of the same double doors she'd once melted. They'd been replaced, but she would never be able to go through them without thinking of Lucas, how he'd been there when it happened and how he'd helped her discover her lightning that day.

It was dark and cold out. She wanted to leap into the sky and escape from everything. The need to fly was so strong that she actually disengaged gravity—and felt a hand wrap around the top of her arm, yanking her back down before she could take off.

"What are you doing?" Orion asked, pulling her down next to him and spinning her around to face him. "You're still grounded, remember?"

"I wasn't thinking," she said absently. She realized they were already yards away from the door. "How could I have forgotten that? Did I just run out here?" she asked Orion, worried.

"Yeah," he replied. "You ran fast, too."

Hector burst through the doors but skidded to a stop when he saw that Orion had ahold of Helen. He spread out his hands in a questioning gesture.

"It's okay," Orion called out to him.

"What's wrong with me?" Helen asked Orion quietly. "It's like I can't trust myself anymore. About anything."

"I'll watch you," he said.

She gave him a dry laugh. "You're one of the reasons I'm not trusting myself right now." She saw a bright aurora of desire course through him again, but he controlled it.

"I would never—" he began.

"I know I can trust you," she interrupted, not needing him to spell it out. "Just don't tell Hector anything about this whole mess yet, okay?" She gestured to the glittering sheen of awareness she could still see under her skin. Then she laughed. "His ego is big enough already."

Orion drew an X over his heart with his finger as if to say *cross my heart*, which Helen found adorable. She rolled her eyes at herself. "How am I going to do this?"

"We'll do it together," he said, taking her hand. He kept her hand in his as he steered them to the parking lot. He put Helen in the back of Hector's car and got in the front seat, while everyone else got into Jason's car. Cassandra stared at Helen through the back windows, her face blank.

"Has Cassandra *seen* anything lately?" she asked as they pulled out of the parking lot.

There was a long pause. Hector was driving and he glanced over at Orion, curious.

"I don't know," Orion answered, looking out the passenger window. "We haven't had a chance to talk the past few days."

Helen watched the dark trees blur by outside. "Because of me."

"Because of all of this," Orion corrected, spinning around to look at her. "It's not like you're to blame for Zeus. Or for what's happening to Lucas."

"No. I'm to blame for Luke," Hector added quietly.

Helen found Hector's eyes in the rearview mirror. "Then you're the only ding-dong in the universe who could blame himself for getting killed by Achilles—who was the greatest warrior ever, mind you."

Hector smiled to himself. "I *almost* had him."

Orion's shoulders shook with silent laughter. "No, you didn't," he said, shaking his head.

"You know I did," Hector insisted.

"I was *there*. You never had him."

Helen watched the two of them taunt each other amicably until they got to her house. Her street was festive with holiday lights that glowed against the snow. She got out of the car, but stopped halfway across the yard, feeling the hairs rise on the back of her neck. She watched her breath cloud in front of her in the multicolored light. She felt a panicked feeling, like she hadn't done something she was supposed to do. It thrilled through her, making her shiver. A black cat bolted, hissing, right in front of Helen and ran into the bushes.

Hector and Orion both jumped and grabbed Helen, one on each side.

"What the hell was that!" Orion exclaimed.

"Cat," Hector replied.

"A warning," Helen corrected. "I think I'm being summoned."

"Hecate?" Orion guessed.

Helen nodded. "I still have a task to complete." She'd wasted a whole day, and she didn't think the Witch Titan was pleased. "But I have no idea how I'm going to do that without Lucas to make a portal to Cronus."

"Let's go inside, figure it out," Hector said.

Helen took a step toward the door and felt the panicky feeling in her grow stronger. "I don't think I can," she said, stopping. "I get the feeling that the cat was a gentle reminder, but

Hecate won't be so nice if she has to remind me again. I need to go now."

"But where? And what do you have to do?" Hector asked.

Helen shrugged. "Cronus wouldn't tell me. He said it was something for his family... so I'm hoping laundry?"

Hector chuckled, but Orion frowned. "Where is Cronus?" Orion asked.

"In the Underworld."

"Then I can take you to him," he said, lifting the Bough of Aeneas on his wrist. "We don't have to wait for Lucas."

"Yeah, but we have to get back to the mainland," Hector said. "That will take hours."

Orion shook his head. "There's another portal here on Nantucket. Lucas told me about it when I saw him."

"Where?" Helen asked.

He looked reluctant to answer, but finally did because he had no choice. "At your house," he said, tipping his chin at Hector.

Helen blinked, stupefied. "How can that be?"

"Because Lucas is the Hand of Darkness, Helen," Orion replied, sighing. "Wherever he lives, the dead will climb up to reach him."

She shrank at the thought, like paper curling up and shriveling as it burned. The dead really were taking him away from her.

"This is why I didn't want to tell you," Orion said, seeing her sadness. He started pacing in a tight, frustrated circle before facing Helen with his hands on his hips. "My offer still stands."

"No," Helen replied immediately.

"What offer?" Hector asked.

"Orion—," Helen warned.

"To take Lucas' place," Orion admitted.

Hector let that sink in for a moment. "What?" His face fell

with something like betrayal before rage flared in its place. "You asshole!" he yelled, pushing Orion's chest and knocking him to the ground. "If anyone's going to take Luke's place, it's going to be me!"

Unsatisfied, Hector grabbed Orion by the front of his jacket and hauled him back up to standing so they could shout at each other properly, but he was interrupted.

"My sister said that we should just leave you be, and you would tear each other apart," called a familiar voice.

A man who looked like he could be Lucas' twin sauntered out of the shadows. It was the cruelty in his eyes and the slightly feral sneer on his lips that gave away his identity.

Poseidon.

Hector and Orion immediately took defensive postures between Poseidon and Helen, but she put her hands between them and moved them aside so she could approach the Olympian.

"I'm not afraid of him," Helen told Orion and Hector. As she spoke, she looked directly in Poseidon's blue eyes. "None of the Olympians can hurt the Scions—as per my agreement with Zeus."

Poseidon's smile faltered. "My little brother made a very hasty oath. Again."

Though his expression was impassive, Helen knew that face too well for him to hide anything from her. She didn't even have to read his heart to know that Poseidon resented having spent the last 3,300 years locked on Olympus because of Zeus' last oath to a Scion, and that he had no intention of doing it again.

"Tough," Helen scoffed. "Zeus swore on the River Styx that none of the Olympians would attack any of the Scions or our mortal loved ones. But I never promised the same in return."

Poseidon's eyes flared and his chest swelled with anger. He took a step closer to Helen and, undaunted, she took a step closer to him. She felt Hector and Orion coil at her sides, but she held out her hands, stopping them.

"He's just fishing," she said.

"And what a catch you are," Poseidon murmured. Then he grabbed her and kissed her.

She felt his hands dig painfully into her hip and shoulder, and his cold tongue push into her mouth. The sudden violation was so startling that Helen froze. Hector did not. Poseidon had no sooner clamped onto Helen when Hector dove on him, hitting him viciously.

Orion shouted, "That's what he wants!" and tried to rein in Hector, but it was too late. Hector and Poseidon traded blows like they meant to kill each other.

Helen blinked, unable to snap out of her shock. It looked like Hector and Lucas were fighting and Orion was trying to break it up, but ... Poseidon was not Lucas. She saw a three-pronged blade flash in Poseidon's hand and her frozen silence turned into a scream.

"No!"

She felt the reverberating shock of that one word, and knew she'd gone too far. Opening her eyes, she saw that she had thrown all of them ten feet in three directions. It was like a bomb had gone off in their midst. The force of her voice had blown the snow on the ground back in concentric circles and the air glittered as the crystals sifted back down like the finest powder.

She ran through the sparkling air after Poseidon. She found him on his hands and knees in the middle of the street. He grinned at her with bloody teeth and though he looked like Lucas he made her skin crawl.

"I can't wait for our second kiss." He licked the blood off his lips lasciviously, and then ran.

Helen watched him go, shaking with rage because he'd gotten what he wanted from her. She heard a groan behind her and spun around. Hector and Orion lay on opposite sides of her front yard.

"Oh god," she whispered, not knowing who to run to first.

Orion was getting to his feet. She helped him up and they both went to pull Hector out of the neighbor's bushes. "I'm sorry. I'm *so* sorry," she kept repeating. As she and Orion helped Hector up, her dad yanked open the front door in a panic.

"Helen!" Jerry called.

"I'm here, Dad," Helen replied, putting one of Hector's arms over her shoulders.

"What happened?" he asked, coming outside in a daze. He looked at the strange pattern in the snow, and at Hector's face. His nose was gushing blood.

"I—I..." Helen stammered.

"Let's get inside," Jerry said, taking Hector's other arm over his shoulder when Orion staggered. "You okay?" he asked Orion.

"Just got the wind knocked out of me," Orion wheezed.

They went inside and brought Hector to the sink in the kitchen. He heaved up blood into it and Helen heard Kate stifle a scream behind her. Still holding Hector up on one side, Jerry turned on the faucet and started splashing water on Hector's face.

"Your nose is broken," Jerry murmured. "All the blood is going down the back of your throat. You need to get it out." Hector nodded in agreement like this was something he had experienced before. He heaved again and puked up more blood while Jerry coached him saying, "That's it. Get it out."

"I need to sit," Orion announced shakily. Helen turned to help him as he half sat, half collapsed on the kitchen floor. She rubbed his back as he put his head between his knees. "Are you okay?" he asked.

"I don't know," she whispered. "Are you?"

"I will be."

"I think I hit you with a sonic... thingy."

"Boom," he finished for her. "The Voice of God. Goddess. Whatever. It *really* hurts."

"I'm so sorry," Helen said again.

"Don't be. I'm happy it wasn't a lightning bolt." Orion looked up at her. He narrowed his eyes at her. "You're not okay," he said. It was a statement, not a question.

Helen shook her head. Creon had forced himself on her once. He was trying to kill her, not rape her, but still there was something disgusting about how he'd pressed up against her. What Poseidon had done was blatant sexual assault. Helen couldn't bear to unpack what she felt about that yet because he looked so much like Lucas, and she didn't want to tie Lucas' face to such a vile memory.

"We need honey," she told Kate, changing the subject.

Kate nodded, her eyes wide and her face blanched. She went to the pantry and came back with a honey bear. "I also have honey buns from this afternoon if you want them," she said numbly.

Orion gave Kate the thumbs up while he upended the honey bear into his mouth. Helen stood for a moment to check on her dad and Hector. He'd stopped vomiting blood and Jerry was in the rinse-off phase.

"I'm gonna kill 'em," Hector said, slurring his words.

"You can't kill him. He's immortal," Helen said, wiping his face with a towel.

"Make 'em wish he's dead, then." He looked at Helen and his face twisted with an unbearable thought. She hugged him briefly and felt him slump against her.

"He's going to fall down," Helen said, and Jerry helped her steady him.

"Who's Hector talking about?" her dad asked as they took Hector over to the couch in the living room.

"Poseidon," Helen said.

Jerry's face went ashen. "Did he do this?"

"No. I did," she said, and then laid Hector back on the cushions. She helped him out of his jacket and his bloodied shirt. Then she started unlacing his shoes.

"Hector, I'm—" she started.

"Nope," he said, clutching his ribs. Red welts were forming under his skin like he'd been caned. "Not your fault."

Helen shook her head while she got the throw blanket off the back of the couch and covered him with it.

"Are you still bleeding?" she asked, worried.

He shook his head and held out a hand. "Honey."

Orion had recovered enough to stand, and he was behind Helen. He handed Hector the nearly drained honey bear. Hector inspected the low level.

"Dick," he said.

"Why did you go after him? That's exactly what he wanted!" Orion shot back at him.

"He grabbed Helen..." he started to shout, then winced.

"He grabbed you?" Jerry asked, turning on Helen with his eyes wide.

Helen crossed her arms over her chest and nodded reluctantly.

"He did it on purpose, to start a fight," Orion said. "That's the only way the Olympians can get to us. We throw the first punch, they defend themselves, and maybe in the process they take out a few of our mortals." Orion glanced at Jerry, then back at Hector. "We have to be smarter than that."

Hector nodded. Beads of sweat stood out on his upper lip and he took a deep, steadying breath.

"We'll get you some more honey," Jerry promised, and then motioned for Helen and Orion to come with him. "Start over. How did Hector get so injured?" he asked quietly when they got back to the kitchen.

"That's my fault," Helen said guiltily, but Orion stopped her.

"It is not all your fault—"

"It is! I lost control and I can't do that no matter how I feel because—look what I did with just my voice!" Helen said, stopping to sniffle and wipe her eyes. She happened to glance out the window as she did so and saw two glowing green eyes looking in at her accusingly. "See?" she said, tossing a hand. "Even that stupid cat knows."

Orion and Jerry turned to look out the window. The black cat from earlier was perched on the windowsill outside. It meowed insistently at Helen through the glass.

"I'm coming, just give me a minute!" she shouted back at it, throwing a dish towel at the window.

The cat hissed and jumped down, but Helen was certain it was still waiting for her outside in the snow. She hugged her dad.

"Can you watch Hector for me?" she asked. "And call Jason and Ariadne. Tell them to come over and help."

"Course," her dad replied, hugging her back.

She stepped back and looked at Orion. "Are you strong enough to come with me?"

He gave a short laugh. "I'm strong enough," he said quietly, turning away before she could figure out if there was a second meaning to what he'd said. He walked to the door and opened it, holding it wide for her. "Let's go follow that stupid cat."

Chapter 12

They followed the black cat across snowy yards, over fences, and diagonally down streets until they were back at the intersection where Helen and Claire had encountered Hecate during the snowstorm.

The cat did not hurry, nor did it care that it was making the humans following it climb through difficult scrub brush and trespass multiple times. When they arrived at the crossroads, the black cat turned into something too big to be a ferret. Helen thought it might be a polecat. Whatever it was, it undulated across the frozen asphalt toward its mistress.

Hecate stood at the joining place that didn't really exist—the almost-intersection of Surfside, Prospect, and Sparks.

"Thank you, Gale," Hecate cooed to the all-black weasel that jumped limberly up into her arms. She petted the clever little creature and then stooped down to set her free before addressing Helen. "Well, Helen Hamilton. Have you figured out what you're supposed to do with the Omphalos yet?"

Helen stared at Hecate, slack jawed. "Ah—no," she replied, like that should be obvious. "How am I supposed to know what to do with it? Neither you nor Cronus have told me anything."

Hecate did not look pleased. "Who is our common enemy?" she asked, forcing patience.

Helen threw up her hands. "Zeus? The Olympians?"

Hecate sighed and shook her head. "They are cogs. Blunt instruments. Please tell me you are not the same."

Helen looked at Orion. He shrugged back, at a loss.

Hecate noticed their familiar way with each other and chuckled. "At least you're finally with the right companion."

Helen startled. Both Cronus and Hecate had told her that Lucas was the "wrong one." Apparently, Orion was the right one. Why? She doubted either of the old gods cared about her teenaged dating drama, so there had to be some other reason Orion was "right." Then it came to her

"Wait. You're the Shield," Helen said to him. She looked at Hecate. "The Fates. They're the enemy."

Hecate nodded. "We Titans have striven against them for eons. Now at your side, you have the one thing they can't see through. A child of Nemesis. The Hand of Darkness cannot help you—he never could. You must use your Shield to complete the final task, or it will not have been done."

"Will not have been done," Helen repeated quietly. "You sound like Cronus. You're both going to have to start being more specific if you expect me to figure this out, you know."

"We can't be more specific. Without the Shield constantly by your side, what you know the Fates would know," Hecate said, two of her three-sided faces regarding Orion. "You were supposed to have been with Orion for some time now."

Helen smiled ruefully. "Yeah. My mom said something like that once."

"I always liked your mother," Hecate said, remembering, until a thought occurred to her and all three of her faces darkened with consternation. "*Like* might be too strong a word. I respected her, and the battle she fought against the Fates is my battle. It is her architecture that we build on tonight."

"Hold on—this is all Daphne's plan?" Orion asked. "You're saying that the tasks you're having Helen complete are something her mother set in motion years ago?"

"Daphne and Nemesis. Even *you* are something they strove to bring into being," she told him. "It was not easy to protect you when the Fates turned so vehemently against you at birth, as they do with every Shield. After Ladon stole their last Oracle from them, they tried even harder to kill you than they did him. It was Daphne who kept you alive, and by doing so, she preserved the Shield of your generation."

Orion looked like he was going to tip over. Helen grabbed his hand and steadied him. She knew he'd had a terrible childhood. His father, who felt the Furies toward his own son, was supposed to have left him exposed on a mountainside because he was an Earthshaker. His uncle tried to kill him to keep the Houses separate. His mother killed her brother to protect Orion and became an Outcast for it; and because of that, she almost killed Orion in a Fury-induced rage. How he'd survived that many brushes with death was like a miracle.

Only it hadn't been a miracle. It had been Helen's mother, scheming with some powerful being named Nemesis, so that she could beat the Fates.

And yet although Daphne was still, even after death, proving to be a manipulative person, Helen now sensed that there might have been more to her mother than just her selfish desire to revive Ajax. Maybe she was fighting fate for all of them. Helen suddenly missed her. Or rather she missed the Daphne she had met in 1993. She felt like that Daphne, the one who was willing to do anything to break fate, was someone she could have been friends with. Maybe. But she didn't have the time to be sad about her mother and got herself back on topic.

"Orion is here, so now you can tell me. What do you need me to do?" she asked.

All three of Hecate's faces smiled and the one set of shoulders beneath them shrugged. "I don't know either," she admitted. "If I did, the Fates would know as well. I have no Shield. Nemesis revealed herself to Daphne and then left us again."

Helen and Orion exchanged a look.

"You're doing *all this*, and you don't know what it's for?" Orion asked, incredulous.

"If I did know, it wouldn't work," Hecate replied simply. "My thread to weave in this web is long, but straight. I know we right a terrible wrong done to one of the Titans, who can, in turn, help Helen reclaim *her* world without destroying *this* one in the process."

"But why do you care about Everyland, or planet Earth at all for that matter?" Helen gestured to the dark and cold around them. "Look, if I don't understand *why* you want me to do all this, how am I supposed to understand *what* to do?"

"Interesting. You feel like you need to understand my motives to know the endgame." Hecate stared at Helen, considering. "Do you know who I am?"

"The Witch Titan," Helen said.

"That is my title. Who I *am,* is Choice," Hecate corrected. She gestured down one road, then another, then the third that met at the crossroads. "I give people choices."

"For a price," Helen remarked, eyebrow raised.

Hecate laughed. "The price is the choice. I want to live in a world—any world—that is of my own choosing. That is why I do this. The question is, who are you, Helen Hamilton? Are you like the Olympians, content to fight wars and sink continents because the Fates deem it so? Will you allow yourself to be a chess piece moved about by higher beings?"

"You know I won't," Helen replied, insulted.

"Then allow yourself to be moved about like a chess piece," she said, aware of the irony. "I can hold the borders of Everyland for only one more week while you figure out what you are supposed to do with the Omphalos. Once you know, tell no one but Orion, not even me. You must never leave his side, or the Fates will see inside your mind. Go to Cronus and complete your final task. And Helen? Hurry." She gave a tired smile. "The Olympians cannot attack you directly, but they recruit lesser gods and other beings to their cause, and I cannot help you hold the borders of your world indefinitely. Nor can you survive these repeated attacks from Zeus. We are both on borrowed time."

With that, Hecate disappeared. Orion and Helen stood on the empty street. They looked at each other for a long time.

"Are you sicker than you're letting on?" Orion asked.

"I'm fine." Helen shrugged.

Orion narrowed his eyes at her. "Helen," he warned.

"I'm really tired, like, all the time now," she admitted. "But I'm not dying right this minute. I'm more worried about these lesser gods Hecate said the Olympians are recruiting." She frowned suddenly. "Shoot. I forgot to ask her about the eyeballs."

Orion looked mistrustfully at the shadows around them. "We need to get you back inside," he said, gathering Helen closer.

They broke into a sprint and arrived at her house in moments. Once they were inside, Orion locked the door and went to draw the curtains. Kate and Jerry had gone to bed. Jason and Ariadne were in the living room, healing Hector. They paused in their work to watch Orion run from window to window.

"What's going on?" Hector asked from the couch.

"The long and short of it is that I have one week to figure out what I'm supposed to do for my final task, because the Olympians are aligning a small army of lesser gods and 'other beings' against us, and Hecate doesn't think she can help me hold the borders of Everyland closed against Zeus for much longer," Helen said.

Hector's face darkened with anger, and he tried to stand.

"Don't be an idiot," Jason said, pushing his brother back down. "You still have a partially collapsed lung."

"Jason—" Hector began warningly, but Ariadne wasn't in the mood for any of Hector's heroics.

"Lie down or I swear I will put you under for so long you'll wake up with a beard," she threatened, one glowing hand raised. Hector reluctantly did as she said.

"Dad and Uncle Castor are outside, running perimeter. Someone needs to warn them," Hector argued.

"I will," Orion said, opening the door.

Helen followed him.

"Wait—where are *you* going?" Hector asked, grabbing Helen's wrist as she passed him.

"I can't leave Orion's side," Helen replied. "I need him to keep me hidden from the Fates while I figure out my final task or it won't work."

"What's your final task?" Hector asked.

"We don't know. And Hecate said we can't tell anyone when we figure it out," Orion said.

"Why?" Hector persisted.

Helen sighed heavily and turned to Orion. "It's like, we tell Hector that a goddess specifically warned us not to talk about it..."

"But he didn't even hear us," Orion finished, grinning. "It's like he can't figure out that sometimes he's just going to have to trust the people around him and not try to control every situation."

Jason stood, frustrated. "And while you guys are joking around, my father and uncle could be getting attacked," he grumbled and stalked out of the house.

"What's up with him?" Helen asked Ariadne, surprised.

"He's still angry about Dad not telling us about the wolf thing," she replied, concentrating on holding her glowing hands over Hector's chest.

"How do *you* feel about it?" Helen asked.

Ariadne shrugged, considering. "Disappointed," she decided.

"Ari, come on," Hector said, frustrated. "They didn't tell us because they were trying to put the war behind them."

"No wonder no one in this family ever gets over anything," Ariadne said. "We spend so much energy trying to put things behind us that we never actually deal with anything."

She stood up and went to the refrigerator, pulled open the freezer, and stopped. "Helen. There's an eyeball in your freezer."

"Yeah, just leave it there," Helen muttered.

Ariadne put her hand in—carefully, to avoid the eyeball—took out an icepack, and brought it to Hector. "You're healed. Put that on your fat head."

Castor, Pallas, and Jason came back inside. Castor and Pallas must have gotten dressed outside because they were both wearing clothes.

"I think you should come back to our house tonight," Castor told Helen. "It will be easier for us to protect you there."

"I'm not leaving Kate and my dad here alone." Helen frowned, shaking her head. "Something about this isn't right. Why did Poseidon pick *now*?" she asked no one in particular. "Was he testing me to see how strong I am?"

"What are you thinking?" Orion said.

"Why haven't any of these lesser gods attacked us yet?" Helen said. She turned to Jason. "Have you spoken to Claire today?"

"Right before I came here," he replied.

"Can you watch her tonight?"

"Sure. Do you think Claire's in danger?" Jason asked.

"More than I am." Helen turned to Castor and Pallas. "I think this whole 'protect Helen' thing has to stop. Clearly, I can take care of myself."

"A few days ago, you fainted on me," Hector reminded her.

"Oh, big deal," she scoffed.

"Wait, Helen," Orion interjected. She knew he was going to go blab about Hecate saying she was on borrowed time, so she turned quickly to Castor.

"Can you find out if any of the Hundred Cousins have been attacked by any of the lesser gods?"

Castor and Pallas exchanged a look. "We'll make some calls," Castor promised.

Helen turned to Orion. "Have you heard from Niobe lately?"

"She hasn't been attacked," Pallas answered for him. Everyone but Castor looked at Pallas questioningly.

"How do you know that?" Jason asked.

Pallas let out a long breath, like he dreaded what he was about to say. "I was with her... last night," he admitted.

There was a long silence.

"Dad," Hector said, like he was rearranging his whole world view. Jason looked visibly upset, and Ariadne didn't seem to know what to think.

Thrown, but not at all prepared to discuss her boyfriend's uncle's love life, Helen turned to Orion. "Um. Okay. Can you check on your dad? Maybe even your uncle Ladon?"

"Sure," Orion replied before returning to his earlier topic. "I don't think Zeus' attacks on Everyland and what Poseidon did to you tonight are just distractions. I think you're in real danger."

"Okay, fine," she admitted impatiently. "But there's something else going on, and we have no idea what it is. We need to figure out who's on our side, and who's on the Olympian's side." Another troubling thought occurred to her. "And why hasn't Cassandra *seen* anything? Isn't that weird? It's like we're flying blind here."

"She goes for weeks sometimes without seeing anything," Castor said.

Helen knew that making a prophecy was physically and emotionally traumatizing for Cassandra, but it seemed a little too convenient that the Fates were hiding from her now.

"Ask her to make a prophecy. If she's strong enough," Helen said, feeling terrible, but knowing there wasn't really any choice.

Castor's lips pressed together, and Helen could see his heart twisting painfully in his chest. He nodded once and left.

"He knows you're right," Pallas said, following him but pausing at the door. He looked at his three children. "Jason. Be careful tonight."

"I will," Jason said, though he didn't meet Pallas' eyes.

"Ari. Hector. Let's go."

Hector looked up disbelievingly. "But—I have to—"

"You have to come home so you can sleep and eat and recover," Pallas insisted. "This isn't a request."

"I'll be here with Helen," Orion told Hector, sidestepping an argument between father and son.

Hector finally gave in and headed for the door. "I'll be back tomorrow," Hector told Helen. "Don't go anywhere without me."

"Go home, Hector. And take the eyeball out of my freezer before Kate finds it and has a heart attack."

When she finally got Ariadne and Hector (with the eyeball) out the door, she leaned against it, letting out a long breath. She and Orion stared at each other, aware that they were very alone.

Orion tilted his head to the side. "Hungry?"

"Starving," she replied.

"I'll make you something." Orion headed into the kitchen.

He pulled some cheese and olives out of the fridge, and then went to the pantry to get bread. He laid out a wooden board and started arranging the food. Helen had seen this exact moment before and her breath caught. Orion looked up at her, pausing.

"You're remembering something," he said, reading her emotions.

Helen smiled at him, impressed again by how skillful Orion was at reading hearts. She couldn't even guess what recalling a memory looked like in another person.

"Your uncle Adonis made me dinner exactly like this the other night."

Orion went back to cutting and arranging his cheese board, smiling knowingly. "He made a big impression on you."

"He did." Helen nibbled on an olive, thinking about that night. "He wasn't what I expected. I thought he'd be this smooth lover man, and he was, sure, but he was also kind. He was a true friend to your uncle Ladon. It was so against type, I guess, to see this perfectly dressed nightclub owner in an abandoned subway tunnel helping an outcast monster."

"Adonis and Ladon were friends?" Orion asked, surprised. "How'd they manage that?"

"I don't know how they met or anything, but Adonis was better at controlling the Furies than anyone I've ever seen."

Orion nodded. "I was never good at it, but my dad told me my uncle and my mom were. That's how my mom and dad got together in the first place."

Thinking about Ladon, a thought occurred to her. "Ladon's a Shield too," Helen said, grabbing Orion's wrist to keep him still before she lost the thought. "Has he ever told you about Antigone?"

Orion shook his head. "Who's she?"

"The Oracle before Cassandra. She said that Ladon was the only person who silenced the Fates for her." Helen felt an urgent rush inside. Like she was tiptoeing around something important, but she couldn't figure out what it was. "We need to see Ladon. He knows something about the Fates. I don't know what it is, but I know he knows."

Orion's face fell at a thought. "My uncle lives underwater, mostly. I can't leave you, and you can't go... not with Poseidon..." He stopped.

"Right," Helen said, looking down. She didn't want to talk about Poseidon. It made her nauseous to think of him.

"Are you okay?" Orion asked.

She was still holding his wrist. She stared at it, just absorbing the way his skin hugged the muscles of his forearm and how harmoniously the dusting of little golden hairs matched the golden cuff that he wore around it.

"Why does he have to have Lucas' face?" she finally asked.

"I don't know," Orion said. "The Fates are being extra cruel, I guess."

"I want the Fates *gone*." She looked up at him. "Can your dad help us contact Ladon?"

"I'll ask him."

Helen felt the churn of hurt in him. His face shifted slightly, tightening subtly into sadness. "It's hard for you to talk to your dad," she said, opening the can to see if any worms needed to crawl out.

"It's easier when I have a reason. Something for him to do, rather than something I need him to say to me, or feel about me," Orion leaned onto his elbows across the table from Helen, bringing his face closer to hers.

She could sense everything he was feeling like it was happening to her. He normally hid himself from her, snatching his emotions away before she could discern them. But now something was different. As soon as the question arose inside of her—had he changed or had she?—Orion pulled away and took out his phone.

"I should have reached out to my dad and Niobe as soon as you mentioned it," he said as he started texting. Then he paused, and looked over at her. "Have you been feeling like there's a gap between the time when you tell yourself to do something and when you actually do it?"

"I don't even know what I'm doing anymore," she replied, suddenly feeling exhausted. "Two minutes ago I thought I was hungry. Now all I want is a shower and bed."

. . .

They went upstairs together. She heard him lean up against the bathroom door and she stood on the other side of it for a moment before she started taking off her clothes. She knew he could hear her undressing, and when she stepped into the shower she imagined him imagining her as she turned beneath the spray. She tipped her head back and felt fingers of water sliding down her scalp, and she forced herself to think of Lucas. But Lucas became Poseidon, and her eyes snapped open.

She finished showering as fast as she could, dried, and wrapped a towel around herself before stepping outside. Orion changed places with her without even glancing in her direction, but she could see a shimmer of iridescent sparks undulating beneath his skin before he shut the door. When he got out of the shower a few minutes later, wrapped waist down in a towel of his own, there was no steam accompanying him and the iridescent sparks of lust had dimmed a bit.

"Did you take a cold shower?" Helen asked, laughing.

"Hell yeah," he replied, grinning back at her. "Go get dressed. I'll wait on the other side of your bedroom door."

Helen threw on pajamas and took out something for him to wear. As she changed places with Orion again, she handed him a pair of soft sweatpants and a black t-shirt that said *No Matter How It Ends/No Matter How It Starts* on it in faded rainbow colors.

"Lucas'?" he asked as he took them.

Helen nodded and shut the door. He opened the door seconds later, dressed and already getting out the inflatable mattress.

"Is it sad you know where that is?" she asked, getting him some blankets and a pillow.

"It is for me," he said so softly she barely heard him.

While he used the pump Helen had finally broken down and ordered, she debated with herself whether she should ask him what he meant by that. She could see how much he wanted her, and he could see how much she wanted him, but causing him to say it would make it real. Helen didn't know if she wanted it to be real.

"I know. Neither of us are ready for that," he said, like he was reading her mind. He was reading her heart, which right now was like a neon sign on a hotel that said *Vacancy* with the *No* before it flashing on and off.

She gave him a weak smile. "This sucks."

"Yeah," he agreed, throwing a blanket onto the inflated mattress. He ran a hand through his wet hair in frustration, and it was instantly dry.

"I love it when you do that," she said. "Can you do mine? I hate sleeping on wet hair. I wake up and it's sticking up all over the place."

"Sure," he said. "Come here."

She stood in front of him. He reached out with both hands, threaded his fingers through her wet hair and lifted. She felt his fingers trace the exact opposite path the fingers of water had made across her scalp, and it felt so good she couldn't help but moan softly. She saw his eyes flare.

"And that's all I can take," he whispered, and his mouth dipped down to hers. But he didn't kiss her. He stopped himself and stepped back.

He was shaking. Helen was shaking.

"Go to bed, Helen," he said.

She scrambled into her bed, switching off the light as quickly as she could.

Orion stood in the near darkness, as if still torn. In the diffuse moonlight, tinted slightly with holiday lights, she could see his chest rising and falling as he fought for calm. His heart looked like heated glass, glowing red, loosening, and flowing over white-blue flame as he debated getting into bed with her.

Orion had never seemed dangerous to her before, and Helen couldn't believe how much she liked it. And she knew he could *see* that she liked it. He got very still.

"Stop it, Helen," he said.

"I'm trying," she replied desperately, burying her head in her hands.

He touched his fingertips to his chest, searching for words. "Lust is something *I* control, not something that's done to me like —" he stopped suddenly.

He looked at Helen through the thin moonlight, like he'd figured it out and said, "That little shit!"

She switched on the light by her bed and sat up. "Who's a little shit?"

"Remember how you asked earlier why the lesser gods haven't attacked us?"

"Yeah."

"I think they have been," he said. "After chorus, you said that you weren't in control over what you were feeling for me and Hector. That's because it's not you. It's Eros, the god of lust."

She let out a long, relieved breath and flopped back on her pillow. "I thought I was going crazy," she said.

"Lust messes with your head. None of us have been thinking straight," Orion said.

"But why can't we block him or stop him?"

Orion shook his head. "We get our power over emotions from Aphrodite, but even she couldn't fight Eros. He might not be an Olympian, but he's very powerful."

"Apparently! But how could they know that I wouldn't just put all this—" she made a vague gesture toward her body underneath the blankets, "*—energy* toward Lucas?"

"They know Lucas is not here at night. And that Hector and I have been guarding you because of Zeus' attacks, which, if you think about it, always seem to happen when Lucas isn't around. They have to be communicating with Zeus. Telling him when to strike to weaken you."

"Hermes," Helen replied immediately. "He can get a message anywhere. Even to another world."

Orion nodded, but then seemed to think better of it, like he was not fully buying into the scenario they were spinning. "But even with all of that going on, you could still hold out. Wait for Lucas to come back and, ah, scratch that itch," he said with a lopsided grin.

"Unless the thought of him disgusted me," Helen said quietly.

Orion looked confused, and then realization dawned. "Poseidon."

She nodded, her heart sinking. "I can't seem to separate their faces in my head. It's like I don't want to think about Lucas anymore because it makes me think of *him*," she said. She looked up at Orion, begging for help. "What do we do?"

"Nothing. This is a war of attrition. There's no enemy to fight except ourselves." He covered his face with his hands, trying to keep in an enraged shout, and barely succeeding.

Helen recoiled from him, surprised. Orion was usually the level-headed one, but this was really getting to him. He was not used to being out of control where emotions were concerned. He swore under his breath and then dropped his hands, staring at the floor like he was giving up.

"We'll figure it out," she said encouragingly. "It'll be fine."

He looked over at her, and he took a breath to say something, and then thought better of it. "Yeah," he said instead. "We'll be fine. Let's go to sleep."

Helen switched off the light and lay back in bed. She listened to Orion shifting beneath his blankets, far too aware of him for comfort. She knew she wasn't going to sleep. She rolled over and faced him. Orion was on his back, staring at the ceiling.

"But why Eros?" she asked. "Of all the ways to attack us, why like that?"

"Poseidon said his sister was betting we would tear ourselves apart."

Helen frowned. Every time she thought about Poseidon she was overwhelmed with repulsion, and fear. She wondered why it was that the way Poseidon had forced himself on her had left her more scared than a full-on battle ever had. Why was an unwanted touch so much more terrifying than any fist or sword? Her fear, and maybe more importantly her avoidance of that fear, left her at a disadvantage. Poseidon had given away this information about his sister, and about her plan to goad the Scions into destroying themselves. Orion had caught it, but *she'd* been so bullied and humiliated by Poseidon that she avoided thinking about any detail of her encounter with him. It infuriated her that it could be so easy for men to disable women in that way.

"Who's his sister?" she asked.

"He has two. Hestia and Hera." He rolled over and pillowed his head on his arm, looking at Helen. "Don't," he said, his eyes soft with care as he read what was in her heart. "What Poseidon did shames him, not you. It's a tactic to separate you from Lucas."

Helen swallowed the lump in her throat. Orion always made

her feel better. Always said the right thing. He never hid things from her or lied about anything. She felt her expression growing softer as she gazed at him.

Orion squeezed his eyes shut and turned his face into his bicep. Then, he rolled over onto his back with an arm flung over his eyes. "I can't even leave the room," he said, his voice shaky.

"I'm sorry," Helen said, but what she really wanted to say was *come here.* He was so beautiful when he was tortured like this, and she hated that she enjoyed watching him ache. She turned away from him. "We need to separate somehow. Maybe I should sleep in the closet?"

Orion laughed. "No," he said, taking a deep breath. "Let's just go to sleep. I'll figure out how to control this. I promise."

Helen sighed, thinking how much she wanted Orion to lose control. She forced herself to shut her eyes and go to sleep.

"No, Beauty, you can't be here without your Shield!" Morpheus exclaimed.

Helen sat up next to him, and then Orion appeared between them as Morpheus summoned him, still sleeping.

She looked at Morpheus expectantly. He shrugged, his dark eyes wide with uncertainty.

"I didn't think," she said, wanting to kick herself. "I forgot I come here in body when others just come here in spirit."

"We're lucky he has this, or I would not have been able to bring him here," Morpheus said, touching the Bough of Aeneas on Orion's wrist.

"Was it in time?" Helen asked in a tight voice.

"Have you figured out what it is the Titans want you to do in this wild goose chase on which they've sent you on?" Morpheus asked in turn.

"No." Helen rolled her eyes ruefully.

"Then don't worry. The Fates can't know either," Morpheus said, relieved. He slid his long, elegant body down beside Orion's slumbering one, eyeing him appreciatively. "He is a sight to behold, isn't he? And he smells divine. Scent is absent from dreams, and it's one of the things I find the most enticing about my paramours."

"Me too," Helen admitted. She lay back in bed as the glowing follow-me-lights wafted in the air like candle flames encased in iridescent bubbles. "I'm practically molten."

"With Eros shooting arrows at you every second of the day I can't believe you've resisted this long," Morpheus replied, propping himself up on an elbow. His long black hair flowed like an ebony river to the silky pillow.

"Can you take me to the nightmare tree? If I could just see Lucas and wipe out this image I have of Poseidon..."

Morpheus shook his head firmly. "No, Helen. Don't."

"Why not?"

He thought about it for a moment. "Do you know how Pheidippides managed to run the twenty-six miles from Marathon to Athens in full armor after having fought one of the most grueling battles in the history of Greek warfare?"

Helen shook her head.

"He didn't stop. He knew that if he'd sat down, he never would have gotten up again."

She frowned. "Didn't Pheidippides die after he said 'nike'?"

"Dropped like a *stone*," he said, widening his eyes humorously. "But he still said it. And he saved legions of soldiers." Morpheus gave her a sympathetic smile. "Let Lucas run his marathon."

"Then help me," she pleaded. "You could be him." She glanced down at Orion. "Or him."

Morpheus closed his eyes and made a humming noise in the back of his throat, tempted. "I can't," he decided. "It would only work in Eros' favor. Your molten body would flow from my bed to Orion's. Then to Hector's." He narrowed his eyes coquettishly. "Then both together."

"But why?" Helen asked, not even bothering to deny she'd pictured it.

"Dreams can satiate certain wants of the mind and the soul. They can bring insight, inspiration, and even comfort when the soul of a dead loved one visits a sleeping mind. But dreams can never fulfill the needs of the body. Thirst, hunger, and desire are only increased by me."

Helen nodded, recalling a dream she'd had once of a world of candy and cakes. She'd awoken the next morning ravenous.

"This is Hera's plan? Get me to cheat on Lucas and the Scions will fall apart?" she asked, her derision obvious. "It seems a bit petty."

"To Hera, infidelity is the greatest crime, and she does love to concoct punishments that have symmetry to them," he said. "Remember, the Trojan War started because Helen was unfaithful."

"Can you help me stop Eros before I do something stupid?"

Morpheus considered. "I can send him dreams that may sway him to your side, but do not put too much hope in this. The gods know how I favor you. Eros will not trust any prophetic vision I send him in sleep."

Helen smiled at him wanly. "Can you send *me* a prophetic vision? Maybe I'll wake up with all the answers."

Morpheus laughed quietly. "I'm sorry, Beauty. I do enjoy

giving people solutions to their problems while they sleep, but with you I cannot help at all. If I were to know how you were to proceed, the Fates would know as well, and thwart all your efforts. But you are not alone."

Helen looked down at Orion's peaceful face. "That's the problem."

Chapter 13

Helen awoke in her bed with Orion spooned against her back. His top arm was draped over her, and his hand lightly cupped her breast. When Morpheus had returned their bodies to this world he must have sent them back together, and in his sleep, Orion had merely found a comfortable place to put his hand. That's all.

That was enough. Her entire body felt like it was moaning.

She held very still while she contemplated how to untangle herself from his arms without waking him. Not that she wanted to untangle herself. In fact, she was imagining how easy it would be to arch her back ever so slightly and wake him in the nicest possible way. But she knew exactly what would happen after that. And then after *that*, she didn't know what either of them would do. Lucas would lose his mind. Cassandra would be heartbroken. Ariadne, Jason, and Claire would hate them. Hector would be the only one who would understand, and Helen knew she'd end up going to him for comfort and protection like she always did, and then when *they* were alone...

Even if it was petty, Hera's tactic was a good one, Helen realized. Infidelity was the perfect way to destroy the Scions.

She felt Orion breathe in, and his hand moving against her breast as he woke.

"Wait," she said, turning over to stop him. Which was a mistake. Facing him brought her mouth to his.

Orion's kiss was so different from Lucas'. His skin was smoother. His lips were fuller and softer. His body yielded as much as it pressed, and Helen shifted effortlessly underneath him, not really knowing who was leading or who was following. They flowed together, like two rivers spilling into each other and gathering strength and speed as they rushed toward the waterfall.

If Kate hadn't knocked on Helen's door they would not have stopped.

"Helen? Are you in there?" Kate asked from the other side of the door.

Orion sprang off Helen and crouched at the end of her bed.

"Yeah!" Helen replied breathlessly, staring at Orion as he looked back at her with wild eyes. "We just woke up."

"And... how many of you are in there?" Kate asked, chuckling uncertainly.

Orion got up and started pacing back and forth. A hand was covering his mouth and his chest was rising and falling with fast breaths.

"Just me and Orion," Helen called, pulling her knees up to her chest and wrapping her arms around them as she watched Orion silently freak out. "We'll be right down."

There was a tense beat, as if Kate could sense there was more going on than Helen was letting on. "Okay," she finally said. "I'll start breakfast."

Helen and Orion stared at each other while they listened to Kate go downstairs. The initial rush of panic they'd both felt was replaced with crushing guilt. Helen had never been so ashamed of anything she had ever done in her life.

"Don't," Orion said, reading her heart and coming to sit on the bed next to her. "It's my fault—"

"No, it's mine," Helen insisted, not allowing him to take the blame. "I should have gotten out of bed as soon as I woke up, but I didn't."

"Don't feel guilty."

"How can you *say* that?" Helen exclaimed, standing up. It was her turn to pace now while Orion watched her from the bed.

"Because Lucas —" Orion broke off and shook his head, like he couldn't believe he was about to say this. "Remember I said I'd tell you later what Lucas and I talked about in the Underworld?"

"Yeah," Helen replied tentatively, already knowing she wasn't going to like what Orion was about to say.

"He told me that he wants you to move on. With me."

Helen stared at Orion. Then a slightly hysterical laugh slipped out. "There is no way in hell—or Hades—Lucas would ever say he wanted me to be with some other guy. Do you have any idea how jealous he gets?"

Orion's mouth was tight, and his eyes flashed with anger. "Am I lying?"

He wasn't. Helen stood very still while the rest of her world turned upside-down. "Why would he say that?"

"I think he's already been down there a really long time," Orion said quietly. "I asked how long and he wouldn't say, but he seemed different."

"Different how?"

"I couldn't read his heart at all. I've never not been able to read someone, but it was like he was switched off," Orion said. "I think he needs to separate himself from all of us. Mostly you. If he knows you've moved on, he can let go. He can't handle the thought of you and Hector together, so I'm the best option he's got."

Helen's legs felt unsteady. She sank down on the bed next to Orion. "He really believes there's no way out of his oath, doesn't he?" she whispered. "He's given up."

"He has." Orion still looked angry.

"I'm sorry. I didn't mean to accuse you of lying," she apologized.

"I know," he said.

"Then, what is it?"

"Lucas just assumed *I'd* do it. Like I'd be fine with being your dirty secret," he said. Then he laughed derisively. "And I guess he was right."

"Hey," Helen said. He was just beating himself up now. "It's not like this is a normal situation. We're literally being attacked by the god of lust."

Orion looked at her and sighed. "That would be much easier for me to believe if I didn't want to push you back onto that bed right now," he said.

Helen dropped her head, half laughing, half groaning. "You're killing me."

"At least it's mutual." Orion stood up like it hurt and schlepped to the door. "Come on. You can use the bathroom first."

Helen gathered up her clothes. When they got to the bathroom, Orion stopped her.

"Let's not tell anyone about this yet, okay?" he asked. "I'm not saying we should lie if we're asked directly, just..."

"Don't say anything to the family." She nodded. "I have to tell Lucas when I see him, though. I can't hide this from him," she warned.

"Yeah, I know," he said, biting his lower lip. "But... I think it would really hurt Cassandra if she knew, too."

They were standing too close together again, leaning against the wall in the hallway, practically touching—her face tipped up to his, their mouths close. Helen rolled away from him across the wall with a groan and spun herself into the bathroom.

She sped through her turn, though she wished she could have stayed in there all day. She wanted to be alone and think, preferably listening to sad music while she did something hypnotically mundane like painting her toenails. But she knew breakfast was ready and Orion was probably hopping up and down on one foot in the hallway, so she rushed and changed places with him, leaning against the door listlessly while he took another cold shower.

He came out, mercifully dressed in his own clothes instead of Lucas', looking as miserable as she felt.

They went down and had breakfast with Jerry and Kate.

Orion left momentarily to answer a call from his father and came back to the table looking concerned.

"What?" Helen asked.

"He said there was nothing. No fights, no sign of these smaller gods. Just nothing."

That didn't sit well with Helen. "Hecate said they were gathering. What are they waiting for?"

Orion shrugged, irritated as he dug into his eggs.

"And Ladon?"

Orion hastily chewed and swallowed so he could answer. "My dad will bring him here when he finds him."

"Great," Helen replied sarcastically. "So we just sit here. Staring at each other. Eating eggs."

It was the staring at each other part that was killing her. Helen realized that this was why everything was quiet. She couldn't fly. She couldn't swim. There were no battles to fight. Nothing to distract her from Eros' arrows. Like Orion had said, it was a war of attrition, and she was losing.

Kate and Jerry tried to engage them in conversation, but it was pointless. Guilt hit Helen in waves, getting stronger every time it engulfed her. She sat at the table, pushing her food around, unable to eat it. She knew Orion was feeling something similar, although for different reasons. He deserved better than to be someone's side piece, and she could see his heart turning like a lava lamp. Gooey shame kept welling up inside him and blooming inside a pool of simmering rage. He was the angriest Helen had ever seen him outside of a battle. He was barely keeping it together.

Eventually, Jerry gave up trying to talk to them and went to watch football in front of the TV. Helen and Orion did the dishes, standing silently side by side while Kate eyed them with a combination of worry and suspicion.

"Are we okay here?" Kate asked, quietly, to keep Jerry out of it. "I mean, I know what must have happened between you two last night. You both look guilty as hell. But do I *know* what *happened*? Does anyone? And do they really need to know if they can never know *all* of it?"

Helen looked at Kate, unable to decipher if what she had just said was extremely wise or absolute nonsense. Before either of them could comment, a pair of shiny luxury SUVs pulled into their driveway, parking behind Jerry's rusty pickup truck and Kate's tiny electric car.

One Aoki and about a dozen Deloses started piling out, including Cassandra. Orion and Helen took deep breaths, steeling themselves for the "everything's normal" performance they were about to give.

Kate grimaced. "Sorry. Noel, Castor, and I need to go over wedding stuff. I didn't know the whole family was going to come, but I should have guessed."

"I really need to hit something," he whispered.

"Well, you're in luck," Helen replied. She grinned at Orion. "Hector's here."

They both started laughing.

"See, this is what I mean," Kate said, watching them. She stood and made her way to the door to let in their guests. "They say love is a two-way street, but sometimes I think it's more like a rotary."

She pulled the door open and there was a flood of bodies and a rush of hellos. Noel and Kate gave each other a long, comforting hug. Noel was still upset about Lucas, and though she tried to make this visit about the wedding. Castor and Pallas strode in and started putting snacks and beers in the refrigerator before joining Jerry to watch the game. Ariadne and Claire greeted Helen; Cassandra tried to get to Orion, but he was already making a beeline for Hector.

"How do you feel?" Orion asked, giving Hector a bro hug.

Hector sucked his teeth dismissively. "I could wreck you right now." Exactly what Orion needed to hear.

"Right. Let's do it," Orion said, waving Hector back outside.

"Sure," Hector replied, thrown. He edged toward Helen. She

leaned against his side easily and he wrapped a thick arm around her. "What's up with him?" he whispered.

"Just go fight him. In the backyard. And don't knock over any of my trees," she scolded, poking his shoulder as they went outside together.

"'Kay," Hector agreed breezily, always ready for a fight.

Before parting he tipped his head down and brushed his lips across Helen's, lightly nipping at her with his teeth—like they'd done it a hundred times before.

Which they had in past iterations of themselves. When he was Arthur, the Great King in his blinding armor, and she was Guinevere, a blue-painted savage from the native tribes of the north, it was their custom to give each other that biting kiss before a joust or battle.

But he was not Arthur anymore and she was no longer Guinevere, his wife and queen.

The kiss had been quick. It wasn't even a true kiss, but they both stutter-stepped as they pulled away from each other before quickly continuing in different directions, hoping no one had seen it. Camelot had been destroyed by infidelity.

Claire and Ariadne closed in on either side of Helen, each of them grabbing an arm.

"What the heck was that?" Claire hissed in her ear as they went around to the backyard.

"I don't know," Helen stammered, petrified by how easily she and Hector had slipped into intimacy. And by the fact that her lips still tingled pleasantly from his rough treatment.

"Did you and Hector just *bite* each other?" Ariadne asked, a little horrified.

"I don't know," Helen repeated. "It was a mistake."

"What? You slipped and fell on each other's faces?" Claire asked sarcastically.

Helen clutched at Claire's and Ariadne's wrists, bringing their little group to a halt. "We're not attracted to each other."

Ariadne guffawed. "I'm a Healer, and we're touching, so I can read your physical condition. Helen? Your panties are on fire."

"No, just listen." Helen sighed in frustration. "Eros is influencing us on the Olympians' behalf, betting that if Orion, Hector, and I cheat with each other it will divide the Scions."

Claire raised her eyebrows. "It would," she admitted.

"That's why you can't tell anyone else, okay?" Helen begged. "Even knowing that we're fighting these feelings would hurt everyone."

Ariadne nodded, then looked at Claire. Claire silently agreed and gave Helen a sympathetic side hug as they walked together into the backyard.

Hector and Orion were already stripped down to the waist in the cold December air and kicking the ground clear of snow.

"You just made a 'yummy' noise," Claire informed Helen. "We'll keep your secret, Len, but you *gotta* stop doing that when you see them."

Helen groaned. "It's Eros, not me."

"Should we just go back inside?" Ariadne asked, trying to give Helen an easy out.

Helen shook her head, tortured. "Orion and I can't be more than a few steps away from each other," she reminded them.

"Oh right," Ariadne said. "You two have to sleep in the same room? How are you managing that?"

"Not very well," Helen admitted.

"What does *that* mean?" Claire asked, alarmed. "You guys didn't...?"

Helen shook her head quickly, noticing that Orion was watching them talk. He clapped his hands together, maybe to keep his blood flowing in the frigid air, maybe to break up the girls' huddle before Helen said too much about that morning.

"Let's do this before we freeze," Orion said.

"What are the rules?" Hector began to say when Orion punched him in the face.

The exchanges came fast, and Jason struggled to keep both combatants in his eye-line so he could referee. Orion and Hector fought brutally, but they both seemed to be enjoying it. They bantered back and forth between combinations, remarking on a good shot, or clever footwork. It was playful, even if they were hitting each other so hard the ground shook. Pallas, Castor, and Jerry joined them, watching the impressive fight.

"Plant your back foot, Hector," Castor called out to his nephew.

"I'm trying," Hector complained. Orion danced out of reach and then back in to land a few more shots.

Pallas winced at the beating his son was taking. Helen noticed that the banter between Hector and Orion had ended.

"Are they going to be okay?" Claire asked after a particularly rapid combination from Hector that included a spinning back fist to Orion's temple. Alarmed, Cassandra took a jerky step toward Orion.

"Dad?" Ariadne said, looking at Pallas to see if he was going to stop the fight.

"They're fine," Pallas assured her. "They'll switch to grappling soon."

Hector tried to grapple. He shot in to take Orion to the ground, but Orion shook off his attempt. He wanted a stand-up fight that ended in a knockout, not a submission. He covered up his head and went in for Hector's body, looking for a beating.

Jason stayed right in the thick of it, making sure it was a fair fight, and it was. Neither of them were taking cheap shots or doing anything that could be called out as poor sportsmanship. It was a clinic in hand-to-hand combat, but they kept fighting long past when they should have stopped, and every hit seemed harder than the last.

Helen saw Castor and Pallas go from being engrossed in watching an amazing fight, to admonishing reckless choices that they wouldn't have made, to exchanging worried looks, like they were finally considering stepping in.

"Stop it," Cassandra whispered after one particularly vicious strike.

Helen heard bones breaking. "That's enough," she cried.

Jason tried to put an arm between the combatants, but they were moving too fast. Helen jumped in and found that she had to push Orion off Hector, when usually it was the other way around. Her palms slipped on the blood and sweat on Orion's chest as she shoved him back.

"Stop it!" she yelled at him, pushing him a few steps away. She felt Hector bump into her from behind.

"We're not done," Hector taunted, coming for more, though his forearm was clearly broken.

Helen blocked him with her body, and he wrapped his good arm around her, pulling her against his side and trying to put her behind him.

Orion didn't like seeing Hector's hands on Helen and he flared with jealous rage. He grabbed Helen by the shoulder and pushed Hector off her.

The switch in Hector was immediate. Helen saw jealousy

flame inside him, like it had long ago when she was his unfaithful queen, and in a heartbeat Hector and Orion fell back on each other viciously.

They were no longer sparring. They were fighting; fighting over her, and that was exactly what Hera wanted.

Helen could think of no other choice. She electrocuted them.

Hector and Orion convulsed as violet-white light danced over their skin and they collapsed onto the ground in unison.

"Dammit," she whispered, looking at the two inert heaps at her feet.

Jason threw his hands out to his sides in frustration. "Really?" he asked Helen. "I just healed him yesterday."

"Sorry," she replied sheepishly as he crouched down next to his brother.

"What the hell was *that* about?" he mumbled, looking up at Helen with an eyebrow raised. She shrugged, pretending that she didn't know, but Jason wasn't an idiot. He understood that they were fighting either over her, about her, or because of her, though he didn't know the details.

Ariadne knelt by Orion to heal him, and the twins' fingertips glowed blue as they revived the two fighters. Hector awoke and groaned, rolling around on the frozen ground. Orion writhed next to him making similar pained noises. They caught each other's eye and were united in agony.

"Damn that hurts," Orion said in a creaky voice like the wind had been knocked out of him.

"Old Sparky. She's a beast," Hector commiserated. The two friends started laughing and wincing in turns, all animosity forgotten.

"Fight's over. You both lost," Castor declared. Relieved,

everyone but Helen, Hector, and Orion made their way back inside.

Orion and Hector sat back on their heels, too beat up to talk yet. She saw them nod at each other in silent understanding and mutual gratitude, and she finally realized why they had given each other such a methodical beating. They had been purposely trying to incapacitate each other so neither of them could do anything romantic with Helen if the situation arose.

"Did you tell him about Eros?" she asked Orion.

He nodded. "Did you tell Claire and Ari?" he asked in turn.

"Yeah," she admitted. "I had to. They saw that... thing we did." She looked at Hector.

"What thing?" Orion asked.

"It was like a love bite, but on the lips?" Helen said, attempting to describe it.

"Right before the fight?" Orion asked.

Helen nodded.

"You drew first blood for him before battle. That's hot," Orion said, nodding. Of course, he understood.

Hector put his elbows on his knees and rubbed his hands over his scalp, whispering, "Stupid. I don't even know where it came from. It just felt like..."

"...Our thing," she finished for him. "It was once."

Helen explained about the memories she'd gathered from touching the waters in the River Lethe—who she and Hector had been.

The three of them exchanged hopeless looks.

"So, this love triangle thing is something the Fates keep repeating?" Hector asked.

"It's more like a love pyramid," Orion commented. "It's three dimensional."

"Yeah," Helen said, replying to Hector's question. "The Fates are setting us up for a fall. And they've chosen infidelity to bring it about."

"Great. What are we supposed do? Keep beating the snot out of each other when we can't take the sexual tension anymore?" Hector asked.

Helen smirked. "How does you two beating each other up help me?"

"Well, if we keep making each other look like this," Orion said, pointing to his swollen face, "resisting Eros might be easy for you."

When they were feeling steady enough to get up, Helen supported Hector and Orion and they trudged inside together. She dumped them on the couch in front of the TV and went to the kitchen to get them food. Behind her, she could hear Ariadne and Jason tell Hector that he could suffer all day for all they cared, but they weren't going to heal him if he kept throwing himself on Orion's fists.

"Just accept it, bro. Orion is a better fighter than you," Jason teased.

"And better looking," Ariadne added.

"You're both dead to me," Hector deadpanned.

Helen chuckled to herself, refusing to engage, while she searched the pantry for honey. Why didn't her dad just order buckets of it? He knew how to stock a shelf for crying out loud, but he seemed to resist the idea that injured demigods would be peppered throughout his living room for the rest of his natural life.

"I'll bring that to Orion," Cassandra said.

Holding a bag of chips and a jar of salsa, Helen turned around. Cassandra stood in the kitchen with the chip bowl.

"I haven't had a chance to ask you, but have you made a prophecy recently?" Helen emptied the chips into the bowl.

Cassandra shook her head. "I think the Fates are hiding something." She turned to go into the living room and Helen caught her arm, stopping her. She told Cassandra about meeting Antigone, keeping her description to the basics. Helen said nothing about Antigone's attempted suicide or how she'd fallen in love with someone who didn't love her back.

"Antigone told me that she could see things the Fates didn't want her to. Can you do that?"

"You mean force them?" Cassandra looked scared.

"Yes," Helen said, hating herself. "You know I wouldn't ask unless it was important. I feel like ... there's something happening and we're all too blinded by personal things to figure it out."

"I've felt the same," Cassandra agreed, gaze falling to the floor. "I'm not saying I'll be able to see anything *they* don't want me to, but I'll try."

Helen glanced over Cassandra's shoulder at Orion in the next room. "Maybe it would be a good idea to stay away from Orion, until you see something?" she suggested.

Cassandra looked up at Helen, her eyes widening with anger. She threw the bowl down onto the ground, smashing it at Helen's feet. Everyone in the other room went silent.

Helen put her hands on her hips, dismayed, and shook her head.

"This is what *they* want," she told Cassandra, who spun away from her and started running for the door.

Orion beat her there. He caught Cassandra's arm. "Woah, wait a second."

They went outside, staying just on the other side of the front door. Helen could see them talking to each other. Orion mostly listened, only saying a few things, but whatever he said calmed Cassandra down. He came back inside and asked Noel and Castor to take Cassandra home, then joined Helen in the kitchen where she was cleaning up the chips and broken crockery.

"She can't prophesy around you. I had to tell her to stay away," Helen said.

"Well, *someone* did," Orion said, bending down to help her.

When Helen glanced at him, she saw him waiting for her to pick up where he left off. "But it probably shouldn't have been me?" she guessed.

"Probably not," Orion said, smiling at first and then looking troubled. "If she were *jealous*, I would like her less and this would be easier."

"She's not, though," Helen said, standing. "She mostly feels unworthy of you." She looked at Orion. "I can't stand us right now," she whispered.

"Me neither."

Helen sat in the corner and tried to catch up on her homework while Hector and Orion napped on the couch and the rest of the family watched football. It was easy to keep a lid on her raging body while they were all hanging out, probably because Eros saved his arrows when he knew they wouldn't be able to fool around; but she could tell that as soon as she was alone with Orion, something would happen between them. Every time she glanced in the general direction of the couch a hot-and-cold ribbon of excitement slipped through her.

She begged either Claire or Ariadne to sleep over. Ariadne took pity on her and agreed. Helen reminded herself that Lucas would be back the morning after next; as soon as she saw him, she'd be fine. But every time she tried to picture Lucas in her mind, he had cruel eyes and a feral twist to his lips. It made her skin crawl. And it worried her. She started to wonder if she was going have that reaction to Lucas in person, and her worry turned to genuine fear. She didn't know what she would do if she couldn't look at Lucas the same way anymore.

After dinner Jerry kindly kicked everyone out and, though he had done nothing but rest all day, he went to bed early. After watching her dad climb the stairs more slowly than he should have, Helen didn't feel much like staying awake either. The general fatigue she'd been feeling was becoming much more insistent. Orion and Ariadne gladly agreed to an early bedtime.

Having Ariadne there as a buffer between her and Orion made it much easier to share a bedroom with him. Orion was asleep in minutes and Ariadne was a close second, but Helen couldn't seem to drift off.

She still had no idea what to do with the Omphalos. It did not escape her attention that this was the first time she had considered her task for the Titans since she had seen Hecate, and it only emphasized how effective this tactic of using Eros against them was.

Finally able to focus, Helen flipped her pillow over to the cool side and thought about everything she had read about the Omphalos. It was supposed to mark the center of the world, and because of that it was called the Navel Stone. It was also supposed to be the strongest thing in the universe after passing through the gut of the Titan of Time, Cronus.

Helen glared at her ceiling. How the hell had Cronus, who struck her as a pretty astute guy, mistaken a rock for his newborn son? It didn't make any sense. Didn't he notice the distinct lack of crying and, um, squishy baby-ness when he popped it in his mouth? There was just no way the Titan she had met would not be able to tell the difference between a rock and a living, breathing baby.

Unless the Omphalos could *seem* alive, somehow? Maybe it did cry. Maybe it did feel like a swaddled baby on Cronus' tongue before he swallowed it whole. Like warm sushi. The idea was not comforting to Helen, though there were many things in the Greek myths that were extremely unsettling, and this was fairly par for the course when it came to father-son relationships in the ancient Greek pantheon. Still. Not a good image to be working with at bedtime.

Family. This was all about family. Cronus had told Helen that. Hecate had told Helen that. But who did Cronus consider family, and who among them did he want to save from unimaginable suffering?

She needed to do some more homework.

After an hour of tossing, Helen decided the widow's walk wasn't too far away from Orion for her to go get some fresh air. She pulled on a woolen, oversized sweater that clearly belonged to one of the boys—which boy, she had no idea—and went onto the roof.

She hadn't been sitting up there for more than a few minutes when an enormous woman wearing full battle armor strode out onto the Hamilton lawn, planted her spear in the frozen ground, and looked up at her.

"Dammit," Helen whispered.

All she could think of was her father, lying a few yards away from this monument of a female, and she jumped over the railing of the widow's walk and landed in a crouch in the yard between them.

Helen rose slowly, taking in every inch of the Olympian in

front of her. She was one hell of a thing. Seven feet tall at least and as thick and muscular as Hector, but every inch a woman. Her armor did not make her look male, but accentuated her breasts, belly, and hips. This was a goddess like Helen had never encountered.

"Athena," Helen said, guessing correctly. She even tipped her head respectfully, because how could you not?

Athena breathed in deeply before speaking. "You smell of Athens, my home. But not as it is now. As it was when I loved it and it loved me back." Her voice was surprisingly vulnerable. "Is this part of the magic that makes you irresistible?"

Helen nodded. "I'm sorry, but I don't know how to turn it off," she said honestly.

"Nor should you," Athena replied. "It is a powerful weapon. Tactically, I would advise you to use it to your advantage."

"You're good at tactics, aren't you?" Helen asked.

Athena frowned. "I am wisdom, and I am war. Sometimes one inspires the other and sometime, it hinders."

In a flash Helen's mind rifled through of all the innovations war created, from Greek fire to the atomic age; and of all the things war destroyed, from art and architecture to libraries and great thinkers.

"You're a blessing and a curse," Helen mumbled.

"Aren't we all?" Athena said knowingly. "And here we are at the end of one Cycle and the beginning of another. Beginnings and endings, blessings and curses."

"Why are you here?" Helen asked, unsettled now. She glanced into the darkness of the cold Nantucket night around her, glowing cheerfully with holiday lights, and expected an ambush. She dreaded that it would come from Poseidon.

"I come to weigh my father's chances," Athena answered. "His sister wife is chomping at the bit for you."

Athena regarded Helen like a thing under a microscope.

"You don't like Hera," Helen said, noticing Athena's tone.

"There's not much to like," Athena replied dispassionately.

"Then why do you obey her?"

"I don't. Hera has always tried to destroy the Scions, usually as babes, easily smothered," she said disapprovingly. "She's a jealous coward. I have only ever helped Scions when they called on me for aid, for you are the next Cycle that *must* happen. Logic tells me that if it is fated, it will occur, and now that I lay eyes on you and find you defending your home—weaponless and barefooted, but unafraid—I say you should take your place Helen, Goddess of Everyland. You are the First in the pantheon of the new Cycle, whether you like it or not."

Helen stood staring, dumbstruck. She gestured down at her bare legs sticking out like two stems from the scratchy fisherman's sweater that ballooned to her thighs and scrunched down past her long, narrow fingers. Before this goddess, Helen looked like a waif.

"Are you *drunk*?" Helen exclaimed. "I'm a shopkeeper's daughter..."

"Shopkeeper, carpenter, shepherd." Athena made a dismissive gesture. "The First of a new Cycle has always had humble beginnings. Zeus himself was raised by a goat in a cave. You are the beginning of a new Forever, but telling the Olympians that the Fates are done with them will only strengthen their resolve to grind you into the dust—as they have done with countless other Scions. But I hope for you, Helen of Everyland."

"Why would you do that?" Helen asked mistrustfully. "You'd be in Tartarus if I won."

"Would I be? I guess that would be up to the victor, wouldn't it?" Athena asked with a sly smile. She suddenly looked up behind Helen.

Helen turned to see Ariadne landing on the ground behind her. She strode forward, barely dressed but ready for a fight. Helen put out a hand to stop her.

"You should have been one of my warrior maidens," Athena said, openly admiring Ariadne.

Ariadne bared her sharp, white teeth in a humorless smile. "The warrior part? Definitely. The maiden part? Not so much," she said.

Athena laughed, amused. "Ready yourselves, warrior women. I will see you both at the Final Battle."

She leapt into the air and flew away. Helen turned to Ariadne. "Well, that was weird."

"She wanted to size you up. It's the smart thing to do before a fight, and she *is* the goddess of wisdom," Ariadne said.

"She also wanted to put it into my head that I didn't have to send all the Olympians to Tartarus if I won. Wink-wink, nudge-nudge."

"Girl's gotta have an exit strategy," Ariadne joked, spreading her hands wide as if she didn't blame her.

"Which means they *are* gearing up for a fight. A real one. Not this war of attrition," Helen murmured darkly.

"Is it bad that I'm actually happy about that?" Ariadne asked. She shivered convulsively and hugged her arms around her chest. "Damn, it's cold. Why are we still outside?"

They went back inside through the door, rather than rattle the whole house by jumping up to the roof. They crept upstairs and tiptoed over Orion's sleeping body sprawled across the floor. Helen scolded the whining voice in her head that kept trying to get her to lie down next to him rather than Ariadne, and got into bed with her teeth chattering.

"Do you think this is going to keep happening?" Ariadne whispered, her voice breaking with quiet laughter. "Gods showing up in your yard?"

Helen giggled. "And not one of them with a casserole."

"So rude. I wonder who's going to pop by next?" Ariadne said musingly as she snuggled in for sleep.

Helen didn't reply, but she hoped it was Aphrodite. She missed her sister. And, as she tried to think of Lucas, but couldn't keep his face from sliding into Poseidon's hateful sneer, she also hoped that the goddess of love could fix her haywire heart.

Chapter 14

She awoke the next morning with a head full of lightning.

She saw it blazing over ocean waves and searing the sand on the beaches. She heard it rolling over mountains and firing down on shaggy redwoods whose resinous bark burst into flame at the lick of it. She felt it rooting down into the soil of her, sending all the furry, burrowing, little bits of her into terrified, squeaky convulsions before they died.

And it ticked her off. How dare he boil her teeming oceans and torch her gallant trees? How dare he kill all her soft, scurrying mousies and her clever little badgers? Helen sat up, throwing her blankets off with a growl—which she immediately regretted.

She balanced her elbows on her knees and grabbed her head, trying to keep it from falling off, until the world stopped swaying back and forth.

"Helen?" asked Orion gently.

"Wait," she warned, holding out a hand with one finger raised. "Might barf."

She felt Orion come and kneel in front of her, putting his hands on her shoulders. She wanted to tell him that he was in the splash zone, but she was too afraid to open her mouth. Not that there was anything in her stomach to throw up. She felt scoured-dry inside, and so hungry that the thought of food made her sick.

"It's okay," he murmured, lifting her up. "I've got you. Is it Zeus?" He carried her to the bathroom. He kicked the closed door with a foot. "Ari! Open the door."

"Yeah," Helen groaned. "He's killing my mousies. That dick."

The door swung open, and Orion carried Helen into the steamy air. Helen felt a cool towel being placed on the back of her neck. "Did she say mousies?" Ariadne asked.

"Zeus is on a rampage," Orion explained.

A tense moment stretched before Ariadne said, "Here. Water. Drink it, Helen," in a brisk voice.

Helen drank the glass of water, feeling Ariadne's hands touching her shoulders. Healing light filled her.

But it wasn't enough. Her body felt fine enough now, but it wasn't just one city, or one grove Zeus attacked anymore. He was raging over Everyland as quickly as he could. It was a blitzkrieg.

"I'm okay," Helen said gently, moving away from Ariadne's healing hands. "There's nothing you can do. It's not something anyone but me can fix."

Ariadne looked anxious. "You have a demon in you."

"And for some reason my demon has decided to be extra evil today, so we have to be ready for something."

"I'll let everyone know." Orion pulled out his phone. He went outside the bathroom and stood on the other side of the door while he called Hector.

. . .

Orion came with her to school and stayed close to her all day. He used his talent to influence teachers and students into accepting his presence as an unremarkable thing.

Some people, though, were more difficult to convince than others. Gretchen seemed particularly tenacious. Passing Helen in the hallway more than usual, Gretchen commented on Orion's presence several times. After lunch she accosted Helen at her locker.

"Isn't your new boyfriend a little old to be in high school?" she asked acidly.

"There's nothing strange about me being here at all," Orion replied with a smile.

Gretchen wavered momentarily, feeling his influence, but then she seemed to brush it away. She refocused all her energy on Helen, and her anger came back twice as strong.

"You should be ashamed of yourself!" Gretchen snarled, like a woman possessed. She stepped forward threateningly, forcing Helen to take a step back. "You think you can get away with doing whatever you want, but you won't!"

Helen was backed up against the lockers, too stunned to defend herself. Orion stepped between them. "There's nothing happening here," he said smoothly while Helen's knees shook.

Gretchen looked at Orion, and the smile she gave him was more like a grimace of disgust. "You think you're blameless because you *feel so bad* about it?" she asked mockingly. "You'll feel worse. Soon." Then she whirled around and stormed down the hallway.

People were staring at them. Helen clutched her books to her chest, her eyes wide, while Orion gathered up the rest of her stuff and shut her locker for her.

"How is she resisting me?" he asked quietly.

Helen shrugged, her heart pounding, and shuffled down the hallway next to him.

During her last few classes, she noticed everyone around her glaring at her scornfully. By the time she got to chorus practice after school she was a nervous wreck. She saw Claire and Ariadne; they crossed the auditorium to meet up with her. Jason was with them as well, but he seemed to hang back. He had a tight, offended look on his face.

"Oh my god, Lennie!" Claire whispered frantically. "The whole school is saying the worst stuff about you two." She glanced at Orion, trailing Helen.

"That can't be," he said, confused. "No one's supposed to care I'm here."

Helen looked over at Jason, but he wouldn't meet her eyes.

Mr. Abebe entered the auditorium, clapping his hands and calling for everyone to take their places.

"Oh, they care," Claire said, breaking away from them to take her place on the risers. "Whatever you're doing you need to do it harder."

All through rehearsal Helen fielded contemptuous glares from people she was normally friendly with, and more than once between songs there was an outburst of whispering, and someone would look at her with narrowed eyes and a smirk.

After two or three songs Hector joined Orion, Jason, and Ariadne in the audience. Soon, Helen noticed that Jason and Hector were arguing. By the end of rehearsal, Helen shoved her jingle bells in her bag with trembling hands, desperate to escape. Jason and Hector looked like they were on the verge of an actual physical fight. She shouldered her bag, eyeing them and hoping she could reach them before they started throwing punches.

"Miss Hamilton?" the choral conductor called.

"Yes, Mr. Abebe?" she said, stopping for him though she didn't want to.

He sighed heavily and gave her a chagrined look. "I'm afraid I'm going to have to ask you to resign from the Christmas Chorus."

It took a moment to sink in that he was kicking her out.

"Why?" she asked loudly, her voice quavering. She loathed chorus, but still. She'd never been kicked out of anything before.

At the threat of tears, Mr. Abebe held up his hands in a placating gesture. "Ninety percent of the choir has threatened to quit rather than sing with you." He shrugged apologetically, but he didn't look too sorry. "One or two complaints I could overlook as a personal matter, but I have to consider that if this many people have a problem with you, you might just be the problem."

Helen took an involuntary step away from him as if she'd been slapped. Glancing at the risers behind her, she saw a triumphant look on Gretchen's face and smug ones on nearly everyone else's. It was one thing to know there were rumors going around, and another thing to face such open hatred.

"Fine. Sure," Helen mumbled, backing away from the derision and scorn that seemed to be closing in around her and trying desperately not to stumble and cry.

She blindly made her way toward Orion. Jason and Hector silenced their fight as soon as she arrived.

"What happened?" Hector demanded when he saw her face.

"I got kicked off chorus," Helen said, laughing through a few stray tears that she couldn't seem to squelch. "Can we go now?"

She tried to bolt, but Hector caught her by the arm. "Why?" he asked, moving closer until his big body blotted out everything else.

"No one will sing with me because, apparently, I'm a pariah now."

Hector's eyes flared with anger, and he pulled her closer. She let her hands rest on his chest and he put his arms around her. His face drew close to hers.

"This is what I mean!" Jason shouted at them. Mostly at his brother, but Helen was included. "What do you think this will do to Lucas when he gets back tomorrow morning?"

"Jason—" Orion began in a rational tone.

"No, *you* don't get to say shit to me!" Jason threw off Ariadne's soothing hands. "Cassandra hasn't left her bedroom in two days because of you. Do you know what that's doing to my aunt? My whole family?"

"Jason, nothing's been happening between them, and I would know!" Ariadne declared, which made Helen feel even guiltier. Ariadne had not been with them the other morning. "Can we please just go and talk about this in private—"

But Jason didn't give Ariadne a chance to finish. He spun away from them with one last disappointed look for Hector and did not come back, even though they called after him. Claire had joined them silently during the argument.

"I'll go after him, Len," she said, patting Helen on the arm before chasing down Jason.

Helen rotated around, her mind in a fog of humiliation and disbelief. The entire chorus was staring at them with satisfied faces.

"I have to get out of here," she whispered, feeling panicky.

Orion took her by the elbow and steered her out.

. . .

Helen was vaguely aware of him putting her in a car and shutting the door, but she didn't really look at anything until they were nearly to the ocean. The long, dark walls of vegetation on either side of Surfside was a mottled shadow outside her window.

"It's happening. We're turning against each other, just like the Olympians want," she said hollowly.

"Yeah. Hector almost kissed you," Orion replied, his tone just as leaden.

Helen's head whipped around, and she gave him a falling look. "In front of everyone?" She knew Hector had his arms around her and she had her hands on his chest, she just hadn't realized he was going to kiss her.

Orion nodded. "He has no control over himself anymore. Jason's right. If Lucas had seen that..." he trailed off. "I told Hector he should stay away from you from now on."

Helen watched his profile as he drove. Each streetlight approached, lightened his features, burned them too brightly, and then slid off them reluctantly before the cycle started all over again. In every type of light, no matter how it shifted, it was a face that was precious to her.

"And what about you?" she asked him, though she wasn't sure what she wanted his answer to be. "How's *your* self-control?"

He graced the middle distance in front of him with a slow smile. "I think I found an ace up my sleeve."

She smiled with him. "What's that? Crippling guilt?"

"Guilt doesn't work. Shame doesn't work. Not against Eros."

"So, what is it?" she asked, curious.

His smile faded. "I can see your heart. I know how much you love Lucas." He glanced over at her surprised face. "And your love for him is even more beautiful than you are to me." He looked back at the road. "That's what's keeping me in line. For now."

Helen let the scenery whip by, thinking that even if Orion couldn't control hearts or shake the earth, he'd still be a god to her.

"Where are we going?" she said finally.

Orion's eyes sparkled. "Exactly where we both need to be."

They took one turn off Surfside and it was clear they were headed to the Delos compound.

"I asked Cassandra to stay away from you so she could make a prophecy," Helen reminded him as he parked.

"And she can go back to trying tomorrow after Lucas is home. For tonight, I think you and I need this," he replied.

Helen nodded reluctantly, her fingers threaded through the door handle. She didn't open it. Orion gave her a quizzical look.

Helen took a breath. "Every time I try to think of Lucas, I see Poseidon and it disgusts me. He disgusts me," she admitted in a rush. She looked over at Orion, terrified. "What if I don't love him anymore?"

His eyes rounded with sympathy. "You do," he said, opening his door. "It'll be okay."

They went in, calling out to announce their arrival, and found that only Cassandra was home. When she came downstairs, she looked confused for a moment but not displeased.

"What—are you doing here?" Cassandra asked haltingly.

"You need a night off as much as we do," Helen said. She saw no resentment towards her in Cassandra. How did she do it? How could she be treated so unfairly in life and not blame anyone, except maybe the Fates?

"Where is everyone?" Helen continued, flicking on lights in the dark kitchen.

"On dates," Cassandra said. "Mom and Dad went out to dinner, and Uncle Pallas is in Boston with Niobe."

"I can't believe they're hooking up." Helen said.

"Everyone's freaking out about it, except my mom. She's totally behind it," Cassandra replied, eyes narrowed thoughtfully over a smile.

"Your mom should have been House of Rome," Orion said from the refrigerator. "Niobe and Pallas are a great match."

"I think Hector and Ari are starting to get that. Jason's the only one who's angry," Cassandra said.

Helen's smiled faded. "He's pretty angry with us, too," she admitted quietly.

Cassandra nodded, like she already knew. Helen glanced over at Orion who was busy making himself a sandwich, and mouthed the word, *later.*

Helen eyed Cassandra warily, but she couldn't see anything in her heart that indicated jealousy or anger. She'd been hurt, but that pain paled in comparison to how happy she was just to watch Orion make a sandwich. All Cassandra wanted was to be near him.

Orion noticed the silence and glanced up and smiled at Cassandra. "Are you two talking about me?" he asked.

"We are *avoiding* talking about you," Helen clarified. "And you better be making me a sandwich, too."

"Make that three," Cassandra chimed in.

They ate and talked and laughed, until Orion announced that he had to do some homework or not even he would be able to charm his professors into passing him this semester.

"Homework. My Achilles heel," Helen groaned, but she dutifully followed Orion and Cassandra to the library, grabbing her backpack from the entryway.

She did her best to focus on her work, though every time she lifted her head, she saw Cassandra staring over the edge of her book at Orion so longingly it was like seeing Echo and Narcissus.

Which reminded Helen of Hera, who had been the one to curse Echo to never be able to say anything, but what had just been said to her. Which made Helen angry because Echo didn't deserve that. None of them deserved this. Cassandra certainly didn't. Lucas didn't. Helen put away her human homework and started randomly choosing Greek mythology books off the Delos' bookshelf to do some goddess homework.

There was a lot to slog through. She put one book away and took down another. What she was looking for was about the Titans, not the gods. Cronus had told her that her tasks were about his family, and that he wanted to save someone he loved from an unendurable punishment. Zeus' punishment.

"What are you reading?" Cassandra asked, intrigued. "Is that Hesiod's *Theogony*?" She tried to snatch the dusty, leather-bound tome out of Helen's hands, but Helen wouldn't let her take it.

"It's none of your beeswax, that's what it is," Helen replied with mock anger. "You go over there and read a romance novel like a normal person. Sheesh."

Cassandra laughed. "I don't think I've ever read a romance novel," she replied.

"Well, that's your fault not mine, now will you go away?" Helen laughed. "Look. It's highly possible that you will figure out what I'm trying to figure out before I do because you and your brother are freakishly intelligent, and then the fabric of reality will explode. Or whatever it is that fabric does when it... you know what I'm getting at, so stop laughing at my horrible metaphors."

Cassandra backed away from Helen with her hands held up, failing not to laugh. "Okay. I'll be over here if you need me."

"I don't need you," Helen said emphatically, but honestly, she really did need some help.

There were twelve Titans, and the Titans had the Hundred-handers and the Cyclopes as siblings. Zeus punished nearly all of them in horrific ways after he won the war between the Olympians and the Titans—called the Titanomachy—and then threw them in Tartarus. Prometheus—not a Titan, but the son of a Titan—was nailed to a mountain where every day an eagle ate his liver and every night it grew back. Atlas, the strongest immortal ever, was forced to carry the weight of the world. The Hundred Handers were ripped to shreds, and they had *helped* Zeus.

Helen got up and paced behind her chair, thinking. There didn't seem to be any logic to it. Zeus just did it to torture beings he thought were a threat to him and his power. It infuriated Helen because she knew her family would be treated just as harshly if she didn't win.

"Helen?"

"What?" Helen slapped the back of her chair in frustration, and ash flew up around her. White and papery, it floated around her, still curling, like it was alive and crawling through the air.

She pulled her hands away slowly and drew in the last of the lightning flashing over them. She'd burnt handprints into the back of the chair where she'd gripped it. She hastily patted out the remaining flames. Orion and Cassandra stared at her wide-eyed.

"Sorry," she mumbled. "I'm a little stressed out." She swallowed, scared of herself.

Cassandra shrugged. "Furniture comes and goes in this house. We'll deal with it tomorrow."

"I think we should go to bed," Orion suggested.

Helen glanced at the clock. They'd been studying for hours

and she was worn down. More than she should have been, probably. She gathered her things and started for the door, but Orion stopped her.

"We're sleeping here tonight," he told her. "All three of us."

Cassandra blushed furiously and glanced at Helen who didn't know what to say. She knew they couldn't be more than a few feet apart and that they needed a chaperone, but she didn't know why he insisted they stay at the Delos house. Orion didn't give them a chance to argue. He led them upstairs. Cassandra went to her room to get ready for bed while Helen balked, standing in the doorway of Lucas' room.

"Helen. It's okay," Orion said, taking her hand and leading her inside. He opened one of Lucas' dresser drawers and pulled out a t-shirt. "Here. Smell it," he told her.

Helen took the shirt and put her nose in it. All she smelled was Lucas.

Relief broke over her when Lucas' face stayed in her mind and was not replaced by Poseidon's. She narrowed her eyes at Orion, finally understanding why he had brought her here.

"How did you know that would work?" she asked him.

He gave her a small smile. "I know how *you* work. Smell is very important to you. I even had a dream about it. Then I remembered that Sunday morning," *the morning we fooled around* he seemed to add with his eyes, "I was wearing Lucas' clothes. I smelled like him."

Helen's brow pursed with conflicting thoughts. He had smelled like Lucas slightly, but that wasn't why she'd cheated. She'd done it because she'd wanted Orion, and the fact that he was wearing Lucas' clothes hadn't precipitated that want. She didn't get a chance to correct him. He took his turn in the bathroom first while Helen waited, sitting on the edge of a bed she knew nearly as well as her own.

Cassandra came and sat next to her, already in her pajamas. Helen took a deep breath but remembered her promise to Orion not to tell Cassandra and shut her mouth again.

"I know," Cassandra said, as if reading Helen's mind. She rolled her eyes. "At least one of us is making out with him."

Helen looked down. "What gave us away?"

Cassandra shrugged. "Kind of everything? I don't have to be House of Rome to figure it out. Neither of you are very good at hiding your emotions, you know."

Helen breathed a laugh and then became serious again. "It hurts you," she said simply.

Cassandra narrowed her eyes in thought. "It's not your fault."

Helen nodded and shrugged at the same time. "I'm just glad you don't hate me."

"I don't," Cassandra answered immediately. "I hate this." She gestured down at her undeveloped body. "I deserve to be a woman, but it's being kept from me by others who've decided what I should be. Why can't I be a woman on the outside if that's what I am on the inside?"

"You should," Helen said simply. She pressed all the sorrow and anger she felt into a tight little nut of purpose. "And we're going to do something about it."

She and Cassandra looked at each other at the same time.

"We will. I have foreseen it," Cassandra said.

"You made a prophecy?" Helen asked, turning toward her.

Cassandra shook her head. "The Fates are still shutting me out, but I had a vision. It's a little different from a prophecy. What I saw I don't understand yet."

"That's great!" Helen grabbed Cassandra's hands excitedly.

"This is what Antigone was talking about. You're seeing what the Fates don't want—"

"No, listen to me." Cassandra stilled Helen's grasping hands. "What I saw was like ... one part of a dream that doesn't fit with any other part of it. And after that, there's darkness. Forever."

Helen sat very still while she thought about it. "Darkness like you can't see the future anymore because you're free of the Fates, or darkness like there's nothing because we created a paradox and destroyed reality?"

"Darkness like fear." Cassandra was utterly motionless, as though there were monsters waiting at the edges of her body and if she turned even a hair's width, they would slip out of her shadow. "But I still want to do it. I still want to break fate."

Helen let out a long breath she'd been holding for them both. They heard Orion finishing up in the bathroom and coming to the door.

"Don't tell anyone," Cassandra whispered.

"I won't," Helen whispered back as Orion came out of the bathroom. She stood up and changed places with Orion while he sat down on the bed next to Cassandra.

"What's the matter?" he asked Cassandra. "You're scared."

"Because my dad is going to lose his mind when he sees us in here," she replied, laughing. Helen tried not to shudder at Cassandra's lie as she shut the door behind her.

She used the toothbrush she kept next to Lucas' in the rack. She washed her face with her soap and put on the moisturizer she liked to use before bed. So many of her things had crept into Lucas's house that it was almost like her own. She could have gone to his dresser and pulled out one of her own t-shirts as well, but she wore Lucas' to bed. Cassandra was under the covers and Orion had made a little bed for himself with pillows and blankets on the floor next to her. They were talking and laughing quietly.

"This is weird," Helen said, shaking her head as she got in on the other side of Cassandra. "And your dad is definitely going to freak out if he comes in here."

"No, he won't," Orion said confidently. "A few weeks ago, Castor and I had a long talk about..." he waved a hand over all three of them. "*This*."

Helen thought about that. "That's even weirder." They all laughed, mostly from nervousness.

"I'd really like to know what you and my dad said," Cassandra prodded.

"Too bad," Orion replied, like they'd already been through this. "But he trusts me. And so does Lucas."

Cassandra turned her head and smirked at Helen. "Chumps," she said.

Giggles turned to smiles, which turned to nervous glances. It was intensely strange to be sharing Lucas' bedroom with his little sister and Orion—and then it suddenly wasn't anymore. Helen realized Orion was using his talent to soothe them until they all drifted off to sleep.

Chapter 15

She didn't dream. She went from nothingness to feeling a hand gripping her shoulder. She wasn't startled. She just opened her eyes and Lucas was standing over her.

A glance to her left showed Helen that next to her Cassandra still slept curled up and turned away. Lucas' room was barely lit by gray dawn light.

She turned her head back to him and smiled, relieved that she saw only him and not Poseidon. She wanted him to lie down next to her and she lifted a hand to touch his chest, but he let go of her shoulder abruptly and stood back, gesturing with a tilt of his head for Helen to get out of bed and come with him.

She slid out from between the covers silently, her heart suddenly racing with anxiety. Lucas didn't look right. He wasn't angry—his heart was calm and even—but he wasn't happy to see her, either.

She followed him into his bathroom, and he shut the door.

They sat next to each other on the edge of his tub. Helen stared at him nervously.

"You're back," she said.

He nodded, barely smiling. Helen rolled her eyes at how stupid she sounded.

"How was it?" she tried again, and realized she sounded even worse. "Are you okay?"

"Yeah." His voice broke. "Sorry," he said, looking abashed as he cleared his throat quietly. "It's been a while since I've spoken."

Helen's face fell. "How long were you down there?"

Lucas looked at the floor, still smiling softly as he gripped his thighs. He shook his head quickly and looked at her. "How are you?"

Helen stared at him, frightened now. "How long, Lucas?" she asked.

He looked away. "I spoke to Morpheus after you visited him. He told me you can't be without your Shield anymore." Lucas tipped his chin at the door. "He explained why you can't talk about your final task with anyone else, so I won't ask if you've figured it out yet. I know you and Orion can do this."

Helen leaned away from him. Something was off about this entire situation. Lucas was stilted and distant, and treating her like he didn't know her. Or like he didn't want to know her.

"Are you making *small talk*? With *me*?" she asked disbelievingly. Her throat tightened around tears.

"I don't know what to say," he said. "I don't know where *we* are."

"Where we always are—I thought. I mean..." she trailed off and ran a hand across her forehead. "Did Morpheus tell you about Orion? Is that why you're acting like this?"

He shook his head. Not believing his denial, Helen continued more fervently, "I'm sorry! It was Eros, and it was stupid of us to stay in the same room that night, but I'm not supposed to be more than a few steps away from him, and I offered to sleep in the closet, but—"

Lucas grabbed her gesticulating hands to quiet her. "That's not it," he said, shaking his head, like she wasn't understanding him. "I kinda figured it was bound to happen."

"I'm so sorry, Lucas."

"I know." He let go of her wrists and moved away from her.

A horrible thought crossed Helen's mind. "You don't forgive me," she whispered.

He looked at her, finally with emotion in his eyes. Even if it was partly angry and a lot sad, it was less frightening than the detached way he had looked at her before.

"Of course, I do." He gave a short laugh. "I'm not going to lie. It doesn't feel great, but I told him I was okay with it. And it was so long ago."

"It was the day before yesterday," Helen said carefully, studying him. "How long were you down there?"

He nodded, accepting that he had to tell her now. "A year for every day."

"Three years?" She said, more to make it sink in for herself than for confirmation from him. His eyes fell into something only he could see for just a second and then he was back—or at least most of him was. She wondered if all of him would ever come back or if she'd keep on losing bits of him like this until there was nothing of her Lucas left.

"I'm just trying to get my bearings," he said. He turned his head to look directly at her for the first time. "Or figure out if I even should."

"What does *that* mean?" Helen asked, confused and little offended. Did he think she wasn't worth it anymore?

She saw a crack form in the wall around his heart—a wall she only just realized he had built, built over *years*—and too many emotions burst through it for Helen to keep track. Lucas struggled to keep his voice down as he spoke.

"So, I'm back," he whispered, biting his words, "and I spent a lot of time making myself not want to come back, because if I did want it, I would want it so much I wouldn't be able to make it. Three years. But I made it. And after all that, when I looked down at you sleeping in my bed, do you know what I realized would finally break me?" He begged her to understand with a look, and she was trying.

"What?" she whispered.

"Finding out that all that time I spent trying not to want you, you were doing the same thing about me. And that you were better at it."

Her father was right about one thing, she thought. Lucas *did* always make her cry. She wiped away the tears that were suddenly streaking down her face as she moved off the edge of the tub and knelt in front of him. He was stiff at first—reluctant to go to her as she put her arms around him. Undaunted, Helen held him, sealing herself against him until he finally gave himself up to her.

In one smooth motion Lucas tipped his chin under her jaw to push her face out of the crook of his neck, and caught her mouth with his. He took her weight in his arms as she went liquid, and crawled forward between her legs, lying her down under him.

He pulled away and hovered above her, looking down at her fearfully. "Have you ever been so hungry that you couldn't eat?" he asked through a shaky laugh.

"Yes," she whispered as she watched the thick walls he had

built inside come tumbling down, revealing the starving heart behind them. "Small bites." She eased his lips down to hers slowly.

They had only a few more seconds together before they heard an alarm clock go off somewhere and everyone in the house beginning to stir.

Helen groaned when he stilled. "Just lock the door," she begged.

Lucas thought about it, but finally pulled away and sat back on his heels. "They're going to come looking for me to see if I'm back," he said, smiling ruefully.

Helen covered her eyes with her hands, repressing a scream of frustration. She sighed and stood up, resigned to the near-constant interruptions, and took his hand as they left the bathroom.

Cassandra and Orion were sitting on the edge of Lucas' bed, side by side but not touching. Lucas looked between the two of them. "My dad is going to kill you," he told Orion.

Orion smiled back. "It's good to see you, too."

Cassandra studied her brother. "What is it?" she asked him, cocking her head as if she saw something Helen hadn't.

Without answering Cassandra, Lucas turned to Helen. "You and Orion should go to school. I'll meet you there later."

"But—" Helen said, keeping ahold of his hand.

"Later," he said quietly. "My family really needs me too."

"Okay," she agreed reluctantly.

"Come on, Cass," he said. He paused to kiss Helen on the forehead. "I'll see you in a few hours," he added, before leaving with his sister.

Helen sat down on Lucas' bed next to Orion. He glanced over

and down at Helen's chest and smirked, noticing the iridescent sparks and the red glow of lust.

"Lucas was supposed to take care of that, not make it worse," he commented.

"We didn't get a chance before someone's frigging alarm clock went off. As usual."

Orion frowned. "I've noticed you two have never—" he trailed off, raising an eyebrow.

"You can *tell* if people have slept together?" Helen was too stunned to beat around the bush.

"Yeah," he said, like it wasn't a good thing. "Can I ask you why you two haven't?"

Helen shrugged. "It's either the wrong place, wrong time, or we get interrupted. Or he's hiding some catastrophic secret and he needs to tell me first because the guilt would ruin it. You know. Normal teenaged stuff."

Orion didn't laugh at her joke. "So, what's wrong with now? What's keeping you apart this time?"

"Ah—his whole family waking up and barging in here any second?"

He gave her a look. "Helen, if you were *my* girlfriend, the only thing that could stop me from making love to you would be you."

It was too easy to picture making love to Orion. Helen felt something catch and turn over inside her. She stood abruptly. "Let's go to school," she said, bolting for the bathroom.

"Yeah," he agreed, also standing too quickly and too stiffly. "I'll wait here."

Helen shut the door and leaned against it, horrified by her own desires and how they could veer so violently and with so little provocation. She could still taste Lucas, and she was fantasizing about Orion. Clearly, Eros was not done with them.

"Have you noticed Eros waits until we're alone?" she said, half-laughing to dispel the tension.

She heard him laugh as well through the few inches of wood separating them. "No, I hadn't. But you're right." He paused. "How does he know when we're alone, though?"

"Good question."

"And how are we going to figure out what your last task is supposed to be *and* keep it a secret if we can never be alone?"

"Stop asking good questions." Helen threw up her hands. "I guess we just have to keep sucking it up."

"Great," he mumbled sarcastically. "Because that's easy."

They took turns getting ready for school, rushing as quickly as they could, though they had plenty of time. They rushed to stay busy and not allow their thoughts to stray to what they'd rather be doing. They heard Hector come home and call out to everyone, asking if Lucas was back, and then heard him join the rest of the family.

Orion barged into Hector's old room like it was his to borrow some of his clothes. They fit him a bit better than Lucas', and Helen was glad for that. She was confused enough as it was without him wearing Lucas' clothes on top of everything else.

They skipped breakfast. The whole family—Castor, Noel, Pallas, Cassandra, Ariadne, Jason, Hector, and Lucas—were in the library together with the door closed. Helen wavered as she passed it on her way to the car, wishing she could go in there with them, but Orion took her hand and led her outside.

"Let Lucas have time with them," he said.

"I know," Helen said, shivering as the cold ocean air hit her face.

Orion looked at her over the hood of the car, his brows pulling up in sympathy. "I always wanted what they have. My whole life." He gestured to the Delos compound. "This was my dream."

Helen knew he didn't mean the impressive piece of real estate.

"*We're* family," she told him.

It was early, an hour before the first bell. They headed into town to get breakfast at Kate's Cakes. Helen went to see her dad at the adjacent News Store and found him talking with people happily and smiling as he rang up customers.

Despite his obvious effort, Helen could tell her dad was struggling. He looked far more tired than he should have. She went behind the counter and gave him a long hug. Jerry hugged her back and didn't give her hard time about the fact that she'd slept out on a school night with only a quick text from her to inform him she'd be gone, which was not normal. And he barely acknowledged it when she said that Lucas was back.

"Great," was all he said, and then changed the subject. "Are you ever going to put your name on the schedule again, or should I just hire someone else?"

"No, I'll work tonight!" Helen promised. Then she glanced at Orion. "You can come in and work with me tonight, right?"

"Sure," Orion said in an offhand way and then went back to his conversation with Kate. She was making him taste samples of her wedding cake, which he did not mind in the least.

"I want the second to last layer to be crème brûlée, but I'm worried it's not going to share well," Kate was complaining.

"It's tough," Orion commiserated, "because you want to crack the crust on a crème brûlée yourself. That's the best part."

"Exactly!" Kate said. "But I want that flavor." She rushed off to tend to customers while Orion ate cake and sipped his latte—

completely at ease. The combined spaces of Kate's Cakes and the News Store ebbed and flowed with people, like a murmuring tide of steamed milk, coffee, and newspaper ink.

This was what Helen thought of as family. This bustling influx of regulars and newcomers in her father's store. It wasn't the traditional hearth and home and blood ties of the Delos family. It was more relaxed than that, maybe less secure as it changed from day to day, but it still had meaning.

Jerry finished a string of sales and closed the register. He leaned over the counter across from Helen. She moved closer to her dad and they smiled knowingly at each other.

"Go ahead and say it," she prompted resignedly. "Again."

Her dad couldn't help himself. "Orion is a really great guy. Maybe not mysterious and brooding like *some*," he said, stopping just shy of disparaging. "But I've always thought he's a better choice for you."

Helen hit her dad's elbow with her own. "Orion is a prince among men," she said like it was a given. "But he's not *my* man."

Her dad nudged her back over the counter. "He'd give anything to be your man. You know that, right?" Helen pursed her lips, trying not to let her dad sway her too much while he continued in a slower, more serious tone. "I get the appeal of someone with a dark, tortured soul. Your mother was like that. Full of secrets." Helen looked at her dad sharply and he gave her a wan smile. "Don't suffer for years when you've already got your Kate waiting right there. Trust me. It's not worth it."

He patted her hand and went to ring up another customer, leaving Helen to her disturbed thoughts. Orion had just asked her what it was that was keeping her and Lucas apart this time, and she hadn't had an answer. It had to be something inside of Lucas, and though it pained her, she had to consider that there might be something else that he was hiding from her.

Kate swirled back to the end of the News Store counter where Orion was happily serving as her guinea pig. "So, what am I going to do?" she asked.

Orion glared at the plates in front of him, thinking deeply. "Your bartender should make crème brûlée shots," he decided.

Kate looked like she'd been struck by lightning. "You're a genius!"

Orion raised his arms in exaggerated triumph. He spun around until he found Helen. "I won the wedding!" he declared, dropping his arms around her.

"You can't win a wedding," Helen said, laughing and pushing against his chest while her father watched them with a raised eyebrow. "You're going to make me late," she complained, suddenly angry with Orion because he made her laugh, and Lucas made her cry.

One of the Hamiltons' neighbors cleared her throat exaggeratedly behind them. "Well, excuse me," Mrs. Loughlin muttered, looking between Helen and Orion disapprovingly. She stepped up to Jerry's register, practically throwing her purchase down on the counter while she eyed Helen with a raised eyebrow.

"Hi, Mrs. Loughlin," Helen said uncertainly. "How are you today?"

Mrs. Loughlin looked Helen up and down. "And who is this? A new friend of yours?" she asked, emphasizing the word friend suggestively.

"Ah—no, actually. Orion is an old friend. You've never met him?" Helen replied, suddenly embarrassed. Mrs. Loughlin looked away haughtily, refusing the introduction, and Helen decided it was time to go.

They said quick goodbyes and headed for the door. Helen saw her dad sit heavily on the stool behind the counter as she and Orion left the News Store.

"That was judge-y," Orion said as they got in his car. "What does some middle-aged lady care who a teenager is hanging out with?"

Helen shook her head to bat the subject away. "Did my dad look pale to you?" she asked as they drove to school.

"Yeah. He did," Orion replied honestly.

Helen looked out the window and chewed her lower lip. Orion took her hand and held it until they pulled into the school parking lot.

"I wonder how many people are going to hate me here today," Helen grumbled.

"Buck up little camper," Orion said, grinning.

She laughed, but only so she didn't kiss him. She loved the movie he'd just quoted, *Better Off Dead.* It was her second favorite John Cusack movie after *Grosse Point Blank*—she loved it way more than *Say Anything.* Of course, Orion knew the exact order of her favorite John Cusack movies. But she wondered if Lucas did. They'd spent so much time either devastated that they couldn't be together, or rapturous that they'd been reunited, that they'd had little chance for any in-betweens. Lucas had asked her if she regretted that they'd never been a normal couple, and now for the first time, she really did because it meant that Lucas couldn't know that *Better Off Dead* was her second favorite John Cusack movie. And Orion did.

"Yeah. Sticks and stones, right?" She sighed as she hiked herself up by her mental bootstraps and walked confidently into school.

Sticks and stones would have been better than what Helen

faced. It was worse than she could have imagined, and she had a lot of experience with being hazed. Nasty looks followed her. Shoulders popped out of nowhere to knock into her as she walked down the hallway. People hissed vile things as they passed her, and Orion nearly got into a fight when a group of junior boys kept stepping in front of her as she tried to go through the door to her first class.

"Hey, Smellin' Helen," one of them said mockingly as he blocked her way again and she stumbled into him. "Excuse you," he sneered.

"Are you trying to go inside?" said the next kid as he took his friend's place, barring her from entering the classroom.

Orion draped one of his big arms around the shoulders of the next kid who tried to step in front of Helen, like the two of them were buddies.

"So, who am I going to beat the shit out of first? Is it you?" he asked casually, almost politely. The size of him, and the tightness of his smile, was enough to scare them off, but Helen was still shaken.

Lucas, Ariadne, and Jason arrived after second period, and Helen nearly cried with relief when she saw them. She and Orion met up with the family in the hallway. Lucas brushed Helen's lips with a quick kiss and a frown on his face.

"What is it?" he asked, worried.

Orion answered for her, describing the unusual amount of hostility leveled at Helen, even though he was doing everything in his power to sway people's hearts.

"Every time I turn a heart, it turns back to hating her twice as much," he finished.

Claire came running up as they all walked toward Helen's locker. "Thank god you guys are here," Claire said. "It's like a war zone in here today."

"Not just in here," Helen said, remembering Mrs. Loughlin. "The whole island is against me."

"It was bound to happen." Jason rolled his eyes at Helen and Orion. "You two have been acting like—" he broke off, wanting to say more. "Everyone's been talking about you two."

Helen saw a muscle jump in Lucas' jaw. "And have you stopped anyone from talking about them?" Lucas asked Jason. He sounded calm, but he wasn't, and Jason didn't need Orion and Helen's talent to read hearts to know it.

"No," Jason admitted tightly.

"Maybe you thought Helen getting shamed would help me somehow?" Lucas continued, still sounding perfectly calm, which was somehow much worse than his usually explosive temper.

Jason looked at his cousin cautiously, aware of how strangely Lucas was behaving. "No, I—" he broke off. Looking like he wanted to climb under a rock, he shook his head. "You're right. I should have stopped it," he ground out, very much like he was answering his father and not someone his own age.

Because Lucas wasn't acting like he was a teenager anymore, Helen realized. He acted much older, and as if he had become accustomed to having others answer to his authority.

She stared at Lucas' profile, wondering what his job in the Underworld entailed. Then everyone else stopped. She felt Lucas' hand tighten around hers and she turned her head to see what they were all staring at.

The word SLUT was spray-painted in bright red letters across the front of Helen's locker.

She couldn't take her eyes off it. She'd had the same locker for two years and she'd sort of moved in there. It was hers. Her locker. It was like a little capsule of Helen at Nantucket High and someone had taken that privacy, security, and familiarity away from her.

She held her breath. She couldn't allow herself to lose control or she could burn down the whole school, killing everyone in it. She stood very still and stared at her locker.

"Jason. Go to the office. Get Mr. Summerton, and bring him here," Lucas ordered quietly. Jason left at a jog.

"Helen? Are you okay?" Ariadne asked.

"Of *course* she's not okay," Claire hissed back at Ariadne angrily. "Lennie? Len!"

Claire's voice shook her out of her torpor.

"It's ruined," Helen whispered.

The bell rang. She didn't move.

"Ari. Claire. Go to class," Lucas said with quiet command.

Helen felt Claire and Ariadne squeeze her arm as they left, but she couldn't take her eyes off that word, or she knew she was going to lose whatever hold she had over her lightning.

Slut.

A part of her spinning mind wondered if it was possible to be a virgin and a slut at the same time. Another part wondered how it was that she felt dirty, simply because the word had been written about her. She'd kissed four boys in her entire life, and one of them was Matt playing spin the bottle when they were in middle school, which hardly counted. And Hector—that was just a crazy love bite, not a kiss. She was not a slut, and yet that word stuck to whomever it was thrown at, no matter how unjustly.

Jason arrived with Mr. Summerton, who immediately started making excuses about how this sort of thing never happened.

Lucas cut right to the heart of it. "We all know who's doing this. And you need to stop it."

"Did you see who did it? Are there witnesses?" Mr. Summerton asked, thrown on the defensive by Lucas' commanding tone.

Helen fought for control while she looked at the shiny red letters on her locker that were only half dried. On impulse, she reached out and touched them. Her fingers came away red, and she laughed mirthlessly. That word *did* stick.

"Do you pay attention to any of your students?" Lucas asked Mr. Summerton coolly.

Mr. Summerton was shocked silent. He visibly tried to remember that he was the one in charge here, though he wasn't. Lucas was.

"I have to wash my hands," Helen said suddenly. She held up her fingers, livid with red paint.

"Come on," Orion whispered to her. He looked at Lucas. "I'll stay with her."

Lucas nodded and turned back to Mr. Summerton. "You know Helen is being bullied. Ignoring it is the same as participating at this point."

"Now wait a *second—*" Mr. Summerton stammered. Helen and Orion turned the corner.

Even just twenty paces away from Lucas and Mr. Summerton, Helen and Orion were accosted by stares and sneers from the gathered crowd of students.

"I'm sorry, Helen. I can't stop them," Orion said in a low tone, pulling her tighter to his side as if he could physically protect her from the verbal assault.

Classmates hissed hideous things as they passed Helen. She looked at her hands, touching her fingers together and pulling them away from each other to feel the tackiness between them, like a tic. Their words kept sticking. Evil words that were worse than slut, though that one was repeated many times as they went down the hall. The red paint darkened to a rusty blood-brown that made her stomach turn. She felt lightning rising inside of her and stuffed it down. She didn't want to kill everyone in her high school. No matter what they said to her.

The closest bathroom was the one next to bio lab that smelled like fetal pigs. Suddenly disgusted with the dirty smear on her fingers, Helen felt like she wouldn't make it to another bathroom without vomiting.

"I'll be right here," Orion told her, standing guard outside while she went in.

She went directly to the sinks and scrubbed her hands with the harsh pink soap from the dispenser, but the paint left a stain.

"It'd be easier to peel off your skin than get that out," said a voice behind her. Helen looked up in the mirror and saw Gretchen behind her, inside one of the stalls. "Want some help with that?"

Helen turned off the water and looked at Gretchen's reflection carefully. She'd known Gretchen since first grade. The tilt of her head was wrong. The way she held her mouth was different. Even the way she stood was off.

"Hera," Helen said, turning to face her.

Hera-as-Gretchen feigned shock. "And they told me you were the dumb one."

"You can't hurt anyone here," Helen said calmly. "Zeus swore on the River Styx."

"Except you," Hera-as-Gretchen replied. "You're not part of the deal."

Helen smiled. "Go ahead. I'll even let you throw the first

punch." Hera-as-Gretchen's lips pursed, and Helen's smile turned into a laugh. "Not much of a fighter, are you? Yeah, I read that about you. You're weak. All you can sling is mud."

Hera-as-Gretchen took a step forward and her right hand dropped open at her side, like she was thinking of slapping Helen across the face. Helen shook her head *no*.

"You can't attack me, Hera. Because you can't get Gretchen injured. She's one of my mortals."

"You hate her," Hera-as-Gretchen snarled.

"I don't. She hates *me*," Helen corrected. "I always wished we could have been friends." She looked Hera up and down. "How did you do it? How did you get inside her?"

"She invited me in," Hera said derisively. "The goddess Ate barely had to use the power of delusion on her at all for me to take over her body. She hates you so much she *prayed* for a way to bring you down. I am the answer to her prayers."

It saddened Helen that someone she'd known for so long could hate her so much, but she wasn't about to let Hera see that. "Why don't you come out of that stall and tell me what your plan is? Are you going to slut-shame me some more? Is that all you've got?"

Hera-as-Gretchen chuffed. "You know, they used to stone women like you to death," she said.

Helen remembered a long-ago version of herself being stoned, and Hera's eyes widened, sensing she had gained purchase into Helen's fear.

"Morals are so lax nowadays, and loose women get away with their shameful crime, but the good people on your little island still have their limits about how much they'll tolerate from a woman before they punish her properly." She breezed past Helen on her way to the bathroom door and stopped there, turning back. "The most powerful woman in the world, even a goddess like yourself, can still be reduced to nothing simply by calling her one of two things: slut, or crazy. And people hate sluts the most. Even more than murderers."

She pulled open the door and swung through it, passing Orion who moved politely off the wall he was leaning against.

Furious, Helen rushed after her and stopped the door from closing. "You won't win this!" she yelled after Hera-as-Gretchen's retreating form.

"I already have," Hera-as-Gretchen called over her shoulder. She whirled around, walking backwards. "Once you've been marked, the stain never comes out." She spun back around, almost like she was dancing down the hall.

Helen looked down at her fingers. They were still red.

"What happened?" Orion demanded.

She took deep breaths, trying to calm herself down. Trying to keep her lightning from arcing down the hallway and frying Hera-as-Gretchen as she sauntered away with her head held high.

Helen was furious because she knew Hera was right. Her reputation was ruined, and she would never get it back. And she was furious because she saw how easy it was to tear down any woman, regardless of who she was or what she was trying to accomplish. Just call her a slut, and everyone hated her. *Hate*. Not the disapproval that men faced if they slept around or cheated—but hate. People hated sluts and they wanted to hurt them, but why? Because a woman had too much sex? Or she didn't have sex with the person she was "supposed" to have sex with? Helen had never even had sex, and she was still a slut because someone had called her that.

That word was a prison. Anyone could put any woman into it at any time. All they had to do was say it or paint it on a locker.

That word kept all women on parole regardless of whether they'd ever committed a crime or not. It weakened all women, and Helen finally understood that this weakening of women was quite often *because* of women like Hera. Because that was their only power, or so they perceived. They felt helpless, as Hera no doubt felt since she had no physical strength or particular gift among the Olympians, and she was saddled with a husband who cheated constantly. Hera's only power was to ruin other women, and there were so many disempowered women with internalized misogyny who, like her, had seized on this dysfunctional control to gain even one shred of power. She was a diseased goddess, jealous and hateful, but many women followed her because they thought it was the only way for them to obtain power. Women like Gretchen.

"Helen?" Orion asked, bringing her back to earth.

"That was Hera. *Wearing* Gretchen." Helen felt hate and fear for Gretchen in equal measures. She looked at Orion. "I think things are about to get very *torches-and-pitchforks* around here."

"Let's go," Orion said, seizing Helen's hand and striking out down the hallway, about to break into a run.

Lightning flashed in Helen's mind so bright and hot that it nearly sent her to her knees. She stumbled and pressed the heels of her hands into her temples. The pain was unbelievable.

"Helen!" Orion said, grabbing her shoulders and pushing his face close to hers.

"It's Zeus," she said in the halting way of a person trying to tiptoe around an internal pain, as if being careful and quiet could keep the pain from finding her.

"It's okay," he said soothingly. He held her bursting head against his chest while he looked up and down the hallways.

Then he tried to pick her up and run with her. Pain shot

through her, like something inside was tearing, and she screamed. Orion stopped immediately and put her down.

"Lucas. He can portal us out of here." Orion cradled Helen's head with one hand and sent Lucas a text with the other. He slid his phone into his back pocket and held Helen. "He's coming," Orion assured her.

He rocked her back and forth trying to help Helen manage the rolling pain that sent sweat prickling through her skin. And then she felt him go still.

"Shit," he breathed.

She managed to turn her head to the side to look down the hallway. Even though it was mid-period, and everyone should have been in classrooms, there were a few figures coming through the double doors at the end of the hallway. They were the same junior boys who had accosted her earlier, but now there was something different about them—something *off* about the way they walked. It took Helen a moment to register that they were walking strangely because they had swords buckled around their waists.

One of Orion's hands went to the back waistband of his jeans and returned holding a long, thin dagger with a wide, flat hilt at the base of the blade. A stiletto, Helen guessed. She looked up at Orion.

"You can't hurt them," she pleaded.

"These aren't your people," he said. "Not on the inside."

"Yeah, but on the *outside*—the part that can get killed—they're just kids."

Orion growled something profane, but he stowed the stiletto in the back of his jeans anyway.

"Stay here," he said needlessly, letting go of Helen. She couldn't stand without him and sank to the floor.

The storm in her mind continued to rage. She barely managed to keep herself propped up on her hands. Her eyes watered, and swaying above her locked arms, she had to keep blinking through the flashes of lightning and the blue-edged black spots of agony to see.

Orion met the junior boys halfway down the hallway. They pulled their swords from the sheathes at their hips. It was four to one, and Orion was empty handed, but he looked calm.

"Here comes a ready lad," the boy in the middle said, sounding not at all like a modern teenager.

"Ready whenever you are." Orion's voice was low and steady. "And who are you, again?" he added mockingly.

The boys passed a look between them before the one on the end replied, "We're the Machai."

Orion nodded. "Ah, the spirits of combat. I see." He laughed under his breath. "I know a guy who would give just about anything to fight you. He's going to be so jealous when I tell him how I kicked all your asses."

None of the Machai liked that.

"How can we fight? You're unarmed," the boy in the middle said.

Orion chuffed. "Not for much longer. I'm going to take *your* sword first."

Like a pressed spring suddenly released, the four Machai fell in on Orion at the same time. Orion did exactly what he said he was going to do. He slid past the boy in the middle, evading his first downward stroke, and as he stepped past Orion grabbed his wrist, twisted, and took the gladiolus out of his hand.

The four Machai spun around to find Orion behind them, holding up the taken sword like it was a bag he'd found left on a bus.

"Look at that," Orion bantered, obviously stalling, trying to throw them off balance.

"We just want the girl," the disarmed Machai said, like this situation was negotiable.

"And I just want to know, whose sword am I going to take next?" Orion asked, his lush upper lip ticking back in a feral, one-sided sneer to show an incisor.

The Machai were incensed by this, and again they rushed Orion as if they were one. This time they moved so quickly and with such precision that Helen cried out with fear. Then the hallway was suddenly plunged into darkness.

Helen saw Lucas' face, nearly phosphorescent in the disorienting blackness, strobe beside Orion's in a ghostly flash. Then they disappeared. Almost instantaneously, she felt an arm around her middle, and familiar lips brushing the outer curve of her ear. She felt the cold void of a portal ending all sight and sound.

Chapter 16

Helen had been to the palace in Hades before. She'd even been inside Persephone's Garden, a rarified place where only three others had ever been permitted. But for all the access she'd been given in the Underworld while Hades had tried to prepare her for her future as a Worldbuilder, she had never been in this particular room before.

Dressed in midnight blues and charcoal grays, and touched here and there with shroud-white draperies, the room stretched wide and high around her. The floors were dark, polished hardwood. Severe Doric columns made of black stone held up the tall, rib-vaulted ceiling. The furniture was oversized and thick, yet simple. Chairs so deep you could sleep in them, were amply padded with velvet cushions. Dressers, chests, side tables and bookcases were lacquered to a high gleam. There were no frills, no ornate carvings, yet everything was so lavish that it seemed to glimmer.

A four-poster bed draped in dark silk sat on one side of the room, and a wall of windows and French doors adorned the other. Outside the windows was a terrace, and beyond it an unruffled pool of water the size of a lake lay like a tranquil mirror to the night. Past that was an ever-expanding field under a sky so full of icy white-blue stars, galaxies in pale opalescent hues, and softly blushing nebula that it seemed to whirl and flow above her like a river of light.

Helen stared at the beauty of it. This had been Lucas' room for the past few years, and she'd never been in it before. She knew it was his because it smelled like him. It felt like him, too—but a different side of him. A side that was more formal, more rigid than the Lucas who played football with his cousins on the beach. More dignified than the Lucas who stole sips from her lemonade, and kisses from her lips in equal measures as they walked through downtown Nantucket on a summer evening after one of Helen's shifts at the News Store.

This Lucas she could envision wearing a crown. She had always known he'd been in there under the high school heartthrob in jeans and trendy sneakers, but here in Hades, this other, more regal Lucas, was out in the open. And she realized that although she'd always known he was there, she didn't really *know* this version of him at all.

"Are you still in pain?" Lucas asked. He held her shoulders between his hands as he crouched down on the floor next to her. They were somewhere in the middle of his vast room—or suite of rooms, now that Helen turned her head and took in the doorways that led out of this space.

"No," she replied, blinking. "Zeus has stopped. That's weird. Why would he stop?" She looked between Lucas and Orion, confused. They were on either side of her, and each supported an arm as she sat up.

"It must take everything he has to sustain a really big attack, and if his minions can't attack your body at the same time, it would be for nothing," Lucas said.

"Right," Helen replied, rubbing her forehead, and yawning wide to pop her ears. "So, he weakens me from within, making me vulnerable, and the small gods, or personifications of battle spirits or whatever they were, go for the kill." She looked at Orion sheepishly. "I'm sorry I told you not to hurt them. That was a little unfair of me."

He shrugged. "It's okay. I didn't want to kill them. They're just kids, with some nasty spirits inside."

"Which ones?" Lucas asked Orion.

Orion's lips tightened before he replied. "The Machai."

Lucas' eyes flared momentarily, and then he nodded like he was reassessing his strategy.

"And Hera was there, too," Orion continued. "She somehow entered Gretchen—"

"She used the spirit of Ate," Helen put in.

"Probably to confuse those kids enough that the Machai could enter them," Orion continued. "Hera spoke with Helen directly."

"Spoiler: We don't get along," Helen added dryly.

"What did she say?" Lucas asked.

Helen shook her head. "Not much. She just wanted to make sure I knew *she* was the one who was going to bring me down. She's vain like that."

She stood up from the floor, with a lot of help from Lucas and Orion, and let them lead her over to one of the deep, inviting club chairs. She sat heavily, realizing how close she'd come to visiting Hades as a spirit rather than a corporeal person. It was starting to dawn on her that she'd nearly died, and she was afraid.

Not just of dying, although that was enough to get her knees knocking, but of what her death would do to the world. Hera certainly would not be kind to women. Well, the women who survived getting raped by Zeus, Poseidon, and Apollo at any rate. The world could very easily go back to the way it had been, when slavery was a given and women were considered little better than animals.

Not that she hadn't been taking this seriously before, but it had seemed removed from her, like the inferno would magically burn itself out somehow if Helen kept stomping on the little fires that sprang up directly in her path. She shook her head at her foolishness. The fires were there to distract her from the inferno.

"I need to get rid of Zeus. Now," she said.

Orion and Lucas shared a look. "Shouldn't you heal first?" Lucas asked.

"I'm not injured, I'm angry," Helen began, but Lucas waved a hand and food appeared on the table nearest her chair. All her favorites were there. Even lasagna, the queen of pasta. She looked up at him. Scions couldn't make food appear. Only gods could do that in the worlds they controlled. Lucas really was Hades now.

"Still, it's lunchtime. You should probably eat and drink something," he said, smiling at her. A tall, thin glass appeared closest to her and began to fill with cold water that rose from the bottom of the glass as Lucas went to the door. Helen stared at it while fog condensed around what she knew would be frigid, pristine mountain spring water.

"Where are you going?" she asked.

"I have to attend to a few things," Lucas replied, standing in the open doorway. "Plus, I need to leave you two alone anyway so you can figure this out." He seemed to think of something sad. Then he forced a smile and left them.

"When did Lucas start using words like *attend*?" Orion asked, looking unsettled.

"I don't know," Helen replied, tiredly. "It's this place. I guess he can't take over Hades without becoming Hades in a way, too."

Orion looked at her consolingly. "Are you okay with that?"

"No," Helen said. "Not at all. Everyone changes, but he shouldn't have to change into someone else. Some*thing* else."

Orion looked out the window and seemed to drift off in thought. He turned back to her suddenly. "Wanna go for a swim?"

She smiled. "Yeah."

On a hunch, she went to the drawer in Lucas' enormous dresser that would have been hers if this were his dresser back home. Sure enough, there was a swimsuit in it. There was everything in it, really. Anything she could go to a drawer looking for was in there if she just lifted a few things and looked beneath. To test her theory, she imagined needing a ball gown, and found one right underneath a Red Sox t-shirt. She even found a pair of swim trunks for Orion in there. This place *was* Lucas, and he always found a way to give her what she needed.

"How'd you...?" Orion began, taking the swim trunks from Helen.

"Don't ask," she replied, heading to the bathroom.

Once changed, they went out through the French doors, across the terrace, and down to the mirror-pool. Helen dipped a toe in skeptically.

"No Poseidon here," Orion said, reading her fear. "No Eros, either," he added, smiling.

"Oh my god, you're right!" Helen said, clutching his arm and nearly shouting with relief. "I mean, you're still hot, but I don't feel like a four-year-old left alone with a marshmallow."

Orion burst out laughing.

They swam for a while and then floated on their backs side by side, gazing at the bright cosmic pinwheels above them in the ever-night sky of Hades.

"Who am I supposed to save?" she asked Lucas' stars. No answer came to her.

After the swim, Helen and Orion dried off and put on big, white terrycloth robes. They sat by the pool and food appeared. They ate it and talked about the Titans, but no answer came.

They went inside and changed. Neither of them were tired so they wandered around the palace, looking in rooms until they found a library. They read books about the gods and the Titans, and they talked again. More food appeared and they ate it, but still no answers came.

They decided they needed to take a walk. They went outside and wandered through a dark forest with old, wide trees that arched over a path lit with floating follow-me-lights in the air and glowing mushroom circles on the ground.

Then there was a river. Helen and Orion sat beside the river. They couldn't remember its name, only that they'd been to this river before, a long time ago, and that they had done something good for someone else there. But they couldn't remember what.

By the time they returned to Lucas' palace, they had talked about everything there was to talk about, both in the pantheon of Greek mythology and in their lives. They knew everything about their ancestors, and about each other. And still they had no answer.

Helen was sitting in a deep chair across from Orion, looking at the four-poster bed that was hung with dark silks and trying to remember the last time she'd slept, when Lucas appeared. She sat up in her chair and smiled at him, only realizing now that he'd been absent for a long time. He wore all black. It wasn't exactly a suit, but it was almost a suit. There was something about the precise fit of it that told her to keep her distance even as it made her want to come closer. He was so beautiful to her. Especially when he was sad and remote like a constellation hanging in the sky.

"Still nothing?" he asked, looking away from Helen and at Orion.

"Nothing," Orion said.

Lucas nodded. He was halfway across the room. Helen wondered why he didn't come closer. "I don't think you'll find the answer here, then," he said regretfully. "I tried to give you a safe place and as much time as I could to figure it out, but I should bring you both home. It's Friday afternoon now. Time for the Winter Choral."

Helen made a disbelieving sound. "It's Wednesday," she corrected.

Lucas shook his head, not looking at her. "You've been here much longer than you realize."

Helen thought back and counted all the meals she'd shared with Orion. Only two. Maybe three? They'd had a picnic in the woods. And later they'd climbed a tree and eaten apples. So, was it five or six? They'd picked berries, too, and there was that time they'd built a campfire and eaten s'mores. Was that seven. No. Eight?

Lucas came toward them finally. "Your dad and Kate know where you've been, and I told them that I'd have you back before the wedding. They haven't been worrying about you, or anything like that."

Helen blinked her eyes to focus them as Lucas took her hand. "Is it really Friday?" she asked him.

He drew her close and she felt like she was falling toward him. Falling in love with him all over again. She saw his eyes round with longing as she swayed closer to him. Why wasn't he kissing her, she wondered?

"It's Forever, Helen," he replied, shaking his head, and turning away. "It's always Forever with you."

Then, the cold of a portal snapped her out of her daze, and they were home.

Helen, Orion, and Lucas appeared outside the school. They were all dressed appropriately for an evening concert and wearing warm coats. Helen felt that her hair had been washed and blown out. She could even taste her favorite gloss on her lips. Lucas had dressed her and done her hair and makeup.

For some reason, that disturbed her, though if they had been exiting Everyland, Helen secretly had to admit she probably would have done the same for him. Clothing and makeup were just a thought away for a Worldbuilder—it's not like Lucas had bathed her and Orion by hand. Still, it bothered her, and a glance at Orion and the creeped-out expression on his face told her that he felt the same. It was unsettling to be controlled by a god, even if you trusted him. Helen couldn't help but recall how Matt had looked at her with so much mistrust and disappointment after she'd built Everyland. She had no longer been herself. Like Lucas was no longer himself.

The Delos family joined them. Hector was with them, and he stopped short when his eyes met Helen's, guilt visibly flooding him. While everyone exchanged greetings, Hector tried to avoid Helen without *looking* like he was avoiding her. Which was so painfully obvious she was relieved when she noticed Orion brush the inside of Hector's wrist to ease his overwrought emotions. Hector lived his life with his heart on his sleeve, which was usually annoying, sometimes endearing, and in this situation, problematic. But Lucas seemed not to notice. Or if he did, he chose not to react to it.

"I'm going to go look for my dad," Helen said, turning away from Lucas. She was annoyed with him. He wasn't acting like himself—or maybe this was himself. The new, emotionally switched-off Lucas who didn't care if Hector was attracted to her. That annoyed her even more because it was better for her to be annoyed with him than heartbroken.

"Oh—Helen. Your dad and Kate aren't coming," Noel told her.

Helen was surprised. They were going to miss Claire's solo. "Why? Where are they?" she asked.

"Kate's family arrived for the wedding. They're at our house getting things ready for tomorrow's big day, and your dad is at home resting."

"Is he okay?" Helen had a bad feeling.

"They were showing Kate's family around the island all day," Noel explained. "He was exhausted."

"Claire already knows they can't come," Jason assured her.

Helen didn't know what to do with herself. She understood about Kate not coming but Claire was basically Jerry's second daughter. A year ago, her dad never would have missed something like this. It's not like he was eighty. The fact that he needed to rest meant that he was more than a little rundown. He was sick. She felt a hand on her arm and startled.

"Let's go," Lucas said close to her ear. "It's going to start soon."

Helen allowed Lucas to draw her alongside, but she noticed

that he didn't say it was going to be okay. Lucas always told her it was going to be okay.

Castor and Pallas went first. Orion fell in on Helen's other side, and Hector stayed close behind her as they entered the school. Ariadne and Jason flanked Cassandra and Noel, who had formed a small, tight cluster in Hector's shadow. Helen realized they were in formation.

"Do you think the Machai will be here?" she whispered to Lucas.

He nodded. "And Hera and Ate and whoever else the Olympians have recruited. But I doubt they'll try anything," he said, his lips pursed with satisfaction.

"Yeah?" Helen asked, a smile breaking across her face. "How do you figure that?"

Lucas glanced at her sidelong and stilled the smile that wanted to answer hers. "Have you ever heard of Hades joining the field in battle?" he asked.

"No," Helen replied, and then off a look from Lucas, she considered why. "How can anyone beat Death?"

"Right," Lucas said. Then he added, "And if any god managed to defeat Hades, there would still be dead souls to tend to, and the victor would inherit them."

As they entered the auditorium every head turned. Helen could see that the accusing eyes sparked with otherworldly spirits. She could name them all, after spending days (or had it been weeks?) in Lucas' library in Hades. She recognized Pheme, the spirit of rumor, and Ate, the spirit of delusion and ruin. The Machai, the spirits of combat, were there with Alastor, the spirit of blood feuds and vengeance, and Lyssa, the spirit of rage. Ancient personifications were inhabiting people she had known her whole life, but only because they had allowed it. In the *Iliad* when the great warriors were described fighting with one of the Olympians beside them, it was a euphemism for being partially possessed by that god.

The town was possessed, and it had turned on Helen. Yet, they kept their seats even as they seethed.

"It's okay. No one wants my job. As long as I'm with you they won't attack," Lucas continued quietly as they walked past baleful glares. "We've won this battle."

Helen's throat tightened as they took their seats. They had only won it because Lucas was Hades. "A pyrrhic victory," she said, the words hurting her chest as she forced them out.

He tipped his head close to hers as the audience lights came down and the stage lights went up. "Not to me," he said. He brushed his lips across hers in one of those brief, fluttering kisses he gave her when they said goodbye, then turned his head abruptly to the stage.

Before Mr. Abebe could wave his hand in the downstroke to start the singing, the auditorium doors opened with a squeak that pierced the silence. A man jogged down the aisle waving his hands and apologizing for the interruption.

"So sorry I'm late!' he said, clasping his hands in a dramatic plea. He looked like a young, hip version of Santa in cool clothes. His eyes twinkled merrily. "But this place desperately needs a little cheer!"

"Who the hell is *that*?" Hector said behind Helen.

She turned around. "I think that's Kate's bartender for the wedding tomorrow," she guessed. "Is it weird that he's at a high school choral concert?" she asked the family.

Orion and Hector shared an *I don't know, do you?* look and shrugged simultaneously. Lucas had no reaction. He just watched the presumed bartender carefully.

The bartender looked dapper, but he behaved like a clown. He climbed over the stiff-backed junior boys who were inhabited by the Machai and almost sat on a girl who was overcome by Pheme, as he made his way down a row. Annoyed glances turned to amused smiles as he bumbled and apologized his way to very middle of the row in the very middle of the room.

"Sorry! Please continue," he called out to Mr. Abebe once his stylishly clad body was folded into a seat.

Mr. Abebe lifted his arms again, and there was the sound of a can pop-hissing as it was opened. Mr. Abebe turned back to the bartender, who was sipping at an overflowing drink.

"It's a sparkling rosé. It just got a little shook up in my pocket. Please. Continue!"

Helen took a breath to comment on the fact that he was clearly drinking an adult beverage on school grounds, and no one was stopping him, when the singing began.

It was marvelous. She had heard every song dozens of times already in rehearsal, but there was something special about this performance. The music swept her away, causing her to completely forget about her troubles. She listened with a glow suffusing her body, and felt Lucas take her hand and rub her fingers as the chorus recreated the feeling of sleigh rides and warm fires and snowy-night magic with their voices.

Claire brought the house down with her solo. There wasn't a dry eye to be found, and as everyone jumped up to give her a standing ovation, the funny bartender screamed *Brava* like a madman, as he waved a bottle over his head and poured champagne into crystal flutes that had appeared in the hands of everyone present. Even Helen had a sip as she chanted in unison with the rest of the audience for Claire to grace them with an encore.

When Claire reappeared in front of the empty risers and sang a killer duet with Mr. Abebe, it was the most elated Helen had felt since the first time Lucas had taken her flying. She met Lucas' blue gaze and mused that her first lesson in flying had been her greatest lesson in falling.

"It's nearly midnight. I have to go," he whispered, which confused her. How could it be midnight? Then he gave her a brief kiss. Helen tried to catch his face and kiss him longer, but he detached himself with a sad smile and put her hand in Orion's. "I'll see you at the wedding," he said. And then he disappeared, leaving nothing but a ring of frost on the floor.

"Come on," Orion said in Helen's ear.

Nearly everyone had left the auditorium. Only a few cheerful stragglers were left who were enjoying the dregs of the night. There was a festive feeling in the air, even though Helen wished she could have shared more of it with Lucas. Claire and Jason were tucked into a dark corner, gazing lovingly into each other's eyes in between kisses.

Ariadne and Cassandra were talking with several flushed-cheeked mortal boys and one girl who obviously had a crush on Ariadne. They were begging them to come out for a little longer —it was *Christmas*, after all, the mortals pleaded—until Ariadne and Cassandra finally agreed. They waved goodbye to their parents as they left. It was the first time Helen had seen Ariadne seem interested in anyone since Matt, and she elbowed Orion and pointed at them excitedly.

"Yeah, I saw," Orion said. Then he frowned. "Cassandra's going out, too." He watched her leave with a mortal boy at her side.

"She's with Ariadne. She'll be fine." Helen looked at Orion's heart and found a strange off-beat rhythm to it. "You're not upset, are you?"

"No, I'm..." he broke off, thinking about it.

Hector interrupted. "Can you figure it out while you help me break down all these risers?" he complained. "Claire asked me to help her and then she and Jason took off."

Hector, Orion, and Helen were now the only ones left in the auditorium, and no one had bothered to strike the set or put anything away before they left to have holiday fun. At least since they were alone, they didn't shy away from using their Scion strength and speed to put all the risers together and pile them on Hector's back.

"I feel like Atlas. Where am I going with this?" he asked from underneath his impossible burden.

"Backstage," Helen directed. She frowned as he walked the huge stack up the stage steps. "Wait—you'll have to reposition, or you'll never make it around the corner without pulling the curtain down," she warned him.

"Okay," Hector said obligingly, sliding the burden off his back as he got onstage.

He braced the stack of risers on the nearest solid object, which happened to be a rock from the set of the long-sidelined *A Midsummer Night's Dream and* chuckled to himself.

"Have they ever made a play about Atlas?" he asked. "Or would that be boring because all he does is hold up the universe. Which must *suck*." He took up the risers again across his wide shoulders. "Worst torture ever if you ask me. And fun fact? He's *still* supposed to be there."

Helen felt a falling sensation inside. She looked at Orion and saw what she felt echoed on his face. Hector continued talking as he brought the risers backstage and placed them behind the scrim curtain.

"Did you guys know that all the other Titans were freed from their punishments, but not Atlas, and you know why? Zeus is afraid of him. Because Atlas is the strongest immortal ever, and Zeus knew he was the only one who could beat him."

"It's Atlas," Helen whispered. Orion nodded.

"I'd frigging *love* to throw down with Atlas, just to see where I rank, you know what I mean?" Hector placed the risers behind the scrim curtain. He brushed his hands together, smiling as he turned towards them. "What's going on? Are you guys whispering about Helen's task?" he asked, joking at first, but his expression fell as he watched Helen and Orion freeze and look at each other with raised brows. "You are, aren't you?"

Orion rolled his eyes. "How can you be both so insightful and so oblivious at the same time?" He turned to Helen. "What do we do?"

"He'll just have to come with us until the task is completed," she said, shrugging.

"Where are we going?" Hector asked, game for whatever dangerous task awaited.

"The Underworld," Orion said. "We've got to get to Cronus."

"Oh." Hector looked less than enthusiastic. After a moment of quiet reflection he asked, "So, the task is about Atlas?"

"Yes," Helen said. She was sure. "Cronus has set this whole thing up with Hecate to end Atlas' suffering."

"How, though?" Orion asked. "He's literally the only one strong enough to hold up the heavens. We can't free him if it means ending the world."

Helen smiled to herself, nodding as other things clicked into place. "I know. But maybe he's not the strongest thing in the universe."

"Yeah, he is," Hector said dismissively. There was obviously some hero worship going on there.

"Strongest *being*, sure," Helen allowed. "But not the strongest *thing*."

"Whatever. How are we getting to the Underworld anyway?" Hector asked.

"Your house," Orion told him, holding up the golden cuff around his wrist. "Lucas' coming and going has created a thin spot between there and the Underworld that I can access."

"That's not freaky at all," Hector mumbled, disturbed.

"Come on," Helen said, breaking the somber silence. "Let's get this over with."

They took Hector's car and parked outside the Delos compound. It started to snow. They got out of the car but didn't go inside the house; instead, they walked around to the back where it had been transformed with heated tents adorned with red velvet and holly trimming and glowing with a million little white Christmas lights for the wedding the next day. Helen couldn't help but pull in a little gasp at how beautiful it looked.

"How do we get down to the portal?" Hector asked Orion.

Orion looked around at the pristine wedding setup and ran a hand through his long hair. "Kate is not going to like this," he said, grimacing, and then he spread his hands wide, and the ground opened.

"Oh no!" Helen exclaimed, jumping back as a series of dirt stairs formed, leading down underground.

"What did you do!?" she demanded, although she could see

perfectly well what he'd done. "There's a huge pit in the middle of what's supposed to be the aisle! What's Kate going to do? Jump over it?"

"I'll fix it when we get back," Orion promised, taking Helen's hand and pulling her down the stairs after him.

"It'll still look awful," Helen complained.

"Maybe the snow will cover it," Orion said hopefully. "Or we could put a tarp down."

"A *tarp*?" Helen glared at him through the last of the aboveground light that was reaching them underground when she realized that Hector wasn't following them. She called up to him. "What's the matter? Forget your keys?"

Hector rubbed his palms on his thighs. Helen had never seen him do that before, and she realized it was because he was scared.

She'd never, in any iteration of her and him, seen him scared. She went back up the earthen steps.

He laughed nervously. "This is stupid, but the last time I was in the Underworld, I—"

"You were dead," she finished softly. She took his wrist between her fingertips and used her talent to stave off some of his fear. "What did you see?"

A pained look crossed his face. "There were three old men, and three young girls—who weren't really young at all—just standing there, watching me. And I remember Luke arguing with Hades. And I saw my heart being weighed."

"It's so big it must have broken the scales," Helen said in a gentle tone.

Hector raised his eyes and smiled at her. He shook his head. "No." He swallowed hard. "It looked too small."

There was a loaded silence.

"Must have been your brain then," Orion said, and they all burst out laughing.

Helen pulled Hector nearer. It was unnatural for him to be afraid, and she refused to allow it to continue. "Come on," she said. Then she grimaced at him apologetically. "I really need you."

"You do?" he asked tentatively, like he was flattered.

"Yeah. I may need you to hold up the universe—but just for a second."

"W-wait, what?" Hector stammered, but she pulled him down the steps before he had a chance to overthink it.

"Where is this portal supposed to be, anyway?" Helen asked Orion, though needlessly. She felt the aching cold before she was done speaking and saw an earthen wall, sparkling with permafrost, standing before them.

Orion shook his wrist with the cuff on it, and from underneath his coat, a branch with green leaves snaked out and weaved over his hand as it grew toward the sparkling wall. With his other hand, Orion reached back to touch both Helen and Hector, and brought them with him through the freezing cold portal and into the Underworld.

Chapter 17

They appeared in the Fields of Asphodels, but it wasn't as Helen remembered it. The Underworld was now lit by Lucas' bright constellations and swirling nebulae that floated across the night in stunning contrast to the cold, implacable pinpricks that had hung stationary in Hades' sky. In the distance, Helen could see the shadowy shape of Lucas' palace and the occasional silver shimmer off his enormous mirror pool.

Hector revolved in a circle, his jaw slack as he took in the nightscape around him. "Wow," he said with his usual economy for words.

"Which way?" Orion asked.

"Cronus' olive tree is in Elysium, on the other side of the River of Joy," Helen said, still staring at Lucas' palace. She wondered how long he had been there since leaving her an hour ago. Months? She noticed there was a long pause, and she shook herself. "This way," she said, striking out in the opposite direction from the palace.

Although time was impossible to gauge accurately in Hades, it didn't feel like long to Helen before she could hear the sound of rushing water. When they reached the banks of the River of Joy, the ever-night of Hades gave way to dawn that they stepped into like a painting. Distance was a relative thing in the Underworld, and they were crossing the bridge into the midday light of Elysium before it was chronologically possible. A smile turned up the corners of Helen's mouth when she considered that Lucas was helping them along. He could feel her in his world as surely as she could feel him in hers. *Thanks,* she thought, wondering if he could hear her.

In two steps they were standing in Cronus' grove. The Titan sat cross-legged under his olive tree with the Omphalos resting beside him. Even sitting Cronus was huge, and the air seemed to whir around him like he took up more than three-dimensional space. He opened his galaxy eyes and Hector and Orion startled at the sight of them.

"It's always good to see you, grandchildren," Cronus said warmly.

"And you, grandfather," Helen said. "I think I've figured it out."

"You always had done," Cronus replied.

Helen let out a frustrated breath. "Here's the thing that's bothering me. If I had always figured out that the Omphalos can shape-shift to appear to be anything—like it appeared to be a baby when you swallowed it—why does Atlas have to suffer so long?" she asked.

Cronus smiled. "He will not have done. *When* you change the Omphalos for Atlas only matters for one thing. The Omphalos cannot speak." His face fell. "But granddaughter. You must know when you want to go."

Helen grabbed Orion's arm and shook it, like that could jog his brain. "Didn't someone go visit Atlas? In some trial? What was it that we read?"

"Herakles," Hector said. Helen and Orion turned to him in surprise. "The last hero to speak to Atlas was Herakles," he added with certainty. He glanced at Helen sidelong. "I had a thing for him when I was little."

Helen turned back to Cronus; her cheeks flushed with victory. "Then that's when we want to go. Right after Herakles leaves Atlas."

Cronus smiled and nodded at Hector. "Ready yourself, grandson. The weight of the world changes you."

Hector was so eager to see where he fit into the lineup of heroes he was practically vibrating with anticipation. "I'm ready."

Cronus gave a deep laugh before they were thrown into the cold senselessness of a portal.

The first thing Helen heard was the staccato burst of a labored breath. The first thing she felt was the gritty cut of flint under her hands and knees. The light around her was tinny-blue and thin, and the air was chilled and dry. Her ears popped like she was in an airplane. The sound of grunting, panting, and straining came and went in bursts between silences that seemed to shake with tortured exertion.

Helen pushed against the rocks, scraping herself, and noticed she was wearing a formal chiton tied about her body in many layers. She shielded her eyes from the raw light and sucked at the thin air of high altitude. The sun was eclipsed by a leviathan figure.

She saw Atlas lit from behind in the merciless mountain light

—his bulging muscles, and the impossible size of him. Above him was nothing but air, and yet he bent under it. Every fiber in his body seemed on the edge of snapping, and each breath was the desperate gulp of a suffocating fish left to die on a beach.

Beside her, Helen heard Orion and Hector gasping for air as well. The three of them helped to right each other on the unstable and razor-sharp rocks, spotted here and there with snow, with nothing but sandals to keep out the worst of the abuse to their feet. They wore knee-length men's *chitons* that were tied about the waist and over one shoulder, leaving half their torsos bare.

"This is a nightmare," Orion said, blinking against the cold, piercing light of the sun, and trying to steady his breathing.

"The Omphalos!" Helen cried, searching everywhere for it among all the other bits of rubble.

"I think this is it," Hector said in between pants.

Helen took one last breath, willing it to provide enough oxygen, and steadied herself. Stooping to pick up the Omphalos, she lifted and carried it toward the longest-suffering Titan. Helen hardly came up to his waist. She put the Omphalos down beside him.

"Who are you?" the Titan groaned.

"Heroes," Hector replied. Helen shot him a look and he shrugged. But, traditionally, that's what the half-human children of the gods were called.

"We've come to end your punishment," Orion said, sounding like he could hardly bear to watch it any longer.

The Titan ventured a glance up at them. "There is no end," he said, blinking at the sweat running into his eyes.

Helen moved the Omphalos so Atlas could see it without moving his head. "Do you recognize that?" she asked.

He gave a ragged laugh. "The Navel of the World," he said.

"The strongest thing in the universe—the only thing strong enough to take your place," she said.

"Only one problem. It must be placed precisely where I stand or the mountain under it will topple over time. How do you propose to do that?" Atlas asked, his voice tinged with desperation.

Helen, Orion, and Hector shared a look.

"I think this is where I come in," Hector said. He picked a nearby spot that looked relatively flat and clearing some of the scree away as best he could. "I'll stand here. You shift the weight of the universe to me for a moment, while Helen and Orion get the Omphalos in the right place."

Atlas seemed to wilt a little under his burden.

"I thank you, but you will surely die, brave hero," he informed Hector. "I can look at a man and know his strength, and I can see that you are mighty. But you are not as strong as Herakles, and this weight nearly killed him."

"I'll help," Helen said. "Orion, you take care of the Omphalos."

"No," Hector and Orion said at the same time.

"I'm stronger than both of you put together," she informed them. She eyed the Titan. "Aren't I?"

He labored to position his head so that he could see all of her. "She is," he declared. "Are you a goddess?"

"Sort of," Helen admitted as she positioned herself next to Hector.

"Still. I do not think you will be strong enough," Atlas said somberly.

"You're not the first to underestimate me," Helen said.

Atlas grunted and strained. "You have heart, young heroes. Perhaps that will be enough."

Orion picked up the Omphalos. "Wait—how do I make this rock turn into you?" he asked Atlas.

"It will become what you need it to be," the Titan said calmly. He gritted his teeth and looked at Hector and Helen. "We must not shake the universe in the transfer. Even the slightest wobble will cause earthquakes like the world has never known."

"Now he tells us," Hector muttered as he re-tied his chiton, wrapping it tightly around his lower back and belly like a weight-lifter's belt.

Helen did the same and took a few deep breaths, trying to force oxygen into her starved muscles. It briefly occurred to her that she should get the Titan's promise to help her defeat Zeus now before she took his burden, but then she decided against it. She wasn't going to charge for her help, or try to trick another god into owing her a favor. That was *their* way. She was going to do things differently.

"Ready," she said, standing shoulder to shoulder with Hector, her arms raised above her head.

She saw Atlas tilt his hands and shoulders ever so subtly, and then she felt an already impossible weight become heavier and heavier, until she thought that her back would snap, and her knees would buckle.

Bent nearly double with the weight of the world on her back, she felt like she had been put into an enormous vice as she was pressed between heaven and earth. She felt Hector's shoulder butting up against hers, rock solid but shaking with strain, and she heard his breath grating in and out of him with surprised, shallow barks. It was agony.

Atlas gave a gusty sigh and Helen saw his feet kicking rocks this way and that as he staggered on numb legs to get out of Orion's way.

She felt something pop inside her head and a drop of blood splashed down on the white chiton covering her shaking legs. "Hurry," she groaned.

"IknowIknowIknow!" Orion chanted with mounting urgency. "Okay! The Omphalos is in place!"

Helen heard Atlas' voice near her head. "I will help you guide the universe onto its pedestal. Gently. Like you're putting a baby down to sleep."

She was almost too afraid to move for fear that half the world's cities would crumble due to her haste to free herself from her intolerable burden.

And then it was over. The weight lifted, and she collapsed onto the ground.

Hector fell next to her, rocking back and forth, making a strained sound. "Definitely... not as strong... as Herakles," he said between gasps.

"Herakles held the universe for half as long as you did," Atlas said with the hint of a smile in his voice. "You carried half of it for twice as long, therefore, I surmise that you *are* as strong as Herakles, young hero."

Helen couldn't even joke with him. Her belly hurt too much. Orion came and knelt between her and Hector, smoothing her hair, and asking, "Why is she bleeding?"

"I think she took most of the weight," Hector wheezed.

"You're bleeding too, you know," Orion informed him.

Helen rocked onto her side and saw Atlas on his knees, hands braced against his thighs as he panted, still recovering.

"Thank you," Atlas whispered, just for her.

Helen swallowed the blood she could taste in her mouth and nodded. She noticed that her vision had a blurry, pink tinge to it. She could barely make out the figure of Atlas behind the real

Atlas. The Omphalos really did look exactly like him. It even grunted and strained against the air as he had.

"I have to get them home. Is there a way back to Cronus?" Orion asked.

"I can bring you to my brother," Atlas said. "They should not stand or walk for the time being, for they have injured their insides. You carry your goddess. I'll take the hero."

Helen blinked repeatedly to clear the pink goo from her eyes so she could see what was happening, but her vision came and went like the tide. Like a heartbeat. She realized that her eyes must be bleeding. She saw glimpses of high peaks and low valleys as Orion carried her a short distance, following Atlas who held Hector in his arms as if he were a toddler.

"Where are we?" Helen asked blearily.

Orion chuckled. "I've actually been here before. It's the highest peak of the Atlas Mountains in Morocco, I think," he replied.

"That makes sense," she mumbled back, and then she felt the frigid sear of a portal.

"Brother. Grandchildren. I am always happy to see you," Cronus said expansively. "Brother, you will have remained with me for all this time. Grandchildren, you were eagerly awaited *when* you belong."

They all assumed rightly that was Cronus' way of saying that they had to move things along. Atlas put Hector down next to Orion and Helen.

"For eons I have been blasted by winds, struck by lightning, frozen by snow and ice, starved for air, and crushed beneath the weight of the world atop that mountain. I cannot tell you the suffering you have spared me," he said solemnly.

"I might have an idea," Hector groaned.

There was a brief pause, and then Atlas' deep laugh filled the olive grove. "I like these grandchildren of yours, brother!" he decided merrily.

"They are eternally amusing," Cronus agreed. "But they must go now. There is one who senses the passing of time in the Underworld no matter when it is, and he is most upset. Well done, grandchildren," Cronus said quietly, and Helen felt another flash of cold.

Lucas was shouting at someone. They were still in Cronus' olive grove. They had not moved in space, but in time.

"...her name on the List of the Dead was never part of the bargain!" he was saying. "Helen!" His tone changed suddenly.

She felt hands trying to tug her out of Orion's arms and she moaned in complaint.

"Stop, Lucas!" Orion ordered. "Let me put her down first."

Helen felt her head being held by cool hands as she was gently placed on the grass. She blinked away the pink goo until she could see Lucas' worried face break into a smile above hers.

"Hey," he said, his expression soft and hopeful. "You're alive."

"Huh," Helen replied, like she wasn't sure about that.

His gaze ran over her face and body, and he tried to hide how upset he was, but couldn't.

"That bad?" she asked.

"You don't look so great," he admitted.

"I got squashed like a bug." She shut her eyes. It hurt to make them focus. "I'll be okay."

Lucas turned away from her to check on Hector. She heard their low, rumbling banter and mentally smiled. Even if she didn't have the energy to make out what they were saying, she knew Lucas and Hector were harassing each other in a brotherly way, as always.

"It is good to see you again, my saviors," Atlas said as he joined them. Actually, Helen considered that Atlas had probably been there with Cronus all along. Cronus did say Helen had always figured it out.

Helen kept her eyes closed and waved at him. She heard Hector and Orion give him confused hellos. They'd just said goodbye, after all, even if it had been millennia since Atlas had seen them.

She felt Lucas stand and step away before announcing, "Helen's three tasks have been completed."

"They have always been," said Cronus.

"And for these thousands of years I have been unendingly grateful," Atlas added humbly.

"Yes, but is she released from her debt?" Lucas pressed. There was a moment of tense silence. "Hecate!" Lucas called, summoning her with a ringing voice.

Helen saw a flash of orange light on the other side of her eyes and peeled them open to find the goddess standing to the right of Cronus, while Atlas stood to his left. Helen found she was no longer seeing red, and that she was able to prop herself up into a seated position with a little help from Orion.

"Is Helen freed from her debt to you?" Lucas asked the Witch Titan.

Hecate's lips were pursed in annoyance. Helen noticed her annoyance was directed at Cronus. "She is. Though what is most needed for her to do is still left undone."

"Patience," Cronus told Hecate. "This is but the first step of many for the young goddess."

Hecate had to content herself with that. "I release you, Helen Hamilton. Though we are far from finished." she promised.

"Wait—what about Zeus?" Orion asked Hecate. "You promised that the Titan we freed could help Helen in return."

"When?" Lucas asked, alarmed he had missed something.

"You weren't there," Helen told him, wiping her hands on the grass beneath her to clean off some of the blood. "Hecate said that whoever we freed in my final task would be the only one who could help me defeat Zeus."

Lucas paused. "And did you make Atlas promise to help you before you freed him?" he asked too carefully, like he already knew what her answer was going to be.

"No," she said, trying not to feel sheepish. Lucas stared at her for a long moment, like he was either too angry to speak or he was trying to figure out how to fix Helen's blunder. Or probably both. She decided to keep talking while he was still stymied. "I know the gods run on payback, but I'm not doing it that way. We're supposed to be better than them." She turned to Atlas. "If anyone had bothered to just *ask* me to help you, I would have, because you needed my help. And now I need your help because you are the only one strong enough to defeat Zeus in battle."

"Apart from you, young goddess," Atlas corrected, smiling. Now that Helen wasn't bleeding out of her eyes, she noticed that his were blue. Like Lucas'.

"Well, maybe I am, and maybe I'm not, but it's still going to take both of us," she replied.

The Titan nodded, and then stepped forward solemnly. "I shall help you. And I do not require anything in return." He smiled a slow, dangerous smile. "In fact, if it means I get to fight Zeus, I would be willing to owe *you* for the pleasure."

"Thank you," Helen said. She turned to Lucas with her palms up as if to say, *see*? He gave her a skeptical smile as if to reply, *I'll believe it when I see it*.

"Question?" Hector interjected. "Can we wait until I can hear out of both ears again before we start?"

Helen chuckled but stopped immediately because even laughing hurt.

"You all need rest," Lucas declared, though Helen noticed he did not include himself. "I'll bring Jason and Ari to heal you." He bowed formally to Cronus. "Grandfather." He turned and bowed to Atlas and Hecate. "We will see you soon."

Helen saw Cronus smile at Lucas in a calculating way, and she realized this was the first time that Cronus had not been the one to end the audience by closing his eyes. Lucas had taken the upper hand. She felt the cold of a portal snatch her breath away, and then they were in Lucas' palace.

After Ariadne and Jason had healed Hector and Helen, it felt like they were home.

Claire and Cassandra appeared as if by magic when Helen mentioned that she wished they were there. They tucked themselves into Lucas' oversized chairs, eating the foods they craved most. They all seemed to have a secret hankering for Kate's pastries, or the tapas Noel used to make in Spain, and those dishes simply appeared on side tables. Even the plates were familiar, as if they'd been summoned from either the News Store or Noel's cabinets.

The mood was akin to that of a bonfire on the beach in the

middle of summer vacation. They were healed and giddy. Running outside, they stripped off their clothes to meet Lucas' whirling star-show. They dove screaming into the mirror pool together. Warm air, soft breezes, and full hearts met in the seam between the water's surface and the yawning depth of the sky lit with the infinite fireworks of Lucas' imagination. Swimming was like dancing, and floating was like flying.

Still soaked and laughing, they parted and slid down different rivulets, like droplets of water after a big splash. Helen found herself alone with Lucas in his oversized bed, and she pulled him closer, kissing him slowly.

"We can't." He pulled away.

She stared at him, waiting for a reason. But he didn't have one. "Why not?" she finally asked.

He shrugged and shook his head. "Because—" he stopped himself.

"Why, Lucas?" she asked.

"I'm tied to this," he said, gesturing the palace around them. "I'm going to have to do things that you won't like."

"I don't care," Helen replied simply.

He looked surprised. "What if it's something that hurts you?"

"I don't care," she repeated. "I spent a good portion of last year slogging through the most terrible parts of the Underworld, so I already have an idea about what Tartarus will be like. If I face Zeus and lose—"

"You're not going to lose," he said, cutting her off with a kiss.

When they made love for the first time, she realized that she had always known the difference between love and Eros. Not to feel scorched on the outside by lust, but warmed down deep into the first fold of her many-layered self by love.

"Are you sure?" he asked, rising above her. "I'm leaving you in a few months."

"You're not leaving me," Helen said, capturing his narrower hips between hers.

"I swore—" he gasped, breathless, when Helen eased him against the cusp of her.

"You swore you'd love me forever," she reminded him. He was vulnerable and unsure, and everything that he refused to be when he was with anyone else. The version of himself that was the most genuine. The one he trusted only with her. She cringed against the initial shock and met his swallowing gaze. "So love me forever, Lucas."

"I will," he said, repeating his promise over and over as he began to move inside of her. "I will love you forever."

Still wrapped around him, Helen felt Lucas sit up suddenly and then hold still, like he was listening to the dark.

"What is it?" she asked, not hearing anything.

"Ari's crying," Lucas replied, getting out of bed. When his feet met the floor, he was clothed.

Helen stood and a long loose dress swept down her body as she took her first step to follow him. They went outside, past the mirror pool, into the Fields of Asphodel. Ariadne stood out there alone, calling for Matt.

"He's not here, Ari," Lucas said sadly.

Ariadne turned around and saw them. Tears were streaking down her face. "What happened to him? Didn't he go to the Elysian Fields?"

Lucas nodded. "For a while he did. And then he passed on."

"What does that mean?" she demanded.

"It's complicated." Lucas smiled, as if trying to think of how to make it simpler. "There are souls that are ready to make their own choices. Some decide to stay in Elysium and wait for their loved ones, some decide to be reborn, and a very small number choose to pass beyond all this." He lifted a hand up to the opalescent galaxy turning above them. "Matt passed on."

Ariadne glanced around, like she was at a loss. "Why didn't he wait for me? Didn't he love me?"

"Of course he did," Lucas replied. Then he looked away. "But his soul needed something else. Maybe yours does, too."

Ariadne looked out over the dark fields for a long time, like she was still asking a question inside. And then it seemed that she was given an answer. "Maybe it does," she whispered.

There was no dawn, but Helen sensed when it was morning and awoke.

Next to her, Lucas was awake, and Ariadne was only just stirring on the couch on the other side of the room. Helen fitted herself against Lucas, wishing they were alone, but Ariadne had needed them last night. Lucas appeared to have been up for a while. Helen recalled the last few times she'd awoken with him beside her. Every time he had been awake first. A troubling thought occurred to her.

"Do you sleep?" she asked.

He shook his head, hesitant to reply. "I don't need to anymore." He looked at her as if scared that maybe he shouldn't have told her that. "But it's nice to lie down with my eyes closed and just... rest. Not make any decisions for a change," he added.

"You love making decisions. Especially for other people," she teased.

He smiled with her, recognizing this foible about himself for a moment before looking away. "I make too many now. And I realize that I tried to make too many for you, too. I was controlling. It's not that I didn't trust you, but if something went wrong, I'd rather you blame me for making the wrong choice than blame yourself. I thought I could protect you from making mistakes, which is just... stupid. I'm sorry."

Helen nodded, accepting his apology. He had been controlling and secretive, attempting to manage every moment of the lives of those around him. Helen was glad he saw that now, but she didn't see any point in rubbing it in or making a big deal out of it. Instead, she tried to pull him closer to show him how much she appreciated his acknowledgment of that, but he stopped her.

He groaned like it hurt. "I want to, but Ari's—," he reminded her, grinning.

"Ari, *shmary*," she taunted, and tumbled him playfully across the bed.

No need here to bathe or change; they simply stood up when Ariadne was fully awake and went to meet the rest of the family outside by the mirror pool.

Orion met Helen's eyes and, looking between her and Lucas, raised a knowing eyebrow. Helen blushed and kicked his foot with hers. He smiled at her in return, but his smile fell quickly. Helen wondered if it was regret she saw flashing in Orion's heart before he snatched the emotion away.

"I'm going to send most of you home," Lucas announced.

"You can't!" Claire argued, sensing rightly that she would be among those sent home to safety.

"Claire, you're not—" Lucas began.

"A fighter. I know. But I am one of the immortals, and whatever happens, I want to be there all the way to the end." She looked at Jason.

He met her smile, and then turned to Lucas. "Luke, I know you want this to be you, Helen, Hector and Orion. But they'll come for the rest of us if Helen loses, and it won't be a clean end for us."

"Exactly," Ariadne said, smiling at her twin. "I'd rather go in a fair fight than face one of those weird punishments that Hera comes up with." Her beautiful face suddenly twisted with disgust. "She turned Io into a *cow,* and then set gadflies to bite her day and night. No thank you."

Lucas and Hector shared a meaningful look, and Helen could tell that Hector and Lucas would send everyone home but the two of them to fight this out back-to-back if they could. Helen put her hand on Lucas' arm before he started opening portals.

"Everyone should make their own choice whether to stay or go," she said.

Orion was staring at Cassandra, worried. He shook his head suddenly. "If she stays, I go," he said, turning to Lucas.

Cassandra barely had a moment to pull in a breath to argue before a portal opened and she disappeared.

Helen whirled on Lucas. "How could you do that? Cassandra should be allowed to make her own choices!"

"She can't defend herself, and she's almost as big a prize for the gods as you are. Orion and I can't be worried about both her and you in this fight," he replied. "Cass will be angry with me, but tactically, this is the right decision."

He looked at Orion and nodded in thanks. Helen realized that's why Orion had done it. To let Lucas off the hook.

Lucas turned to Claire. "Please reconsider," he said gently.

"Jason can't take his eyes off you on a normal day, and I need his eyes on Helen for this."

Claire turned to Helen, her face frozen in dismay because she'd just been given an impossible choice. She rolled her eyes. "Fine," she replied, relenting. "But you'd better not lose. I'm going to be so ticked off if Hera turns me into a frigging cow."

Helen smiled, suddenly misty-eyed. "I'd never let her lay a finger on you, Gig. Love you."

"Love you too, Len," she said. Then, she turned to Jason. "Come back to me and I'll marry you—but *after* college." Jason perked up, surprised. Before he could respond Claire turned to Lucas. "Send me home before he tries to get me to walk down the aisle right after Kate," she said quickly, and with that she disappeared in a ring of frost.

Ariadne pointed a finger at Lucas. "Don't you dare," she warned.

"Come on, Ari!" Hector pleaded with his little sister. "You aren't immortal."

Ariadne shook her head, her lips sliding apart in a feline grin. "I have to be there. Athena challenged me personally."

"No way!" all four guys exclaimed at the same time.

"She did," Helen said, backing her up. "She said Ariadne should have been one of her warrior maidens."

"Damn," Hector whispered, impressed.

"Well, then, Ari's coming," Lucas said, like it was decided. He turned to Jason. "Are you sure?" he asked. "With Ari on the field you're our only Healer, and you're much more valuable—"

"I *know*. Dad's been lecturing us about that since we were born," Jason said, frustrated. "I still want to fight."

"Okay," Lucas agreed. "Let's gear up."

He waved a hand and their clothes changed into black armor

that was lightweight and modern. By the feel of it, Helen guessed it was made of a durable resin of some kind, rather than metal. It moved easily at the joints and fitted like a second skin over her body. Everyone but Helen had a sword on their hips and a shield on their arms.

"Nice," Hector said, drawing his gladiolus and cutting through the air in smooth arcs.

"Where's Helen's sword?" Ariadne asked, still flexing her arms to test her mobility.

Helen shook her head. "Zeus and I can make electromagnetic fields. Anything with metal is useless against us."

"Remember Phaon's dagger?" Hector said with a half-smile at Orion.

"Oh yeah," Orion replied, looking at Helen. "Didn't you melt it?"

"She melted *Luke*," Jason said.

They shared a laugh, and when that died down, a round of nods passed throughout their group, signaling that they were ready. There was a flash of cold, and they were in Cronus' grove.

CHAPTER 18

Cronus opened his eyes as they appeared. To his left was Hecate and to his right was Atlas, dressed and armed with a staff for battle. Instead of telling his grandchildren that he was always happy to see them, as had become his custom, Cronus looked at Lucas and frowned.

"You will not have been fighting," Cronus said.

Lucas started to argue, but Cronus held up a hand and silenced him. "Your oath," he reminded Lucas in a sad voice.

"I've kept my oath!" Lucas shouted back at him.

Cronus shook his head once. "If the Olympians had won you would go to Tartarus. To fight is to risk your oath. To the dead, this is always unacceptable. You do not fight."

Lucas' breathing sped up and he gripped the pommel of his sword with a white-knuckled fist. He looked at Hecate. "How is this any different from fate?" he asked her.

All three of her faces smiled wryly, as if she was aware that he was trying to catch the Titans in a technicality. "The difference is that you made your choice when you willingly became the Hand of Darkness. This is but one of the many repercussions of that choice."

Helen put a hand on Lucas' arm, but he wouldn't look at her. She knew he must have been expecting this. Hades never fought, and neither could he anymore. She wanted to tell him that it was okay, but it wasn't, not for him, so she didn't say it.

Atlas stepped forward. "I will fight in your stead," he promised Lucas.

Lucas nodded tightly, but he wouldn't look at any of the Scions. Helen saw anger in him, and shame at not being able to fight alongside her.

"I should be with you," he whispered, his head canted close to hers so only Helen could hear. "I hate this."

"Me too," she said, knowing any comfort she tried to give him right now would only make him feel worse.

Though it cost him to accept this, he did it because he knew they needed him to. His face broke into a smile, and he looked up at her. "You're going to win," he said.

She took a quick kiss from him. "That's not goodbye," she replied as she stepped back. "That's see you soon."

"See you soon," he agreed, including all the Scions with his look.

Helen faced Cronus. "We're ready," she said. The cold of a portal shrank her lungs.

They appeared on top of the Atlas Mountains. Not at the very peak, where the air was thin and cold enough to make them gasp, but high up enough that they were surrounded by desolation.

Ariadne and Jason looked around in confusion. "Why are we here?" Ariadne asked.

Atlas' eyes narrowed with dark thoughts. "This is the place of my long suffering. Always, I have imagined fighting Zeus right here," he said. Then he threw his huge hands out to the side and raised his thick brow humorously. "Also, there is not much here to destroy during our fight."

"That's a good enough reason for me." Orion turned to Helen. "What's the plan?"

"The plan is for you to stay back when I let Zeus out. Atlas and I are the only two who can fight him," Helen replied, looking meaningfully at Hector.

"I will make sure Zeus remains here to fight," Hecate said. "I will guard the boundaries."

"And what are we supposed to do?" Hector complained.

"Zeus will call the other Olympians," Atlas answered. "You must be ready to keep them at bay until we have subdued Zeus."

"Okay," Jason said reasonably. "And then what?"

"And then I'll end it," Helen said, her jaw tight. She looked at Orion. "An earthquake up here could be devastating," she said.

"I have just as much power over the earth as Poseidon does. I can stop him from making one," he assured her.

She turned to Hector. "Apollo can fly."

He chuffed. "I've fought Luke enough to know how to keep a flyer right where I can beat on him."

Helen smiled and shook her head at him. Somehow, he always managed to say the right thing in a way that made her want to punch him. She turned to Ariadne and Jason. "Athena's already called out Ariadne. Hestia, Hera, and Aphrodite never fight physically, and the only other Olympian I can think of who does, is Hermes."

"I figured he'd be mine," Jason said, his mouth ticked up in a smile like he had a plan.

"He's fast," Atlas cautioned.

"Not if he's unconscious," Jason countered. He glanced at Ariadne, and she smiled at him like she knew what he was planning.

Helen took a deep breath and let it out. "Ready?"

"I've *been* ready," Hector commented impatiently.

"Okay," Helen replied, rolling her eyes like Hector was annoying her, but really, she was grateful he was the brave, over-confident brawler she needed him to be. "I'm going to open a passageway to Everyland right in front of us, and hopefully Zeus will come through it."

"He will," Atlas rumbled and the muscles across his shoulders flexed, like he was recalling the weight of universe on them. "He cannot resist this world."

Helen mentally filed that comment away for another time. She took a moment to look around at her family. "Here we go," she mumbled, then she opened the boundary to Everyland.

She felt a blast of cold in front of her, and then a tingle of electricity as Zeus appeared not three paces away from her. He looked just as Helen remembered him, like a male version of her. He had brown eyes, blond hair, and a lithe, muscular body. He was as handsome as Helen was beautiful—flawless, really, as the king of the Greek gods should be—but the haughty, over-confident sneer on his face ruined it.

His smirk of triumph slipped when he realized who was standing next to her. Atlas. A ring of orange fire sprang up around them, stretching for miles around the crown of the mountaintop.

"You will not make a portal and leave this fight," Hecate

announced. They were on sacred ground now, like when they had fought the Olympians on the beach, and there were rules that neither side could break.

Backed into a corner, Zeus stared Helen down. "Seven against one?" he mocked. "This fight is between the gods and the Scions, yet you bring Titans. How is that fair?"

"There was no agreement between you as to who could or could not fight," Hecate intoned. "Or the numbers allowed each side."

Zeus narrowed his eyes at Hecate. "It's dishonorable, and you know it."

"Call your Olympians," Helen said with a shrug. "One for each of my Scions. But let them know that I swear whoever fights for you will be imprisoned with you."

The Olympians appeared, arrayed behind Zeus. Poseidon to his right, Athena to his left; Apollo stood beside Athena, and moving in a blur behind them was a younger teen. Hermes was smaller, but he never stood still, and it hurt Helen's eyes to try to focus on him enough to discern his features distinctly.

But there was one more among them, someone Helen had not even considered. Behind Poseidon was a grizzled and bent figure. His back was misshapen, his features irregular, and he was covered in soot. The tanned animal skins he wore were patched together haphazardly, but the weapon he carried was like no other Helen had seen. Part scimitar, part spear, it shone with light, and the knife edge was so keen that it glistened. It was a work of art, certainly made by the incongruently gnarled hand that gripped it.

"Hephaestus," Ariadne said on a surprised exhalation.

"Does anyone know what he can do in a fight?" Hector asked, his voice low and his words clipped with urgency.

"He has never fought in a battle before and is therefore unseasoned. But he is immensely strong," Atlas replied, sounding slightly concerned. "And his weapon is made of adamantine. Impossible to shatter."

"New plan!" Helen shouted desperately, but too late.

She didn't know who moved first, the Olympians or the Scions, or if the opposing lines snapped simultaneously like over-wound guitar strings, but the combatants fell on each other as if ravenous. Each warrior collided with a foe, their battle cries curtailed by grunts of effort and the clanging of sword on shield.

Hephaestus engaged Atlas before the Titan could reach Zeus, and with a nasty wink in Helen's direction to make sure she knew her plan to capture him had failed, Zeus took to the air.

Helen followed with a snarl, bursting from the ground like a geyser. Zeus climbed higher and higher until Helen's lungs shriveled and her vision blurred. With a burst of speed, she closed the gap between them and grabbed onto his ankle. Switching instantly to her super-massive state, she dragged Zeus down with her, intending to drive him into the rocky mountainside beneath her.

They struggled in mid-air. Tumbling over each other, switching from buoyant to massive, they wrestled for position; each of them maneuvering to be the one on top when they hit the ground. Plummeting, floating, wrenching limbs, Helen never let go of Zeus though he tried several times to wriggle from her grasp. As the ground rushed up to meet them with Helen on top, Zeus struck her with lightning. It had no effect on her, but he was desperate.

Seeing the fear in his eyes as they neared impact, it occurred to Helen that Zeus might be the strongest, but he was not a great fighter. He relied on his bolts, which had always been enough until now. Helen had been trained by Hector, Orion, Ariadne, and Lucas. She'd worked on other skills besides the one weapon of her lightning, and although she had hated nearly every second of it, in that moment she smiled with satisfaction.

They hit the ground and Helen drove him into the mountain, plowing a great trench through the rubble with his body. She did not let him get up or release her hold on him. With Hector's coaching in her mind, she straddled Zeus, pinning him between her legs, and rained down heavy punches on his face. He covered his head with his forearms, bucking beneath her uselessly, but Helen knew she had him.

Then she felt something connect with the side of her head, sending her sprawling beside Zeus.

Not knowing who or what had hit her, Helen saw Zeus trying to get airborne to flee again, and she latched onto his arm and dragged him back down. She felt another blow to her head but did not release Zeus. She wrapped one of her hands around his throat and craned her head left and right, looking for her attacker while she struggled to keep Zeus pinned beneath her.

On the next rise, Helen could see the battle rage between the Scions and the Olympians. In a glimpse, she saw Ariadne and Athena as they fought with sword and shield, trading blows expertly. Orion and Poseidon were in a close knife fight, their bodies crouched and their forearms blocking viper-fast strikes. Hector had already won, but unable to kill Apollo, he settled for dragging the unfortunate god around by one leg and smashing him into whatever he could find. Atlas had Hephaestus pinned beneath one of his enormous knees while he searched for Helen. He met her eyes, nodding at her in acknowledgment of his swift victory over Hephaestus.

The only pair missing was Jason and Hermes. Out of the corner of her eye, Helen saw a blur and snatched at it. She caught a boy, maybe eleven or twelve, by the hair. He shrieked and struggled. She held him until Jason, who Helen guessed had been chasing him this whole time, caught up, sucking in strained breaths in an alarming way after having run from one mountain peak to another. He tackled Hermes and touched the sides of Hermes' face with his glowing healer hands. The god fell to the ground, unconscious. Jason collapsed next to him, still heaving breaths.

Helen glared down at Zeus. "You've lost, and your Olympians are being defeated one by one. Yield."

Panicking now, Zeus doubled his efforts to get away, but Helen tightened her grip on his throat. "Yield!" she shouted into his face.

"Never!" he gasped back at her, barely able to form words. He somehow managed a hateful smirk. "Everyland... mine. Can't put me... Tartarus."

Helen felt a chill go down her spine. She loosened her grip slightly, just enough so that she could understand what he was trying to say. Golden ichor leaked from the corner of his mouth and from the many cuts on his face.

"Say that again," she said.

He grinned up at her wolfishly. "You can open and close the boundaries to Everyland, but you can't use it to make portals anywhere else, because Everyland belongs to *me*. Without full control of it, you can't travel through it. Which means you can't open a portal to send me to Tartarus, Helen."

While Zeus looked up at her triumphantly, Helen tried. She could open a portal into Everyland, but she couldn't go through it. If she couldn't go through Everyland, she couldn't open a second portal from Everyland into another place—in this case Tartarus. If she couldn't open a portal to Tartarus, she couldn't put Zeus in it. She simply didn't have the power to imprison him, not without her world.

Enraged, she squeezed his throat. "Give it back to me!" she screamed in his face.

Though Zeus choked and sputtered under her hands he mouthed the word *never.*

She looked at Jason. Their eyes met and widened with dawning dread. Why would Zeus ever give Everyland back to her? Doing that would damn him. And without it, she could not imprison Zeus anywhere.

Gathering all that as quickly as Helen did, Jason asked, "What do we do?"

She shook her head in a daze. She searched her mind for a solution but found nothing of any use. Then the ground next to Helen shook. Atlas had jumped from the neighboring peak where the other Scions still fought and landed next to her.

"Zeus will not yield," Jason told Atlas. "And without Everyland Helen can't send him to Tartarus. Can you do it for her?"

Atlas shook his head. "I cannot make portals for I am not a Worldbuilder," the Titan said. "Cronus is."

Zeus' expression was smug. "The orange flame—no one else may come within the boundaries of our fight until it is resolved. No one can send me to Tartarus but those who are already here. If Helen can't do it, it won't be done," Zeus said, watching her face fall with terrible understanding and enjoying every second of it. He attempted to laugh but coughed instead under Helen's choking hand, yet not even that momentary indignity could put a damper on his gloating.

She glanced at Hecate, pleading with her eyes for a way out, but saw only implacable acceptance in the Witch Titan.

"No one else may enter the ring until there is a winner,"

Hecate said. "And I cannot send him to Tartarus. I am an adjudicator, not a combatant."

Helen sensed a growing presence behind her as the Scions and the Olympians gave up their individual battles and jumped or flew across to be present at the outcome of this one, the only one that mattered.

"You may as well let me up," Zeus said pityingly. "What are you going to do? Stay here on top of me forever?"

Helen wavered. Though she searched her mind for a loophole, she knew he was right.

"You will not rise!" Atlas boomed. The ground trembled and Zeus' eyes flared with fear at the rage he saw in the Titan.

Atlas moved Helen out of the way and put his knee down on Zeus' chest. "You will never rise again," he said resolutely.

"What—no! You have no right to... to..." Zeus quibbled, pinned beneath Atlas' knee, but his objections ran out.

"Holding you down for the rest of eternity is a joy compared to holding up the entire universe," Atlas said. He looked at Helen and smiled. "I will gladly stay here with him beneath my knee forever. Tartarus be damned."

"No!" Zeus screamed. He started discharging bolt after bolt into Atlas, but the Titan merely shrugged them off.

"How many times have I been struck by lightning standing atop this mountain? There is no torment you can dole out that is more than the merest fraction of what I have already endured at your hands," Atlas said. He settled in, a look of peace across his face. "At last, I will have my revenge."

"Brother!" Zeus called to Poseidon, but Poseidon averted his eyes. "Daughter!" he shouted at Athena, who would not look at him.

Orion and Ariadne tensed, ready to beat back the Olympians if they tried to help Zeus, but neither of them moved.

"You have lost, father," Apollo said simply.

"We cannot aid you," Athena added with a helpless gesture toward the orange fire on the mountainside. "Honor demands—"

"I decide what is honorable!" Zeus raged. The Olympians shrank further away from him, as if embarrassed.

Helen gazed first at Orion, and then at Hector, Ariadne, and Jason. They all looked as uncertain about this strange stalemate as the Olympians were, and though Atlas seemed perfectly happy to make good on his promise, it made Helen uneasy. This was not solved yet. Only one thing could end it.

"You could give me back Everyland," Helen said.

Zeus calmed himself, panting under the pressure of Atlas' knees. "Give you back Everyland, so you can send me to Tartarus?" he asked, incredulous. His gaze moved across the Olympians. "She will send all of you down with me! She swore it!"

"She did," Hecate intoned, the orange fire glowing brighter.

"I swore that everyone who fought for Zeus would be imprisoned with him," Helen clarified. She waited a beat. "But what if, instead of imprisoning you in Tartarus, I imprison you on Olympus?"

The Olympians paused, surprised by her offer.

"There is nothing in her oath to Zeus that disallows that," Hecate confirmed, and the Olympians appeared enticed. Zeus looked from one to another, as if sensing that his control over his family was slipping.

"You'd have to swear on the River Styx never to leave Olympus again, of course," Helen added.

"It's a trick," Zeus spat. "She lies!"

"She does not," Apollo, the Falsefinder, countered in a ringing voice. "I hear truth in her words."

The Olympians passed a questioning look amongst themselves. They all seemed decided.

"Olympus," Athena said, as if casting her vote.

Apollo nodded. "Olympus." He glanced at Hephaestus who was nodding already.

"No!" Zeus pushed at the Titan's knee ineffectually. "We must stay here!" he nearly wailed.

Helen frowned in thought at that. To be in complete control of everything meant that nothing was ever at stake. In theory, omnipotence seemed like the ultimate prize, but in practice it leached meaning out of everything. *This* world was the only one in which anything mattered to the Olympians—or to Helen. Earth was where none of the Worldbuilders were in control because something *else* was.

The Fates.

And even the gods and Helen herself were subject to them. Things mattered here on earth because here was the only place none of them were omnipotent.

"Exile in Olympus is still a punishment, maybe even a kind of torture," Helen said, meeting Atlas' eyes and finding agreement there. "Or you can stay here. Trapped under the knee of a Titan. For eternity."

To punctuate her point, Atlas drove his knee into Zeus' chest. "I could make this much worse for you," he growled.

"Olympus!" Zeus cried out in agony. Atlas relented slightly and Zeus glared at Helen. "I choose Olympus and exile."

Helen narrowed her eyes at him. "Return Everyland to me."

He huffed in frustration. "I give you back Everyland," he said, and the orange flames licked higher.

Helen felt the return of her world like a familiar hand slipping into hers. She didn't realize how much she had missed it, but she quickly hardened her expression. She wasn't done with Zeus.

"And now swear on the River Styx that you will go to Olympus with all who fought for you and never leave it again," she demanded.

Zeus' face trembled with hatred, but Helen saw the pride leave his eyes, and knew that this time she had not simply outsmarted him. She had won. "I do so swear on the River Styx," he rasped.

Hecate folded her hands in front of her with finality. "You may go," she pronounced.

Atlas rose, releasing Zeus, who stood slowly. The rest of the Olympians moved away from him, most in embarrassment at his failure, but there was anger in one of them. Poseidon openly sneered at his brother.

"You promised me you had this in hand," he growled.

"Don't worry, brother. It's not over yet." Zeus smiled coldly at Helen, though he spoke to Poseidon.

"Really? It kind of feels over to me," Helen said.

"You're not going to like the job," he promised. All bitterness had left him, and for the first time in her dealings with Zeus, Helen felt as if he was speaking to her as an equal. "In the end, when the Moirae call on you to perform that final task, you're going to wish you'd left the world to me."

The orange fire went out and Zeus and his Olympians disappeared.

"It is done," Hecate said, a rare smile lighting up all three faces.

There was a long moment where everyone stared at each other, disbelieving. Then Ariadne let out a held breath and her shoulders suddenly slumped with fatigue. "I'm so glad that's over!"

Jason sat down, exhausted. "You? I ran my ass off," he said, letting his head drop between his knees, and everyone seemed to uncoil.

Helen looked at Orion, just now noticing that he was bleeding. She pointed, concerned, but Orion only shook his head. "Poseidon got me in the shoulder," he admitted, gripping his injury with his good hand. "But I almost had *him*."

"You did not," Hector teased.

Atlas extended an enormous hand to Helen in congratulations, and she shook it. "I am glad that Zeus is defeated, but I wish I had been the one to bring him low," he admitted.

"He's actually not that good of a fighter without his lightning." She shrugged. "I think you would have been disappointed."

"Nah. You're just a beast," Hector said, pulling her in for a hug with one arm and Orion with the other.

"Can we hug it out down here?" Jason asked from the ground. "I don't think I can stand."

"Aw, is my baby brother tired?" Hector teased. He leaned and tipped the pile of Scions over onto Jason, making him regret his request.

After a short groaning tussle where everyone, including Hector, admitted that they were more beat up than they'd let on, Helen opened a portal into Cronus' grove.

Lucas was waiting there with Cronus. He smiled and embraced everyone—cracking jokes and trading banter—but Helen could see he was working hard to push past his own feelings to celebrate with them. He seemed separated, even as he laughed at Hector's boasting.

"Helen Hamilton," Cronus said in his rumbling voice. The commotion died down and she stepped forward. "Our thanks are everlasting. You will have been starting your greatest task now that you have completed the first."

Helen thought about that for a moment. She looked sideways at Lucas standing next to her, but he didn't seem to know what to make of that, either.

"But Helen has completed all of her tasks, hasn't she?" Lucas clarified haltingly.

Hecate stepped forward. "Helen is free from her debt to me," she said, her middle face intent as she regarded the pair of them. "But she still has much to do."

"Ah—good?" Helen said after a moment. "I like to make myself useful."

Cronus and Atlas thought that was hilarious for a reason Helen couldn't quite discern. "It is always good to see you, granddaughter," Cronus said, still amused. "You will have been coming back soon, and I am glad for it."

Helen opened her mouth to ask a question she hadn't quite figured out yet when Cronus waved a hand, and she felt the cold of a portal snatch her words away.

Chapter 19

Helen was late again. But it wasn't her fault.

As soon as she and the rest of the Scions appeared in Lucas' room at the Delos compound, they could hear the bustle of preparations downstairs.

Helen cringed. "The wedding!" she said, looking around at everyone.

They hurried downstairs together to find caterers and florists and other hired help setting food and flowers and chairs into final position for the service. At the center of it all was Noel, who was organizing the last few details before the guests arrived.

"Do you have any idea what time it is?" Noel asked them angrily.

"Ah—?" Helen began, because she really didn't. She looked at her dad, who was standing behind Noel with a slightly traumatized look on face, and he just shook his head at Helen as if to say *don't even try to answer her.*

"Where's your dress?" Noel barreled on, gesturing to Helen's armor. "Why do you all look like the X-Men?"

"Mom, where's Dad?" Lucas asked through a laugh. "We have really good news."

"Helen kicked Zeus' ass," Hector announced in his usual unceremonious fashion.

"Well, not alone," Helen clarified. She looked at her father who, like Noel, now looked pleasantly shocked. "But yeah. I solved my pest problem, sooo if someone wanted to have the perfect honeymoon, I've got a great spot."

"Helen—that's wonderful!" Jerry stammered.

"It is, and I'm happy you're all safe, and we'll celebrate this properly at the reception," Noel said, still flustered and now at war with herself because she was relieved and stressed out at the same time. "But there is a *hole* right where Kate is supposed to walk down the aisle."

"I'll fix it," Orion said, heading for the backyard.

"I'll—help him," Hector said, just to get out of there.

"No, Hector! You go upstairs right now and get in the shower!" Noel yelled after Hector, Ariadne, and Jason who were scattering in different directions to get away from her.

"You look nice, Dad," Helen said. "You're really pulling off the all-white ensemble thing. Very stylish."

Jerry chuckled. "If you don't get into your all-white ensemble, you're going to be black and blue in a minute," he warned.

Helen kissed him on the cheek and grabbed Lucas' hand. "Be right back."

"Helen," Jerry called after her. "Are you *really* okay?"

"You don't have to worry about me anymore," she said.

Jerry smirked at her. "Like that's ever going to happen. Now hurry up."

Helen grinned at her dad and pulled Lucas into the downstairs bathroom.

"What are we doing in—?" Lucas began, but the portal Helen created into her bedroom cut him off.

She looked at his disconcerted expression with triumph. "It feels so good to be able to do that again," she said, as she slipped into his arms.

"It is *very* strange when someone else does it," he admitted with a grin, his eyes sparkling as he pulled her close.

"Payback. Especially for that portal you made directly onto Broadway from Ladon's cave. *So* weird." Nothing made Helen happier than causing Lucas to smile, but the levity was short-lived.

"I'm sorry I wasn't with you today," he said, his face falling.

"There was no way you could have been."

"I should have helped—"

"You've helped me with everything I've ever had to do. You've always been there for me," she countered as he shook his head in denial.

"Not for this. Not when you needed me the most."

She thought about what she was about to say before speaking. "Oddly enough, I didn't need you today. I fought Zeus and I beat him on my own."

He narrowed his eyes at her and smiled slyly. "I knew you could." He hugged her tightly rather than kiss her, a little groan escaping him. "You know what I'm going to say, right?"

"That we don't have time?" Helen hazarded. He pulled back and nodded.

"Put your dress on before my mom loses it."

"I can't believe you're still scared of your mom," she teased, as she went to the closet and took down the garment bag.

"You're scared of her too," he countered, stretching out on Helen's bed.

"I'm no dummy." She paused on her way to her bathroom. "What about you? Aren't you going to get ready?"

Lucas smiled devilishly, disappeared, and almost instantaneously reappeared with a blast of cold air. He was dressed perfectly in a dark suit and lounging on her little bed like a model in a cologne ad.

"Ready," he said.

Helen gasped. "I forgot about that!"

She grabbed her dress and opened a portal to Everyland. Though she was momentarily struck to see the beauty of her world again, she knew she couldn't linger. Time ran differently in the Underworld, but not in Everyland, where it passed as it did on earth. Helen took a deep breath of the sweet air and simply thought about being in her dress with her hair and make-up done, and she was. Then, after a quick internal promise to herself that she would be back soon, she portaled back to her bedroom.

Lucas stared at her for a long moment, and she stared back. Things had shifted between them, and they'd barely had a moment alone to process it. Thinking about their one night together in the Underworld, Helen felt shy standing in front of him seeing the churn of love and lust in his chest, but not embarrassed.

"I should have taken you to prom," he said, sounding a little sad. He sat up suddenly and came to her. "Come on." He took her hand. A quizzical look crossed his face. "Should I portal us, or do you want to?"

"I can drive," Helen joked, and then she flinched at something pricking her.

"What is it?" Lucas asked.

Helen twisted her arm behind her and felt at the seam on the bodice. "I think there's still a pin in this. Can you unzip the back and check?"

"Ah—sure," Lucas said, hesitating. He slid the zipper down and Helen could feel his hands shaking a little as he parted her dress. "New bra, huh?" he asked, his voice higher than usual.

A laugh fluttered in Helen's throat. She could feel his breath on her bare skin and the hairs on the back of her neck rising. "Do you see anything?"

"Uh-huh," he murmured, his voice lower than usual. He zipped her dress back up. "But no pin."

She shifted in her bodice, testing for pokes. "It's okay. Whatever it was is gone."

"Oh really?" He narrowed his eyes and smiled. "Nice try."

Helen's jaw dropped in astonishment. "I did *not* do that on purpose!"

"Of course you didn't," Lucas replied innocently.

Still huffing, she portaled them back to Lucas' room in the Delos house. He looked pointedly at his bed. "Still not falling for it," he said. He captured her hand and they went downstairs together into the chaos of last-minute wedding prep.

"Helen, you look gorgeous, but can you help with the chairs outside?" Noel said, looking frazzled. "Orion just fixed the hole, but now we have so little time to set up—"

"We got it, Mom," Lucas interrupted calmly, and the two went outside to the heated tents, their hands still linked and their strides in step. None of the chairs were set up and the florist looked like she was about to have a melt-down.

Thinking about how easily she'd gotten herself ready in her world, Helen said, "Wouldn't it be great if I could portal everyone to Everyland where I could have an exact replica of your house and the wedding all set up?"

Lucas looked intrigued as he thought through the details of that scenario. "No one would notice the cold of a portal. They'd just think it was a chilly gust of wind."

Helen paused, seriously considering it. "I could make the wedding perfect, too. Everything would be exactly as Kate planned. Nothing would go wrong, and if it did, I could fix it with a thought." She shivered and rubbed her bare arms. "I could even make it a little warmer. Why did she pick *December* to get married? *Outside*."

Lucas smiled at her tone, but he was still considering the logistics of moving the wedding to Everyland. Finally, he shook his head. "What if someone shows up late? The house would be empty." He glanced through the clear siding on the tent to the house where some of Kate's fully mortal family and friends were talking with Castor and Pallas.

Helen nodded, accepting defeat. "You're right. I'd have to portal everyone at once as they stepped outside so they didn't notice we'd gone anywhere."

"Nice idea though," Lucas commented as he started unfolding chairs.

"I guess we'll just have to do this the old-fashioned way."

They managed to get the tent set up in time, and Helen even stole a few minutes to chat with Kate's mom and dad while Lucas, Hector and Orion, pulled Cassandra, Castor, Pallas, and Niobe aside to give them a full account of how they'd defeated Zeus. Helen excused herself from Kate's family and tapped Cassandra on the shoulder. Cassandra gave her puzzled look, but she followed Helen up to her bedroom.

"So. I have Everyland back," Helen began.

"Yah, I know," Cassandra replied uncertainly, and then it dawned on her. "Can you, you know... make me..."

"A woman." Helen nodded. "If you want me to."

"Yes!" Cassandra practically shouted, like it should be obvious.

Helen took Cassandra's hand and portaled them into Everyland, right into the middle of Helen's redwood forest. Helen took a deep breath of the fresh air while Cassandra looked around in awe.

"This is amazing," she whispered. Then she looked expectantly at Helen. "How does it work?"

"Well, I don't want to suddenly make you twenty or anything like that. I figured we could do this in a few trips. Maybe this time we just make you sixteen, like you're supposed to be?"

Cassandra nodded briskly. "Okay. Do it."

Helen laughed at her eagerness. "Done," she said, looking at a slightly older version of Cassandra.

"Oh my gods, let me see!" Cassandra squealed, so Helen portaled them back into Cassandra's bedroom in front of her full-length mirror.

Cassandra turned slowly in front of it, holding out her arms so she could admire the new curves she saw straining against the hips and bust of her dress. The change was subtle, but unmistakable. She was not a little girl anymore. Her eyes filled.

"You're a stunner," Helen said, pulling her into a hug. Her chin nearly rested on Cassandra's shoulder, when normally she would have to bend down. "And you're *taller*."

Cassandra laughed and hugged Helen so hard it almost hurt. "Thank you."

Helen pulled back. "Now get down there and flirt with Orion like you're supposed to."

Cassandra did not laugh. Instead, she looked down. "What if he's still not interested?"

"Then he's an idiot." Helen squeezed Cassandra's hand one last time. "You might need to give him a minute to adjust but trust me. You two are going to be great."

It was time for the wedding to begin. Helen went to Ariadne's room where Kate was ready and waited with her until the wedding march started up. The florist handed them their bouquets.

"Game time," Kate said, sounding jittery.

"I'll run interference for you," Helen said, giving Kate one last hug and kiss.

Kate grabbed her arm. "Just please don't tackle anyone," she replied, only half joking. Helen squirmed inside her itchy bodice until she set it to rights, and then began walking down the aisle.

She felt giddy and a little dizzy. She was so happy she practically skipped, and because she wore the Cestus as always, her joyous mood was infectious. Everyone she passed on her way up to the alter looked back at her with smiling faces, suffused with joy.

Except Lucas. His heart was a tangle of opposites—happy and sad, frustrated and content, detached and passionate. Nothing emotional was ever easy with him, though. Helen met his gaze and pushed her joy at him until he rolled his eyes and gave in, finally allowing himself to enjoy the here and now with her.

Her dad grinned back at her from his spot at the alter and Helen had to resist the urge to high five him when she got there.

"Smartest thing you've ever done," she whispered instead as

she took her place opposite him. Kate started down the aisle, and everyone turned to look at her.

"I know," her dad whispered back.

She noticed he was flushed and sweating a little, like he had a fever. Right after the reception was over and no one was looking, she decided that she was going to take him to Everyland and cure his mysterious illness. Whatever it was, it was going to end as soon as she could steal him away for a few moments.

Helen only cried twice while Jerry and Kate exchanged vows. She noticed that Hector had to brush a few tears away as well, confirming Helen's long-held suspicion that he was the softest-hearted of all the Delos boys. And then it was done. Kate and Jerry were married, and everyone was on their way over to the other tent for the party.

Kate had wanted an informal reception. No assigned tables or awkward speeches or overly enthusiastic DJ's announcing the bride and groom's first dance. Helen helped Kate get from one tent to the other with no dress mishaps and stood back, her maid of honor's job done. She felt Lucas' hand on her waist and turned into his arms.

"One dance before I go?" he asked.

Helen glanced at the darkening sky through the clear side of the tent. It was barely late afternoon, but the sun was already setting.

"You really can't stay?" she asked, trying not to sound upset about it.

He shook his head and pulled her against him. Helen laid her cheek against his shoulder as they swayed, determined to enjoy what little time she was given with him as thoroughly as possible. She felt lightheaded again and closed her eyes, but after just a few moments she pulled back. Lucas seemed anxious, somehow. Distracted.

"What is it?" she asked, looping her arms around his shoulders and neck.

He untangled himself from her and pulled back, not even trying to sway to the music any longer. "I have to go," he said.

Helen nodded and dropped her hands. She tried to give him a smile but quit when she realized a forced smile would make him feel worse than none at all.

"Tomorrow," she said firmly. Then, at a thought, she did find a true smile. "Kate and my dad are going to be gone for a week, you know," she reminded him saucily.

A desperate, falling look swept across his face and he stepped back into her arms too quickly and hugged her too hard. "I love you. No matter what," he practically growled in her ear. Then he let her go abruptly and bolted for the exit before she could read his heart.

She stared after him, knowing something was wrong, but having not a clue what it could be. She felt a large, reassuring presence join her.

"Just pretend he's a doctor who's always on call," Hector said behind her. Helen turned to smile gratefully up at him.

"I got ditched."

"Me too. Want to dance?" he asked, opening his arms wide for her.

She fit herself against him easily and they flowed right into the music as if they'd done it a thousand times. Maybe they had.

"No Andy?" she asked Hector, concerned. Helen hadn't been paying much attention to anything that wasn't actively exploding in her face over the past few weeks, but she did remember that Hector had said Andy might not be back for the wedding.

He grimaced ruefully. "Not even a phone call. Not since we were at your dress fitting."

"I'm sorry," Helen said sadly.

He shrugged, looking away. "Pretty sure I've been ghosted."

"That doesn't make any sense," Helen said, shaking her head. "Andy loves you. I know she does."

"Apparently she's found something she loves more." Hector's face was stony. He wasn't trying to hide his emotions. He never did that. Rather, he was trying to not have emotions, which Helen decided was worse and very un-Hector.

Resting her spinning head on Hector's enormous shoulder, Helen looked around. She saw Jason and Claire gazing at each other lovingly as they danced. Pallas and Niobe were talking with Kate's family—they made a stunning couple—and even Noel was taking a moment to enjoy a dance with Castor. Orion and Cassandra weren't dancing, but he was looking at her with a surprised expression on his face as she talked with Ariadne. As Helen suspected, Orion had noticed the difference, but wasn't quite comfortable with thinking of Cassandra as a woman yet. Helen suddenly felt overheated and her throat was dry. A reckless mood overtook her.

"Want to get a drink?" she asked Hector.

"Like, alcohol?" he asked, his eyes flaring at her with surprise. "You don't drink."

Helen made a *pshaw* noise. "You do. I saw beer in your fridge in New York, and wine bottles on the counter."

"The wine is Orion's," he said defensively, like it besmirched his reputation to have it in his house. "Damn Roman won't drink beer like a normal college guy."

The giddy feeling was back. She grabbed Hector's hand and pulled him to the bar, picking up Orion on her way there.

"What are we doing?" Orion asked as he let himself be dragged along.

"Lucas ditched, Andy never showed, and Helen's got it in her head she wants a little drinkie," Hector replied with one eyebrow arched meaningfully.

"Oh great," Orion replied, looking worried.

"Come on, it'll be fun," Helen said, trying to catch the bartender's attention. "Where's Cassandra?"

"She's over there," Orion said in an offhand way, although Helen could tell his nonchalance was forced. He knew exactly where Cassandra was, but Helen guessed that sixteen was still too young for him. She made a mental note to fix that over the next few weeks. "You know what? Get me a whiskey," he decided suddenly.

"That's the spirit," Helen said, and then smiled at the bartender when he made eye contact.

It *was* the guy from the winter concert. He looked as dapper as he had the night before even with a red nose, pink cheeks, and eyes that were hazy with drink. Or maybe it was just the heat. Helen could feel a flush in her own cheeks and pressed a cool hand to the side of her face.

"Are you okay?" Orion said.

"It's stifling in here," Helen said. She wobbled on her heels. Orion caught her arm and steadied her.

"Have you already had a few?" he asked.

"No!" Helen replied, shocked. Though she did feel a little dizzy.

The bartender upended some liquor bottles over a shaker of ice, popped a pint glass opposite it and shook the frothy, caramel-colored concoction while he strode toward Helen. Setting up three iced highball glasses with his free hand, he dropped a maraschino cherry into each, and with a flick of his wrist poured out equal measures of the well-shaken drink while saying, "Did I hear you ask for whiskey sours?"

Someone bumped raucously into Helen from behind and Orion shoved the stumbling person off, saying, "Easy."

"You were at the winter choral," Helen said, continuing her conversation with the bartender, elbows on the bar, leaning toward him.

He pushed the drinks toward them with a sparkle in his eye. "I love a good performance. Can't keep me away from the theatre," he replied.

"Who are you?" she asked in a lowered voice, knowing there was more to this guy than a fast cocktail.

Crowds of people Helen didn't recognize were howling for service, but the bartender ignored them and leaned onto his elbows, mirroring her, his face a breath away from Helen's.

"Just another mortal-born god stuck in this, like you," he replied. For a moment his edges stood out, like he was more real than other people.

Helen looked down at the shaker, and then at the bottles of wine lining the back bar. "You're Dionysus," she said, stunned.

He tilted his head in acquiescence. "I've done my best to keep the party light for as long as I could, but there's always a point when it gets... savage. I'm sorry, Helen. She made me come."

Helen wanted to ask what he meant, but a disturbance had already caught her attention.

A group of women seemed to be trying to start a mosh pit on the dance floor. They screeched and tore at their clothes, flinging their bodies about with fierce ecstasy as they skipped and leaped, knocking others to the ground. They seemed possessed; when they threw their heads back, their eyes rolled, showing solid white.

Helen searched across the tent and found her dad. They shared a confused look. Neither of them knew who those women were.

A fight broke out. Two guys went at each other, trading violent blows. Castor and Pallas jumped into the fray and managed to pull the two men apart, but the Scions looked as if they were actually struggling to keep these mortals restrained. There was no way Castor and Pallas couldn't easily contain full mortals.

Then the wild women fell on Castor and Pallas, shrieking horrifically and tearing at their skin and their clothes with claw-like hands.

"Maenads!" Castor shouted at Pallas. The entire crowd seemed to erupt into a frenzy.

Helen lost sight of Kate and her dad. Hector and Orion darted into the chaos, and Helen took a step to follow them, but her knees buckled, and she nearly fell to the ground. It was like she was on the deck of a ship in a storm. She threw out one hand to steady herself against the bar and put another to her spinning head. What she'd dismissed as natural giddiness at the excitement and high emotion of the day, was now obviously something much more serious. She tugged at the bodice of her dress. She couldn't breathe and it felt like her skin was on fire. There were too many people inside the tent, everyone screaming and thrashing around in a mix of terror and euphoria. She got knocked down as she tried desperately to right her blurred vision and felt several people stumble over her and land on top of her.

A pair of hands pulled her from the pile. Helen blinked her eyes and popped her ears until she saw Ariadne yelling into her face and heard her say, "You're bleeding!" as if from far, far away.

The world was swirling and smearing around her. Helen

looked down at her dress and saw prickles of red blood seeping through the silk.

Ariadne tore a hole in the side of the tent to let them out and dragged Helen over the snowy sand toward the water. She heard the waves fizzing in the surf nearby. *Sister*, the waves whispered. Helen closed her eyes.

Morpheus's face hovered in front of hers, looking desperate. "You must not sleep!" he roared at her. "Wake up!"

Helen's eyes snapped open. A blue glow lit Ariadne's determined expression.

"Your dress is poisoned!" she hissed as she ripped the silk away with her illuminated hands.

Helen retched, the world flipping over sickeningly as Ariadne rolled her into the frigid saltwater. The burning turned to stinging, and the stinging turned to itching. Helen started clawing at herself as if to tear off her tortured skin, preferring pain to the maddening itch.

Ariadne submerged Helen in the churning surf, her healing hands working in tandem with the water to rinse away the poison. The bubbles sparkled against Helen's skin and the burning faded. Helen stopped thrashing around in blind agony.

"Did you get any on you?" she asked, her speech garbled.

"I'm okay," Ariadne replied, struggling to keep Helen close in a tug of war with the waves.

Numb and shivering, the girls climbed up the beach and away from the tide that sucked the sand out from under them.

"Someone's coming," Ariadne said through chattering teeth.

Ariadne stood in front of Helen, her back to the wedding tents farther up the beach, and faced the figures stalking toward them along the water's edge. Helen propped herself up on shaking arms, her head bobbing weakly on her shoulders. The Cestus swung about her neck and Helen scowled at it. It made her impenetrable to weapons but not, apparently, to poison. She dragged her bleary eyes up off the sand and forced them to focus on the pending danger.

The group that approached made no sense. Struggling to remain conscious, Helen thought she must be hallucinating. Hera, still wearing Gretchen like a human shield, was at the center back of the group, flanked by the three junior boys who were possessed by the Machai. Before them strode Gus, the maker of the poisoned dress. He wore a long, dark overcoat that bunched around the shoulders and neck, and Helen recognized him as the man who had been watching her from the edge of her yard. Under that, he wore the same flashy royal blue vest he had worn when Helen had come in for her fitting. Next to him was *Andy*. Helen only knew that she wasn't mistaken because Ariadne groaned in dismay when she recognized her.

"What have you done to Andy?" Ariadne asked Hera, bracing herself in front of Helen.

"All I did was keep her distracted by her research up there in that frozen wasteland. Time, distance, and doubt did the rest," Hera replied. "Really, once she heard Hector was sleeping in Helen's bedroom she practically begged me to possess her."

"We defeated you," Ariadne snapped back. "You should be trapped on Olympus."

Helen shook her head mutely, already understanding where she had gone wrong.

"I didn't fight for Zeus," Hera replied, obviously pleased with her own cleverness.

"I didn't—I never said—" Helen explained brokenly to Ariadne, shaking her bent head at her own stupidity.

She could hear Hector and Orion shouting somewhere far off as they searched for her. Even if she'd had the strength to yell back, she didn't know if she would have. It would destroy Hector to see Andy aligned against them, no matter how addled she seemed; she obviously wasn't herself right now, but Hector would still hold it against her.

"Argus. Take her," Hera commanded, and the tailor stepped forward.

Sand flew through the dark and Helen shielded her eyes as Ariadne intercepted Hera's minion. There was a wicked exchange of blows as they fought. Ariadne beat him back and then engaged Andy who was trying to get around them to take Helen. The two girls slammed into each other, but Ariadne was the better fighter by far.

"Don't," Ariadne pleaded through gritted teeth as she wrapped Andy in a choke hold.

Argus righted himself and made a startling squawking sound. A magnificent peacock tail fanned out behind him, dotted with a multitude of iridescent eyes—cobalt blue eyes that moved as the tail did. One even blinked. He jumped into the air, grabbed Ariadne about the shoulders with clawed bird feet, and tried to haul her off the ground.

Helen summoned her lightning but saw only useless sparks fizzling away between her fingers. She was so thirsty. The poison had left her too dehydrated to summon a bolt, and the saltwater that seemed to kiss her feet in apology was of no use to her.

Desperate, Helen crawled forward and lunged for Ariadne's

legs. She caught them before Argus could fly away and switched to her super-massive state, hauling Ariadne and Argus back down to the beach. While Helen was stretched out and exposed, Andy took the opening and kicked her savagely in the ribs. Helen curled up around her middle but did not let go of Ariadne.

The Machai rushed forward, swords drawn, and began hacking away at Helen's back—in vain.

"Get her necklace!" Hera commanded shrilly. "Rip it off her neck!"

Helen heard Hector and Orion shouting as they neared.

"Let me go!" Ariadne said. Helen obeyed, and Ariadne sprang up just as Hector and Orion appeared.

Hector skidded to a stop, throwing up a rainbow of sand.

"Andy?" he said, his voice strangely high and plaintive.

"You take the Machai!" Orion yelled, shoving Hector and facing off with Argus.

"I've got Andy," Ariadne said grimly.

Hector threw himself at the Machai as if possessed. He disarmed one, kicked another, and had the third by the throat in a matter of seconds. Ariadne subdued Andy as gently as she could, one healer hand glowing as she touched Andy on the temple. Andy gave a gasp and a startled shake, as if while she fell unconscious, she was simultaneously waking up to what she had done.

Orion and Argus traded swift blows that flashed with steel. Argus' hands had turned to scaly talons, and Orion's stiletto blocked and stabbed in staccato bursts. A glancing cut across Argus' chest and shoulder left a gaping hole in his clothes, exposing his chest. It was covered in the same blue eyes that had been scattered across the island to watch Helen.

Hera backed away with mounting fear as she realized the battle was lost. "Argus!" she called out to her servant, and he broke away from Orion. He grabbed Hera by the shoulders and flew away with her over the ocean. Orion waded out into the water as if to follow them, but stopped with a frustrated shout when he realized that he could not.

He came out of the water and went to Helen. Ariadne touched the temple of the last Machai with her glowing hand and the boy, too, had a moment of clarity before he passed out. Hector was already kneeling, gathering Andy's unconscious body in his arms.

Orion took off his dress shirt, placed it over Helen's bare shoulders, and helped her thread her arms through the too-long sleeves. He wouldn't meet her eyes as he buttoned his shirt on her.

"My dress was poisoned," Helen said, misunderstanding his worried look.

He shook his head. "That's not—" He stopped and took a deep breath, steeling himself. "It's your dad."

Helen went numb. The sea-foam gathered at her feet whispered, "*Sister,*" as if to comfort her.

"What about my dad?" Helen asked, her voice breaking, and her tongue dry and heavy in her mouth. He shook his head and picked her up in his arms rather than answer.

Ariadne swiftly pulled the junior boys farther up the beach to keep them away from the tide and left them there to wake on their own, hopefully remembering nothing. Hector picked up Andy and Orion carried Helen back to the wedding tent. They said nothing on the way. And Helen knew.

She knew before she saw Claire and Kate on their knees beside him, crying. She knew before Jason looked at her saying, "He was dead before I got to him. There was nothing I could—I'm so sorry, Helen."

She knew before Orion put her down next to him and she touched his cheek.

"Helen," Kate wept, devastated. She collapsed on Helen in a clinging hug.

Helen held Kate with stiff arms, her body wooden. She let Kate cry, draped over her like a mourning cloak, while she stared at her father's face. He was empty. Nothing but a used cup. There were no injuries. His white suit didn't even have a smudge on it.

"How?" Helen asked.

"Aneurism. He was gone in moments," Jason said. "He didn't feel any pain."

"I'm sorry, Helen," Cassandra said, looking like she blamed herself for not foreseeing this. "I knew the Fates were hiding something from me. But I had no idea it was anything like this."

Helen just stared at Cassandra blankly, holding Kate. She recalled saying many times in the past few days that the Fates had been strangely silent. Helen had been moments away from making her father and Kate immortal with a thought. But now it was too late. She couldn't bring him back. She knew that as sure as she knew her own name. Her father's soul, the thing that made him her father, was in Hades.

Noel's tear-streaked face suddenly filled Helen's field of vision. "I'll take her," Noel whispered, pulling Kate from Helen's arms.

Helen put a hand down and pushed herself to standing. Her legs shook under her, Orion's shirttails reaching down to her thighs, the sleeves dangling past her fingers. Like she was a little girl again, wearing her father's clothes.

"Wait." Orion clutched her by the shoulders. "What are you thinking?" he asked, scared. "What are you going to do?"

She looked at him until he let her go. And then she opened a portal to Hades and went through it.

She appeared in the great hall in the palace of Hades. Marble columns stretched up until they were swallowed by the darkness. A throne sat upon a dais. No one was in it.

"Lucas," she whispered.

"I'm here." He coalesced out of the shadows before her.

"My father—" she began, a breath bursting out of her. And then the tears came. Horrible, choking sobs that twisted in her chest and on her face until they ached. She bent forward, pressing against her breastbone, trying to push back against the hollowness, vainly trying to fill the spot that had been emptied.

"I'm so sorry, Helen," Lucas whispered, over and over. But he didn't come to her. He didn't try to hold her.

Helen pressed and pressed against her chest and the intolerable feeling that was lodged there. "Please, Lucas," she begged. "Please give him back."

He was silent. Helen drew in a breath and then let it out, letting go of tightness. She looked up at him.

"I can't," he said.

Helen heard the lie. She stared at him. "You're lying to me," she said, confused. Tears still streamed down her face, dripped off her chin, and wet the marble of his great hall.

He nodded, swallowing hard. "I won't," he replied.

She took a step toward him, holding out her arms, and he stepped back three paces.

"Go home, Helen," he said, his voice shaking. "Go home to Kate and Orion and let them comfort you."

Helen felt the sweat from her weeping chill on her back and

on her forehead. She took another step toward Lucas. "Please," she whimpered, reaching out again, and letting her arms drop when he avoided her. "Give me my father back."

He shook his head.

"My *father*, Lucas!" she shouted, suddenly flaring with anger and confusion.

He had never refused her anything. She stood in front of him, unable to make it stick in her head that he wouldn't do this for her.

"Why?" she asked, the word falling out of her like the first pebble before the landslide.

He refused to give her an answer. "Jerry is dead," was all he would say.

For a moment his eyes swam as if he were looking up at her from beneath a wave that was drowning him.

Rage clawed up from her thighs to her belly. It roared through her chest and came crawling out her mouth, misshapen and evil.

"I hate you," she said.

Lucas looked back at her, as blank and dead as her father had been.

"Goodbye, Helen."

Outcasts

Please enjoy the following brief excerpt from OUTCASTS, book six in the STARCROSSED saga.

Daphne
House of Atreus

I'm not used to being happy.

It's not something I was raised to believe was an attainable goal for me. My uncle Deuce disabused me of any hope of happiness at a very young age. Not to be cruel, but to give me a leg up on what was almost certainly in the cards for me. I remember him telling me that for our kind, fairy tales were often true.

Not the sanitized, pink-and-glitter version of fairy tales that they make cartoon character movies out of in Hollywood, but the original ones that are more like those Scared Straight presentations from ex-convicts. The princess usually suffers a hellish childhood where her whole family dies and she's either locked in a tower or forced into indentured servitude. In most cases, she not only doesn't get the prince in the end, but they also both either die or get turned into animals. Being turned into a swan sounds romantic until you consider the fact that you'll probably get eaten by a fox.

I admit it. Being happy was never something I considered, and because I'm not primed for it, I'm waiting for the other shoe to drop. Maybe I'm paranoid, but I can't help but feel like there have been too many accidents, too many near misses for me to swallow it as coincidence, and when I hear Ajax gasp and curse under his breath I think, *this is when I lose him.* I run across the deck of the *Argo IX*, our home since faking our deaths two months ago, to where Ajax has been painting all morning.

"It's nothing," he says, wrapping a rag around the gash in his wrist.

"I'll get the kit," I say, and rush below deck to our medical supplies. When I come back topside Ajax's blood has already seeped through the rag and started to run across his hand.

I open the kit and he peels the rag back away from the wound. It's deep. I meet his eyes. "Do you need a Healer?" I ask. Not that I can take him to one. We're supposed to be dead.

"I'll be fine. Just give me some clean gauze and I'll put pressure on it until it closes."

I do as he asks and stand back, my fists clenched around the lightning in my fingers. "What happened?" I ask.

"There was a gust of wind and the mast swung. When I put my arm up so it wouldn't knock me across the head, I cut myself."

While he bears down on his wound, I check the mast of our

ship. "Cut yourself on what?" I ask, baffled. There's nothing sharp anywhere near the sails.

He shrugs. "I think it was the edge of my easel."

Ajax's easel has been tipped askew and there is some blood on the top corner of it, though how he managed to cut himself on it so badly is beyond me. I look out over the calm waters of the Aegean Sea. The steady, light breeze hits my face from one direction. There are no gusts of wind now. The mast is a bit loose, but it's not swingingly violently. I yank on the ropes, pulling them tighter anyway.

"It was just an accident," he insists, watching me.

"You're not clumsy." I double check my knots before I turn to face him. "How many accidents have happened to you since we ran away together?"

He smiles through a sigh and comes to me. He doesn't try to tell me I'm jumping at shadows anymore, but he's still not ready to be convinced, as I am, that the universe is trying to kill him. Holding onto his wrist, he loops his arms over my head and pulls me against him. He kisses my temple until I go from stiff to pliant in his arms.

"You can't fight the wind, Daphne," he says.

I wrap my arms around him, wishing I could unzip my chest and stuff him inside me. "That's what scares me."

Scheduled for release October 2023

For more information visit Josephineangelini.com

Also by Josephine Angelini

Starcrossed Series

Starcrossed

Dreamless

Goddess

Scions

Worldwalker Series

Trial by Fire

Firewalker

Witch's Pyre

Thriller

What She Found in the Woods